The House
with Blue Shutters

Lisa Hilton read English at New College, Oxford and studied History of Art in Paris and Florence. She is the author of three historical biographies, *The Real Queen of France*, *Mistress Peachum's Pleasure* and *Queens Consort*. She currently lives between the south of France and London, where she works as a journalist and broadcaster. *The House with Blue Shutters* is her first novel.

The House
with Blue Shutters

LISA HILTON

CORVUS

This paperback edition first published in Great Britain in 2010 by
Corvus, an imprint of Grove Atlantic Ltd.

9 8 7 6 5 4 3 2 1

A CIP catalogue record for this book is available from
the British Library.

ISBN: 978-1-84887-466-4

Printed in Great Britain by Clays Ltd, St Ives plc

Corvus
An imprint of Grove Atlantic Ltd
Ormond House
26-27 Boswell Street
London WC1N 3JZ

www.corvus-books.co.uk

For Nicola

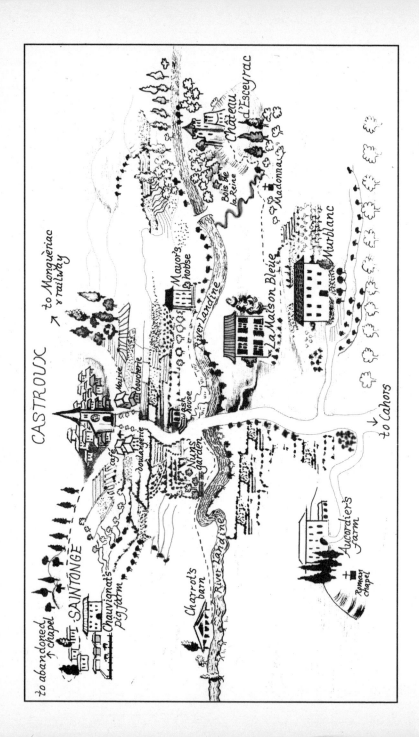

'Y a souffert las pénos del diable: attendré et beyré ré béni.
Ayma et n'est ré pas ayma. Habé talen et n'abé rés à minstsa.'

'To wait and see nothing come, to love and not to be loved, to
hunger without food. These are the sufferings of the devil.'

Occitan proverb

PART ONE

SUMMER HOLIDAYS

'What shall I give them for pudding?' asked Aisling.

'Pudding?' said Jonathan.

'I must say, it's absolutely typical of your brother to arrive on Thursday, with the bloody PG barbecue, so I thought either the chocolate parfait with chilled pistachio custard, or just the strawberry crème brûlée, which always comes out, but then I think we gave him that at Easter, didn't we, not that he'd remember so I don't suppose it matters really, but I was thinking with the PGs, we'll be late, so I thought just melon and the good *jambon* and then a chicken tarragon, so the pistachio would look a bit more like trying. Do you think this Claudia's a vegetarian? I could do a *gratin de courgettes* in case, but in this heat?'

'Why don't you do the strawberry thingy? I'll get a bottle of Monbazillac down.'

'Good idea, darling,' said Aisling.

The Harveys smiled at one another. They had been five

years at Murblanc, and variations on this conversation had passed between them several times a week. Aisling had a blue leather book from Smythson's of Bond Street, in which she wrote down the details of who had come and what she cooked, so as to be sure of not serving the same combinations of dishes and guests. The book had been a Christmas present from Jonathan and was always casually on display on the kitchen dresser. In a series of orange plastic-backed exercise books with ruled squares Aisling kept a similar record of the food she made, in July and August, for the paying guests. She lived in fear of a wandering boarder discovering one of these volumes on a prowl about her huge stone-flagged kitchen, since she had got into the habit of adding comments on the visitors in the margins. She flicked through now, to remind herself of what the Lawses had eaten nearly two weeks ago for their welcome dinner. The entry for last Friday week said 'Welcome dinner. Laws Family. Chilled sorrel soup with parmesan toasts. Slice foie gras with apple chutney. Guinea fowl. Cheese, salad. *Tarte aux framboises*. Mrs L fat. Perm. Children horrid.' Somehow, Aisling was unable to break this secret practice of judgement, which was inconvenient, really, as it necessitated her hiding the current book behind the cream china flour bin or in the larder with the cat food, and usually being unable to find it, causing her to wake sometimes in the early hours of the morning, beset by chimerae of repeated recipes.

The paying guests were a disappointment to Aisling. She had worked hard on La Maison Bleue, a square stone barn with powdery turquoise shutters at the dormer windows, which the Harveys had transformed during their first winter into a four-bedroomed cottage with a terrace and a small walled garden. Murblanc lay at the bottom of the hill opposite the village of Castroux, beneath Aucordier's farm. The guesthouse, in turn, was below the main building, beyond the swimming pool. The Harveys and their own guests dined on the terrace above the house itself, overlooking the valley, while the PG perspective was brought up short by the square line of the chateau wood, yet the presence of the visitors, in the form of obese, shrieking toddlers or the television turned up loud to Sky Sports, was a permanently irritating reminder of what Aisling believed herself to have left behind, a mosquito-itch of small but significant failures. She had spent more than she ought on furnishing La Maison Bleue, determined that it should not display the usual tasteless collection of half-broken surplus furniture with which many English filled their shabby gîtes. Each room was painted a different soft-faded pastel, inspired, as Aisling informed potential renters in her brochure, by the famous frescoes in the church at Landi, the two bathrooms were large and modern, there was a dishwasher and a microwave and, against Aisling's aesthetic judgement, the 'digi-box', so beloved of ex-pats, which everyone pretended they installed merely to keep up with the cricket, but which gave access to all English television channels.

Aisling had been delighted when the inspector from *Charme Français* had pronounced La Maison Bleue fit for inclusion in the guide, particularly as the woman, a weary-seeming divorcee who lived in one of the grander parts of Provence, had arrived during a particularly raw weekend in March, when the countryside was stripped and ragged, and Aisling's *crema catalana* had, according to the blue leather book, come out stodgy and too full of aniseed. Oliver had commented most unhelpfully that it tasted like cough mixture, and both the boys had refused to show off their French. Mrs Highland was indifferent to Aisling's food, claiming that she preferred a salad and a huge lump of cheese, and had grimly shone a torch under the beds and inspected the lavatory cisterns. She and Jonathan had had a long and apparently satisfactory discussion about drains, oblivious to Aisling's increasingly frantic attempts to divert her onto the delights of Castroux market or the view from the pool terrace. Nevertheless, Aisling felt that the credit for the entry, 'Stunning location, highly comfortable, large swimming pool. Sleeps ten', was hers, rather than the plumbing's, though it was a pity Mrs Highland hadn't had room to say anything about the frescoes.

Mrs Highland's lack of interest in Aisling's attempts at elegance was reflected in a similar obliviousness on the part of the readers of *Charme Français*. They came, numerously, to loll by the pool drinking beer and to stuff the fridge with cases of nasty white wine bought en route at Calais, they microwaved pizzas for their children, and watched the television, and altogether, they claimed, had a wonderfully relaxing holiday, but they did not visit the monastic museum at Landi, or the grottoes at Saux, or take any of the walks Aisling had so painstakingly marked in pink highlighter pen on a large-scale map. Occasionally, Aisling would meet one of the wives at the Saturday morning market in the village, surly sunburned husband trailing behind with an absurd rustic basket, and Aisling would smile gaily to conceal her cringing at their bulging shorts, and suggest that they try the goat's cheese that dear little Monsieur le Filastre made himself and brought wrapped in fig leaves and brown string, or the walnut bread for which Castroux was known. Inevitably, the straw basket was filled with scented soaps attached to wooden paddles, impractically small bottles of flavoured olive oil, and tins of cassoulet. Aisling imagined them, these gastronomic souvenirs, lingering dusty and reproachful in the back of English kitchen cupboards until the obese toddlers grew up and threw them out when they shunted their parents to a nursing home.

Aisling herself did not wear shorts, or wilting patterned skirts, or foolish straw hats. Her hair was neatly and expensively shaped into a collar-bone-length bob once a month in Toulouse. In the mornings, particularly if she was busy with the garden or the ducks, she happily drove into Landi in jeans and a grubby sweater, with a fleece thrown over, when she was not working she wore linen tunics in white or navy, with fitted trousers, leather flats, and lipstick. Shorts, she felt, were one of the many elements in which the PGs were not quite up to the mark. She was perfectly aware of this snobbery, professing on occasion to hate herself for it, although she did not, admitting in franker moments that she was merely being honest, but it coloured her relationship with her visitors, rendering it at once bumptiously didactic and guiltily genial. Jonathan was better, repeating the same remarks about motorways and routes with the husbands at the welcome drink, cheerfully shifting suitcases and changing lightbulbs, even occasionally watching a match with a bottle of beer (the Harveys did not have Sky Sports), and otherwise apparently unaware of the boarders' existence. Aisling asked too many energetically pleasant questions of the wives, insisted that Richard and Oliver play in the pool with the children, and caught herself agreeing with enthusiastic insincerity as to the lost and unmourned advantages of Sainsbury's and Tesco.

She had imagined, she thought, resentfully rubbing in a *pâte brisée* for the individual blueberry and ricotta tarts she would store in the big freezer in the barn until Thursday, that La Maison Bleue would attract different sorts of people. People who were artistic, who would spend long evenings chatting over wine about opera or the latest prize-winning novel, who would admire Aisling's cooking instead of poking at it suspiciously, who would speak French with her boys. There had been a winter rental, a gloomy young couple with a goatee and stringy dreadlocks who claimed, respectively, to be a painter, the goatee, and a writer, the dreadlocks, but they had stayed three weeks and barely emerged from the house except to drag car-loads of shopping from the Landi hypermarket indoors. The fumes of what Aisling was sure was hashish lingered about the doorway. Madame Lesprats had shown the sheets to Aisling, with great disgust, when they departed. The couple had apparently made love during the woman's period, and Aisling's carefully chosen old linens, bought especially at the annual *brocante* in Lille, were a mottled, liverish abstract of stains. Madame Lesprats had refused to have anything to do with what she referred to as *leur saloperies*, and Aisling had boiled the sheets herself and eventually cut them up, sadly, for dusters.

Oliver and Richard trailed into the kitchen, slapping wet footmarks on the limestone. 'Mrs Laws,' said Oliver, then hunched into a fit of unattractive sniggers. 'Mrs Laws,' took up Richard, then collapsed exaggeratedly onto his brother's back. 'Mrs Laws,' they howled, 'has grey pubes! We saw them,

Mum! Sticking out of her bikini! It's sick!'

They shuffled off. Aisling looked at the clock, went to the fridge, and poured herself a glass of white wine.

That evening, Claudia Wesson lay in the guest bathroom at Murblanc, rubbing bubbles off her new Tiffany engagement ring. Alex would so absolutely have gone to Tiffany. Claudia had accepted Alexander Harvey's proposal the day after she knew for certain that she was pregnant with Sébastien's child. She repeated this information to herself, in the third person, as she reached into the pocket of her discarded pyjamas and extracted a cigarette. Alex hated her smoking. She lay back in the water, but the sharp nicotine mingled foully with the steam and she lurched forward, flipped up the loo seat and vomited, discreetly flushing at the same time in case any of the Harveys should hear. Crouched, shuddering, her knees in the water and her breasts squashed against the taps, she rested her chin on the rim and thought that she would have to give up now, anyway. Alex tapped on the door, 'Aisling says supper in half an hour, darling.'

Claudia closed her eyes. She wanted the evening to be gone; she wanted darkness and cold air on her skin, to be alone and numbing herself with cognac. She had begged Alex to take her to France when she had received Sébastien's letter, a few days after she had fled from that terrible, humiliating, drunken scene in Paris. She had worked out cleanly in her mind the announcement of the pregnancy, had gone through her diary to fix precisely where she would muddle the dates. It was a mercy at least, she thought, that Alex was dark like Sébastien, with brown eyes, and a greater blessing that, exuberantly and magnanimously in love, he had declared to her a few weeks before that he wouldn't care if she threw away her pills. She was quite safe.

There was just this evening to be got through. 'I will bear it,' she thought, constructing the words as though she were a character in a book, a penurious Victorian heroine about to hold fast against a drawing room of terrible aunts. There was just the dinner, and the announcement, to which she could respond demurely and blushingly to the questions about churches and dresses that would surely follow after the congratulations. He would understand when she told him, not feel it too much when she would explain that she preferred something simple and low-key, under the circumstances. There was a strain of meanness in Alex upon which she relied to console him for her projected rejection of a showy wedding. He tended to look too closely at bills, even for presents or restaurant meals, had a troubled laugh for the price of her face cream. This strain had offended her in the past, as when, on holiday in Greece, she had gone into rather forced raptures about a hotel room in Santorini, very bare and plain, with rich blue shutters and a view of the sea. She said that she had always dreamed of such a room, that it was inspiring in its austerity. 'Yes,' Alex had said, 'and it costs nothing.' Now, thought Claudia, this penny-pinching could be pushed into necessary practicality, into the tedious business of selling their two flats and organizing a mutual life. She had already employed it, persuading him into a month at his brother's house by showing that two extra weeks of unpaid leave would not be a great loss, since they would save the price of two weeks in a hotel if they stayed with Jonathan and Aisling for nothing.

Murblanc certainly was fetching, a long, low house, creamy-stoned as the name suggested, with a hump of third storey slouching on one side. Jonathan had taken her over it proudly as soon as they arrived, the kitchen, the dining room with the big beamed fireplace, his study (though, apart from a stack of computer games, Claudia thought, it looked unused), the drawing room on the first floor, the three bathrooms, five bedrooms, attic sitting room for Aisling, who had always wanted a room of her own, high up. Jonathan had gone on rather, about the bathrooms, particularly the lavatories which seemed to involve some personal triumph with a recalcitrant builder and the location of the *fosse*, and Claudia had thought about Sébastien because she thought of nothing else.

This bath was huge, standing alone in front of a large window with floor-length linen curtains, striped in primrose and ivory. The room gave on to the front of the house, where Claudia could see a track, turning lilac in the sunset, leading up to a line of slender, pointed trees surrounding a plain square farmhouse high on the hill. She must mention the lovely view to Aisling. She would be safe here, if she could not, not think of Sébastien. She touched her ring again, screwing it around her finger so that it wrenched at her skin, white and puffy from the cooling water. Lucky after all, really. She would be Mrs Harvey, and there was nothing better to hope for.

NOVEMBER 1932

Pop pop pop, the tiny screech of the ball in the air, and the whistle behind, intense as a soap bubble in sunlight, bursting in the silver weight of the mist. Oriane hears the guns, knows the hunt is out. She sighs, drops the broom and runs out into the yard, her eyes searching the skyline to find where, for sure, William is.

Pop! Pop! Sucking the noise around the whorl of William's ear, way down the valley from Saintonge, up over the hill at Teulière, swooping along to the meadow of the chateau, where the peacock cries steady against the staccato of the guns, the lacy whisper of the leaves drawn in now, dense and crisp where the boar are running, crunch and thud along the bottom of the fields, delicate in the high chestnuts the squeak of a crow against the scream of the green and blue birds in the high walled park, Papie Nadl's donkey gasping like an ancient horn, pop pop pop the guns, and always the tendrils of the thrushes' tongues lapping at his ear, high fluttering kisses of noise, and

William breaks from the row of hunters, runs whirling and dancing along the line of the guns, whilst trilling for freedom the boar and her two babies escape down the bank and William claps his hands at their excited snorting. Red pain makes silence. William holds his icy hand to his burning ear and howls, roars so the whole valley can hear his sound, collapsing hiccuping crazily on the wet grey ground.

William rolls up like a beetle and rootles his nose into the grass, warming it with his breath. In the earth, he hears his sister's boots, pounding down the field.

'For shame,' shouts Oriane. 'Don't you know the boy is not quite finished?'

William does not look up, but he knows Oriane will have her hands on her hips under her apron, bunching the cloth so her body stands even skinnier between the folds, like a poppy-dolly. Her knuckles stroke his sore face. 'Look at him! All over mud. You should know better, the lot of you! Come on now, William, come on home.'

Shame is a word William recognizes, a hissing word with the sting of a slap within it. The sound and the sense come usually together. 'For shame, William,' says his mother, reaching across the table as he dribbles his soup, cuffing him with a bent hand so that her knuckles crack hard across his cheekbone, 'For shame,' as William rolls howling across the kitchen floor, her anger dull and hard as the crack of the iron ladle across his skull. Sometimes Oriane uses the word, and then its power dims, quietens, leaking its force until the house is silent.

'For shame, Maman,' gathering a bundle of William into her arms, as her mother lays her head on the long oak boards and sobs too, the sound passing back to the wetness of her despair. 'For shame, for shame,' until William hears the poplars bow in the shudder of her sobbing breath and creeps back to her crabwise across the smooth dirt floor and lays his head against her broken heart, drumming to the hum of his blood outside in the darkness of the trees. Shame is stilled then, the logs shift in the fire, William forgets until the next day or the next when Shame grows strong, dances in the tightness of his mother's lips until her hands are possessed by it and reach once more to batter it from her.

Shame hovers around Aucordier's. The square pale stone house and the two barns scoop and cup it like the wind that scrapes forever across the plain and pauses between the roofs, twisting down the chimneys and sidling under the doors, whipping the wash into contortions and scattering the chickens with dust until it emerges as a whisper of a breeze, unfelt in the village down the valley. Oriane knows, as William does not, the elements of shame, can count them clear as fat clouds in a blue summer sky.

Her father was a shame, a roaring stinking storm of it, until he subsided in their mother's bedroom into a whimpering puff, worn out with the drink. One.

Her mother wore his shame in the purple lumps of her eyes, which, when they paled sufficiently for the Aucordiers to go to church, glowed horribly bright and obvious against the faded mauve of her Sunday hat. Two.

William is a shame, poor thing, dumb and hopeless, a lolling child whose scent is the high sour smell of the less than loved, the ferment of loneliness carried in the skin of the old and the ugly. Three.

Oriane knows that William's shame is her parents', the result of something too much more than cousinly affection in the Aucordier family. Four. This is a dripping shame which has seeped into her, she does not know how, curdling inside her and sticking like the sucking mud of the yard after rain. '*La terre amoureuse*' they call it, when the mud clings so and there's nothing to be done in the fields and Oriane goes to school, scraping soft new words on to her slate. The schoolhouse has a big stove and the floor is made of wood. School is for rainy days, and Oriane likes the French lesson, because the pictures in the story book have nothing to do with Castroux, or mud or shames. Cécile and her brother Jean live in a pale, precise world where the sun is always shining and Papa takes them for a ride in *le bateau* on *la mer bleue*, while Maman waits behind in a long white dress and a big hat with a pink ribbon to prepare *le goûter*, which is *du pain* with *de la confiture*. French is clear, it forms itself cleanly, dividing the world into *le* and *la*. Cécile and Maman have pink ribbons, Jean and Papa blue shirts. Mademoiselle Lafage the schoolteacher says that Occitan is a dirty, primitive language, and she raps at the big boys with her ruler when they whisper dirty things at the back. Oriane sits up very straight, so straight it hurts the bottom of her spine, and tries to take no notice when big boys howl at her like her brother the werewolf, dribbling and biting at their arms, hunching one shoulder up to their ear and letting the other arm swing low to the ground, grunting.

Four shames, one for each corner of the house, like the scallop shells carved to welcome pilgrims.

Oriane is too busy, mostly, for the counting of shame. William stayed at first in the kitchen with their grandmother, porridge and saliva oozing tepid on two formless chins, two bewildered mouths straining for words they couldn't find. It was quite a surprise when William outlived her. Now William is old enough at least to be trusted not to fall into the fire, and Oriane no longer has to secure him to the laundry pole with a long loop of rope when she goes outside. Now he wanders about the yard like a chicken, unable to help Oriane with her easiest jobs, like sacking potatoes. She tries to teach him, dragging him to the pump with the bucket, giving him a line of string to hold as she ties up the peas, but William makes no effort, merely wanders peacefully away with the bucket spilling in the dirt, and lies with his huge ear to the ground, as though he were listening for moles. Sometimes Oriane wants to rush at him, to beat him with her dirty fists and splayed nails, she feels her mother's fury within her as she strains to carry the logs or mend the high door of the big barn that the wind bursts through, contemptuously, several times a week, but she stops herself, as four shames are enough for anybody.

Oriane sleeps with her mother, now that her father is dead. They get up just after the light, and Oriane slices the hard bread and makes the coffee as her mother dresses. Aucordier's had been a big farm once, but the fields mostly went in her father's time, and Oriane's mother sold the last but one to old Papie Nadl, down the hill at Murblanc. Sometimes Papie's donkeys escape and Oriane has to chase them from the plum trees. In the evening, if she is not too tired, Oriane walks down the hill towards Castroux, to meet her mother who goes out for the grapes or the cherries, the melons or the apples, to the chateau for the laundry or sometimes across to Saintonge to Chauvignat's pigs. Oriane minds William, hoes and weeds the vegetables, washes the clothes and fetches the water, feeds the chickens and the three goats and the baleful, scabby rabbits, milks and collects eggs, sweeps the house and makes the beds, sweeps the ashes and fetches the wood, hoes William and feeds the vegetables and washes the goats. As she goes about, she names things in French, *le grenier, la poule, mon frère*. Many of the children in the village hardly speak French at all, and many of the mamies and papies too, though Mademoiselle can't rap at them with her stick. Oriane speaks Occitan with her mother, but she likes to translate the words inside her head as they talk, so that there is always a part of her that is somewhere else.

William is a musician. High up on the plateau, he seeks sounds beneath the dull bass of wind that curries forever along the plain. His ears can separate the song of the fat little oriels from the swish of the poplar leaves and the cries of the children playing *rescoundut* far below in the village square. Long ago, he beat time with a metal spoon as his mother scoured the pots at the pump, jigging his grandmother's compliant hand as accompaniment. The air made an organ of the spread of bone beneath a hawk's wing, carried the soprano scream of a rabbit beneath a fox. William danced to the angelus as it sang up the hill from Castroux, bounced to the chop of the tractor blades as they hummed in Nadl's fields. Everything he knows, he knows through sounds, the rain comes when the wind gathers the clouds together, the soup will taste thick and salty when Oriane moves the paddle through the bacon and barley, sleep is the knock of the loose shutter that bumps through the nights.

Sophie Aucordier rarely takes her children as far as the village. They go to Mass on the Days of Obligation, but do not linger about gossiping afterwards in the square. When Oriane goes to the school she is to come straight home immediately, for the devil finds work for idle hands. Sophie suspects that she may have married the devil, and even though she saw him expire with her own two eyes, yellow and shrivelled and muttering about the fiends hidden in the walls, she would not be surprised if the demons grew tired of his company and sent him back to torment her. So she remains vigilant, because decency and hard work will preserve her. No children come up so far as Aucordier's begging for eggs for May Day; on the first of the year Papie Nadl walks his wreathed donkey straight down the hill, leaving Oriane and William to the mercies of the Israelites. Sophie Aucordier keeps herself to herself and the village lets her, confirming her belief that the world is a cold, uncharitable place, making a sorry little virtue of her loneliness. William is the proof that she has no right to joy, and in the still summertime, when the sound of Yves Contier's accordion and Papie's violin can be heard all the way up the valley, she puts the bolster over her head. Oriane pretends not to hear her weeping.

SUMMER HOLIDAYS

Claudia's resolution about Sébastien lasted until three o'clock the next morning. The dinner had been got through, and mercifully Alex had been so tired after the drive and the drinking that he had gone straight to sleep. Claudia was longing for the relief of tears, the tension was balled in her lungs, but in a sudden, terrible intimation of what marriage could be like, she lay raw-eyed in the darkness and realized she would have to find somewhere to cry.

The silence around her was vacant and terrifying. In London, a day could be filled with a walk across Kensington Gardens to Hyde Park, a trip around Selfridge's Food Hall to choose some wine for some fucking barbecue, then a crawling drive to Wandsworth or Clapham. All of Alex's friends seemed to work in the City and live in garden flats in South London, with wooden floors and Ikea kitchens, expensive stereos and lurid eighties-yellow walls. The men were bankers or lawyers, as were most of the women, with the occasional financial PR or dim primary school teacher thrown in. The primary school teachers were usually prettier than the lawyers, but otherwise Claudia had difficulty telling the couples apart, an inability that Alex claimed was pure affectation, but which struck her sincerely at Sunday lunches or the dreaded barbecues, when she wasn't certain whether she was talking to Anna solicitor who lived with Tom banker or Lucy banker who lived with Gordon solicitor. Claudia was aware that everything about her, her clothes, her job, even her cigarettes, was an anomaly in Alex's circle, a distinction that had relieved her when she first began to go out with him, but which tonight left her dumbly dismayed.

There was nothing wrong, she told herself over and over, with Alex's friends. They were intelligent and well educated, more intrinsically able, she felt, than herself. They travelled, for weekends in Europe and long trips to Asia or South America, they skied and played tennis and went to the opera and the latest films, but Claudia nevertheless sounded a false note within their cultivation, a boorishness that derived, she thought, from the fact that their ideas extended no further than the obviousness of Sunday newspapers. She felt herself to be superior to them, although she had no logical right to, a superiority based, she feared, on no more than the fact that nearly all of them were unattractive, the men paunchy or spotty, the girls thick of chin and ankle, and hopelessly dressed. Claudia had the knowledge of her own beauty that comes easily from a lifetime of admiration, she was precise about the extent and limitation of her power, grading it according to the groups in which she moved. In Alex's world it shone more brightly than in her own, where it was challenged occasionally, by fashion models or the impeccable grooming of the women whom she taught.

Claudia worked in the education department of an old and distinguished auction house. Four days a week she lectured on British Pictures from 1700 to the Present Day to small classes of earnest American graduate students, idly interested financiers' wives (they of the impossibly manicured appearance) and an ever-evolving pool of easy Europeans, constant only in their cashmere, who rarely lasted a full term, and who would politely disappear to Gstaad or St Tropez without ever appearing to feel that their course constituted some sort of commitment. Claudia had written her postgraduate thesis at the Sorbonne, on Elisabeth Vigée-Lebrun, and on Friday mornings she gave a class on history of art to the baccalaureate students at the French *lycée* in Kensington. She occasionally contributed a bilingual review or a short article to an expensively produced and little read journal called *Diréctions*, edited by an old university friend, not because such work particularly pleased or suited her, but because it gave her access to dinners with journalists and film people at the Groucho or Soho House, to fashion shows and talks at the ICA, and private views in the East End. Her presence at these events, to which Alex of late had awkwardly and excitedly accompanied her, gave her, she felt, some sort of status beyond that of a teacher, a sense of inhabiting a private and more engaging London than the resolutely English city known to his friends.

There had been a dinner – Charlie and Fran? Emma and Henry? Sébastien's book was lying on the Heal's coffee table. For all that its presence was like a prop in a bad film, it had stabbed at her. His photograph was on the back cover, a Hollywood film version of the French intellectual. The men had already gone through to the garden.

'Are you reading this?' Claudia asked.

'I should. Did you see him on the telly?'

'Yes,' said Claudia.

'Oh, God, of course, you probably know him. He is *so* gorgeous.'

'I do know him,' answered Claudia, 'a little.'

She smoked too much and drank a bottle of Australian red by herself. There was a glabrous potato salad. Claudia watched Alex eat it in the dying light. He pretended to mind about food, but she wondered sometimes if he knew what anything really tasted like. Pudding was ice cream from an expensive box. All the time, Claudia had seen Sébastian's face, the hollow above his collar bone in the shadow of his jaw as he moved inside her in the dark. The image rasped at her like dust motes dancing in the tilt and whistle of an invisible wind.

Claudia's handbag slumped on a bentwood chair, carefully repainted and then distressed by Aisling. Sandpaper, she said. Claudia took the bag in both hands, so it shouldn't clink, and went back to the bathroom. Then she lay face down on the floor and wept. For a while, she was unconscious of the sound she made, then gradually the high keening that had hummed and pushed in her ears since she had woken was released, and she heard it away from her, like a ship's horn caught across a beach, coming closer and closer until it subsided into great hissing sobs that crossed her like blows. She gasped for air and rolled on to her side. Here I am, she thought. On the floor in the bathroom. She sat up and pushed her hair with wet hands from her wet face, saying nothing to herself. In her bag, tucked into a book Sébastien had given her, was the letter he had sent. The book was a beautiful edition of John Donne's poems, over a hundred years old. The letter said:

My darling Claudia,

Alarms and excursions. I am so sorry that you left Paris that way. I am sorry, also, that we had the conversation we had, and if I loved anyone at all, my own, it would be you. I don't see the inevitability of our parting any more than I see the inevitability of that, but I am sorrily flattered when you say you could not bear it. I don't think, though, that I told you, when you forced me, anything you had not known when we met. You know where I am, my love.

Ever your,

S x

Claudia looked at the letter for an hour, the last five minutes of which she saw go by on her watch. She tried to get a signal on her mobile, but was reduced to slithering painstakingly downstairs to the phone in the kitchen. At precisely three a.m., she dialled his flat in Paris. He would be up, he liked to work at night. She whispered that she was sorry, that she had not meant to be so pleading, so undignified, that he ought to know her better than that, that she didn't know what had come over her and that she had decided to marry Alex. They had laughed about Alex in bed together. They called him Old Faithful. Sébastien said, 'Well, lucky Old Faithful. Shall you be a faithful spouse?'

'Terribly,' said Claudia. 'You're invited to dance at my wedding, of course.' They laughed.

Claudia went back to bed with a glass of water as a prop and surprised herself by falling asleep rather quickly.

Claudia's hair was the colour of acacia honey, thought Aisling, and she was quite insufferable. It was Friday, changeover day. Aisling was doing what she called 'the chapel walk', a path that led up through the woods behind Murblanc and passed a small, pink brick church whose foundations, according to a sad little printed card, were Roman. It was displayed with the modest and, to Aisling, infuriating diffidence to tourist attractions so typical of the region. The track looped around the plain square block of Aucordier's farm, isolated on the high purple-grey plain, where ancient Mademoiselle Oriane lived alone – except for poor Ginette, who came occasionally to help Madame Lesprats with the ironing – and then doubled back along a poplar avenue to the Castroux road, dipping towards the river and a wonderful view of Murblanc on the right, which Aisling had photographed for her brochure. There was smoke rising from Aucordier's, scenting the still air with a brief autumnal reminder of mouldering wood, but Aisling was alone today in the landscape, her figure progressing across the ridge with the permanence of an illumination from a mediaeval book of hours. The idea soothed her, gave a resonance to the contact of her feet with the ancient road, a little pilgrim marching stolidly beneath a bright sky bordered in golden curlicues and peacocks entwined in mounting, green-inked boughs. There seemed always to be a breeze in the poplar avenue, and their branches today made a sound like water rushing far away. 'Soughing,' thought Aisling, pleased with the justice of her word, and she stretched her arms so that her knuckles met behind her back, and turned her face up to the sky, breathing the remaining freshness of the morning, which still smelt green, though throbbing already with the gold promise of the heat.

Aisling had been up at seven, diligently seeing off the ghastly Lawses before their long cross-country drive. As she crossed back from la Maison Bleue, she heard Madame Lesprats' car pulling in at the bottom of the hill, and thought that she should really have brought the fresh linen for the turnover down with her, to save Madame Lesprats, who was at least sixty, a hot climb. Yet she felt selfish today, a little careless, and wanted to be away from the house before anyone woke up to claim her. It was Claudia's tone, she decided, which had so ruffled her, an imprecise suggestion of patronage. Too small to be in any way reasonable to mention in bed to Jonathan after dinner, and unkind perhaps, as the girl was probably nervous, uncertain before what was after all to be her new family, though Aisling didn't in the least believe that, didn't believe that Claudia was the sort of person who was ever nervous. She had said to Jonathan, 'What do you think?' hoping that if he, too, had some reservation, she might be able to analyse her own aloud. But he was muffled with drink, *digestifs* and red wine on top of the vintage champagne that Alex had produced with City-ish ostentation to toast the engagement, and had only said, 'Seems like Alex has done pretty well'. Aisling understood this clearly to imply that he found Claudia sexy, too sexy to mention. Jonathan only felt it safe to comment on women's looks when they did not interest him. He thought this prudent and diplomatic, without realizing that Aisling was perfectly aware that if he said a woman was 'very attractive', it meant that he didn't really think so. He had no idea that the quality of his silences was a more precise indication of interest than if he had denied having noticed that a woman had any allure.

Claudia was very pretty, Aisling recognized, pretty enough for it to be surprising, almost, that she should be with Alex, but jealousy was not the source of her discomfort. Aisling had never had any claim to be particularly good-looking, had been sensibly aware of the fact since she was quite young, and had simply made the best of herself so as not to look, as her own mother would have put it, 'a fright'. She took care with her clothes, her hair and her make-up, but with little vanity, content that she should look nice and not aspiring to more. Rancour at other, more beautiful women had never troubled her, and now, at forty-two, this calmness about her appearance gave her an attractiveness that other women of her age who had perhaps been far more so a few years ago might be glad to possess. Having no special looks to lose, Aisling did not make the mistake of trying with pathetic tenacity to retain them. Her figure had always been average, but was little changed after two pregnancies, and she was fit from walking, gardening and swimming. She never dieted, or squeezed herself into unflattering clothes a size too small. Her hands were protected by gloves and lotion when she worked outside, and though she guarded her fair skin from the sun, she did not mourn the wrinkles around her eyes or the grooves that ran from her nose to the edge of her lips. The other English women she knew from around Landi seemed to fall into two categories. There was a depressing carelessness, like her friend Charlotte Glover, who occasionally ornamented her shapeless blouses and sensible slacks with an ill-advised scarf or slash of lipstick, which served to accentuate her general grubbiness. Equally depressing was the attempt at glamour, spongy pink bodies, bloated with alcohol and idleness, spilling out of brief bikinis, low-cut tops and too much hard jewellery. In comparison, Aisling felt quite satisfied with her own appearance, which she judged in the language of her magazines to be elegant and understated. Jonathan usually complimented her when they dressed up to go to a dinner party or an occasional concert in Toulouse, and in groups with other husbands she felt less invisible than she had at twenty.

Claudia's looks, Aisling decided as she started down the road towards home, were definitely not the problem, though it was disturbing to see Alex mooning over her so, jumping up to fetch her cigarettes or her pashmina, attentions that Claudia seemed to demand as little as she took them for granted. No, it was her tone. Last night, with the PGs safe, prodding mirthlessly at her carefully marinaded chicken breasts, Aisling had felt relaxed, expansive, proud of her home and her beautiful view, of Oliver and Richard, neat in pale blue shirts, of the fragrance of her food, so she had felt awkward when Claudia had turned the conversation to the fact that after their two years in France, the Harveys had not really made any French friends.

'Really?' she had said, exhaling a long plume of Marlboro Light over the remains of the strawberry brûlée. 'Are the people here unfriendly to strangers, then?' Her inflection was entirely solicitous. At home, Aisling thought, she would have asked the girl to put it out.

'Incomers, eh?' put in Alex, snorting as though he had said something clever.

'Not quite that, I think,' defended Jonathan, 'more that, well, the people around here have lived here for generations, and, well ...'

'They're not quite PLU?' suggested Claudia, her head on one side.

'Darling!' said Alex, with mock sternness, taking her hand and turning it to kiss the inside of her slim wrist, so that her ring caught in the candlelight, his eyes turned up to her face. Claudia pulled away, the movement slightly exaggerated with Armagnac.

'Since we're in the country, darling, let's call a spade a spade. Or a peasant a peasant for that matter. Shall I help you clear, Aisling? Gorgeous pudding.'

Scraping and stacking the plates for the dishwasher, Aisling had felt an unaccustomed urge to explain, to justify herself to Claudia. But why should Claudia make her feel insecure? What would she know about living in France, or the countryside, or the French? She was obviously a snob, probably intimidated by Murblanc and trying to feel superior at the Harveys' expense. Yet, distressingly, she was right, in a way. Aisling's acknowledgement of this blended with her certainty that she would find the little tartlets she had made for the Laws family untouched in the morning, and that somehow, this was connected to the fact that she and Jonathan had never been asked for drinks by Monsieur d'Esceyrac when he stayed at the chateau that overlooked the village, even though he had been perfectly affable to them that time they had met at the *chasse* lunch in February, and had told Aisling that she was welcome to the walnuts and plums that fell from his strayed fruit trees on to Murblanc land.

Aisling had meant to make a warm clafoutis of these plums for the new PGs, who would arrive that evening, but along with the linens, she had forgotten to take the labelled bag from the big freezer, and now she would have to think of something else that would be quick, as she had to drive the boys to the riding stables in the afternoon. Oliver and Richard were not quite yet at the age when hours of fusty morning sleep were an urgent necessity, and although it was only half past eight she heard them in the pool as she let herself through the side door, quickening her pace as she stepped down the narrow corridor with the pantry on one side, the boot room and the *buanderie* on the left, thinking that she must consult the dreaded exercise book for the welcome dinner. She could feel the calm of her walk draining from her, parched out by the strengthening sun.

The kitchen was full of cigarette smoke, blue and nauseating. Claudia was perched on the worktop in a pair of baggy white pyjamas, holding an Emma Bridgewater coffee mug with a pattern of fig leaves and staring into space.

'Morning,' said Aisling tightly. 'Sorry, do you mind putting that out?'

Claudia started, rather guiltily, caught out. 'God, Aisling, I'm so sorry,' she rushed, stubbing the end into a saucer and ineffectually waving her hand at the smoke, as smokers do. 'Look, it won't happen again. I'm really sorry. So rude of me.'

She looked genuinely distressed. 'It's all right,' said Aisling, and surprised herself by adding, 'I used to smoke myself. But Jonathan hated it.'

'Alex, too,' said Claudia, with a hint of conspiratorial smile.

Aisling disliked her even more. 'I've got to get on, actually,' she said in a brisk, housekeeper tone. 'All the breakfast things are under the cloth on the side terrace. The boys can show you. Perhaps you might like a swim?'

'Is there anything I can do to help? You seem awfully busy.'

'I'm fine, thanks.'

'Well, I'll go and get dressed, then.'

Aisling retrieved the exercise book from beneath three large aubergines in the vegetable basket, which brimmed at one end of the long oak work table. She wrote 'Tartlets not a success (too tart?!). Mrs Laws said we have lovely home, but didn't we miss England, I said this is home. Awful, really.' On a new page, she added, 'Welcome dinner. Froggett Family. Aperitif PG white with ratatouille toasts. Prawns with aioli. Poussin with citrus sauce, haricots verts, almond rice. Brouilly chilled. Cheese, salad.' If she used some of the hard, sharp ewe's cheese, she could drizzle it with the excellent local chestnut honey. But the Froggetts would expect a proper pudding. Aisling scribbled, 'Baked peaches with rosewater crème fraîche.' She could pick the fruit up while the boys were riding. That would have to do.

MAY 1934

The new road into Castroux had been built in Napoleon's time. It had been planned to pass through the village and follow the crest of the hill above the Landine river, through the hamlet of Saintonge, and on another fifty kilometres to the departmental capital of Monguèriac. The road came to Castroux and never left, a quibble in a sub-prefecture, a favour unreturned, an intractable landowner; no one remembered why, but it had never been finished, so the road stopped short at the corner of the church, opposite the optimistically classical facade of the *Mairie*. The new road formed a branch of the 'Y' shape of the village, with the church sitting in the crook, the old road dipping to the bridge across the river, and the track to Saintonge rising obliquely to the left. Aside from the *Mairie*, the new road had changed nothing in the aspect of the village, which staggered up the eastern side of the hill as it had done since the convent had been burned to the ground in the forgotten intensity of the Cathar persecutions. Coming up from the river, the walled garden of the nuns, bowed out with ancient, ligneous apple trees, was the first sign of the village. The ingenious irrigation channels of the garden had been diverted to the wash-house, which now faced the gateway, but herbs grew there still, great humps of sage and rosemary, full of butterflies in summertime. Though the walks had vanished long ago, the grass was rich, and this enclosed half-acre retained – without the quotidian business of the village-proper where trees that did not yield were good only for burning – an air of tapestried enchantment, as though unicorns might still lie down there.

If the ghost of a hollow-eyed, white-draped nun were still to walk in Castroux, it was unlikely she would be sighted near the church itself, which was of a later and altogether more prosaic date. The Madonna in the Lady Chapel, a snug wooden personage of the early seventeenth century, was convincingly matronly, almost rotund, and though the brightness of her cheeks had faded, they were still sufficiently pink to suggest that she had plenty of energy to spare from the cheerful Christ-child plumped stolidly in her lap to go about such matters as the strangling of ducks and the bottling of apricots, should that be required. She suited Castroux much better than the delicate, etiolated remnants of more mystical piety. Superstitions that had been old in the days of the convent remained in the village yet, but they were of a practical cast, concerned with the burying of rabbits at full moon in potato patches, or the efficacy of a pregnant woman's urine to bring on the artichokes. Père Guillaume, whose name had been manipulated on his arrival in Castroux to Poire William, a great joke in 1920 and still good for a laugh more than a decade later, had been troubled initially by the increases to the poor box brought about by his predecessor's having sold vials of holy water, which were apparently of great benefit to the melons. He resigned himself quickly to the mysterious workings of the Lord, blessed a barrel of it in front of the church on Easter Monday, and permitted the congregation to siphon it off in cans, greatly benefiting in turn a charity for orphan apprentices that was dear to his heart. Castroux, correspondingly, was noted for the sweetness of its melons, and for a viscous eau de vie stewed out of them in a barely concealed still by Papie Nadl at Murblanc every September, to whose effects, within bounds and bearing in mind his nickname, Père Guillaume turned another blinded eye.

The orphan apprentices possessed a fine new headquarters, with schoolhouse and dormitories, on the edge of Monguèriac, and it was to this long, yellow-washed building that Père Guillaume turned his thoughts when Sophie Aucordier, poor woman, passed away leaving an idiot son and a daughter not yet fourteen. Père Guillaume was concerned for the child; it seemed to him she had a hard life, even by Castroux standards, with a drunken father and an imbecile brother. The mother had been decent enough, though she had never struck the priest as a kind woman. She had brought her children regularly to Mass, and when Père Guillaume had tried to speak to her about Oriane's more irregular appearances in the schoolhouse she had met his criticism with resignation rather than excuses, to which, from what he knew of their hardscrabble existence up there on the plain, he would have listened sympathetically. The Nadl family, at Murblanc, had been good to the orphans, he believed. Madame Nadl had come for him when it was time for the last rites, and had supervised the arrangements for a respectable funeral, but charity in Castroux began strictly at home. Oriane Aucordier could not expect her neighbours to take responsibility for long.

Père Guillaume had made inquiries at the apprentice school, and at the *Mairie* concerning what remained of the Aucordier farm, and, as he set out on his bicycle on a raw wet day in May, he believed he had found a solution to the poor girl's future. If the property were to be sold, and Oriane spent a few years in Monguèriac, she would have enough to support the brother decently until such a time as God called (and Père Guillaume, calculating on the back of a missionary pamphlet in the presbytery one night, had guiltily considered that William's type rarely live long), and to leave a small competence for herself that would enable her to find work, as a lower standard teacher perhaps. Mademoiselle Lafage, at the school, said she was quite able, and then, perhaps, she might get married.

Père Guillaume freewheeled all the way to the bridge over the Landine, then dismounted for the climb to Aucordier's. He thanked the good Lord for his bicycle, which kept him fit enough for emergency rushes about his hilly parish. The basket had been fitted with a rainproof leather fishing box, which was most convenient for the oil and wafers of extreme unction, or the lugging of the censer up to Saintonge, where he said Mass monthly in the little ancient chapel. At the seminary, Père Guillaume had thought of getting up a cycling club, but had been advised that the bishop might have something to say about it, and he felt a little rush of pleasure at his independence now, each time he mounted the machine and bowled along a lane with his cassock hitched up and billowing out behind. It seemed impossibly far away, that world where a bicycle might be seen as encouraging immorality, though he could delineate clearly the twenty years of his own life that had passed since he had daringly purchased his first Follis. He felt that time had expanded so, since the War, even here in Castroux, that those memories of his cautious bishop might have belonged to his own grandfather. Still, it was certainly a wholesome activity, and he felt rather wistful that he couldn't interest the lads in the village in a club, but the idea of taking physical exercise for pleasure in Castroux was seen as an absurd affectation. Fit for the lady guests of the d'Esceyracs perhaps, who might occasionally be seen, encumbered with easels and parasols, wandering about in the park of the chateau, but unreasonable for hardworking Christians, who obeyed the commandment to rest on a Sunday with an alacrity that Père Guillaume wished they might spread more evenly over the remainder of the Catechism.

Oriane Aucordier was stooped over a fork in the kitchen garden when he rolled his bicycle cautiously through the churned sludge of the yard. He thought irritably of splotches on his mudguards, and that later he would have to brush dried muck from the hem of his cassock. The girl wore man's rubber boots with her thin bare legs showing, and a shapeless brown overall, lumpen and sexless, but Père Guillaume noticed that she had put up her thick braid of dark hair under a cap since the funeral. She greeted him politely and invited him to step into the house, without any of the flapping apologies for unwashed floors or ill-arranged husbands with which women customarily welcomed his visits. The fire was banked up high, and the dirt-floored room pleasantly warm after the dripping chill outdoors. The priest noted with approval that the pots stacked by the hearth were scoured, as was the huge wooden table of creamy oak, while the brother, squatting harmlessly under the stairs and occupied with a bird-scaring rattle, appeared equally well tended. His deformed ears, splayed wide like an overblown cabbage, were pink inside and out, and his green wool jersey had a thick darn like a caterpillar on the collar.

'William,' said Oriane clearly, 'look, Father is here to see us.'

Père Guillaume understood a little Occitan, after ten years, and Oriane's speech was slow enough for him to catch the words. What astonished him was the acknowledgement in the boy's eyes, and the fact that, after some straining with his poor misshapen mouth, William produced a sound that might, kindly interpreted, approximate to '*Bonjour*'.

'Well done, William!' answered the priest heartily, and Oriane spoke again more quickly now, and again the boy seemed to make sense of her, for he put down the rattle and sat quietly, staring placidly at his sister.

Oriane made no explanation for him, as though it were perfectly usual that this dumb child might, after a fashion, speak, and switched to French. Her accent was heavy, with the thin, strained 'i' sound short and mean, as was typical of the region, but her grammar was good.

'Please sit down, Father. Can I serve you a glass, a small glass, of wine? We have plenty left over from—' she breathed, recovered herself, 'Madame Nadl was very kind, we have a whole jug.'

This was the right form, and it amused Père Guillaume to see this child so gravely observe it. He accepted the wine, of which he would taste, as was his habit, one or two polite sips. This practice saved him, he thought, both from insulting his parishioners, to whom a refusal would be a serious breach of etiquette, and from falling into the bibulous habits so distressingly associated with country priests. Oriane poured the wine from a glazed pot, lifting it effortfully with both hands, and then sat down at the table facing him, her hands still in her skirt.

'How have you been, Oriane?' asked the priest kindly.

'Well, Father, I could not truthfully say well, of course, but I think I am managing. There's a lot of work, but I'm used to that.'

He had not expected such containment. Perhaps she might weep, ask for help, advice, suffer, but she was measured, strangely dignified, not pathetic at all.

'Have you been able to think, my child, of what you might do?'

There was a pause, her eyes passed over the room, over William. 'Yes, Father. I am going to stay here and take care of my brother. I went up to the chateau yesterday, and they'll take me as an out-servant, to help in the kitchen and the laundry. Cathérine Nadl works there already. Madame Nadl says she will keep an eye on William, but I think, in time,' and here she looked hopeful, childish for a moment, 'that I can teach him how to be useful, carrying things and so on, and he might be able to help, with simple things. I can manage the farm in the evenings. I'm going to let the back field to the Nadls, so I shan't have to worry about that.'

'Let it? Oriane you can't, that is, the law won't allow you to do such things. You are what is called a minor, you can't just—'

She cut him off, not boldly or impertinently, but precisely. 'Forgive me, Father, I don't mean to be rude, but it is mine isn't it? Mine and William's, the house and the land? Monsieur Nadl says that it can be done legally, with papers.'

'I'm sure he does,' said the priest drily.

'And if I can't yet, about the field I mean, then it can go to grass and I can still live here, can't I?'

'No. It's not right, not decent. You are very brave, Oriane, but you are too young.'

She was quiet, thinking. 'If my mother was still, still here, then I would do exactly the same things that I do now. I can do everything, really. I do the goats and the chickens, and the vegetables, and I can cook, I wash the clothes, everything. I've always done it. And I am not leaving William, or putting him into a hospital, they do terrible things there, they cut pieces out of people's brains and take photographs of them, and it's not a sin to stay in your own house, you never said it was!'

The tears were starting, her lower lip pulled tight against her teeth in an effort to stop them falling. Père Guillaume felt it was time to be firm. 'I am here to help you, not to listen to silliness, Oriane. Now, there's a place in Monguèriac for you, where you can receive a good education, and find a better way to take care of yourself and William than going into service. Wouldn't you like that?'

Oriane Aucordier turned up her face to the priest and she wept at him. She did not cry like a woman. She did not snuffle shamefacedly into a handkerchief or pass a grubby sleeve across smudged and coarsened eyes, or grab mortifyingly at his shoulder. There was a pure quality to her beseeching, neither affected nor ashamed. She let the water stream defiantly from her black eyes and down her cheeks, so pale the skin, grained fine as expensive soap, wept like a statue, like a miracle.

Père Guillaume took out his handkerchief, and she wiped her face, but did not duck her head away. She handed him back the bunched wet cloth, and said nothing.

'Let us pray together, my child,' he said, and she folded her hands obediently on the table, but he knew, and she knew, that she had won.

SUMMER HOLIDAYS

The Froggetts were not expected until six, and Claudia appeared to be reading by the pool. Jonathan often felt vague when Aisling was gone, as though she drew the energy of the house, its point, away with her. He thought he should ask Alex to accompany him in his appointed task for the afternoon, driving to the co-op at Saintonge to collect the wine, the PG white, which they often actually drank themselves, and the rich, heavy local red about which Jonathan invariably remarked to visitors, as he poured it from one of Aisling's big white china jugs, that it really deserved an *appellation contrôllée*. Wine was something the PGs didn't seem to understand, they preferred lugging precarious bags of bottles from the supermarket, regarding the idea of wine *en vrac* as dirty and industrialized. Jonathan took pleasure in loading up his ten-litre containers, their plastic moulded in an utterly unconvincing and yet somehow authentic imitation of wood, the two funnels, one stained dark berry-colour, and their loyalty card, an innovation recently introduced by Madame Chaveau, and of which she was touchingly proud.

It was a short drive, and Jonathan spent it informing Alex about the various grape varieties of the region. Alex listened peaceably, storing the information for production later over a wine list. He imagined himself presenting a bottle of Madiran to Henry, saying, 'You really ought to try this. Quite as much depth as a burgundy, really smooth. My brother's a bit of a wine buff, lives over there.' In the airy, corrugated iron shed, so unsympathetic to paying guests, Jonathan filled up his flagons from a hosepipe. 'We've got guests arriving tonight, so I'm filling up!' he remarked brightly to Madame Chaveau, but he spoke rather too quickly, his French falling over itself in his effort to impress Alex. She looked at him as though she had never seen him before.

'You know, at Murblanc. We've got guests.' He waved a flagon encouragingly.

'That will be fourteen euros sixty, please,' said Madame Chaveau, pressing a button on her computer and presenting Jonathan with a briskly printed receipt, which also gave the price in francs.

Jonathan suggested going into the village for a beer at the café. He did not tell Alex that he sometimes went there with the boys to play pétanque, and that it had really taken quite a few visits for the owner to realize they weren't French. There was no one to say hello to today anyway, because the bar was empty. It was not Castroux's most attractive building, a newish two-storey house in yellow plaster with a concrete terrace scratched out from the bus stop. Posters of women in frilly lingerie astride violently coloured Japanese motorbikes adorned the walls. 'Bit early for a drink around here,' said Jonathan as they carried their demis briefly through the sharp light to a table in the shade of the plastic awning, 'only tourists have nothing better to do.'

'Good beer,' offered Alex politely.

Jonathan and Alex were essentially uninterested by one another. The ten-year gap in their ages meant they had never been companions, playfellows. Jonathan had been married with his own business and two children when Alex left university, and was perfectly aware that if he saw more of his brother now than he had when he lived in England, it was because Alex thought Murblanc a smart place to invite girls. Jonathan felt affectionate towards his brother, and they did not bore one another, letting Aisling take the burden of conversation and confining their own to comments about cars, Alex's work at the bank, Jonathan's boys, and sports. They both supported Chelsea. Alex had given Jonathan quite a profitable tip about some shares in a Moroccan mining company a few years ago; Alex played the metropolitan mover and shaker to Jonathan's country squire. They did not investigate their mutual belief in these roles.

'So,' said Jonathan, 'here's to the joys of marriage.'

Alex took this defensively. 'I really am sure, you know. Claudia's a wonderful girl.' He paused, coy with sincerity. 'I love her very much.'

'Of course you do,' said Jonathan quickly, 'she seems very nice, attractive, bright.'

They sipped their drinks.

'Do you know her family?'

'The father's dead. Claudia's an only child and her mother

lives in Spain. They don't seem very close. I had lunch with her, the mother, when she was over for a weekend. She's fine.'

'Selling the flat?'

'Claudia wants us both to. I'd rather hang on, to be honest, see what the market's going to do.'

'You think you'll make more if you wait?'

Alex told Jonathan about a friend of his who had made a fortune with two ex-council properties on a buy-to-let mortgage in Hackney. Jonathan asked which areas he thought were up-and-coming, Alex talked about nought per cent finance deals on prospective rental properties, and the advantages of living a bit further out. They finished their beer and had another. It was a very satisfactory conversation.

The Glovers came to supper on Saturday evening. They lived in a little stone barn at Saintonge, part of what had once been a pig farm. Charlotte, who used to teach ceramics at a College of Further Education, had cleverly turned one of the sties into a kiln. Malcolm had worked in a bank.

'Oh God!' laughed Claudia charmingly, 'I came here to escape from bankers!'

Malcolm Glover looked a little offended.

'Who were you with?' asked Alex, certain that they would know someone in common. Malcolm explained that he had been a branch manager at the HSBC in Tunbridge Wells. Claudia stopped herself from saying how funny, I didn't think anyone truly came from Tunbridge Wells.

Malcolm smiled and said, 'Disgusted of Tunbridge Wells?'

'You must show Claudia my jug, Aisling,' said Charlotte, later.

Aisling went indoors and returned with a green jug. 'How pretty,' Claudia exclaimed. 'What kind of a glaze did you use to get that effect of depth?'

'Well,' answered Charlotte, 'the colours here are so inspiring. I made a series called seasons, you see, each inspired by the different colours of the seasons, and this jug is "June" for the colours of the leaves when they are so full on the trees.'

Malcolm said, 'Contented of Tunbridge Wells, I should think. I don't know how you do it, Aisling. I wish Charlotte could cook like you!' Everyone laughed, this was a familiar topic.

Aisling arranged her face. 'But Charlotte's cassoulet is divine. I can never get that depth of flavour. Do you use a special pot?'

Aisling had cooked individual goat cheese soufflés, a Portuguese-inspired fish stew with pancetta and chickpeas, and the pistachio custard. The Froggetts had not seemed distressed by the baked peaches, though the elder daughter was a vegan, which was a bore. She had decided that she really disliked Claudia, and listening to her make poor Charlotte look small was in some way satisfactory. Claudia drank a lot, she thought, finishing her aperitif before anyone else, and knocking back Armagnac like a man. This was also satisfactory. Aisling did not particularly like her friend Charlotte, when it came to it, she found her woolly, though she was certainly more interesting than Malcolm, but then living abroad did mean that one had to find one's friends where one could, and poor Charlotte had a kind heart.

Malcolm and Charlotte made love vigorously on the sofa in their converted barn. They liked it there, because Malcolm could enter Charlotte from behind while her head was propped comfortably over the back. Afterwards, Malcolm lit a lavender candle and poured them out a glass of whisky to share. The Glovers had very little money. Charlotte lay naked on the ethnic cushions, stroking Malcolm's shoulder and occasionally raising her head to give it a soft, clinging kiss. Malcolm stroked her plump tanned thigh.

'Aisling hates that Claudia girl,' said Charlotte, 'I could tell.'

'What did you think of her, wise beloved?'

'I thought,' said Charlotte, raising her head, 'that she seemed terribly unhappy. But then who wouldn't be, engaged to that awful Alex?'

'He seemed sound enough.'

'Exactly, darling,' said Charlotte. The Glovers smiled at one another in the candlelight.

Claudia had decided to tell Alex about the baby on Monday. They would go to dinner at a restaurant that Aisling had recommended in Landi, and she would tell him over coffee. She would say, 'Darling, we must give Aisling a night off,' and then she would tell him. Once she had done so, she thought, it would be irrevocable. Claudia had no illusions that she was doing anything but wrong. The baby ought to have a father, she said to herself, and Alex would do very well. He really did like children, always asking Jonathan about the boys, he wanted to marry her, as she had known he would the first time she had dinner with him, and he had not the imagination for flamboyant or humiliating infidelity. Claudia's father had been exuberantly unfaithful to her mother, and though Claudia had to some extent sympathized with his motivations, they had caused complications. The Wessons had divorced eventually. Claudia's mother had moved to Spain, becoming in the process, Claudia thought, rather vulgar, and then Claudia's father had died. Her mind shied from that, with Alex sleeping next to her, his arm ironically protective across her waist. Her mother played golf a good deal.

Alex began to snore. Snot gurgled in his throat and Claudia wanted to kick him. She lifted his arm gently away from her and he turned over, quiet. Claudia turned too, shoving the sheet away from her and dangling her feet into the coolness, but it was no good, she was awake. The wide varnished planks of the floor were cool under her feet as she found her cigarettes and lighter on the bureau, and crossed the landing, a spectre, she thought, in her white pyjamas. From their bedroom, three crooked steps twisted to the drawing room, where the balcony doors were open to the air. Claudia sat cross-legged on the broad stone parapet, not yet cool in the night. She was surprised by the moonlight, real silver moonlight, sharpening the white edges of the house and filling the lawn with deep, reptilian shadow. She could pick out the lustre on the shutters of the guesthouse, and beyond that the square tower of the church over the river at Castroux, backed with bright stars. There were no stars in London, she thought, but here she could see what few constellations she recognized, the Plough and Orion, and trails of unknown others, childishly abundant, so clear she thought she fancied she could see moon-dust hovering in their radiance. There were no lights in the valley, but the night was not peaceful. There were owls here, peacocks, Aisling said, in the garden of the chateau, boar and deer that sometimes came to drink from the swimming pool, foxes. She tucked her hair behind her ears to prevent it falling into the flame of her lighter, and as her thumb clicked the little bevelled wheel there was a rustling from the trees at the end of the lawn. Claudia held her breath, excited. There was something big there. She held the unlit cigarette and peered into the trees, half expecting to see a figure emerge, some terrible moon-faced idiot from the village creeping around the house, or a mysterious man, secret and purposeful in the shadows. There was no more sound. Claudia felt foolishly disappointed, as if she were on a safari and had missed a glimpse of a lion or giraffe. She lit her cigarette.

The baby would be born in March, the doctor had said. Claudia had made an appointment at a private clinic, wanting to deal efficiently with a stranger, and the doctor, sensing her recalcitrance, or perhaps being polite at the bare evidence of Claudia's left hand, had not congratulated her or shown any enthusiasm.

'You intend to have the baby?' she had asked, although if Claudia had not intended thus she would have approached the appointment differently, making it apparent from the start that she needed an abortion. The doctor had given her some leaflets, suggested a book she might buy, asked her if she smoked (Claudia lied), warned her about drinking alcohol and over-exerting herself at the gym. Claudia wondered what the doctor thought of her, this quiet young woman in her expensive suit, if she wondered at all about her patients.

'Good luck, then,' she had said, as Claudia had thanked her and gathered her handbag.

The idea of a baby Claudia was sure she wanted very much. She had no sense of herself 'giving birth', no excitement at the thought of breast feeding or tiny clothes. Shopping on a Saturday morning, or taking a ski lift, she and Alex, like everyone else, would point out sweet little children to one another, determined muffled bundles, showing their own sweetness to one another. None of Claudia's friends had babies. Alex knew a couple in Surrey with two, but Claudia had so far avoided going to lunch with them. She had briefly, stupidly, imagined Sébastien shepherding her proudly through a market in Paris, lying in bed with him with their child sleeping on his chest, scenes from a film or an advertisement. Sébastien was impossible, and Claudia believed that she was acting practically. She supposed that if she had the baby with Sébastien's knowledge, he would agree to give her money, to visit and take an interest, but deceiving Alex relied on Sébastien's ignorance, and she could not risk making him part of it.

The newspapers were always talking about the expense of childcare. If Claudia had the child on her own, she reasoned, even if Sébastien were dutiful about it, she would have to give up her job, at least for a time. This would necessitate her selling the flat in Lexington Street, which she had bought outright with all the money left by her father, and moving somewhere cheaper, so that she would have money to spare when she did not work. There was something about the thought of herself pushing a pram around Stoke Newington or Queen's Park that she couldn't bear. Fat, she supposed in the Queen's Park version, and covered in milky sick. And it would be years and years before it could go to school, you were always reading about how mothers couldn't afford to work because nursery was so expensive. As Claudia saw it, she was making an exchange, herself for her child. She would be Alex's wife, they would live in town, she would be able to work or not as she chose, there would be money for school fees and holidays. She did not pretend to herself that there was anything admirable in this, it was just that she could imagine no other possibility that would be tolerable. She had not seriously considered selling her flat and taking off to Mexico or Andalucia, there was nothing she found enticing about setting herself bravely against the world, there was not the strength in her for that.

Nor did she tell herself that she loved Alex. There was nothing at all in her feeling for him that even resembled the pride and longing she had for Sébastien. Claudia and Alex had met at a large party given by one of Claudia's former students, an Italian girl who had been dating someone at Alex's bank. She had given him her number and had not been remotely surprised when he called the next day. They had dinner somewhere obvious. Alex was not good-looking, but he was tall, and his face was kind. Claudia's relationship with Sébestien was long past the point of even nominal fidelity, and Alex was a good lover. His cock was long and thick, and, perhaps because Claudia was unconcerned as to his opinion of her, she came easily with him, felt quiet when she slept in his arms. That Alex was not Claudia's 'type' caused less comment than she expected amongst her girlfriends, who themselves as they moved into their thirties, were considering men at whom they would not have looked two years before. If she had put off calling Annabelle and Sally, she told herself when she accepted Alex, it was because she needed to have everything straight first.

There was this too, Claudia thought, in her relationship with him. A sense of imminent compromise, unspoken of between her and her friends, who had dissected and analysed every incident of one another's lives over years' worth of wine bottles and coffee cups. This new reticence, a mutual, gentle refusal to insist or to question where once they would have dismissed, even laughed at one another's lovers. It came from a decade of London loves and London disappointments, infatuations that collapsed into disillusion, men unremembered and unmourned after ten years of bed-hopping. There was a gravity to this restraint, a required discretion, which was not entirely derived from the fact that it was no longer quite form to mock masculine inadequacy, sexual inadequacy, for the amusement of the girls. If Claudia and Sally and Annabelle no longer laughed at their boyfriends, it was because they needed one another to believe that these men were possibilities, loves rather than affairs, and this magic cloak of love was necessary to maintain the invisibility of doubt. They participated, they knew, in a narrative where desperation to find a man was funny and also rather risible, the stuff of novels read by secretaries on the Tube, but there was to be no admittance, even in unspoken desperation, of the possibility of something other than True Love. Mr Collins had still to be Mr Right, thought Claudia, pleased because that was rather clever. Claudia knew that her engagement, once announced, would carry with it a similarly unmentioned taint of spinsterish anxiety. It was a loyalty they needed now, she and her friends, this mutual pretence that they were the same careless creatures who had come to London together after university, and that if they chose such or such a man, it was because they loved him as they had once believed they loved other, less suitable incarnations, more beautiful, or cleverer though they had been, but that there was nothing in the quality of their love that had changed. That was the essential thing, this new silence.

There was a woman standing on the terrace below her, holding the handlebars of a bicycle. Her appearance had come so silently that it took a moment to realize, so Claudia's gasp of shock sounded stagy. She was breathless, Claudia could hear her urgent panting, she looked around, confusedly, then saw Claudia's white pyjamas in the moonlight, and called out in French, 'Quick, please, I need to telephone! For the doctor.'

'Who are you?'

'Oh, Ginette. From Aucordier's. I need the phone for Mademoiselle Oriane.'

Fear resolved into the simpler timbre of domestic emergency. Claudia jumped off the parapet and ran through the drawing room, up the stairs to Aisling's bedroom, knocked peremptorily and poked her head into the darkness. 'Aisling, Aisling,' she hissed in a half-whisper, 'Aisling wake up! There's some woman downstairs who says she needs the phone. It sounds urgent.'

The woman waited at the back door. Claudia dithered, London discretion fighting with drama, then turned the key, stepping back quickly along the passage. 'What do you want?'

Jonathan, down the stairs, 'What's going on?' Aisling in the doorway in a long nightdress. Claudia thought it was typical that she would keep up the rustic charm even when she slept.

'Oh, it's you, Ginette,' sighed Aisling, as though she were disappointed. 'It's only Ginette!' she shouted over her shoulder.

'The phone?'

Aisling proffered the portable and Ginette fished in the pocket of her nylon overall for a scrap of paper. She dialled carefully, pressing her fingers precisely on the digits, hunched over.

Jonathan appeared in a maroon towelling dressing-gown. The sweat of his sleep came thickly to Claudia's nose in the cooler air from the passage. 'What's up?' he asked in English.

'They haven't got a phone, you see,' said Aisling, as though that explained everything.

'Who hasn't got a phone, for God's sake?'

'Ginette and Mademoiselle Oriane, from Aucordier's up the hill. There must have been an accident. Claudia found her.'

Ginette turned back to them. She was thin, feet snub in green felt slippers. Claudia saw that Aisling had on a patient encouraging smile, as for a child. 'Mademoiselle Oriane had one of her nightmares. I heard her scream, then she fell out of bed on to the floor. I think she's broken her arm. I best go back up.' Her speech was rapid, in the thick nasal accent of the region. There was a moment of hesitancy on Aisling's face.

'The other lady is hurt,' Claudia offered.

'My God!' said Aisling dramatically, then quickly in English, 'I'll go up in the car. Jonathan, will you put the lights on and watch out for the doctor, he mayn't know the way up? Just a moment,' she added imperiously to Ginette.

Claudia followed Aisling up the stairs. 'Shall I come, too?' she asked, feeling that Aisling minded about something.

'You might as well, since you were up anyway.'

Alex was still sleeping. Claudia pulled his light sweater over her pyjamas and shoved at her espadrilles with her feet. On the way back down, she picked up a bottle of cognac from the table in the drawing room, Aisling reappeared in jeans. 'Right then, Ginette.' Jonathan was making tea. The three women loaded the bicycle into the boot of the car and Aisling manoeuvred carefully up the narrow Murblanc lane to the road, only slightly wider, steel coloured in the moonlight. The road climbed to the left until they stopped at the large square house that Claudia had seen over the brim of the hill. The door was open, a harsh neon strip frosted the yard from indoors. 'It's only me,' called Ginette loudly, 'and Madame Harvey.'

Mademoiselle Oriane was propped on the floor against a high wooden bed. Ginette had clearly been too afraid or too weak to move her. Aisling stepped forward purposefully, her voice matronly. 'Now, Mademoiselle, what's going on? You remember me don't you, Madame Harvey? From Murblanc? I bought your lovely table for my kitchen.'

The old woman's eyes were so pale that it was hard to discern where her floury, crinkled face began. Her hair was absolutely white, tucked into a blue web of hairnet. As Aisling approached, she spat at her, viciously. She called her, in a high, strong voice, the son of a whore.

Ginette rushed forward. 'I'm so sorry, Madame Harvey, she's confused, she gets like this. It's one of her spells, oh dear, when she fell, she was screaming so.' Ginette stopped short and began to cry, her sobs mounting into wails, she hiccuped breathlessly, uncontained, and began to gulp like a frog, her shoulders convulsing, saliva running down her chin.

'Oh Christ!' said Aisling.

Claudia cautiously put an arm around Ginette's shoulders, but the gasping continued, the frail muscles bouncing beneath her housecoat. Claudia shook her a little, then raised her arm and cut a short slap across her face.

'Now,' Claudia said firmly, feigning confidence, 'come and sit down, Ginette. I'm going to give you a little drink, and we're going to put Mademoiselle right. Come on.' She led Ginette to a dingy brown sofa, looked to the cupboard next to the huge old fireplace, occupied by an oil stove, and retrieved a glass. She was still holding the bottle of cognac. 'Now you drink that,' pouring a measure, 'and we'll get on. The doctor will be here soon.'

'She's not right, you know,' said Aisling in English, meaningful on the word 'right'.

'Should we lift her back?'

Mademoiselle Oriane had closed her eyes. With an arm each beneath her shoulders, they pulled her up until she half sat on the bed. She winced, her left arm dangling, Aisling slung her legs around, covered the horrible lumpen feet with sheet and blanket. Their swiftness was tender. Claudia fetched a glass of water and propped it to the slit of mouth. 'Is that better, Mademoiselle?'

Aisling unbent. 'We'd better wait for the doctor. It's a good half-hour drive from Landi. I'll make some tea.' Ginette was silent on the sofa, clutching her half-empty glass tightly, her eyes far away.

'What about her?' asked Claudia.

'Just shock, I suppose. I don't think it's serious. She comes to help Madame Lesprats sometimes, at our place. Madame Lesprats always calls her "pauvre Ginette".' Aisling was setting a pot of water to boil, pushing aside a saucepan from which a bone and a lump of carrot protruded.

The large room, hard in the neon, was floored in turquoise lino. Aside from the bed and the sofa, there was a fridge under the angular wooden staircase, a formica table covered in a wipe-clean plastic cloth printed with sunflowers, and four wooden chairs, a calendar from the church in Castroux on the wall next to the fireplace, a television half covered in a crocheted pink doily on a huge dark *buffet*, and a small folding table with a vase of plastic lilies and a framed photograph of a black and white young man with a Proustian moustache. There was too much space, like a set in a theatre before the actors come on, and a strong thick smell of soup. Around the fireplace, saucepans and casseroles were piled, neat but homeless, and the table was set with two striped coffee bowls, an orange plastic dish of white sugar cubes, and two teaspoons, ready, Claudia supposed, for breakfast. She had never seen such a poor room, a room whose sparseness had nothing artful in it, whose shabbiness was merely shabby, not deliberate or bohemian or charming. She had never been so stupid as to believe that there was anything picturesque about poverty, but the room grated at her nonetheless, in a way it would not have done if it had been squalid. It was ugly, and the ugliness was painful, the calendar with its photograph of a nun at Lourdes was painful, the orange bowl was painful.

Aisling had appropriated the coffee bowls and filled them with boiling water, into which she unenthusiastically dunked two Lipton tea bags. Claudia always associated those yellow labels with France, the way Lipton tea always left a white scum on the surface of the water.

'It's a shame, isn't it?' Aisling continued in English, following Claudia's eyes. 'It could be a wonderful house. I don't know why she doesn't sell it. The *maison de retraite* at Teulière is really wonderful, they have a marvellous time going on coach trips and playing boules. She could get a fortune for it you know, there's the barns too, but you know what the French are like.' She paused, then added in an accusing tone, 'I didn't know you spoke French.'

'I'll look out for the doctor, then.' Claudia took her tea to the doorway and looked down the hill for headlights.

1934–9

Propriety put the rout to Père Guillaume's good intentions. Mademoiselle Lafage, the schoolteacher, let it be known that she was looking for lodgings in the village as the Board had seen fit to appoint a master to the schoolhouse, and it was not decent that two unmarried people should share their quarters. Mademoiselle Lafage knew her rights, and applied to the *bureau* in Monguèriac for a boarding allowance. If the Board wanted to throw good money after bad, it was their own affair. Mademoiselle Lafage thought that no schoolmaster would be any more capable than she of prodding knowledge into the lumpish heads of the bigger Castroux boys. Monsieur François Boissière might well be from Toulouse, but she had taken her diploma in Paris, and was more than equal to him. If he thought she was going to waste her education teaching crochet and catechism he would have a surprise, that was all.

So Mademoiselle Lafage went to lodge up at Aucordier's with that poor child Oriane and her idiot brother. Laurent

Nadl came with a chalky bucket and distempered the walls of the best bedroom, which Oriane had the sense not to mention was where her father had twitched and raved to death. Mademoiselle Lafage's possessions were dragged up from Castroux on a cart. They included the artistic blue and yellow curtains that Mademoiselle had sewn and hung herself, and which she couldn't see were deserved by the new teacher. For the first time in Oriane's memory, a fire was lit upstairs. Mademoiselle Lafage arranged her books, hung up the framed copy of her diploma, and unpacked, to William's joy, a large elongated bellows of an instrument that she explained was called a bassoon. She let it be known that she would take her evening meal at the small table in her own room, and afterwards, if William did not become too excited, she allowed him to stand in the doorway as she practised, her legs stretched out in front of her, toes in their black shoes straining to a point on the high notes and her eyes squinting with concentration behind her glasses. The schoolmistress provided her own coffee and sugar, and washed her underthings in the flowered china basin that had belonged to Oriane's grandmother.

Oriane felt neither obliged nor ungrateful to Mademoiselle Lafage, though she was thankful for the simplicity of her presence. William was now able to wash and dress himself, and in the early mornings she allowed him to watch the coffee on the fire as she went about the yard, releasing the hens, stuffing bread and hay through the bars of the rabbit cages, watering the goats. On cold days, the little animals were reluctant to leave their warm, pungent stall, and she set William to chase them, flailing his arms and making a strange deep lowing noise that never failed to startle the silly creatures and send them hopping out into the wind. Sometimes Mademoiselle Lafage would look out of her window, a scarf tied around her sheared brown hair, and laugh as William pursued the goats enthusiastically into the mud. Oriane peeled the vegetables for the soup and left them in a pot of water, wiped coffee and mud from William and set off with him in her clogs, her clean apron rolled up in a bag.

William hated cold days, the wind slashed painfully at his ears and he yelped, rubbing his palm against the vulnerable holes. Oriane tried to protect him by tying a shawl of their mother's around his cap, so that his head bobbed monstrous large in the silver mist. In the unpredictable time between January and March, when dense, icy fog was succeeded by days of startling brightness, the sky as rich as ink, the braziers were lit in the dawn orchards. Some were oil stoves with lids to protect them from the wind, some just little clay pots filled with coals, which glowed orange all along the valley, around the chateau hill and up over the brow at Saintonge. Stumpy figures stood around them, wrapped into mushrooms, with the tips of their noses poking out of their scarves. They could be frightening, Oriane thought, these strange little goblin fires, if their purpose was not so tender. If the blossom was not saved, there would be no fruit, so the men of Castroux, even men like Camille Lesprats who got drunk in Dubois's and beat his own grandchildren, rose in the dark and coaxed the precious heat from the braziers, watching the newborn flowers until the sun rose as if they believed they could warm the trees by their own human presence.

Madame Nadl, Papie, Laurent and Cathérine were all kind.

William spent each morning at Murblanc, though Oriane feared at first that he would be in the way.

'Don't worry,' Madame Nadl told her, 'he's willing enough and it's company for Papie. They can keep each other out of mischief.' In the village, she said that it was a shame the way Sophie Aucordier had treated that poor child, he wasn't really dumb at all, just strange, and his sister kept him very nice, you had to say that for her. William trotted happily about with Papie, watching Laurent at work in the barn, driving the cows into the meadow each morning. They were beautiful cows, the Murblanc animals, seven big Blondes d'Aquitaine with cream-coloured hides and soft pink noses. His favourite was called Alice, and Madame Nadl taught him to milk her, pressing his face against her warm patient flank and smelling the sweet grassy smell of her cud. William waited in the barn, stroking Alice's ears and singing to her, when the Nadls went in for their lunch, until he saw Oriane coming down the track from the chateau.

They went to Mass every Sunday now. Amélie Lesprats boasted that she was going all the way to Landi to take the School Certificate, and Oriane thought it would have been nice to go to Landi too, but Amélie came to work at the chateau all the same afterwards, and it was still possible to speak good French with Mademoiselle Lafage. She didn't much mind leaving school, she had never gone there regularly, and Amélie didn't seem any cleverer for it. Laurent said he didn't see much point in girls going to school, it only made them ugly like Mademoiselle Lafage, and his own mother had managed quite well without it. Laurent's sister Cathérine said he was an old stick, and when she had enough money saved she was going to get a husband in Monguèriac, a man with a shop maybe, and sit behind the counter all day on a stool and never get up to milk an old cow again. Madame Nadl laughed and said how was Cathérine going to persuade this marvellous shopkeeper to marry her if her jam came out stringy and she burned the meat? 'He will love me for my great beauty,' replied Cathérine saucily, pushing her bosom out and patting her meagre bun, and they all laughed because Cathérine was as plain as a saucepan, but it wasn't cruel, because she said so herself.

Cathérine was always laughing, but Laurent was quite stern. Every week after Mass he set off on his motorbike, and no one knew where he went. La Moto, people called him. The machine was blue and black with polished silver pipes and Laurent could mount it quickly, despite his leg, twisting the handlebars into a triangle with his body and then supporting his whole weight on his arms as he started the engine. It looked as though it must have taken a lot of practice.

Oriane asked Cathérine why he hadn't got married, there'd be plenty of girls who would have him, and Cathérine said he was very serious, he wanted a serious girl, because he'd been in the war. Yves Contier had come home from the war though, and he had got married to Magalie, who wasn't that old, and they had four children. Bernard Vionne, too, had his boy Marcel. Oriane thought that maybe Laurent was ashamed because of only having one leg and felt very sorry for him. She knew about that, because of their father and William. Laurent was gentle though, and he always came up to Aucordier's when his own work was over if she asked him for help.

Most homes in Castroux did a big wash twice a year, in April and October. Two or three washerwomen came with a wagon from Landi, and for a week or so the wash-house opposite the nuns' garden was filled with steam and the scent of wet ash. Poplar wood was best for ashing, as oak and chestnut stained the clothes with tannin. If the wind was not high, the women draped the linens over the big rosemary bushes inside the sheltered walls so they would absorb the scent, and it looked as though it had snowed, with all the shrubs white and bulbous. When Sophie Aucordier was still there, Oriane had gone down to wash with her mother as it was too expensive to pay one of the women. They had hauled the sheets and clothes down the hill in the barrow and pushed them back up again twice a day, soaked and heavy, to dry and air in the breeze of the yard. Sophie said it was the only time the hateful wind ever came in useful. Oriane liked pouring the blue into the vat, it made the sheets and her father's shirts so white that you had to squint to look at them in the sun, and she was proud to smell the fresh scent of iris root as the wind beat it about the yard, hiding the smells of the chickens and goats.

At the chateau, there was a proper indoor laundry room, and Oriane poured soda instead of blueing into the copper, which Cook said didn't get the soiling out so well as blue, for all it was more modern, but then perhaps the d'Esceyracs were not so dirty as the people in the village. On Monday, Oriane rubbed the wash with soap, and brushed at any stains, then screwed the fabric into long sausages and left them in two cotton bags submerged in the rinsing vat overnight. Next morning she filled the ash bag at the fireplace and placed it in the bottom of the copper, which she lined with a fresh sheet. She filled the boiler with three buckets from the well, and when it bubbled she used the long wooden scoop to transfer it to the vat for the first washing. There was a plug at the top of the vat from which the water could run down a funnel to be re-heated in the boiler and scooped back, and that was the most difficult part of the work, plucking it out before her hand was scalded. While she waited for the water, the clothes had to be rubbed against the ridged side of the vat, stooping and kneading until her arms ached and her kidneys stabbed with pain. When the water ran clear, the wash was ready for bleaching, and then it had to be rinsed three times, hot, cold and cold, transferred between the two tubs with great care so as not to drop it on the sodden stone floor. Oriane worked barefoot, so that no dirt was trodden into the laundry room. Though it was hard and made you breathless, she liked the heat and the steam because afterwards her face felt so clean when she splashed it with the cold fresh rinsing water, though Amélie and Cathérine teased her and said she would grow a red porous nose like Camille Lesprats.

Madame's things had to be done separately, in the china sink, and they were put to dry in her own linen cupboard, off her dressing room, so that no one should see. The silk underwear was washed with a dilute solution of *Savon de Marseille*, and Oriane poured lavender essence that Cook distilled at the end of August into the rinse. At first Oriane had felt nervous, handling such fine things, but she saw after a while that sometimes they were marked with little spots of blood, or rims of grime, or other things, and though Oriane would never have said so to the other girls, it was comforting to think that the Marquise was just like everybody else. You learned things, washing. For instance, Monsieur and Madame did not sleep in the same bed like ordinary married people, they had separate rooms, but Oriane knew when Monsieur had visited Madame in the night, and whether he had stayed to breakfast with her, since he took coffee whilst Madame liked her chocolate in the morning.

Oriane sat down to lunch with the others at eleven o'clock. Cook served everybody at the long table in the kitchen, she said there was no point in doing separately for maids and men these days, though Clara had to be sent up with a tray for herself. 'Herself' was the nurse who looked after the Marquise's baby, little Charles-Louis. He was a lovely little boy, with fat red cheeks, staggering about in the nursery, sucking on a worn yellow bobbin from which he was inseparable. Everyone thought it was a shame for him, his mother leaving him alone so much when he was just two, but no one felt sorry for herself, Mademoiselle Cleret, who was from Paris and gave herself airs. 'It's not as if she is a governess, even,' sniffed Cook. Oriane thought Mademoiselle Cleret must be rather lonely, pushing the baby carriage up and down the lanes all day with no one to talk to. She went to Mass with Cook and Clara on Sundays, but she barely spoke to them the rest of the week, keeping to the nursery and her little bedroom on the third floor, where she had her own wireless and a big pile of fashion magazines passed on from Madame. Mademoiselle Cleret wasn't old, but she looked it in her starched navy uniform. It was English style, with stiff white collars that Oriane had to press, all seven, when she ironed on a Wednesday. Perhaps she could be friends with Mademoiselle Lafage, though Oriane would never dare to suggest it. When Mademoiselle Cleret did speak, it was to tell tales of the d'Esceyracs' house in Paris, which was in the very best part of town, a place called St-Germain, where there were always parties with the very best people, and she took little Charles-Louis for walks in a park called the Luxembourg gardens with the babies of duchesses. 'The very best duchesses, no doubt,' said Cook. Mostly though, Mademoiselle Cleret was stuck with Castroux, where she grumbled about the dust and the heat, or if not that, the mud and the cold, and she made Amélie scrape at the clogged wheels of the baby carriage with a stick.

Clara and Amélie lived in, sharing one of the attic bedrooms next to Cook, who snored something terrible. The long dormitory above the stable was empty now, a place of sunlight and cobwebs. Two of Amélie's Lesprats cousins saw to the horses and the odd jobs, though they were very superior about their real job as chauffeurs, which meant they polished the Marquis's car when it was there and fiddled unnecessarily under the bonnet. There were Lesprats everywhere, old Camille had been one of fifteen and had had thirteen children himself, so Amélie had relations from Landi to Monguèriac. The boys had made a snug, smelly nest for themselves in an alcove off the tack room, which had a fireplace, and on Sundays they went for their dinner to Amélie's parents in the village. Monsieur Contier, Yves's father, was the gardener, though he was nearly as old as Papie Nadl. He was too old to farm, but he had a wonderful touch with roses, Madame said, and she was so proud of the sweetness of the d'Esceyrac melons she would often drag old Monsieur Contier out to meet her guests when they came down from Paris in the summer. He mumbled and touched his cap, but didn't tell them about the holy water. In fact, there were not guests from Paris so very often, Monsieur le Marquis was usually away, and Madame was often with him, fetched in a car from the station at Monguèriac and driven away to dance with the very best people in St-Germain.

Cathérine slept at Murblanc, but though she walked up with Oriane in the morning, she worked the full day, so Oriane returned alone, taking the track down through the woods to fetch William. Sometimes she would stop and sit down at the little shrine to the Madonna and leave her a posy, or just trail her fingers in the brook. It was nice to sit and think, and plan the chores for the afternoon. Cook allowed her to take some bread and a bit of cheese or sausage for William, so often they sat on the bridge over the Landine while he ate his lunch, and then they walked into Castroux. Oriane felt very grown up as she counted her own money from her own purse to pay for a few nails or a loaf from Charrot's bakery. Sometimes she left William playing in the square and stuck her head into the kitchen of the café, where she would share a *sirop* with Betty Dubois and tell her about the doings up on the hill, how the funnel of the copper had got clogged with a ball of string, or how Charles-Louis had escaped into the drawing room and broken a porcelain figurine. Betty liked to hear about the food Cook made, though that was better when Monsieur was there because Madame liked odd meals, dry toast, a nasty sour thing called a grapefruit, the size of a football, or just a plate of steak chopped up raw with capers. Betty said it was because she was slimming. It was all the rage, slimming. Oriane liked *sirop de grenadine*, but they usually had lemon because it was cheaper and Betty said her father would have her if he knew she was giving the other kind away for nothing.

It was a long walk home, but if there was a wagon passing, the driver would usually give them a lift up the hill, and that gave Oriane a chance for a rest before beginning the afternoon's work. She had to be extra careful about keeping the house nice because of Mademoiselle Lafage, so she was glad on the whole that she did not have a pig. When her mother was alive, that had been one of the shames of Aucordier's, because even the poorest people had a pig, but her father had sold their last one to a carrier before it was killed, and had hitched them both a ride to Cahors with the money. The carrier had pushed him out of his cart at the entrance to the yard five days later, covered in his own red sick, and all the pig money was gone. Sophie Aucordier left him in the dirt for a whole day, stinking and covered in flies, but when night fell and she tried to get him to the privy to clean him off he had pulled out a plank of wood from the queasy-looking fence of the sty and broken it across her back. So when Laurent Nadl asked her if she would like a *penong* bringing back from the fair at Landi the first spring she had gone to work up at the chateau, Oriane had thought about it and said no. William always hid when the pig killer came, even from Saintonge he could hear them screaming. That autumn, when Madame Nadl kindly offered to let them share the fricassee of fresh throat meat, fried with flour and lemon, Oriane said it upset him, and they stayed at home.

The rabbits were difficult too. Oriane loved them when they were small, blind and writhing in the straw, but as they grew they became sullen, shuffling resentfully behind their wires, snapping at her hand even when she pushed a bunch of fresh sweet grass through to them. They knew their fate, and they hated her for it. She told herself they were cruel, nibbling up their own children like that sometimes. Laurent showed her how to grab them by the soft loose skin on the back of their neck and twist the supple little throat, but the first time, Oriane dropped her rabbit and it lay screaming and rolling in the dirt of the yard until Laurent finished it off with a lump of brick. She learned to be deft and quick then, though she always had to close her eyes at the little pop of bone that meant the warm body would grow heavy and still in her hand. When she had enough clean skins, she made a cap for William, and she cooked the rabbits with vinegar and olives, or with mustard, or sliced them up for a pressed terrine. All the same, she never stopped hating the way those skinned eyes rolled at her, because they had trusted her, once.

SUMMER HOLIDAYS

Sunday scratched, half past three was endless. The air felt
stagnant, even the water in the pool blood-warm. Nothing
moved in the valley aside from an occasional car passing at
the bottom of the hill, the sound of its passage stretching the
length of the road in the stillness. Beneath the milky sky the
family at Murblanc moved with a fellahin slowness, a dogged
un-English lethargy. The house knew centuries of such heat,
would remain cool enough for sleep at least until the sun
banked, with the shutters closed and the thick stone walls
sweating a last chill of winter. Yet some Northern inability to
see light and heat as anything other than a blessing, too
precious to be squandered, kept them irritably out of doors.
The Froggetts baked stoically on their terrace.

Claudia had thought she had slept late, it had been after
three again when she had got to bed, but she was disappointed
when she woke to find it was only nine-thirty. Alex,
maddeningly, slept on. Richard and Oliver lay on the grass

under the chestnut tree, sighing with exaggerated boredom. Aisling had woken at the same time, and was irritable at starting her day behind. Her first thought was that Claudia spoke perfect French. She had forbidden the boys the pool when she found them dive-bombing the Froggett daughters. Alex and Jonathan were liverish, it was too hot to eat and there were no papers because Aisling had missed the market. In the breathless shade they flicked resentfully at a three-day-old *Telegraph*. Aisling thought about dinner and wondered if she ought to ask the Froggetts up for a drink.

Charlotte Glover telephoned to say thank you.

'I thought I might walk up to Aucordier's to see how the old lady is,' said Claudia to no one in particular, pronouncing the name lightly, as though it had always been familiar to her.

'Yes, you could take some cherries. They're a bit manky, I was going to do a clafoutis, but it's the last, they'll do in a basket.' Aisling sat with a pile of recipe books with greasy yellow Post-its marking the pages.

'I'll come,' said Alex.

'Are you sure, darling? It's very hot.'

'Do me good.'

At breakfast, the men had listened politely to Aisling's explanation of the adventure, Ginette's breakdown, the arrival of the doctor, the broken wrist. They both felt, though neither said so, that it was tiresome of Aisling to be so interested in the neighbours, bothering over silly old women whom she would not have noticed in England. Excessive somehow and not worth hearing about. You expected women to be kind like that, they were feminine. Richard put in that the old woman from Aucordier's was a witch, and that he had seen her pissing in her artichoke patch on his way back from tennis. 'But we loved the artichokes that Ginette brought for us,' said Aisling mischievously.

'I didn't,' declared Oliver, 'they're disgusting and hairy. Sick.'

Richard whispered something about Mrs Laws, the boys collapsed into their habitual huddle of wheezing sniggers.

'There could be something in it,' Jonathan smiled at them, 'maybe we should try it on Mum's tomatoes.' Aisling swatted him with a napkin, everyone laughed.

'They're nice kids, Richard and Olly,' offered Alex as they began the climb. He was gallantly carrying the basket of cherries, huge and bulbous, the colour of clotted blood. There was something cancerous about them, Claudia could hardly stand to look. Her mouth was dry, but she felt a horrible gush of sour gastric juices lurch in her throat, gulped it back. She could tell him now.

'Do you think they get bored here?' she asked.

'Are you bored already?'

'Not at all. It's heaven.'

'Bloody hot.'

They carried on in silence. The steepness of the hill had been disguised last night in the car, Claudia felt the pitch of it a little in her lungs. Was this over-exertion? she thought suddenly. Alex was red-faced, she could sense him breathing carefully through his nose so as not to let her hear him puff. His belly bulged a little over his belted shorts; released from his scaffolding of suits and tailored shirts, Alex was soft all over, less convincingly male. Sébastien did not have that look of peeled, grub-like Englishness. Sébastien would be wearing jeans, ancient worn Levi's sitting low on his tanned hips, his T-shirt would not be neatly pressed navy blue from Hackett's, but something overwashed to the texture of fine suede, bought ten years ago in the rue Oberkampf. In photographs, the same T-shirt or jacket would appear over and over, a snapshot at the beach in Mexico, the magazine pictures of the Venice Biennale, eventually arriving at Claudia's time, the T-shirt smooth against her breasts, pulled from the tangled floor in the morning, the corduroy jacket warming her one cold October morning in Florence. An American woman had Polaroided them kissing in the Piazza della Signoria and shyly given them the picture. Claudia, though she knew it was not original, touched Sébastien's clothes like talismans when she found herself alone in the flat in St-Germain. He did not have many things so Claudia had once been pleased by the continuity of his clothes, the way they bridged the time before she knew him. She realized now that the presents she had given him, a black cashmere sweater, a heavy printed silk scarf, would complete Sébastien in time for a woman whom he had perhaps not yet even met. Hopelessly, Claudia felt tears start at the back of her jaw.

'Darling! Darling, what's the matter?' Claudia loathed herself for the concern in his voice. She scrubbed at her face with a dusty balled fist, screwing up her eyes.

'Nothing, I'm just feeling a bit dizzy.'

'Ought we to go back?'

'No, no, sorry, we're practically there. I'll be fine when I have some water.'

Aucordier's was as lifeless as the day. Claudia knocked hesitantly at the door, this was the wrong time to come, the two women would surely be sleeping. But Ginette appeared promptly, smiling, normal, her hair heartbreakingly twisted in plastic rollers.

'How are you?' asked Claudia. 'This is my fiancé, Alex.'

'*Enchanté*, Madame,' said Alex gravely. He proffered the basket with the ghost of a little bow. He is kind, thought Claudia, so kind to me.

Ginette insisted they come in, and though Claudia was reluctant to see the room again, it was surprisingly cool, no soup, only the vinous combination of old beams and stone. The air felt suddenly watery, smooth and greenish as a plunge into a lake after the glare outside. Mademoiselle Oriane was on the sofa, straight backed but nodding, in a white blouse and broad dark grey skirt. The hairnet was covering Ginette's rollers today. On the television, Romy Schneider trilled through the Alps in a crinoline. 'Oh, it's *Sissi l'Impératrice!*' Claudia realized that she had exclaimed.

'We love her. Isn't she beautiful?' Ginette looked wistful.

'How is Mademoiselle?' asked Claudia.

'Oh, fine, fine.'

The night before, Claudia had left Ginette still immobile on the sofa as the doctor washed his hands, and, not knowing how much she now recalled, given Aisling's cleaning-lady's claim about fits, she did not wish to confuse her with details misplaced or provocative of embarrassment. Ginette did not seem inclined to say much.

'And the wrist? All fine?'

'Oh, yes.'

'Well, we don't want to interrupt your Sunday.' Claudia tried to direct Alex to the door with her eyes, but he was smiling expansively and indiscriminately, not attempting to keep up with the French.

'Please, stay and have some tea.' There was a long pause, Ginette's mouth hovered open. 'Very English?' she produced in English, and Alex beamed at the effort.

'We'd love to,' said Claudia, thinking with dread of the viscous foam floating on the surface of the hard water in last night's coffee bowl. Ginette beamed too, for much too long. She did not make any move towards assembling the tea, but remained where she was, smiling hugely. Claudia avoided Alex's eyes.

'Poke her with that,' came a voice from the sofa. Mademoiselle Oriane was alert, straining out over her bound arm with a grey plastic-tipped crutch.

'Go on. You hit her last night. Give her a good poke.'

'How are you, Mademoiselle?' asked Claudia stupidly.

The old woman set the crutch on the floor and hauled herself up with her right arm, bigger and obviously much stronger than she had appeared slumped against the bed in that white light. Alex stepped back out of her way, she transferred the crutch to her left armpit and jabbed at Ginette's pink sprigged blouse with the right. Ginette's eyes immediately refocused, the smile melted, she blinked rapidly and said, 'What are you doing up? Doctor told you to rest. Look, we've got visitors.'

'I had seen that,' muttered Mademoiselle, turning to look at Claudia. 'There you are. Thank you for coming last night. Is Madame Harvey your mother?'

'No, my sister-in-law, at least she will be.' Claudia smiled her bride-like smile and gestured at Alex.

'I see. When?' Mademoiselle nodded to her.

'Well, we haven't really decided on a date for the wedding yet.'

'No, the baby,' the old woman smiled kindly, 'when are you due?'

Claudia fainted, for the first time in her life.

Giles Froggett was attacked by the Marquis d'Esceyrac's Alsatians at the same moment that Claudia's head made abrupt contact with Oriane Aucordier's turquoise lino. He had heard them first, the quick bounding patter of paws on dry leaves, but the sound meant so little to him that the dogs were upon him before its identity was clear to his thoughts. They hurtled from the woods at the side of the path, not barking, two of them, ears pressed back against the long narrow heads, black lips snarling. The first brought him down in a leap of nightmare, its weight barrelling against his chest, he knew he would fall only as his back painfully struck the ground. He curled over on his side, tucking in his chin and squeezing his arms to his sides, a gesture unlearned, the body reacting swiftly as the brain struggled still with the shattering of his holiday afternoon. The second dog nipped his bare ankle, too quickly still for fear, the other was upon him, hot and fetid, snouting at his neck. He rolled foetus-like, eyes closed, heart hammering now but aiming at motionlessness, dogs could smell fear couldn't they, hoping passivity would keep their evil yellow teeth from his veins. They circled him as he scrabbled in the desiccated leaf mould, barking triumphantly. If he moved they would kill him. He could not cry out.

'You're stupid.' An English voice, a child's voice. Giles opened his eyes. A little boy, six or seven, stood on the path in blue shorts and long blue socks, a white shirt. The dogs abased themselves, jaws to the ground, one of them licked amiably at Giles's face as though it had just been joking. Warily, Giles sat up.

'I am the Comte d'Esceyrac,' said the little boy, adding conversationally, 'my father had a cancer.'

There were leaves sticking to Giles's knees, his polo shirt was torn. He wanted to brush at himself, but was afraid the movement might bring on the dogs.

'You're bleeding,' said the Comte d'Esceyrac.

'Are you French?' asked Giles. The scene was beyond him.

'Yes, but my nanny is English. She is called Sarah Ashworth.'

'Do you think I should get up?'

'Well, you can now.'

The child held on to the dogs by their collars, their shoulders well above his waist. A voice called through the trees, 'Charles-Henri?'

Giles stood, his back smarting. There was blood in his sandal, quite a lot of blood. He felt dizzy. Charles-Henri answered in a rapid staccato, then looked contemptuously at Giles. 'You had better come up.'

Tea was being served on the oval lawn before the chateau, white cane chairs, white cloth dappled with leaf-light beneath a huge tree. A smaller boy, neatly identical to his brother, sat quietly to one side with a picture book, a couple, oldish man and younger, fair-haired woman in a dark blue dress, talked quietly. Like a painting, Giles thought. The tree was probably an oak. He scrambled after Charles-Henri through a rhododendron bush. A young woman in large shorts, hair in an Alice band, ran forward. 'Sarah Ashworth, I presume?' said Giles, attempting to recover himself.

'Oh, you're English. I'm so sorry, what has Charles-Henri done to you?' She had a clear, ringing voice, 'Plummy', Giles said later to his wife.

'Actually,' asserted Charles-Henri, 'I probably actually saved his life. Zola and Balzac were eating him, to tell the truth.'

'Oh dear,' said Sarah Ashworth.

'I'm bleeding.' Giles hoped he didn't sound whiny. Charles-Henri, his heroism unappreciated, wandered off.

'This is, I'm sorry? This is Mr Froggett. The dogs bit him.' Giles limped a little, affectedly if he were honest, as they approached the tea table. 'I've already met your dogs!' he called cheerfully.

'The Hounds of the Baskervilles?' said the man, his English more heavily accented than, presumably, his grandson's. He was obviously pleased with this remark, more pleased than concerned.

'Vicious, I would say,' answered Giles defensively, conscious of the man's soft linen jacket, his gold signet ring, irritated even further by the consciousness.

'They were only, as you would say, doing their job. I am very sorry. I hope you are not badly hurt?'

Charles-Henri reappeared, crumbs on his mouth, tugging at the jacket and speaking French.

'I see,' said the man to Giles, 'you were lost?'

'That's it, I'm staying down the hill there, at Murblanc.' He pronounced it 'moorblonk'.

'Of course, at the Henrys' house. Well, would you like Sarah to find you a bandage? A glass of water? Or perhaps you would prefer to be driven home?'

This was clearly the right choice. Down the hill and back up the lane to Murblanc in Sarah's capable little Renault, Giles wondered why he had said 'Yes, please' like a child who has behaved badly at a birthday party.

Dinner at the Harveys' that night was a surprisingly gay affair. Eventually the sky was streaked yellow and purple like a new bruise, Sunday was on the way to being dispensed with, everyone took a late swim. Claudia, her bikini top thoughtfully attached, practised diving with Oliver and Richard. They tried to teach her the pike, and she plunged again and again, sopping hair trailing her mouth as she resurfaced, laughing, unable to get it right. She had forbidden Alex to mention her collapse, the relief, as she surfaced in his arms, of the knowledge that he could not possibly have understood what Oriane had said, was cooler than the water. She felt loving towards him again and thought that the faint could introduce nicely her resolution to tell him the truth. She flexed her legs, trying to bring up her knees and shoot them out straight as she turned in the air, the pool meeting her body too soon each time before she had executed the movement, and she tumbled splashily until she felt truly tired, an incipient languorousness in her limbs promising real sleep. She would drink water tonight and leave her cigarette packet upstairs.

Aisling thought 'Sod it' and cooked a great crock of spaghetti with tomato sauce and a salad. No one changed, they ate outside, slurping in their damp bathing costumes. Magnanimously, she told the boys that they really ought to practise their French with Claudia, she spoke perfectly. Claudia questioned Jonathan, intelligently ignorant, about wine, she leaned her head on Alex's shoulder. When it was dark, the men lit citronella candles in yellow ceramic pots against the mosquitoes. Alex found a CD of baroque music and turned the stereo in the drawing room up loud, so the sound of violins poured over the balcony to the garden. Claudia said, 'Aisling, you must be dying for a night off from cooking for us ogres. Alex and I thought we might go out to dinner tomorrow night.'

'Fine, what about going into Landi, guys? We could go to the pictures and then have a pizza.'

'*Star Wars The Prequel*? Kevin says it's in VO.'

'Oh, God, all right.'

'Cool.'

At ten o'clock, Mrs Froggett appeared, looking morose. She asked Aisling if she had any disinfectant. 'Giles was bitten by a dog,' she explained.

Aisling glared pre-emptively at her sons. Poor Mr Froggett was a geography teacher, apparently the saddest profession known to man, and nearly as funny as Jaffa Cakes. Richard and Oliver constantly rehearsed a mysterious dialogue that they found endlessly hilarious.

'Jaffa Cake, Vicar?'

'Don't mind if I do. I must say, I do enjoy a seedless fruit.' Jonathan had no clue as to why Jaffa Cakes provoked this reaction, he said they hadn't been invented when he was at school. She ought to ask Alex, maybe.

'How dreadful,' she said aloud. 'Look, why don't you all come up for a glass of wine? You must tell us what happened.'

Mrs Froggett assented and reappeared shortly with her family. The Froggett daughters wore acne and surly expressions, their father a surgical stocking bulging out of his sandal, which had obviously come from the hypochondriac's paradise of the pharmacy in Landi. They sat down, Jonathan fetched more glasses. Giles told the story of the assault.

'So you met the d'Esceyracs?' asked Aisling nosily.

'It was the grandson who found me. He said he was a Comte.'

Richard and Oliver nearly suffocated with glee.

'Well, do you know, he probably is. I'd heard there were two little boys, living in Paris. The father died.'

'I thought it was the other way round,' said Claudia, 'Marquis and then Count. Like de Sade.'

Alice Froggett, the vegan, had just finished her A levels and was going to Cambridge. She said, 'I think it depends on the antiquity of the title.'

'I didn't think the French had an aristocracy any more?' queried Alex.

'They still have the titles, but they don't really mean anything. Like Italians,' said Claudia, 'contessas all over the place.' This information was a relief to Giles Froggett.

'He didn't seem that posh to me, anyway. That castle looked like it was half falling down. There really should be a sign about those dogs, they could kill someone.'

'Maybe we ought to do something, Jonathan. Speak to the Marquis?' It was clear to Claudia at least, that Aisling's interest in such an encounter had nothing to do with the state of Mr Froggett's ankle.

'It's absurd, isn't it, that they still go around using such antediluvian titles?' said Alice Froggett hopefully, but no one disagreed with her, which was disappointing.

JUNE 1939

In the summer of 1939, no one in Castroux was at all surprised
when Mademoiselle Lafage moved back to the schoolhouse
to become Madame Boissière. The bride was married from
Aucordier's in a fawn crêpe de Chine coat and skirt made up
in Monguèriac; for a week, William was forbidden to go in
pursuit of the bassoon in case he smeared the costume with
excited grubby hands. Mademoiselle Lafage's mother was
coming from Paris, and her friend Simone from the training
college was to be bridesmaid, so Oriane did out William's
room and put a jug of lavender stalks on the washstand, so
that Mademoiselle Lafage might wake alone on her wedding
morning. Oriane thought that would be nice, for the last time.
There was to be lunch in the café and dancing afterwards,
with lights in the square. Mademoiselle Lafage had hoped for
something quiet, some cake and champagne before the drive
to the train (they were to take a walking tour in the Italian
Alps), but François had persuaded her that they had to have

a real country wedding. In Castroux, everyone attended everybody's wedding whether they were invited or not, funeral too, come to that, so Mademoiselle Lafage resigned herself, and discreetly asked Betty Dubois to make sure that all the café's shutters were kept wide open.

Monsieur Boissière had purchased a new necktie with a pattern of daisies, and half a dozen bottles of champagne. He told Betty to make sure it was poured out for the right people, and gave her a list to learn to be certain. The Marquise d'Esceyrac who might well stay after the Mass, Monsieur Larivière, the mayor, himself and the bride and the bridesmaid and the bride's mother, Père Guillaume, the three teachers from the schoolhouse at Landi, and poor Oriane Aucordier, though not that brother of hers and certainly not Camille Lesprats and his cronies, who were filthy boozers. It was Camille Lesprats and his rustic odours that caused Mademoiselle Lafage such worry. Castroux was countrified enough for someone of Simone's experience without smelly old peasants, high and gamey in the June heat, crowding around and showing people up.

Oriane got up at half past four on Saturday morning. She had boiled water the night before and left it with a stem of rosemary to soak. It smelt crisp and spicy as she washed her neck and under her arms. It was not quite light, she pushed the shutter a little so as to see better, and could smell that it was going to be hot. Her eyes were peepy, she rolled the cloth in the cool water and pressed it to her face, yawning, wishing she could climb back into the bed where William still slept, his arms wrapped around his head to cushion his ears. He was decent, she had made him climb into the tub the night before and scrubbed roughly at his throat and face while he howled and splashed. She put on a skirt and blouse over her bodice and knickers and wrapped her head in her mother's print scarf. William opened his eyes. He heard the faded silk squeak against his sister's clean hair. She was standing by the window, folding her best dress into a flour sack, a blue dress with a pattern of violet-coloured flowers. Oriane felt him stir, gave him a big smile, put her finger to her lips. William followed, 'Shhh', then pointed to the dress, and whispered '*Polida*'. Pretty.

The church clock struck six as Oriane reached the nuns' garden. From Aucordier's, she had seen fine plumes of smoke across the valley at Saintonge and clear over the village, but as she reached the bridge she plunged into dawn vapour, swimming waist deep in dense, silvery mist, tangible to her spread fingers and thick as a January morning. Two wagons passed her as the road began to rise again over the river, she stepped politely to the side of the road and the drivers wished her good morning, though they were not Castroux men. The white stones led up from the ghostly river until where the bells rang it was bright again everywhere. There was no gate to the garden, just a stone archway with an empty niche set in the wall, opening on to a modern gravel path through the trees, which stopped against the wall at the other end. The wall had been built up, but beyond it, Oriane knew, were vague mounds, ploughed over now and joyful with sunflowers, but where in winter it was possible to imagine the outlines of the buildings that had once stood there, the hospital, chapel, cloister. Along the river bank, by the barn owned by the baker, Monsieur Charrot, there was a single stone pillar that was used as a boundary marker between the Charrot and Teulière plots.

The relief was worn almost smooth except at the base, where, if you pulled away at the grass, you could see that the carving had once been a filigree as sharp and delicate as lace.

Oriane felt that it was precious, this between time. She picked a sage leaf from one of the huge bushes that flourished in the shade of the old apple trees and rubbed the velvety scent on to her fingers. It was so rare to be not just alone but absent, with no one knowing where she was and no sense that there was work she ought to be getting on with. Walking slowly, she touched the spikes of the rosemary and closed her hand around a wizened grey apple branch, breathing deep until she felt her lungs strain to open further in the swashy shade, spreading her arms and relishing the coolness in the soft morning shadow. She wondered what it would feel like to slip from her clothes and lie naked in the damp grass as though it were a beautiful green carpet. But imagine if someone came by! They would think she was as silly as William. She untied the neck of the flour sack and fastened it again around the branch, tying the ends so the bag was raised up and her dress would not be spoiled by wet stains. The orange flowers by the wall were still furled tightly where the sun had not reached them, treasuring their scent inside. They would open up nicely by the time the cake was served. All the same, as she knelt to gather them, she lifted her skirt to where the sudden white skin above her knees showed, and settled her legs apart, so the juicy grass brushed her, and grew warm on the inside of her thighs.

The Nadls were going to the wedding in the wagon, so William could leave with them. It was a shame Cathérine couldn't come, but she hadn't a half day, although the girls might be allowed out in the evening, for the dancing. The Mass was at eleven. The bridal party, Oriane liked the sound of that, so smart, the bridal party were to come in Monsieur Larivière's motor car, driven by the mayor himself. There was bread and coffee and strawberry conserve laid out under a cloth in the pantry, and three madeleines for the ladies in a saucer. Oriane had fetched them from Charrot's herself yesterday and told William she would lock him in the goat shed for a week if he so much as sniffed one. Downstairs, the floor was swept and there was another jug of lavender on the table, laid with bowls and spoons. Perhaps the best coffee cups, the wedding cups from the *buffet*, might have looked well, but they didn't hold much and Mademoiselle Lafage was greedy for her breakfast, though she might, Oriane supposed, feel obliged to hold back today on account of nerves.

Betty and Andrée didn't think much of that. 'Rubbish,' Andrée snorted, 'she can't wait to get into bed with old Boissière!'

The kitchen at the café had a damp terracotta floor and smelt of spilled wine and yellow soap. It was built down into the ground so that the only window, above the porcelain sink, looked out through fronds of honeysuckle to the bottoms of the tablecloths airing on the washing line. Oriane was breaking eggs into every basin that could be assembled.

'Do you think they've done it already?' asked Betty.

'In the schoolhouse on Wednesday afternoon!'

'No, in the woods by the Virgin, with her knickers flapping in the breeze!'

'No, at your house, while she was practising the bassoon!'

Andrée grabbed Betty from behind and pumped her hips

at her fat backside while Betty blew at a wooden spoon with her eyes screwed up.

'She played the scale of C major to cover his huffing and puffing!'

Andrée and Betty looked like 'Happy Families' cards swapped around, Oriane thought. Betty Dubois, the café owner's daughter, looked as though she belonged in the bakery, plump as a brioche with soft pale skin and light hair, a big bosom and stomach under her apron. Andrée, the baker's daughter, was dark and skinny with a big nose that pecked at gossip, and small bright eyes that gleamed like crème de cassis. Andrée was a fine cook though, she had made the *pièce montée* for the wedding the day before and it would be she, not Betty, who supervised the twenty big truffle omelettes. No one could say that Monsieur Boissière was stingy, everyone was excited about the feast. There would be foie gras, of course, with fig bread, then the omelettes, then capon with roast potatoes and ceps, the salad and cheese, made in the dairy at Murblanc by Madame Nadl, then the dessert of cherries in red wine, then the tower of choux pastry and caramel decorated with the white blossoms that Oriane had picked in the nuns' garden. They lay on a plate in the larder covered with damp paper.

The short country term was already over, but both the classes from the school were assembled on the steps of the church with a painted banner that said '*Vive Les Mariés*' in meandering primrose letters. The Marquise d'Esceyrac attended the Mass with her little boy and graciously accepted a glass of Monsieur Boissière's anxiously proffered champagne. Camille Lesprats got roaring drunk, and everyone laughed about 'Poire William' when the *digestifs* went round.

Mademoiselle Lafage's friend Simone had purplish lipstick and a rather revealing apricot costume, she drank Papie Nadl's eau de vie from a glass like a man instead of coyly dipping a sugar lump. Monsieur Larivière, who had given away the bride as well as performing the legal ceremony, proposed the toast, looking quite the thing in his sash. Then the bridegroom seated himself at the piano and played a soft, wandering piece whilst gazing at his red-faced wife, while all the guests respectfully pretended to listen.

The benches were moved outside and the old ones sat down to watch the youngsters dance. Yves Contier settled himself on a chair in the shade, important with his accordion. Papie Nadl stepped forward with his violin, but instead of nodding at Yves to begin he raised his bow for silence. He spoke up in his high, reedy voice, 'As we know,' he began, coughed a little, 'as we all know, Madame Boissière has made her home up at Aucordier's for the past few years. William Aucordier has made a present for her. All by himself.' The amiable quality of the quiet shifted a little. Oriane clenched her hands in the skirt of her dress.

'Go on, William,' said Papie.

William got to his feet. There was a dribble of yellow crème patissière on his jaw. He reached out to Papie, his arms wide and anxious, as though to receive a child, and made a little squeak. Someone tittered, and Madame Boissière frowned. William took Papie's violin, holding it delicately in his big raw hands, and settled it under his chin. He dipped his torso in an awkward bow. Then he arranged his fingers around the bow and began to play. He played softly at first, his eyes closed, a little tune that ran up and down the fret, then gathered itself, and dipped, and soared, mounting like a bird hopping from branch to branch, pausing, swooping back, rising higher and faster as his elbow sawed and he nodded forward into the music, pushing it on and tapping his foot until it ran under his hands like the river in winter, and then he curbed it, softening, ending on a long full note, dying away and holding them all there, spun for a moment a little above the dust of the square. The silence was new again. That was what was remembered of that day, that William Aucordier astonished everyone in the village when he played the violin for the first time in his blue shirt at the schoolmistress's wedding.

Oriane was breathless with happiness and surprise. Papie was beaming, though he had not been the only one to wipe a tear from his eye. 'We had you there, eh?' he asked everyone. 'Oh, that's a good one! We had you there!' Cathérine said she had heard music coming from the cow barn for years, but she thought Papie must be playing to William to pass the time, although it did seem as if he was improving with all the practice. Everyone laughed and laughed, there was not a bad word to be said. Père Guillaume said it was an example. What Oriane remembered later was the rapid flutter of the light, how it danced in the dappling leaves of the chestnut trees, the same light the wind had pushed so cruelly around the eaves of Aucordier's now gathered up so wonderfully in William's music, how it spun between the pale massed bow strings, and how it cancelled out shame.

SUMMER HOLIDAYS

Charlotte Glover was drawing a batch of pots from the kiln next morning when Richard Harvey appeared on his bicycle. It was already filthy hot, but August was the busiest season for the markets, and she was making a load of the thick, brightly coloured salad bowls that had really sold well last year. If they were popular again, she and Malcolm might be able to return home for Christmas. 'Mum said, can you babysit tonight?' asked Richard ungraciously, disgusted with the description. 'She said to say she phoned, but there was only the answer machine and she needs to know.'

Charlotte set the blistering rack down slowly on the wall of the old pigsty. What did Aisling think she was doing, she thought self-righteously, it was Monday morning! Lolling around in a negligée painting her nails? She was working, and so was Malcolm, who took odd jobs in the season on English gîtes and had got up at six-thirty to drive fifty kilometres to see about the filter in some hysterical woman's pool. The

Glovers did not have a pool. Then she felt mean and asked Richard if he would like a glass of Orangina.

'Is your mum going out then?' she couldn't help asking, wondering where it was she and Malcolm hadn't been asked.

'Yeah, it's sick. We were meant to be going to see *Star Wars*, but now she's going to drinks at the chateau,' he pursed up his mouth to inject pretension into the last syllable, 'and we have to stay at home with Caroline.'

'Caroline?'

'Caroline Froggett. She sucks. She's a PG and she's got a sister, but the sister's grown up and her parents are going too. It's crap, actually,' he said, daring the semi-risk of the word.

'Oh dear, that is disappointing. I didn't know Aisling and Jonathan knew the chateau people.'

'They don't, but my mum can't wait to have a nose. You know what she's like. And the dogs at the chateau tried to kill Mr Froggett, that's Caroline's dad, so they're all going to have a meeting about it and drink loads of wine, probably.'

'Well, tell your mum it's fine, but a bit short notice. I think Malcolm's got some videos of Monty Python, we could watch that instead.'

'Yeah, all right. Thanks for the drink.'

On the way home, Richard jerked his bike into a skid around the wall of the bridge, like Valentino Rossi. He and Oliver consoled themselves for the general crapness of living in France with the thought that next year he would be old enough for a moto. That's if dad let him have one, because they couldn't even have a Playstation, even though you could get the converter plug in Landi. Also, you could buy spliff in the bar in Castroux, which was cool, though he hadn't actually had any spliff yet. Claudia had caught him filching a cigarette and had been pretty cool actually, saying that if he was going to smoke he might as well do it properly, and she showed him how to inhale in the barn. He pretended not to know how, although he'd been smoking since he was like, twelve, a year ago. Richard definitely fancied Claudia, although her tits weren't that big, but she was really pretty and smelt of perfume and her clothes were all droopy and a bit see-through. He wondered if she sexed with Alex a lot.

It was a bit sad, but he actually missed school. He and Oliver boarded in England, which was fine, because he didn't want to go to the *lycée* in Landi with all those rubes, no way. School was a universe away. School was internet and skiing trip and sneaking into town on the bus and it wasn't weird to live in France because lots of people's parents did, even though to hear his mum you'd think they were the only English boys to speak French at all. His parents' French made Richard cringe. He hated, detested, loathed and despised the way they always carried on speaking unnecessarily, chatting to everyone in the shops instead of just saying thank you and going like they would in England. The way they smiled too much and made mistakes, and those awful pantomime actions to make up for it. French was not another world, it was just what you spoke when you played football in Castroux or hung around the café sharing a cigarette with Jean-Luc or Kevin, who both had motos and were not at all impressed that Richard and Oliver spent half the time somewhere else. Mum kept asking about his friends in the village, asked him to invite them for supper, but Richard didn't know how to explain that Kevin's mum would think Aisling was mad, and that they just didn't talk about who was English and who was not, it wasn't important. He liked having a pool though, because only English people did, and when it was hot and there were no fucking PGs he could say 'Fancy a swim?' and they'd all troop up the hill and Aisling brought down cold bottles of Coke and cake, which everyone ate like it was nothing special, although he'd never even been in any of his mates' houses.

Richard pumped hard up the lane, swerving tightly around the gatepost, Rossi well in the lead, wasting Biaggi. Maybe Dreary Malcolm had that cool Monty Python with the shrubbery. He might try to neck with Caroline Froggett. She was a minger, but she was a girl, and no one at school would know she had spots.

Claudia told herself that she felt like Tess when she discovers that Angel hasn't read the letter. A jolly gel who introduced herself as Sarah had appeared with a note at breakfast time, and Aisling had martialled the household into acquiescence. Claudia knew she was being silly, she could perfectly well tell Alex at any time, if not today, tomorrow, but she had pictured the moment so clearly that it had become talismanic. Thwarted, there was a sense of reprieve, she still didn't have to go through with it. Sébastien would be at his parents' place near Biarritz. She wanted to call him, to have him come to claim her without explanation. Biarritz was not so far away, she could get a train, appear there and just refuse to move, lots of women did that, would do just that. The fact that Sébastien simply did not love her did not make him any less responsible. Surely they could work out some form of a civilized, mutual life?

Claudia did not blame Sébastien for not loving her, she was even honest enough to question whether there was not, in her own love for him, some element of rankled pride, some urge to conquest, since he was the only man she had ever cared for who hadn't cared back. She couldn't blame him because he had never made a secret of it, never disguised the fact that he slept with other women, offered exactly what he had to give and never a promise of anything more. She had been convinced for a long time, for the first three years of their odd relationship, that he must come to love her, if only by virtue of propinquity, but when she had seen finally that this was not true, her bewilderment led to shaming jealousy, to the awful accusations in Paris.

The evidence for her long self-delusion was confusingly positive. Since their first meeting, at a dinner party organized by Annabelle, who edited *Diréctions*, he had been erratically attentive. They had met about once a month, at first for weekends of bed at the flat in Paris, odd nights when he was in London for work, then trips to Italy, to the countryside in France, a magical New Year in Bruges. She had met his friends, had cautiously and over-casually (for one of the many irrationalities of their affair was its retaining an air of the clandestine; Claudia had not at first thought it in good taste to discuss with Annabelle the fact that she was fucking her star writer, and the feeling persisted long after Annabelle had been mollified), introduced him to hers. Sébastien was not rich, but he sent her presents, wonderful, surprising presents, antique books, a cashmere overcoat, tiny pots of truffled foie gras from Fauchon, a jam jar of water from the Grand Canal. He was lavish with compliments, he bought flowers and cooked dinner and read to her, asked her opinion on a paper he was writing or a lecture he was giving, he remembered her birthday, had dashed to London and held her through the night when her father died. They were intimate, made good stories of adolescent miseries, talked about difficult colleagues, watched movies grubbily on Sunday afternoons. His concierge knew her name. It was real, as far as she could see, no abbreviated romance perpetually stalled in its first stages, something rich, and in her mind at least, teleological. She told herself that loving him meant she had no right to question, to demand. They talked freely of her lovers and his, which Claudia felt was very sophisticated, yet somehow she had been certain that she, Claudia, held him. But his pained, embarrassed confusion when she made her furious declaration, his letter, made it as clear as it had been all along that he was just not available, to her or anyone else, for the kind of love she trusted that she deserved. It had been so embarrassingly obvious, during that long night, that he pitied her, and she could not bring herself to hate him even for that. Were it not for the child, she knew that she would have persuaded herself that this was good enough, as she had so many times before, and to make what dignity she could from choosing so, but she knew, even as she lay by the pool with a paperback collapsed across her nose and ached for him and dreamed of release, that he would not come, because she had pride enough, at least, not to make him.

The Marquis d'Esceyrac had not written that morning to Aisling out of any sense of duty to their bitten and frightened guest, but to please and distract his daughter-in-law, Delphine, who was making her first visit to the house, from which she had been married, since Charles-Edouard's death. The Comtesse d'Esceyrac had her own interest in the Harveys (efficient Sarah Ashworth had rectified the doubt as to their name), equally unflattering to Mr Froggett. Despite the evidence of the chateau, and the equally imposing *hôtel particulier* in St-Germain of which the Marquis now occupied just a single floor, the d'Esceyracs were in a somewhat straitened position. The Marquis had been elected Vice President of the Jockey Club twenty years ago, a victory by default achieved when the two other rival candidates discovered at the last moment that they were both shareholders in an extremely dubious mining enterprise in Morocco; exposure of which by either of them for the purpose of social prestige meaning certain ruin for both. They had a cheerful lunch at Le Grand Véfour and withdrew mutually from the race leaving d'Esceyrac as the only contender. The ambition of his life thus attained, the Marquis spent most of his time and, to Delphine's chagrin, his capital, in the Hôtel Drouot. Charles-Edouard had practised indifferently as a stockbroker before the terrible shock of his illness, and Delphine, by her own estimate at least, was now not only widowed but poor.

The chateau simply must be turned to account. The Anglo-Saxon love affair with La Belle France showed no signs of diminishing passion, and judging by the number of horrid old farmhouses sold around the Marquis's land to English people in the last few years, the English were making a fine profit from pandering. Delphine had refused a number of kind invitations to the Côte d'Azur this year in order to bring her boys to spend some time with their grandfather, and their grandfather around to an idea. Why should not Esceyrac become a sort of hotel? Like many women who have only ever seen work as a means of passing the time, Delphine was untroubled by her complete ignorance of the hospitality business, or any business. She had it all worked out. The chapel would make a marvellous restaurant, the two upper storeys bedrooms, the ballroom a lounge, the kitchens were already suitably vast, and the paddocks and woods, stripped, could be a golf course. Perhaps it would even be possible to have a spa in the painted gallery, something Eastern, a wooden jacuzzi bath fitted in an alcove. Delphine saw tennis courts, a new swimming pool, Americans arriving in chauffeured black Mercedes, taking tea in the library.

As for the family, there was a perfectly wonderful old *grenier*, with a cottage next door, at the bottom of the hill on the opposite side to Murblanc, of which an architect might make a large and beautiful house. Heaps of people had done it, in England too. Charles-Edouard's colleague Armand had assured her, when she discreetly mentioned her plans over a consolatory lunch at Laurent, that it would be simple for him to produce the necessary investors. He had ordered two glasses of Château d'Yquem and a rather unnecessary *soufflé aux framboises*, and pressed her hand earnestly over the tablecloth.

'If there's anything I can do, Delphine, anything. For Charles-Edouard's sake.'

She had worn her black Chanel suit, eaten the soufflé with the air of a woman starved, thrown up neatly before Sarah brought the boys home from the Luxembourg, and dined on a fat-free yoghurt with bifidus. Armand LeSaux had a beautiful villa at Saint-Cloud, and a 1930s racing yacht at Portofino. Possible, certainly possible.

Madame Lesprats, who 'did' at the chateau on Monday mornings, had been conveniently voluble on the subject of the Harvey woman. Apparently she had spent a fortune on the old cow barn at Murblanc, and it was filled with boarders from May to September. Delphine was sure the cleaning woman knew precisely how much they paid, though of course she had not asked, but Madame Lesprats needed very little prompting to divulge details of Madame Harvey's decorations, the expensive sheets that had come all the way from Lille, and the unreasonable number of bathrooms the English seemed to require. According to her, the renovated barn was a positive goldmine. Delphine was eager to meet her neighbour, since a few hard facts about the possible income from taking guests might easily introduce the possibility of imitation to her father-in-law. Once he had agreed in principle, it would not be difficult to convince him that the golf course and the Americans were entirely his own idea.

The Froggett daughter seemed very earnest and intelligent, thought Aisling, but it was a shame that the French could not be relied upon to pick up nuance, the difference say, between Jonathan's Turnbull and Asser shirt, foxed to white thread around the collar and cuffs, and Giles Froggett's glaring sky blue from Marks and Spencer. Wendy Froggett was not so bad, she spoke a little French and was perfectly presentable. All the same, Aisling did not wish Harveys and Froggetts to meld together in an amorphous English mass. Like many people who professed to love France, the Froggetts betrayed an innate suspicion of it, a sense of divisiveness, as though France would be better off if it admitted that it was really just England with better weather and fewer ugly buildings. Malcolm Glover, Aisling felt, was rather similar.

Aisling was in the kitchen again, preparing a chicken gremolata for the Glovers and the boys. If the drinks invitation at the chateau turned out to be just that, there would be enough over for everyone, and if not it would freeze. She grated lemon zest while the golden chicken pieces bubbled in her favourite shallow cast-iron pan and shredded parsley from the garden with a mezzaluna. She couldn't understand how people made such mess of food. Charlotte Glover's dire cassoulet, for instance, or the greasy navarin of lamb, really just a big Irish stew, which they had been served last time they dined at the Kendricks'. Lucy Kendrick had made such a fuss about her blasted lump of meat, but the boiled potatoes had been as raw and weepy as new cheese, and the carrots she claimed to have queued for in the market bobbed dingily in their viscous sauce. If people couldn't cook, they shouldn't try, was Aisling's opinion, there were so many wonderful things to buy, boned poussins rolled with pine nuts and Armagnac-soaked prunes, fresh langoustines from the van that parked outside Castroux church on Tuesdays, charcuterie and pâtés, glistening fruit tarts from the patisserie, bottled peaches and tiny Mirabelle plums in syrup. She would much rather eat a dinner assembled from the shops of Castroux, simple and delicious, than the pathetic concoctions her neighbours insisted on boasting about. She was sure that Charlotte Glover had put tomato ketchup in the cassoulet last time.

Aisling's mother said that one could always taste the

resentment of an angry cook, and many of the Harveys' friends seemed to bear out her description. Occasionally, they spoke wistfully of Marks and Spencer, murmuring names like chicken tikka or steak and kidney pudding, like prisoners, or exiles on a barren island recreating the lineaments of their lost city. To Aisling, this seemed feeble, yet there was a form of arrogance in the covert refusal to adapt, a kind of colonial resistance, as though fresh goat cheese and brimming, iron-juiced tomatoes were inconveniences to be endured before the next consignment of tins from the Army and Navy. Living in France might not presuppose an interest in food, but it seemed to impose one, an insincere standard to which the English community required themselves to pay homage. Each summer produced a newly fashionable bible, lavish with gluttonous adjectives, and the latest location of paradise found, the Languedoc, Gascony, the Auvergne; Aisling saw them, crack-spined on sunloungers and listened to discussions of their wonderful mysteries whilst eating food worthy of an English school canteen. The dissonance did not appear to strike with the disciples, who were seemingly unaware of the glaring dissociation of sensibility between palate and brain. Aisling's disgust at this hypocritical lip-service was associated with the secret, spiteful remarks she wrote in her exercise book, a deeply felt, hidden anger that people who did not understand food, did not understand France, should be allowed to be here at all.

Since her arrival at Murblanc, Aisling's enthusiasm for cooking had deepened to a point of such private sensuality that she now barely spoke of it to anyone. Like most truly excellent cooks, Aisling was not greedy, she was inflamed by taste, not satiety. She did not attempt to explain to herself the source or nature of the satisfaction that came from her food, but felt it in a sense of stillness or peacefulness that was with her more and more often, as she worked in the garden or pottered in the market, touching and smelling, as she stood silently at the top of the orchard, watching the sunset behind the tower of Castroux church, holding a basket of velvety plums. Last autumn, she had risen at five whenever it had rained and followed a tiny, ancient path along the base of the Esceyrac hill, passing a little hidden shrine with a startlingly crude wooden statue of the Madonna, wilted flowers at her feet, to gather ceps and chanterelles for frothy omelettes and deep, woody sauces. Aisling learned the pleasure of patience, of anticipating the appearance of the first thick spears of creamy asparagus, the tiny, nutty potatoes whose seed she had sown herself in drenching January rain, the brief rosy season of quinces. She felt she understood now the slow balance of the seasons, the rainbow delight of summer fruit, the rich luxury of winter game. She was less and less inclined towards the elaborate dishes she had prepared in London, felt no regret for chillies or lemon grass, no desire for papaya or Turkish sweets; the exotic was mussels and oysters from Brittany, black truffles from the Périgord, wild garlic or the May acacias, so surprising in batter. She was surprised at first when this sufficed, at her own willingness to repeat the same dish twenty times to perfect the method, even something so simple as a chicken roasted with butter on a plate of the watercress that she could gather in the broad trout pools of the Landine, where the little river flattened out by the abandoned watermill below Saintonge. One afternoon, she had seen otters there, two old Chinese philosophers with thin, ponderous moustaches.

'I still don't see why we have to go,' said Wendy Froggett at seven o'clock. She felt hectored. This was their holiday after all, they owed no social obligations to the Harveys, and she did not see why she should waste her precious evening making conversation with people she didn't know.

'It's just to be polite,' said Giles wearily. They had been having this discussion ever since Aisling had popped down to La Maison Bleue to tell them of the invitation. Wendy had been furious that he hadn't made up an excuse, but since they were clearly going, now, he didn't see the point in arguing about it.

'And what about Caroline? It's not fair to leave her on her own.' Wendy was not going to let up until he admitted that it was all his fault for trespassing in the first place.

'I think Caroline's quite happy to have an evening with those boys. They seem to get on.'

'This is supposed to be a family holiday. Alice will probably want to do her own thing next year, with university, it's just a waste of an evening.' Wendy was putting on her lipstick all the same, Alice was lolling downstairs, ready. It couldn't last much longer.

'I'm sorry,' said Giles, 'it's my fault, I know. Look, we'll have one drink and then we'll go to that bar in the village and get a meal. Caroline'll be fine.'

Giles was pleased to be going. It wasn't every day you got invited to cocktails in a castle, and Wendy was deluded if she thought either of their daughters gave a stuff about family holidays. Caroline was no doubt dying for a chance to snog with young Richard Harvey, and Alice could accuse someone else of being bourgeois for a change. Giles hoped that the prospect of some genuinely dissipated aristocrats might incense her to the point where she stopped lecturing her parents about Marx for a couple of evenings. Secretly, Giles thought it was hard cheese to spend his holidays dealing with sulky teenagers when he had them all year at school, and he was looking forward to a bit of adult conversation.

It was still very hot when the Harveys and the Froggetts decamped from two cars on the circle of weedy gravel in front of the chateau at half past seven. Jonathan had been for walking, but Aisling didn't want to arrive looking tousled from the climb through the woods, although she said that they ought to drive just in case the dogs were on the prowl again. The Froggetts' Mondeo followed the Harveys' dusty Saab down to the little bridge over the river and then right along a white unmade road on the opposite bank. Aisling swivelled around in the back seat and pointed enthusiastically to La Maison Bleue, which was just visible on its rise above the tall poplars that flanked Murblanc land. Giles and Wendy turned their heads too late and nodded politely. They crossed over again, a more impressive stone bridge with columns at the corners, which gave on to the avenue. Tall wrought-iron gates, with a large '*Proprieté Privée*' sign, stood rustily open.

Aisling had walked here many times, hovering nervously halfway across, alert to the sound of approaching terrible barks. Though she had never dared to step beyond the bridge, she felt almost proprietorial about the avenue, pleased that it sustained the beauty it had held in her memory, pleased at the reaction it drew in Claudia and Alex. In the high growth of

August, the avenue was a green nave, cut dead straight through the woodland, rising beneath the yellow barked, summer-asperous horse chestnuts in a clean perspective cut off at the summit of the hill by what seemed to be the doors of the chateau itself, black inside a white stone archway.

They stood about on the gravel, uncertain if they should look for a bell, no one taking a lead. Aisling wore a white tunic and loose navy trousers, as she didn't want to look as though she had tried. Claudia was in an expensive-looking linen shift in a sludgy greeny-bronze that would have looked horrible on anyone else. Wendy Froggett wore frosted pink lipstick, unfortunate with the ruddy beginnings of her tan, and a white T-shirt tucked into a drooping floral skirt. Giles Froggett was still wearing his shorts. Alex tugged at the waistband of his chinos and wished that Claudia didn't have views on shorts. The Marquis appeared from under the stone archway at the side and shouted 'Welcome' in English, so they trooped the length of the eighteenth-century façade, fourteen windows long, as though they were on a school trip.

'How pleasant to see you again, Madame Harvey,' said the Marquis, bending over Aisling's hand. Wendy Froggett was next. As he dipped his face to her knuckles she suppressed an absurd desire to curtsey.

'And this is Claudia,' announced Aisling.

'Hello, Marquis,' said Claudia, confidently, in French.

'Claudia, what a surprise! How are you?' The Marquis kissed her on both cheeks, laughing, 'What are you doing here in the middle of nowhere?' He continued to hold her hand.

'This is my fiancé, Alex . . .'

'How do you do?'

'. . . who is Jonathan's brother, that is Aisling's husband Jonathan, here.'

'How do you do?'

'We're staying at the house, with Wendy and Giles, of course. And their daughter, Alice. I believe you and Giles have already met?' Claudia smiled as though she had executed a conjuring trick, her hand still lying familiarly in that of the Marquis. 'I'm an idiot, I didn't think,' she continued, 'but then I don't think Aisling told me your name. You were just the mysterious Marquis on the hill.'

'Well, what a wonderful coincidence. Delphine will be pleased. Please, everyone, we thought we would have drinks outside, where it's cool.' The troop filed off. The Marquis led the way with Claudia.

'How enchanting!' exclaimed Aisling, a beat too quickly, since she really couldn't see anything but Jonathan's back. To Giles, the arrangement on the lawn seemed not to have shifted since the previous day. He could see the path through the woods beneath the big tree where he had emerged with Charles-Henri, and had an odd sense, now, of being inside the composition that had been waiting so placidly as he had staggered bleeding into the light. The back of the chateau seemed older than the front, more romantically irregular, with a slim, round tower, cone-tipped in grey slate as for a cartoon princess, completing the wing at the left. In the centre, a broad flight of worn steps led from a terrace to the round lawn, where the white furniture was grouped around the table and the Comtesse was rising to greet them.

'Look!' cried the Marquis, 'here's Claudia!'

Claudia was a good liar in the main because she had an excellent memory. All the time that introductions were being made, the guests settled into chairs and the circumstances of Giles's adventure recounted with determined hilarity, she reviewed the occasions on which she had met the Marquis and Delphine in Paris. The first time, she was sure, Sébastien had taken her to a small drinks party, a *vernissage*, in the Marais, where people stood in the hot street with plastic cups of white wine and talked to one another without bothering much with the exhibition in the little beamed gallery. Sébastien had introduced the Marquis d'Esceyrac, explaining that he had been so kind as to allow him to look at two Bonnards he owned for his last book. Claudia recalled the oddly deprecating language buyers self-consciously use about pictures, 'rather lovely', 'very pretty', as though discussing some domestic acquisition, like flowered china rather than things that hang in museums. Claudia knew the right language, and had been confident at the time that Sébastien was pleased with her, though now she doubted honestly whether he had even noticed.

The second occasion, she had seen Delphine, elegant in that fussily skinny French way, at a guest lecture in the Christie's education building, the Hotel Salomon de Rothschild. The Marquis had invited her to sit with them whilst Sébastien spoke, and afterwards, when she saw how insistent Delphine was to emphasize the length of her own acquaintance with her lover, Claudia had felt a little vicious stab of pleasure that she, and not this perfectly finished Parisienne, should be leaving with him. The third time, Sébastien and a guest had been invited to a dinner at the Marquis's St-Germain apartment.

Claudia swiftly ran through the details. She was certain that there was nothing in any of these meetings that could give her away, nothing to suggest that she had been 'with' Sébastien in any sense other than that of a friend visiting from London who worked in the art world. Of course, she would have assumed, herself, that they were together – they arrived and left together and seemed to know one another well. She was protected, she thought, from an accidental betrayal by the distance of French social conversation which, to her, was less personal and individual than what one expected in London, and by the fact that Sébastien had never gone in for that cubbish physicality (which Alex, arm slung around her shoulder, was displaying now), which marked newish couples in England. And then Alex was aware that she was friends with Sébastien, she had made no secret of having seen him, at least occasionally, on her trips to Paris. Alex seemed incurious, though unflatteringly it was not wisdom, she thought, that prevented him from asking questions, but indifference to her life except insofar as it related to himself.

Claudia accomplished this analysis while a woman in a black skirt and white blouse poured white wine and offered tiny square linen napkins and dishes of olives, chunky local sausage and rounds of *ficelle* spread with terrine.

'Bought,' thought Aisling. The conversation was taking place in English, in consideration of the Froggetts and Alex, though Aisling had greeted Charles-Henri and his brother Jules in French and said pointedly that it was all the same to her and Jonathan whichever language they spoke. Sarah Ashworth took the boys away to their supper.

There was a pause. Wendy Froggett stared quietly at the

view. Alice was running a belligerent eye over the chateau, as though calculating how many cringing serfs its cellars contained. Jonathan and Alex swigged at their wine. Neither the Marquis nor his daughter-in-law seemed inclined to speak, though they smiled pleasantly.

Aisling felt sweat dampening the armpits of her tunic. 'Well,' she said brightly, 'how kind of you to ask us.'

'Not at all,' replied the Comtesse graciously.

Alex reached for a lump of sausage. Aisling felt murderous towards the Froggetts.

'Delphine,' said Claudia smoothly, 'I remember last time we met you were thinking about an English school for the boys. Aisling's sons board in England, I'm sure she has heaps of advice.' She turned energetically to the Marquis and asked him whether he had seen anything 'nice' at the rooms lately, keeping at it until the conversation creaked into life, with Aisling comparing the merits of various public schools, Jonathan and Alex chipping in with recollections, and Giles Froggett explaining about league tables. Even Alice ventured a remark on the odd difference between public and private. No one minded Wendy, until she said, 'So how do you know Claudia?'

'Oh, we were introduced by a celebrity,' replied Delphine. Claudia suddenly felt very hot, and prayed she wasn't blushing. Delphine, in her achingly plain black silk dress, was transformed into an allegory of malice. Claudia had feared some unintentional reference, easily explained away to Alex, but she was quite aware that Delphine had been waiting for the chance to make trouble. But she did not interrupt.

'Sébastien Marichalar, the art critic. I believe he's very well known in your country? Tell me, Claudia, how is Sébastien?'

'Do you know, I haven't seen him for ages? I've hardly been in Paris, and then he's so busy. Such a shame, I haven't had the chance to introduce him to Alex yet.' That was the best she could do, Claudia felt.

'Oh, he's on the telly,' chimed in Wendy, 'you know, Giles, we loved that programme didn't we?'

Giles Froggett felt it was common to talk about the television, but then this was a friend of Claudia's, and the Comtesse had brought it up. 'Yes, very interesting. Not that we watch much.'

Claudia thought that rather dear.

'He's gorgeous, isn't he Claudia?' Wendy chimed on. 'You better watch out, Alex!' Her daughter cringed visibly.

'No need,' said Claudia, knowing she was being winsome, looking at the Marquis, 'Frenchmen are just too charming for me. They can't be trusted!' Everybody laughed. Aisling and Claudia both thought about sticking a cocktail stick in Wendy Froggett's eye.

Jonathan asked where the Marquis had learned his excellent English, and was told that, as a little boy, he had spent the war in England with his mother. This gave rise to several remarks, but it became clear, after an hour, that the English party was not staying to dine. The wine glasses remained emphatically empty.

Aisling, alert to the awfulness of people who came to drinks and stayed put, picked up her handbag determinedly and Claudia followed suit. The Froggetts looked rather surprised. As they said goodbye, Delphine told Aisling, in French, that she would love to come down some time and look at La

Maison Bleue, she had heard Aisling had done such clever things with it.

'Of course,' Aisling replied, as casually as she could. 'Why don't you bring the boys? I'm sure they'd love a swim.' Later, she asked Jonathan whether he thought that might have seemed rude, that she had made it obvious that there was no pool at the chateau.

'I can't imagine she cared,' he answered, which was unsatisfactory, especially if he were right. When the chicken gremolata was eaten, the Glovers thanked, and Richard and Olly in bed, Aisling sat on the balcony with a glass of wine. Alex said rudely in the car that it felt as though they had been there about a decade, but on the whole she was pleased with the evening. Claudia had surprised her. The girl had been gracious, it must be said. And how did she become so friendly with the Marquis? This Marichalar person must be well known if Wendy Froggett had heard of him, and Claudia, it appeared, had a life, a French life, which brought her into easy contact with such people.

Aisling did not analyse this shift, this softening, of her initial dislike, nor acknowledge that its source was cupidity. Claudia was clearly an interesting person, and her elegance, her cigarettes, were recast by Aisling as symbols of a sort of bohemian glamour. Claudia was possessed of something that she, Aisling, craved, something that she did admit was surprising to find in connection with her husband's family, but which she saw the opportunity to cultivate. She saw herself with Claudia in Paris – a shopping trip for the wedding? They would pop to the opening of a new gallery, and go to supper with Delphine in a little bistro on the Left Bank, well-dressed women, speaking French. She saw a house party, perhaps next summer, long tables on the lawn of the chateau, a sprawling easiness, someone playing a piano, and the sound drifting down the broad staircase in the twilight. She could do the food. Aisling thought of tureens of chilled green sorrel soup, and quails, lacquered with honey, plump in nests of caramelized Chasselas grapes.

Alex was fucking Claudia on their broad white bed. She was on all fours, a pillow bunched beneath her stomach. She let him pump away in silence, glad that she'd managed to take her linen dress off before he crumpled or ripped it. On either bedpost, Aisling had hung a white muslin bag with a green ribbon, filled with Murblanc lavender. Alex took hold of her hips, pulling them up and hard against him, and Claudia moaned approvingly, as though barely containing her need to scream with pleasure. He moved faster. Claudia put her hand between her legs and scrabbled at herself until she reached some sort of orgasm, relaxed and fell forward a little, tightening her thighs to encourage him to finish. She reached around, straining her shoulder in its socket to prod unenthusiastically at the dry crevice of his arsehole. Alex paused, dipped his mouth to the back of her neck, then pulled out and turned her over. He knelt between her legs, stroking his cock, showing her how stiff it still was. Behind his dangling balls she could see the rindy rims of his feet, the colour of Lancashire cheese. She ran her tongue over her lower lip, keeping her eyes fixed on the spongy helmet of his prick. He settled himself inside her again, the whole weight of him. 'I can go on as long as you want,' he rasped, with a look of stupid cleverness. He ground away at her, until she felt hot and dry and extremely bored. 'As long as you want, baby.'

'Oh, Christ,' thought Claudia.

JUNE 1940

Cathérine waited for her as usual at the top of the Murblanc lane as she walked down to work, but before she was close enough to speak, Oriane had known that something was wrong.

'They're here,' was all Cathérine said.

That was the day they listened to the radio, Père Guillaume's radio that he'd brought out from the presbytery. All the Nadls went, and when they arrived in the village nobody was at work, the men were already grouped around the door of the *Mairie*, smoking, and the women in the square. None of the Castroux girls had gone up to the chateau, the Chauvignats were there from Saintonge. Some women had their hands occupied, wiping a dish over and over, holding a loaf or a baby, darting quick glances at the men and talking, talking, with their heads close together. No one was doing anything but it seemed no one thought to sit down. Laurent held Oriane's arm, he squeezed it above the elbow as he went off with Papie to join the other men. It was already hot again. William was fretting, wanting to play. René Larivière hushed everyone, then they listened to the broadcast in the *Mairie* and sat waiting through the long afternoon.

Everyone was weary of it, but it was impossible to move until something happened, something that could be reacted to, but nothing did. Maréchal Pétain said it was time to stop fighting, that things had to be finished. The church tower was like a giant sundial, the shadow swung slowly around across the square until the *Mairie* was in the evening sun. Monsieur Dubois and a few of the men pulled out more benches from the café, Betty brought a few jugs of wine and orange *sirop* for the little ones. The women went to their houses, Hilaire Charrot fetched the bread, which had been warm that morning and had lain neglected all the day. Terrines were put out, a blue dish of boiled eggs, a plate of radishes. The priest twiddled at the dials of the radio, irritably pushing back the sleeve of his cassock where it flowed forward over the machine, all that came out was dance tunes. They ate, more wine was brought for the men, and someone said, 'Give us a tune, William.' At first he copied a few things he had heard on the radio, American music, fast and snappy. Then he played a tune that Oriane did not recognize. Laurent said later it was a song from the war, the first war, a song about Alsace. Oriane was never sure if William had understood why he played it. Laurent was seated next to her, she touched his shirtsleeve and saw that there were tears on his face. It was growing dark now, and the men's faces looked paler, bluish. They clasped one another's hands as William played, and bowed their heads.

Like everyone in Castroux, Oriane divided the time of the

war between before and after their arrival in France. Hardly anyone in the village had paid much attention to the declaration of war a few months after Mademoiselle Lafage got married. Before they came, it was William she remembered more than anything, William playing. Later, when she thought of the wedding, she remembered distinctly the song he played outside the *Mairie*, the night they all waited there, though that was the year after the wedding party, and she had not been wearing her dress with the flowers. Somehow those times ran together, the recollection of the heat in the square, and the people watching, and all that Oriane knew was that she had been happy then, although she should not. The Marquis d'Esceyrac had arrived that night, she remembered, in his big car from Paris with his man in the seat next to him, so it must have been the next day that the chateau was closed up, but time had got mangled, she couldn't smooth it out. What was left was William with Papie's violin under his chin and the heat draining out of the day, under the chestnut tree.

When Pétain's speech was over, the gay music had continued, interspersed with alarming gunfire bursts of crackling static. That hideous music that seemed suddenly so coarse conjured to François Boissière the squalid gyrations of a decadent time. François remembered that he had burst out in protest, trying to galvanize the silent men who clustered hopelessly around the radio, gazing at it as though it would magically deliver them, sputter into life and tell them the world had not changed. François raced back to the schoolhouse and fumbled for a magazine from the box of cuttings he saved next to his chair in the parlour. His wife stood amongst the other women.

He read excitedly from the turned-back page, holding it high to block his eyes against the sun. At first the men listened respectfully, since he was the teacher after all, as he described the Gauls as the greatest cuckolds of Christianity, who had left nothing of their souls or their speech in France. Nic Dubois, Jean Charrot and Marcel Vionne stared at him with the same surly expressions of incomprehension he had seen on their faces along the schoolroom forms only a year or so before. Marcel's father had fought and returned, Dubois had lost an uncle and Charrot two. He raised his voice. 'So you see, you see, if the word "shit" is left of the French language in generations to come, we'll be lucky! Do you understand? We have to accept,' he paused, his customary fluidity diverted by agitation, but it was no good. Père Guillaume said there was no need for bad language.

It was Laurent Nadl who talked about the hero of Verdun. The Maréchal knew better than to waste more French lives. Laurent looked meaningfully at Jean-Marc Teulière who had been pushed up quietly in his chair. Men raised their voices, the word 'Communist' was spoken, and they looked shiftily at François and his magazine when the schoolteacher tried to explain that he agreed with Laurent, that was the point of the example, that they must avoid destruction. The English had betrayed them. The Jews had betrayed them. Emile Chauvignat spoke up and said that there could be something in it for everyone if they went along with it, and a few heads nodded, though the Chauvignats were not well liked.

It was too late to say so later when no one believed him, but René Larivière said to himself that not a man of them had talked of fighting. Hours passed as they stood there. René's head was aching, he wanted to sit down, he wondered stupidly if he ought to put on his mayoral sash. Père Guillame led them in prayer, they bowed their heads dutifully, as they had listened to François, and over the square the women crossed themselves. René heard that day described as unforgettable, but it seemed to him that nothing was recalled with any clarity, and the only sensation that remained honest in him was the astonishment he had felt at his own fear.

As René saw the Marquis's car drawing up by the church, he felt relief. At least there would be news, some sense of direction. He felt he had no authority, that there was nothing he knew how to do or was certain ought to be done. The telephone lines to Monguèriac were deaf. Perhaps he should have asked Nadl to go, on his motorbike, but until the Marquis appeared, he remained with the others in the square, pointlessly returning to the radio as Père Guillaume turned the dials, sometimes slowly, as though there was information to be caught if only it could be pulled in, like a sleepy trout from the Landine, sometimes abruptly, trying to wrench some certainty from the shrieking whine of the airwaves. He drank a glass or two of wine, but did not share the food the women had brought out. When the car arrived he felt ashamed of his own eager deference. He did join the group that immediately surrounded the Marquis but hung back in the open doorway of the *Mairie*, where the mosquitoes hummed under the yellow strip of light. Monsieur d'Esceyrac climbed out, wrapped in a pale motoring coat, flexing his fingers where they had been gripping the wheel. René remained in the doorway, feeling he should not approach unless he was asked, wondering whether he should not walk authoritatively to the centre of the group and speak up. He saw a few women pointing down to the *Mairie*, and the Marquis came towards him. René was pleased that it was the other now, who hung back, though he was ashamed of himself for thinking such a thing.

Monsieur d'Esceyrac was pale and his face looked pulled tight. When he spoke, René could smell the staleness of his breath, tobacco mixed with a dirty cabbagy scent, as though his mouth had been dry for a long time. René beckoned to Betty Dubois and whispered to her to fetch some water and a glass of wine for the Marquis. The men shook hands. 'Won't you sit down, Monsieur le Marquis?'

The Marquis smiled wryly, 'Thank you, but I've been sitting down since Paris. We left this morning.'

Betty brought a glass in either hand. The Marquis swallowed the water quickly, then looked down into the wine glass without drinking. Betty hovered until René sent her off with a jerk of his head. They stood there a moment, two shadows in the warm yellow doorway, then the Marquis asked if they had heard the radio.

'It's true then?'

'They're in Paris.'

René had to look up to see the Marquis's eyes, conscious of his own sweat-marked collar and dusty boots. The Marquis lifted his head and drank off the wine. He gave a dry laugh.

'I wish I could tell you something, René, but that's not—' His voice did not falter, just stopped short, and when he spoke again René had the sense that he had rehearsed the words as the car ran along the roads. 'I have made certain arrangements. I'm shutting up the house tomorrow. There'll be something left for the servants of course. You must do your best, René, you will need to be firm. That's the thing. I don't think you'll be much affected down here, although you'll see, half of France is on the road. I should get organized, set up some stores, that sort of thing. Things will be back to normal in a few days and you'll hear from the Préfecture. I should tell you good luck, I suppose.' He gave the same dry little cough that passed for a laugh.

Then, René despised the Marquis for using his first name. There was an appeal for understanding, René felt, as though the familiarity would charm René into accepting his abandonment of Castroux. René thought he should speak up, say something about courage and duty, show that at least he, the mayor, had some sense of what was right. As it was, he nodded and replied merely, 'As you say,' and he never saw Charles again. They did not shake hands.

As the Marquis returned to his car, the village was on its feet. They expected him to speak, they looked for it almost pleadingly in his face as he walked on, drawing his cloth driving gloves over his hands. He crossed through the group of women and seemed to recognize Oriane.

'You work up at the house, don't you?' he asked.

'Yes sir. My name is Oriane Aucordier.'

'And you have a brother, don't you?'

Until now, Oriane had not been afraid. There was too much and too little happening to ignite fear, but now she felt it, cold and sick, squirming in her and catching her breath in her throat so it was difficult to speak. The Marquis had never addressed her before.

'I do, sir. William.'

'Quite so. Well, I would like you to bring young William

when you come to work tomorrow, as early as you can.'

'He's not, that is, he hasn't done anything wrong, sir. He's strange, I know that, but he's as good as gold. You can ask Père Guillaume, really.'

'Please don't worry, Mademoiselle. I need your brother to help me with a job, then he can go home with you. It won't take long.'

The car drove away with the smart man from Paris upright and disdainful in the passenger seat. They could hear the engine travelling down to the river, until it vanished in the thick trees of the avenue. Nothing was said, but it was true dark now and the lights about the square looked meagre and lonely.

The governess, Mademoiselle Cleret had vanished. She must have been listening to her wireless, because Cook said that when they went to look for her she and her little trunk of starched collars were quite gone, and the baby howling alone in his crib. Everyone laughed a bit at Amélie Lesprats, who could not conceal her disappointment at not being taken instead, though no one except her vain self had expected that she would leave with the family. The Marquise had departed with just her own maid and the boy. Monsieur Mons the valet was to take those servants who were leaving to the station at Monguèriac in the wagon. There was just himself, Cook, and Clara, who was returning to her family in Lyons. Amélie had packed her suitcase ready, she had been nurserymaid after all, and she was convinced that Madame wouldn't be able to dispense with her, and that she would soon be kicking up her heels in Monte Carlo. Now she was just going along the valley to her parents, like Cathérine.

'What did you think Madame would be wanting with you anyway on the Côte d'Azur?' asked Cathérine nastily, and Amélie cried into her apron and said well, at least it would have been a bit of life. Clara embraced them all and said that she would write, so not to mind. But when Cook and her bundles had been helped into the wagon and they had waved goodbye to cold, silent Monsieur Mons, the three girls sat down suddenly on the terrace steps and looked at one another.

'I suppose we'd better get on,' said Oriane.

They trooped back into the house. Monsieur's instructions had been quite clear. Everything was to be covered in dust sheets and the carpets rolled, the china and the glasses and all Madame's pretty knick-knacks to be wrapped and put in the big trunks Monsieur Mons had dragged down from the attic. The windows to be washed and covered with paper, the shutters closed and locked. Cook had said they might as well help themselves to the preserves, she and Clara would take what they could carry, but there was no sense in leaving them because you never knew. Monsieur Mons heard that and looked as though he might have something to say, but Cook had given him a look. She did not finish speaking. Oriane was to fold all the linens with mothballs and lock them in the laundry room in baskets, along the drying racks, not on the damp floor. The curtains were to come down and be stored in sacks, the saucepans swaddled in newspaper, the candles sorted into boxes, the whole house was to come to pieces as though it were a spring cleaning, but not be put back together.

In the salon, Cathérine sat down on a sofa. She arranged her dress fussily, reclining backwards, and spoke in French, in a refined voice, 'Oh, my head is dreadful with this heat!

Cathérine, do fetch me a tisane.' Amélie giggled, but Oriane felt dismayed.

'Cathérine, get up! What if someone sees?'

'Who's going to see?' said Cathérine in her usual voice. 'They've buggered off to Monte Carlo and left us.' She continued in her Marquise tone, 'Oh, really, the crowds at Monte this year were quite dreadful!'

Emboldened, Amélie sat in an armchair. 'I thought we might try Deauville this season,' she announced. Oriane couldn't help it. 'No, look, you've got it wrong.'

The cigarette box was on the table, she took one, lit it with a match from the silver stand attached to the ashtray, pursing up her mouth and blowing a feather of smoke towards the ceiling, 'We find that Monte is still more select, my dear.' Cathérine and Amélie helped themselves too, and they lolled there, smoking, bored ladies on a hot afternoon.

Cathérine jumped up. 'Come on,' racing into the hallway, her clogs clattering strangely on the newly naked stone of the staircase. When they followed, panting and laughing to the door of the Marquise's bedroom, she had the wardrobe open and was throwing clothes on to the bed. She had a fur stole wrapped around her shoulders and a pale blue hat with a mauve silk ribbon jammed on her head.

'Look,' she said, 'you have this, Amélie!'

'Oh, we can't!'

'Yes we can.' Cathérine's face was set, this was a test of loyalty. She had kicked off her clogs and was trying to work her foot into a pale pink suede dancing slipper. Amélie obediently undid her apron and skirt and stepped into the matching evening gown. The satin strained at the back and her bodice showed under the delicate shoulder straps, but she grabbed a forlorn powder puff from the dressing table and minced about, swishing the train and dabbing beige dust at her nose.

'And this is for you, Oriane!'

A bunch of fabric the colour of milky coffee landed in Oriane's arms. It was a silk negligée, trimmed with chocolate-coloured lace. Oriane put her arms through the wide sleeves and tied the thick, slippery sash.

'Those shoes simply won't do, my dear,' said Cathérine the Marquise, 'do try a pair of mine!'

Oriane ducked as they hurtled towards her. She stooped, gathering the silk carefully where it pooled around her ankles, stuffed her toes into the tiny yellow slippers figured with scarlet flowers. She went up to Amélie at the mirror and peered over her shoulder, then unfastened her hair. It fell down her shoulders, darker than ever against the creamy fabric. That looked right.

'I'm going to tell my brother!' hooted Cathérine. 'That would get him going, seeing you like that!'

'Would it?' asked Oriane foolishly. She thought no one had guessed that Laurent Nadl was sweet on her. Her glance slid swift, involuntary, to the Marquise's big carved wooden bed.

'Look at her, the dirty cow,' shrieked Amélie, 'she can't wait!' She tittered coarsely, rolling her eyes, and Oriane felt cold. She began to unfasten the negligée.

'Come on, now,' she said quietly, 'we'd best get on.'

Next day, the girls continued their work scrappily as the d'Esceyracs departed around them. William was behaving very hard. He said all his words in French and looked at Monsieur's face like Oriane had told him. Madame had a hat with a feather, which startled him, and there was a big clock near the wall that fizzed and muttered so he wanted to lay his ear on the fragrant wood and listen to the beat of its polished heart. He contented himself with resting one fist behind his back in his open palm and flicking his fingernails secretly in counterpoint to the clock's clicks, ssi-tum, ssi-tum, like blood throbbing from a chicken's neck when Oriane killed it with the little knife that looked round but was very sharp so he mustn't touch it, except it didn't slow down like the chicken. Perhaps one ssi-tum escaped from his lips, but that was nothing serious like Oriane said when he did things that were bad but weren't really bad. The clock room was big and had long windows that showed the lawn and the woods, not Papie's house because that was lower down, but Monsieur pointed and said, 'That's your farm, isn't it, William?' so William saw that it looked much the same as it did when he was there, the big barn and the grey square roof, except smaller. It was hard to leave the clock, but Monsieur said he had a special secret to show him, and they went together right through the windows and across the scratchy grass that was full of footsteps.

Monsieur had one big box and William had another. He had to carry it very carefully, like his violin. They went down to a clearing where there was a little house with a pointy roof, then down again through the wood where the brook was, with the statue of the lady who was in the church too. The bridge crossed the brook where the water was muddy and crowded, humming with thorns. Monsieur scrambled underneath, holding back the branches. William did not want to go there, it was dark and nasty, but the box was so heavy and Oriane would be angry if he did not, so he followed Monsieur to a damp, chilly hollow where a few tumbled bricks crawled with lichen. In the wall was a little door. For sure, William would not go in there. He shook his head and began to bounce the box in his arms until Monsieur put down his own and took it from him. Monsieur took out a little bottle of oil and rubbed it on a key, then he disappeared inside. William climbed back up the bridge and waited in a patch of sunshine.

They went back to the big house where Monsieur put the key in a little cupboard that smelt of horses. It looked like the baby of Papie's cupboard, all over flowers and dancing creatures. 'Shhh,' said Monsieur and put his finger to his lips.

'Shhh,' said William, so hard it made bubbles of spit.

William liked the next part much better, when they broke the bottles. They made a wonderful noise, some of them were green and they smashed deep and sad but the best ones were yellow and made a huge spluttering burst. Breaking things was very bad, but no one came to shout at Monsieur ever ever. Yellow and black wine ran into the ground as Monsieur cracked the bottles over the mounting block in the empty stable yard. It smelt like Mademoiselle Lafage's wedding and a bit like Papie in wintertime. William was allowed to break them too, he swung the bottle up and whammed it against the stone which was all purple now and threw the splinters into the pile, a beautiful church noise like tiny bells.

'That's right, William,' said Monsieur, and laughed, but it was not a happy sound, more like the thudding gasp of the green glass tearing on the stone. There were two bottles left.

He had one bottle as a present. Monsieur cracked the other one carefully, just the neck, so that it was jagged but still whole. He held it out so William could see the label. 'This is an Haut-Brion,' he said, 'and it was made in 1913.' He tipped back his head and poured a little of the wine carefully into his mouth. 'Do like me,' he said, so William opened his mouth too and it was filled with wine.

'Shall we have a toast, William?' William wasn't sure he hadn't done something bad, so he just kept quiet.

'Never mind, you're a good boy. Go home now.'

They said goodbye and William remembered to take off his cap. As he set off down the track to Murblanc he heard the last bottle crack once, like a gunshot. He wished Oriane could have seen how he said 'Merci Monsieur'. Maybe he would break the last bottle on a rock, just to hear that noise again, but that could be a shame because it was a present. He gave it to Papie, even though at Murblanc they had real wine from a jug. Papie said he was pleased all the same and while he waited for Oriane to fetch him home William had a piece of clafoutis with cherries and a stick to scrape on Madame Nadl's washboard as much as he liked.

Oriane went home by the village road with Amélie and Cathérine. They were to leave all the keys to Monsieur Larivière at the *Mairie*, so Amélie could take them as she was nearest. There was nothing to stop them leaving through the main door, but somehow that didn't seem right after their long day of work had worn out the giddiness, so they came out as usual on the kitchen side, solemnly, stretching their arms and rubbing the backs of their damp necks. They took turns to carry Amélie's suitcase, bumping it along the swathe of grass in the middle of the avenue where the twilight was hot and green. Nothing was different outside, the scent of the woods came up to them as though the thick air had deliquesced into the soil. Their clogs stirred autumn.

'Do you think they'll come back, then?' asked Amélie timidly.

'Them?' Cathérine was scornful. 'I daresay, when it's all over. Leaving us stuck here in the meantime. What do you expect?'

'You don't know that,' said Oriane, though she believed it. 'Laurent says—'

'Laurent thinks he knows everything because he's been to the pictures in Monguèriac. They're here, and they've won and we lost. We have to put up with it, that's all, see?'

It was true that Oriane did not feel she had the right to say much. She had never seen a film or a newsreel at the pictures. She hadn't even been to Landi. Mademoiselle Lafage had sometimes read *La Dépêche* out loud when she lived with them but Oriane had not bought a copy since the wedding, it was a waste.

It seemed sad, suddenly, that none of them really knew anything at all.

'We're best off minding our own business,' added Cathérine, as though she knew what Oriane was thinking.

They reached the bottom of the hill in silence and left Amélie at the bridge. They watched her for a while, dragging the scuffed case up the hill. The light was growing blue now, thickening around her.

'They put people like William in prison, you know,' Cathérine announced, 'they round them up and take them away for good.' She could be like that, cruel because she was clever.

The wine dried slowly on the cobbles of the stable yard. Even after several hours when the moon came up, little rivulets ran stickily between the stones, showing a red bonfire of razors where the glass sparkled as its light caught the edge of the heaped shards.

SUMMER HOLIDAYS

When Delphine d'Esceyrac telephoned on Wednesday evening, Claudia had still not told Alex. Murblanc contained them, they moved into a rhythm. Claudia continued to rise early, and took one of the bicycles across the river into Castroux for the bread. Olly and Richard were pleased to get out of a chore that, for them, had neither novelty nor charm. Breakfast was on the terrace, and Aisling suggested, every day, some sort of activity for the visitors, a drive to the cathedral at Albi or the lovely old square at Monguèriac, but they were not bored, they saw no reason to go rushing about. Aisling was happy that her house drew them so, that they were content to remain within its orbit. Alex helped Jonathan in his potterings; they were building a low wall around the herb beds with pretty, pinkish local bricks, a cache of which Jonathan had found buried when the *fosse* was dug. The pool was PG territory in the morning, but they spent most of the afternoon there, chatting, reading, snoozing. As it got cooler, everyone took a turn at watering, and Claudia helped Aisling to gather the salads and herbs for the evening. The leaves of the lettuces were delicate, translucent, straining in the dry red earth. While they had drinks, the boys disappeared into the village for an hour or so, and they ate at nine, with music and wine in the cool, thick jugs.

Pushing the bike up the lane, a plastic bag with two *flûtes* swinging from the handlebars, Claudia had to slither into the ditch to make way for an open lorry stinking of fumes. The truck was half full of melons, some split and oozing, and half full of skinny, ratty men wedged amongst the fruit. They wore baseball caps and filthy T-shirts and stared down at her incuriously, slit-eyed in the sun. Jonathan said they were Albanians or something, brought in for the harvest. As the days passed, Claudia realized that the stillness of the landscape was an illusion. Silence sharpened as it was so often broken by tractors clanking heavy farm machinery up the lane, or along the valley, from where the sound carried for miles. Smoking a cigarette on the balcony before she went in for her bath, Claudia saw that the fields were full of little Brueghel figures, loading, tying, creeping across the earth. Old people worked on through the late twilight, squat bundles in the orchards, pruning and trimming now the fruits were over, occasionally a gun went off in the chateau wood, although the season had not begun. Claudia was absorbed, comforted. London seemed far away.

Aisling suggested that Delphine bring her sons to tea on Thursday afternoon. Madame Lesprats would be in to do La Maison Bleue in the morning, so she could be sure it would look its best after almost a week of Froggett depredation. A shame that the flowers were so poor in August, but she could put bunches of rosemary and lavender in the rooms, and the geraniums on the PG terrace were lovely. It was too hot for much, but she could do that fragrant almond and orange-flower cake, thinly sliced, on white plates. Could the Froggetts be got rid of? It was hardly fair to show Delphine around and not ask them for tea, and anyway, they were bound to hover even if she didn't. When she hung up, Claudia was in the kitchen rubbing a garlic clove on slices of bread for bruschetta, wearing a loose embroidered tunic, silver on white, over her turquoise bikini. Her bare feet were tanned.

'Thanks,' said Aisling. She peeled the clingfilm from a bowl of broad bean and sage purée and handed Claudia a spoon to smear with.

'Your friend from the chateau just phoned. She's bringing Charles-Henri and Jules over for a swim tomorrow.' Aisling settled on this unsatisfactory conjugation because she did not like to say 'Delphine' in front of Claudia, as she had not actually been asked to use her Christian name, but 'The Comtesse d'Esceyrac' sounded too overawed. What, really, should she call her?

'That's nice,' replied Claudia, spreading, 'although I don't know her all that well. I've just met her a few times.'

Aisling decided on playful frankness. 'Actually,' she said, with an affected smile, 'I'm a bit overwhelmed. *La plume de mon oncle* and all that. Do I say Madame d'Esceyrac to her?'

'I should say Comtesse,' said Claudia thoughtfully, 'and then she's bound to say call me Delphine. If she doesn't, just stick to *vous*. More to the point,' she smiled more sincerely than Aisling had done, 'what's to be done with the Froggetts?'

Aisling felt grateful, though defensively so. 'It would be nice to get to know her in her own language, so to speak.'

'Alex and I haven't been to the lake yet. What about a picnic lunch, a late one? We could do *pain bagnat* with the ratatouille.'

'They're not so ghastly, really. Wouldn't you mind?'

'Not at all.' Anything to avoid mention of Sébastien. 'I'll go down in a minute and ask them. I'll get the chaps to come, too.'

They had a glass of PG white, and Aisling told Claudia about the Shirleys, last year, who had brought frozen chips in a cool bag all the way from Hemel Hempstead.

Claudia told Aisling that Delphine's husband had, she understood, died suddenly from cancer. Aisling was most sympathetic.

Madame Lesprats steered her navy Clio carefully around the barn at Aucordier's and honked. Ginette appeared at the door, waved, then stuck her head back in to say something to old Oriane. Her overall hung between her broad hipbones, which protruded like the shanks of an old horse. She was really a few years younger than Madame Lesprats, but a glance in the rear-view mirror was reassuring. Time had got the better of poor Ginette, but Madame Lesprats's tightly permed hair was hennaed a nice shade of claret, and there was something to be said for a few extra kilos after a certain age, as Cathérine Deneuve observed. Like many of her friends in Castroux, Madame Lesprats was a devoted reader of *Oh La!* Sometimes she brought a few back copies up to Aucordier's. Today, she was in a hurry to get on, as her son was coming to lunch with his wife, although it would not be kind to mention that to Ginette.

Ginette got out at the top lane, from where she would go to the main house to collect the linen. Madame Lesprats continued down the hill and turned right before the bridge, at the edge of Murblanc land. She took the gravelled path the guests used and parked next to the Froggett car at the side of La Maison Bleue, as Madame Harvey insisted on calling it. She remembered perfectly well when the house was no more than Nadl's cow barn. The cleaning equipment was in a specially built cupboard under the oak staircase – once again Madame Lesprats marvelled at English extravagance, as she tugged out the plastic bucket and went to the kitchen to fill it. A spotty girl with sunburned shoulders was eating baguette and Nutella at the table. She said '*Bonjour*,' and Madame Lesprats returned her greeting curtly, clattering a pile of washing up as she forced the bucket's lip beneath the tap. The girl took the hint and sloped off, carrying a book, leaving her dirty cup and a stream of crumbs. Madame Lesprats thought Madame Harvey was foolish not to get a wipe-clean lino top, they had some lovely bright patterns in the market, and it was so much more hygienic.

An hour later, the two women had done the bedrooms and bathrooms and changed the sheets. At least this lot were tidy. Between them, they carried the vacuum cleaner back down the stairs and got started on the floors.

'That Claudia's pregnant.' said Ginette above the wheezy drone.

'How do you know?' Madame Lesprats was irritated. She considered the Harveys her own private area of expertise.

'Oriane spotted it. She fainted.'

'That makes sense. Still, she's getting married, isn't she, to Monsieur Harvey's brother?'

'I daresay.'

'Well, she is. Mademoiselle Oriane should keep her nose out of other people's onions.'

Rebuffed, Ginette bent her head and continued sweeping out the empty fireplace, terrible for dust in the summer. Madame Lesprats felt mean.

Later, at lunch, she reported to her daughter-in-law that she had asked 'that poor Ginette' to come with them to the *chasse loto* on Friday evening, she knew Sabine wouldn't mind, and God knows, it will be nice for her to get out of that house. Ginette could come on her bicycle, and afterward they could put it in the boot of the Clio and drive her home. Sabine worked in a pharmacy at Landi. Already, in her mother-in-law's kitchen, with the blinds drawn and the cheese on the table, she could feel the sharp ache between her eyes that always came when they went to the loto. She hated sitting in the *Mairie* for hours under the violent yellow strip light, smelling sweaty old women and their graveyard breath. She said, 'Well, that should be a change for her.'

Aisling's table looked lovely. As the Froggetts had obediently gone off to the lake, marshalled by Claudia at two o'clock, she considered serving the tea by the pool, but it would be nice for Delphine to see the house itself, so she put out the plates and teacups on a white cloth spread over a corner of the big table on the terrace. Just the china, and glasses for the boys' lemonade; it would look pretentious, she thought, to scatter some rose petals on the white, though she had been tempted. Lapsang with lemon, the cake and a sticky banana loaf to slice up for the children in case, though French children loved almonds. Sitting with Delphine (who was Delphine, of course, now, she had corrected Aisling's tentative Comtesse immediately), Aisling thought the garden couldn't look prettier. The tour of La Maison Bleue had been lovely. Aisling had tried to go quickly, not wishing to bore her guest, but Delphine had seemed avid for every detail, keen to know who had done the work and how quickly, charmed by what she called the 'delicate' colour scheme and how clever it was of Aisling to leave some of the original byre in the kitchen to make a feature. The ghost of Mrs Highland shrivelled and evaporated in the brightness of Delphine's exclamations and the swift tap of her tongue – so lovely to hear a pure French voice and not that dreadful thick accent Aisling was worried her boys might pick up.

Charles-Henri and Jules munched enthusiastically at both almond cake and banana loaf, and then asked their mother, whom they addressed, extraordinarily, as *vous*, if they could return to the water. Delphine looked dubious, so Aisling suggested they carry their teacups down to be on hand in case of fatal cramps. The French were so old-fashioned about these things. Though Delphine's English was far superior to her hostess's French, they chatted in her own language, and Aisling felt she kept her end up very well, though it was frustrating not quite to have the means of satisfying her curiosity discreetly, without appearing nosy, a trick that was difficult even in English and impossible with the addition of the rather aggressive *est-ce que* at the beginning of a question. She tried the French method of making a statement preceded by 'and' with a rising interrogative inflection, but Delphine seemed to think she was reiterating her own remarks and merely agreed. Still, by the time the third cup of tea was drunk and the second slice of cake refused, Aisling had discovered a good deal.

The husband had died quite suddenly last year, though Aisling did not attempt to probe into the details, moving the conversation along after a suitable arrangement of countenance and a murmured '*je suis desolée*'. Where the cancer had been she couldn't make out. Delphine lived with her children in the same apartment in the fifth, the rue de Vaugirard, where La Maintenon looked after La Montespan's children, so charming, poor thing, and lovely for the boys being just across from the Luxembourg, which was much prettier than the Tuileries, didn't Aisling think? Aisling wondered why La Maintenon was a poor thing. She had tried to read a popular French novel about her called *L'Allée du Roi*, but had never got beyond the prologue. Clearly it was done to speak about historical characters as though one knew them personally. Sarah Ashworth was a treasure (Aisling noticed that Delphine did not feel the need to express any obviously insincere regrets that she hadn't the time to bring up her children herself, which is what, Aisling thought, an Englishwoman would have done). Charles-Edouard had insisted on an English nanny, he had had one himself, like his father Charles-Louis when the old Marquis was with the Free French. This took a moment to unravel, particularly all the Charleses, but Aisling said how funny, she had always had a French au pair girl for Oliver and Richard when they were still in London. Delphine said that she hoped to spend a lot more time in the country. 'I was married there, you know,' she added, looking across over the roof of the guesthouse then staring suddenly at her plate.

Aisling stood up and called to the children in the pool, making a noise.

Claudia wished Alex wouldn't jiggle so. He wore tropically patterned swimming shorts, his flanks trembled like just set custard above the ruched waistband. Dressed, he was fine really, compared to some of his friends, but like this – Claudia knew she was hateful, but she didn't seem able to stop herself. She tucked her chin forward and looked over her lower lids at her own brown stomach. Two hollows of muscle ran either side of her navel and a clean half centimetre of space showed beneath the bikini bottom stretched over her hipbones. The bikini was a waste, really, no need for Missoni around here. It made no difference. She thought of the baby, she thought of Sébastien, she hated Alex. It seemed as though, if she could just be alone for long enough, she could think her way to some resolution, knowing at the same time that this was just procrastination, there was no answer that differed from what she had. Yet her head drummed with the want to be away from all of them, from Aisling and her food and her enthusiasms especially. It had been a mistake to come, her pleasure in the landscape was making her weak. She ought to have changed their plans, made Alex take her away for an expensive break somewhere she had to change her dress a lot, and then back to London to just get on with things.

'The boys' were playing volleyball in the muddy shallows of the lake, Giles and the Harvey sons against Jonathan and Alex. Wendy Froggett was reading a book about one man's struggle to start an olive farm in Extremadura. Alice looked hot and self-conscious with *The Idiot*. Caroline appeared to be asleep. Claudia got up determinedly and went to the lake, avoiding the volleyball. It was brackish close to the edge, but after a few strokes she was out of her depth, it felt cool and fresh. She dipped her head and opened her eyes to greenish motes, stuck out her tongue to feel the softness. She flipped on to her back and propelled herself gently with her hands. It was beautiful here, really, just the sky and the hills and the green water. Perhaps she should phone Annabelle, but to say what? 'Sébastien's knocked me up so I'm marrying Alex. Don't tell anyone.'? It would be in bad taste to inflict her secret on Annabelle, dangerous moreover, and what could her friend actually do? Annabelle would be sympathetic, but there was no solution she could propose that Claudia herself had not rejected. All she had to do was tell Alex, get it over with and after that it would be irrevocable, once he thought it was his.

She imagined it, hunched like a bean inside her with stubby Thalidomide limbs. It seemed so abstract, the baby. At times she felt a protective longing that was almost violent; she supposed that this was the fierce mother love she had so often read of, and then she felt reassured that this was what she ought to feel. Yet there were moments when she sought some sense of connection with it, the bliss she should anticipate, and it stubbornly refused to be present at all, except as a lever that would drive her life onward, a curled, horribly potent cog. Claudia felt tears on her face, hot in the lakewater, then wondered if anyone had ever drowned here. Some farm girl, pregnant and terrified, greening limbs in the swimmy weeds, rising up to clutch at her. A fish splashed close to her hand and she gasped, swallowing water, and swam as fast as she could towards the shore.

★

Delphine telephoned Armand LeSaux. She had to take her phone on to the lawn, there was no mobile reception in the house, that would have to be seen to. He was at Porto Cervo – could he not persuade Delphine to come down for a few days? There were flights from Nice. Delphine considered, but thought it would be better, in the long run, not to seem to wish to leave her boys.

'Of course,' said Armand, 'naturally.'

Delphine explained what the English woman had told her and Armand suggested they might meet in Paris as soon as everyone was back. Perhaps dinner? There were some Americans he knew who might be interested in investing. If Delphine could convince her father-in-law... Armand thought the Bristol for dinner, not very *sympa*, but the food was excellent, and the Americans would like it because they only ever went to the Tour d'Argent and were surprised when they had a dreadful time. He would make some calls. Maybe some photos could be organized? Delphine promised to speak to the Marquis. She found that she was quite excited about discussing the plan with Aisling Harvey, who really did seem nice, even if she had clearly never heard of the subjunctive.

Madame Lesprats was beating a rug over a line by the little summerhouse. When Delphine finished speaking she continued swinging the beater, thwack, thwack.

JUNE 1940

Monsieur Mons had given Oriane twenty francs before he left for the station, explaining it was from the Marquis. This seemed like a lot of money, three months' wages, but when Oriane woke next morning she was already worried about what would happen when it was gone. She wanted to enjoy the strange feeling of lying in bed a little, as though it were a Sunday, but she was wide awake with anxiety, and William would be wanting his breakfast. He was already banging on her door. When she let him in, he did not kiss her, but pushed open the shutters, squeaking and pointing excitedly. It was one of those rare, hazeless days when from the height of Aucordier's they could see right across the valley, beyond the church tower and away, far away to where the mountains began, with Spain on the other side. This morning it was so clear Oriane could make out a sharp line from grey to white where the snow began on the great peaks. There had been only a few times in her life when she had seen as far as the mountains, but today her eye was caught by a line of figures on the Landi road. Castroux itself was invisible from here, hidden except for the bell tower by the wooded hill on the Saintonge side, but the new road was plain before it dipped to the village, and today it looked like the procession of the Madonna, crowded with walkers, several carts and bicycles and a big truck caught in the middle of them, its horn booming across the river like a strange angry bird. For a moment she was afraid, but the light was so fine today that the different colours of the travellers' clothes were visible, even a red bow in the hair of a little girl sitting on a loaded wheelbarrow. The group disappeared down towards the square, and after a few minutes they saw the truck emerge on the Saintonge side, picking up speed and throwing a cloud of blue smoke that hung still in the air behind it.

William was still humming with pleasure and it took Oriane a moment to remember that his excitement was due only to the simple joy of seeing the mountains again. How gentle it must be, to think so simply. Those people must be escaping, she thought, emptying their stables and their barns for whatever could carry them, moving south to safety with their children. They were lucky, she realized. Despite the atmosphere in the village, they were lucky.

Oriane was keen to go down to Castroux and see what news had come, but perhaps it was best to carry on as usual, so after they had dunked their bread in the coffee, she put on her overall and went down to the yard. There were plenty of things to catch up with, jobs she had been meaning to do but had never found the time for lately. She thought she might use the Marquis's money to buy a few more goats, maybe even get Laurent to take her to Landi in the wagon, and move the goat house down the hill, where they would have more space to graze and the smell wouldn't blow into the kitchen. There were strawberries to pick, she could finally start the jam, and the birds had been at the peas again, she had meant to make a scarecrow. She set William to the strawberries, hoping he wouldn't eat too many, and went to the barn to find two bits of wood to make a cross for the legs and arms. She would need a hole in the *potager* to stick it in deep, and the salads were looking parched and mottled, they needed water around the roots. If she fetched the water for the salads after she'd dug the hole, she could moisten the earth to make the scarecrow stick, though perhaps it was already too late for watering, if the sun caught any drops on the leaves they would scorch. She was standing in the pea bed, thinking about the best order to do things in, when a man pushed a bicycle up the road, loaded with panniers on either side, followed by another man with a wheelbarrow, a woman, and the little girl with the red bow in her hair.

'*Bonjour!*' the man called to her. He was a bit fat, red in the face and puffing, and had taken off his cap, which was stupid with this sun. The others came up behind him and stared at Oriane. The man spoke again.

'Is this the road to Cahors? We're trying to get to Cahors.'

Oriane nodded. A pink cardboard suitcase protruded from the barrow, and there was a collection of lumpy bundles with a flowered cloth dragged over them. William stuck his head from the strawberry leaves and made a grunting noise. The little girl began to snivel. Oriane had thought at first the people looked quite well-dressed, but up close they were dirty, the woman's shoes were filthy and one heel was broken. She stepped forward and spoke gently, as though she thought Oriane was simple. 'We're just passing on, see? We thought you might be able to give us a glass of water, maybe some bread. Look! We have money.' She fumbled at a little leather purse.

'You've come from the village,' said Oriane.

'Yes, but they said we couldn't stay there.'

'Who said?'

'Our friends have a truck, but it's full of our things. There wasn't room. We tried to follow, but when we got to that place,' she pointed, squinting down the hill, trying to make out the direction.

'Saintonge?'

'There. By the little church. They'd blocked the road with a cart and some tables. We asked for some water, but they said it was a drought and it would be ten centimes for a jug.'

'Ten centimes?'

'We've come all the way from Orléans,' the other man said. 'We've been on the road a week. The others turned back, but we need to get to Cahors, that's where our things will be.'

Oriane looked about her. She saw the scallop shell on the corner of the house and remembered, suddenly, how she used to count shames. Beyond the mountains the pilgrim road led to St Jacques, people had been walking here for a thousand years. She felt the blood gather in her face, hot and furious.

'You're going away, from them?'

'Yes,' answered the woman, 'from Orléans. We had a shop.' She began to cry.

The little girl's name was Claire. She sat at the table stuffing her mouth with strawberries, her chin and hands stained with juice as red as her hair ribbon. Oriane had broken all the eggs in the bowl and made an omelette with wild garlic from the hollow where she planned to put the new goat pen. There wasn't much bread in the house, but she had wrapped every bit up in a dampened cloth to keep it fresher and given it to the woman. She poured wine from the jug for the two men, and put cheese on a plate, with the tiniest leaves ripped from the hearts of the lettuces, which would die now, anyway. William would have to make do with just the soup later. It was the Chauvignats, Emile and Cécile, who had tried to take money from these poor people. They had the pig farm at Saintonge where Sophie Aucordier used to go down to work. She had always complained of their meanness.

'But what about the people in Castroux?' asked Oriane. 'Didn't anyone help you?'

'Everything was shut up,' said the bicycle man, 'all the windows had their shutters up, there was no one about. We knocked on a few doors... Then our friend drove up the hill and we followed, but those people had blocked the road. Our friend was so angry, he drove right at the barrier and they had to pull it out of the way, but we didn't want little Claire to see anything, you know.' He stopped to take a big bite of cheese, as though he was too hungry and confused to go on with the story.

'So no one helped,' Oriane repeated.

'We thought of stopping at that big farm down the hill—'
'Murblanc?'

'I suppose, but it looked a rich sort of place and we don't

want any trouble. Our friend said he would deliver our things and drive back to find us on the Cahors road.'

Oriane asked the woman discreetly if she would like to wash and use the privy. She went off hand in hand with Claire.

'Ten centimes for a bit of water,' said the bicycle man, shaking his head. 'Is that how things are here?'

There was nothing else in the house to give them, but they seemed refreshed as they dragged the loaded barrow back to the road. Oriane and William waved goodbye, and William played them a little tune, which made Claire laugh.

'I hope you find your friend,' Oriane called as they reached the top of the rise. They turned and waved. Oriane looked at Aucordier's, feeling sad and angry at the same time. She never spoke of the people from Orléans, although the village was full of stories then about the dangers of the beggars on the road, how many of them were Jews and Communists. Each time she heard someone speak of it, even Betty and Amélie and Andrée, she despised them in her heart and made a mark of shame there against them.

SUMMER HOLIDAYS

'Well, that's them gone,' said Aisling, as the Froggett car trundled across the bridge. She dropped the arm that had been waving. 'Do you think Caroline had a nice time?'

'S'pose,' said Olly. They walked up the garden together.

'Do you think they enjoyed the barbecue?'

'Prob'ly.'

'Are you going to the village later?'

'S'pose.'

Aisling gave up. She had gone to more bother than usual for the Froggetts' barbecue, marinating some spatchcocked quail and making four individual pockets of roast vegetable ravioli. The white chocolate and cardamom mousse had really come out well, very light. Wendy Froggett had left a thank-you card and an unattractive arrangement of dried flowers from the market, which was more than most did. She would give those to Ginette, and would actually be quite pleased if they booked again, though Wendy had said they were thinking about Spain next year.

'I hate the fucking PGs,' said Oliver.

Briefly, Aisling considered slapping him, then being mature and asking him why. 'Don't be boring, Olly,' she sighed instead.

'You're boring. It's boring here. I hate fucking France too, come to that.'

Aisling wanted terribly to laugh. 'It's not particularly clever to say "fuck" all the time, you know.' She would have to say something to Jonathan, but she couldn't bother about it now. Olly looked a bit crushed, and she put her arm over his shoulder, non-committally, in the way she had learned with her sons in the last few years. 'It's not long now, just two more weeks and they'll all be gone, Claudia and Alex too. And then you've got riding camp.'

Oliver thought about saying that riding camp was boring too, but Mum looked a bit upset. It was pathetic actually, how excited she got about cooking and PGs and stuff, but then she didn't have a job like Claudia, in London. She was stuck here the whole time. There wasn't anyone looking, so he put his arm around her.

'Sorry, Mum.'

'It's OK. But don't say fuck any more please. I don't do PGs for fun, you know. You do understand that?'

'Yeah.'

Olly tried to think of something he could do to please his mother.

'It was pathetic, actually,' he said as they went up the steps to the terrace, 'Alice Froggett's French.'

His mum smiled.

★

'I should say,' said Alex that evening, 'that the Sternbachs are "A Cut Above".'

'You're a dreadful snob about Mondeos.'

'Guilty as charged.'

'Shall we switch to red?'

'Thinking on it, you're right. Maybe the PG white was a mistake. Do you think it looks mean?'

'It was good enough for the Froggetts.'

'Exactly,' said Aisling, and everyone laughed.

Actually, Aisling thought, the Sternbachs had been most appreciative. Ella had said the bakery in the village looked lovely and that she had heard the Saturday market was fabulous. She'd even noticed the bathrooms, remarking knowledgeably that they were exceptional compared with what one usually found even in places that were supposed to be smart in France. Otto, the husband, had remarked that the view across the valley, broken by the poplars on the river bank, reminded him of a Cézanne. Ella had been wearing a very elegant pair of cream linen palazzo pants with beige suede ballerina flats, and a huge chunky silver necklace, which always looked so wonderful on the kind of women they looked wonderful on. Aisling had experimented with the look herself, but it had never got further than the bathroom mirror. Not the sort of thing one associated with Amsterdam somehow, but then she probably got her clothes in Paris, or Italy even.

Richard and Oliver sat on the roof of the poolhouse. The PGs had the lights off. Richard was smoking a fag he'd sort of nicked from Claudia, at least she'd left the packet on the table and not said anything when she saw him take one. Olly had a drag because he'd threatened to tell otherwise, although it was gross.

'D'you think they're sexing?'

'Gross, they're well old. Older than Jonathan and Aisling.' Richard liked referring to his parents by their names.

There wasn't much going on, but it was dark and they were away from the music and the wine jug on the terrace. 'Kevin's getting an MBK,' said Richard after a while.

'Rice eater.'

'So's Honda, actually, dickhead.'

'Claudia was crying today,' added Oliver, to get back some ground, 'I heard.'

'You were spying on her, you dirty little bastard.'

'Actually, I heard her through the door. I was only going to the loo. She was hysterical, practically.'

'Prob'ly had a row with Alex.'

'Prob'ly.'

Richard reluctantly ground out the cigarette and put the end deeply in the pocket of his shorts, to be wrapped in loo paper and flushed away. 'Alex knows piss anyway. He said their car,' he jerked his head at La Maison Bleue, 'was a three series. As if.'

'X5,' said Oliver eagerly.

They were quiet for a bit. Richard said, 'Kevin wouldn't actually know if we said that car was our uncle's, would he?'

'It's got a Dutch number plate. Dickhead.' They rolled on the roof of the poolhouse, pretending to try to kick one another in the balls.

★

There was a storm that night. As the two houses slept, the clouds banked thickly over the plain, bunching around the moon, and the first smash of thunder came with a tearing sound, as though they were being peeled roughly from the sky. Claudia woke with the lightning, a shaft as bright and quick as if someone had switched on the light. It felt suddenly colder, she reached for the sheet where she had kicked it off, and pushed the hair from her eyes. There was a rustling sound outside, she thought of an owl beating its wings against the shutters like an irritated ghost made suddenly corporeal, then she realized it was the rain. She lay on her back and listened, counting between the claps of thunder and the lightning. Five at first, then three, three again, then four, six as the storm travelled towards the Pyrenees and the rain picked up in the space it left, settling into a steady rhythm like dropped needles. She thought of going outside, to stand on the balcony again and let the cool water soak her skin, but the gesture seemed obvious even if it were performed only to herself, and she turned on her front, wrapping her arms around the pillow, sending her ears away into the freshening dawn, far from the gargle of mucus in Alex's throat that slurped each time he inhaled.

It was a surprise, next morning, to see that the sky remained the mauve grey of skimmed milk, that the air was not soft and rich over the saturated earth, but chill and thickened, a sullen day that looked unlikely to shift its mood. 'Typical,' said Aisling as Jonathan came in with the duck bucket in his hand, looking foolish in wellingtons and shorts.

'What is?'

'This weather. On the Sternbachs' first day.'

'Well it's not your fault. They'll hardly hold you responsible. Anyway, it'll burn off by this afternoon.'

Aisling felt like kicking him on his rubber shin. 'It won't.'

Jonathan put two large blue eggs in the basket on the dresser. 'Suit yourself.' He spent the morning in his study with the door closed.

Aisling took a jar of last year's apricot jam down to the guesthouse. She rapped on the glass door and called '*Bonjour!*' Otto and Ella were looking tidy and composed, eating *pain aux raisins*, which had obviously been fetched that morning from Castroux.

'You're up early,' exclaimed Aisling brightly, 'I hope you slept well?'

'Delightfully, thank you,' replied Ella. These Dutch really did have fabulous English.

'I feel dreadful about the weather. It's been absolutely perfect up until now, almost too hot. It's always the way, isn't it?'

Neither of them said anything, though Aisling fancied that Otto looked amused.

'Well, I'd better get on.'

'Thank you for the jam,' said Otto after a swallow of coffee, 'and please, we don't mind the rain. In fact, we're driving to Monguèriac today, to go to the museum.'

It was unjust, thought Aisling, that the sun had shone so for the Froggetts. The pool would have to be skimmed, it was full of all sorts of rubbish from last night, and that wasn't nice for the Sternbachs, was it? Not that anyone else would think of it. She could ask Alex maybe. Still, there was plenty to do, and bad weather was a good chance to catch up. If Alex did the pool, Claudia could help her finish the cherry compote, and the barn could do with a good tidy, the boys could do that. She felt purposeful, her irritation with Jonathan lifted, but her sense of injustice returned when she got up to the house and saw Ginette's bicycle outside the back door. 'What now?' she hissed to herself.

Ginette looked even more depressing than usual in a blue mackintosh on top of her overall and green plastic clogs. She was talking in French to Claudia, who had a pink cashmere sweater over her pyjamas.

'Good morning,' said Aisling a bit tightly.

'Morning,' said Claudia in English, then turned back to Ginette. 'That's fine, really, I'll be along about seven.'

'Very kind,' muttered Ginette, made a sort of bob at Aisling and scurried away.

'Oh, I feel saintly, Aisling,' Claudia smiled.

'What did she want?'

'Oh, it's sweet really. She's going to some knees-up in the village with your cleaning lady. Madame Lesprats? And anyway, apparently she's worried about leaving the old lady on her own, because it goes on quite long, the bingo or whatever, and Mademoiselle Oriane gets a bit nervous, and she wanted to know if one of us could possibly look in and keep her company for an hour. Poor thing, I doubt she gets out much around here.'

'So?'

'So I said I'd go. You can't possibly, you're much too busy, and I don't mind a bit. Good practice for my French.'

Aisling felt unreasonably cheated. She had planned to be a bit annoyed with Claudia for presuming, and here the girl was doing favours for old ladies. 'Well, I do have a lot to get on with today. The bad weather's such a good chance to get caught up. Thanks.'

'I feel so worthy I should feel guilty, really. And I can give you a hand this afternoon. I was going to suggest Alex drove the boys into Landi, for an ice cream or something. They'll only get on our nerves hanging about.'

Aisling felt played, although it was unfair. Still, perhaps she would get to sit down with her book for once. She brought a box of novels and biographies back from England every time they went over, and they were lined up in the drawing room, making her feel guilty. There was just so much to do in the country.

Claudia had to know how the old woman had known she was pregnant. Ginette had given her the opportunity, and it was always nice to be praised for something that cost one no effort. Besides, the thought of an evening of Sternbach-speculation in the kitchen was dreadful. It was pathetic the way Aisling got so involved with her guests, for better or worse, it made her life seem impoverished, which Claudia supposed it was, stuck here with dreary Jonathan, but why be so transparent about it? Claudia wanted to let Aisling know just how unimpressed she was by the Sternbachs, in the same way she thought she had given the impression of not really noticing that the Froggetts were awful. That 'Otto' was a doctor and 'Ella' a painter could not have been less interesting to Claudia, though the woman did seem to have nice clothes. She thought it vulgar of Aisling to make it obvious that she had noticed what was obvious anyway, that the Sternbachs were rich. Were doctors very wealthy in Holland? Claudia wondered why they had come as boarders for their holiday when presumably they could have afforded something much smarter, and then felt irritated, because that was the sort of thing Aisling might wonder about.

Ginette, in a drooping olive skirt and patterned blouse that did no more for her than the overall, was waiting anxiously at the door when Claudia turned into the yard, warm from taking the steep road at a march, angrily combating her previous weakness. She fussed about showing Claudia the tea things and explained that Claudia need only stay an hour or so, Oriane went to bed early and she could manage for herself, it was just for a bit of company. Madame Lesprats arrived and honked imperiously, there was a small crisis regarding the whereabouts of Ginette's worn navy handbag, and they were off.

'Have a lovely evening!' called Claudia, waving at the angry little car. Indoors, the television was showing a quiz game.

'Shall we turn this off?' asked Claudia brightly.

'If you like.' Claudia did so, then sat down on one of the wooden dining chairs, dragging it towards the sofa. She was waiting to see if Oriane said something surprising again, but the old woman looked at her mildly, without hostility or interest. Nothing in the room seemed to have been touched, the harsh electric light was on, though it would be two hours before the sun moved. A fire had been laid, but not lit, prepared with spills of glossy coloured paper. Johnny Hallyday's sinister lizard face smiled stiffly under a log. Claudia thought that perhaps she had not been recognized, and wondered how to explain who she was without being rude. She began to talk about the drinks party at the chateau, thinking that would interest Mademoiselle Oriane and also that it would remind her that she was Claudia, staying with Madame Harvey at Murblanc. Oriane nodded along as Claudia talked of the garden and the wonderful view.

'I used to work up there,' she interrupted. Claudia's French was not quite so good as to be able to make many distinctions of timbre, but she thought Oriane had a nice voice, surprisingly deep and much younger than the rest of her.

'Really?'

'Yes, before the war.'

'That must have been interesting.'

'Not really. Why would it have been? I was a servant, I did the laundry and the ironing and I helped with the cleaning. There was nothing interesting in all that.'

'But the family, I meant. Didn't they give parties, have guests to stay?' The chateau was a coveting sort of place, no matter how one tried to help it. It would have been fun to hear about its grandeur, but Oriane did not seem much interested in the conversation. Old people were supposed to like telling stories.

'Monsieu d'Esceyrac was away a lot, gone to Paris. There was the Marquise and her little boy, the Monsieur d'Esceyrac your friends the Harveys are friendly with. I didn't see Madame much. The house was lovely though, and I suppose there were the usual things. Tennis, dancing. I didn't see much of that, I just did my work and came home.'

It seemed to Claudia that Oriane's idea of life was a sort of upstairs downstairs gleaned from the television, nothing to do with her actual memories. Perhaps she had forgotten, or didn't care.

'You didn't live up there?'

'No, I had to come home to take care of my brother.'

'Your brother?'

'He was killed in the war.'

'I'm sorry.'

'Why should you be? But it's nice of you to come anyway. Would you like something to drink?'

They had sickly *sirop de grenadine* diluted with tap water, the kind that Claudia had clamoured for as a child on the beach in Brittany. She felt tears starting and twisted up her face to contain them.

'It's no good, you know,' said the old woman softly.

'What isn't?' Claudia asked, trying for brightness.

'It's not his, is it?'

There was something so certain in the question that it seemed pointless to feign surprise or anger.

'No,' she replied, 'it's not.' Claudia could hear the wind outside, louder than it ever sounded down the valley, tugging about the yard. She put her arms on the table and rested her head upon them for a moment, swallowing the beginning of a sob. Then she lifted her face and said in a calm voice, 'I don't want to get married. It's not Alex's fault. I just don't.'

'No.' Placidly. 'I don't suppose that you do. It's not something we choose, is it?'

'What?'

'Who we love.'

Oddly, Claudia considered afterwards, she did not feel stupid, nor damaged by her confession. She did not ask how it was that Oriane seemed to know so surely what she had so carefully kept hidden, nor expect her to say something wise. They were silent for a while, then Oriane pointed to the black and white photograph Claudia had noticed when she had come in the night with Aisling. 'That was my son. Jacky.'

'Your son? Did he—'

'He went away. When he found out who his father was, he went away.'

Claudia stared at the old woman opposite her. Had she understood properly?

'When he found out who his father was? He went away then?'

'Yes, he was ashamed, you see.'

'Ashamed?'

'I met his father there. At the chateau. We had to keep it a secret, of course. And then when I knew I was expecting, I quarrelled with him.'

'Of course.' Claudia felt certain that she knew who the father must have been, it was so predictable and yet one didn't really believe in these things, they were sad stories from history books. Cautiously, she reached out to touch Oriane's hand. She had not expected a response, but the touch seemed to quicken something in her and she grasped Claudia's hand strongly, holding it tight until Claudia began to feel embarrassed, there was something so starved in it. She pulled away gently.

'I'm very sorry. You must have been very unhappy.'

Oriane did not reply. They both looked at the television, and after a time the old lady seemed to doze off.

Later, when Claudia said goodbye, Oriane kissed her, right left right, the way they did here. 'Perhaps you'll come again,' she said, though it wasn't a question. The old eyes had seemed bright and beady, but close in Claudia saw that their shine was filmy, bleached out. Her face was cool against Claudia's cheek, above the neckline of her blouse was a growth of some sort, or a cyst, purple and bulbous. A witch's teat. Claudia thought it was disgusting, and wondered why it hadn't been removed.

'Oh yes,' said Aisling, 'it's terrible the way people suffered around here.'

They were in the drawing room upstairs where Aisling had decided not to light a fire all the same. It had been clear when Claudia returned that the men were gone, there were no belongings lying about the terrace and Aisling had lit a candle that smelt of honey.

'But the son didn't die in the war,' Claudia objected.

'Madame Lesprats told me that his father did, as well as Oriane's brother. Can you imagine? Though it's not unusual around here, if you look on the monument in the church for example, the same few names over and over. Terrible.' Aisling was warming up now.

'And Madame Lesprats said that there was some sort of a scandal with poor Ginette. Apparently she was engaged to this Jacky character and then he went off and left her,' she added excitedly.

'So she lives there because Oriane felt guilty or something?'

'Maybe. But they weren't married, she and the father that is, because she's Mademoiselle Aucordier and the farm was in her family. But it was the war, I suppose, GI brides and all that.'

'It's so sad.'

'Mmm.'

Claudia had no intention of telling what she had discovered, even for the satisfaction of the gossip. She imagined that

Madame Lesprats probably knew that the Marquis had fathered a child on one of his servants, but Oriane's prescience had been so disarming, her confidences so touching, that Claudia felt both protective and superstitious about betraying her. She did allow a little smile at what Alice Froggett would have made of the story.

'What?'

'Oh, nothing. It's funny in the country isn't it? People seem so much more interesting.' If that was a bit near the bone, Aisling didn't notice. Claudia refilled Aisling's glass of red and took another from the *buffet* for herself.

'Have you been to the River Café,' Aisling asked, 'in London?'

'Yes, a couple of times. Why?'

'Well, I've got this book of theirs, those two women, thingy Rogers, and there's a recipe for sourdough I thought I might try, but it's very longwinded.'

They made conversation about recipes and menus until they heard Alex's car in the lane.

Next day was hotter than ever, as though the sun had had a holiday. The Sternbachs drove away again after breakfast, and Aisling was inclined to fret about this, thinking that perhaps it meant they didn't like La Maison Bleue, until she reminded herself that this was precisely the kind of guest she had wanted, *doing* sort of people. Perhaps they had gone to Cahors, or even to Albi, to one of the huge August markets. PG-less, everyone was down at the pool when Ginette drooped up on her bicycle.

'Bloody hell,' said Jonathan loudly, 'doesn't that woman have a home of her own?'

'There does seem an awful lot of coming and going,' added Alex.

'We only notice because bugger-all happens in between.'

'Don't be unkind,' hissed Aisling, sitting up and putting on her sarong. 'How are you, Ginette?' she called loudly in French. 'Did you enjoy yourself at the lotto?' Even to herself that sounded a bit duchess-like.

'Madame Glover was there from Saintonge. She won the fridge freezer.'

'Really? Well, that's nice. Did you win anything?'

'No, nor did Madame Lesprats.'

'Oh dear.'

Ginette hovered. Aisling felt that she had been caught out being lazy, lolling in her bathing costume, though it was Saturday afternoon. That was a problem here, that there were just no barriers. Should she offer Ginette something?

'I just came to say thank you to Claudia for sitting with Mademoiselle Oriane last night.'

'Well, that's nice.'

'No problem, Ginette,' called Claudia gaily from her sun lounger, 'any time you feel like partying!' She was already determined to go back to Aucordier's as soon as she could.

'I'll get on then.'

'OK. See you soon.'

Ginette turned her bicycle around and wheeled it down the track.

'Honestly!' said Aisling, but the others had turned back to the sun. No one seemed inclined to discuss Charlotte Glover and the fridge freezer.

JUNE 1941

Laurent Nadl had lost his right leg at Verdun the year that
Oriane Aucordier was born, and when the rest of him was
sent home to Castroux he felt, bitterly, that he was not
accorded a hero's welcome. Stumps of various sorts had never
been uncommon in the village. Old Vionne the butcher had
only two fingers (the right ones at least, as he was fond of
crudely reminding the women) on his left hand, Camille
Lesprats had only a lump of right arm, the rest of it shredded
by a threshing machine. He hadn't even been drunk at the
time, though he'd been making up for it ever since, challenging
the remaining elderly boozers in the café to call him a coward
and sobbing into his wine about the lost limb that would
surely have made him the terror of the Boch, had he only
been allowed to fight. To Laurent, it seemed that people felt
that coming home at all was more than he had a right to
expect. He was not about to apologize for surviving. It did
not occur to him that Castroux's reticence was moved in some

quarters by a delicacy towards families who had lost sons, brothers, young fathers, and in others by a grief so huge and dulling that those possessed of it endured at first only by indifference. One life more or less could have very little meaning. Four men, finally, had come back to Castroux, from the nineteen who had gone. Laurent had left his leg behind, and Jean-Marc Teulière his wits. Yves Contier was sound, so, it seemed, was Bernard Vionne. Jean-Claude Larivière, the fifth survivor, never returned from his demob leave in Paris.

He'd been a real chum, JC. For a while they had been in it together, all of them, until JC was made corporal and moved along the lines. He had always been a bright spark, reading things from the newspaper, spending money on books that he sent away for. Laurent didn't care much for talking politics, but JC had been a great one for it, always on about the working man. As far as Laurent could see, the working man did the graft and took the bullets when the time came, but JC said it didn't have to be like that, that big changes were coming for sure, and Laurent tried to seem like he understood, he'd even got into a fight or two, sticking up for him. JC wasn't a big man, like Laurent, but he was a scrapper. Laurent could see why he wouldn't have wanted to come back to Castroux, though his mother had taken on something dreadful; JC was a livewire, someone who wanted to be where the action was. Even Flanders hadn't knocked that out of him.

When Laurent took the habit of walking up the hill from Murblanc to Aucordier's after supper in the long summer evenings of 1941, he still did not quite comprehend that he had only one leg. Accustomed to its absence, he nevertheless had not entirely discarded the belief, sustained unquestioningly on the train ride south more than twenty years ago, that it would somehow grow back. This arbitrary state of the leg's being permitted Laurent a quick recovery from the practicalities of his disability and the repugnance it aroused in him. Since matters were only temporary, it was easier to make the best of them. The stump was smoothed over with skin, though it still had a tendency to develop a greasy fungus, which itched deliciously and left pale lines of weak, vealy blood when Laurent raked his nails through it beneath the bedclothes. The wooden leg was so heavy, the leather strap chafing painfully on the now hairless skin of his thigh, that Laurent only wore it for church, preferring the relative mobility of his crutch. With his stump tied into a woollen stocking and covered by the trouser leg, which his mother had sewn into a bag, he could move quite quickly, hopping around the pivot of the crutch when he needed to turn, and balancing so well, when stationary, that he could use his right arm almost freely. He did exercises every morning, drills he had learned in the Army, press-ups and curls of an iron bar filed off from the frame of a rusting plough. Muscle had slabbed on to his arms and chest, he worked his left side more to balance out the effort of the crutch to the right. Laurent was tall for Castroux, and in his Sunday suit, with a stuffed boot laced over the false leg and his massive shoulders squared above his still-narrow waist he looked, if not handsome, at least strong and healthy. There had been no question of him spending his life as an invalid, even had he wished to. His mother was a widow, he was the only son and there was work to be done.

Laurent could not have explained, even had anyone ever asked, why it was that he felt his life so spoiled. He rarely thought of the war. At first, Bernard Vionne seemed urgent with the need to speak of it, always coming up to Laurent in the café or asking him for a glass of wine at market, wanting to tell his stories, even to hear Laurent's. After a time Laurent avoided him and the group he formed with Yves and Jean-Marc, who Bernard insisted on pushing through the village in his chair. Now and again Jean-Marc would call out violently from the trench where he had left his mind, and Bernard would hold his arm tightly, staring into his face and saying 'Now then' until he was quiet. They became a familiar sight, the three of them, sitting in the square on fine evenings, and after a while no one took much notice of them, except to leave the wooden bench at the café door free, by unspoken consent.

Laurent had no wish to join their reminiscences. He got on with his work, the work he had always intended to do, the work he had dreamed of returning to for two years at the front. His injury was no stay on what ambition he had had, which had only ever been an assumption that he would remain at Murblanc, yet he felt now a sense of constraint there, a movement in himself towards unnamed and unknown chances of a different sort of life, and he grew convinced, as he would never perhaps have done had he returned to Castroux as whole as he appeared on Sundays, that something to which he was entitled had been taken from him.

Murblanc had been bought from the d'Esceyracs, Laurent knew, though he did not know and would not have much cared that the house was older, in parts, than the chateau, and that the d'Esceyracs had farmed there before they became grand and moved up the hill when Henri IV was king.

Murblanc land began in the little wood below the rise of the castle hill, the Bois de la Reine, which the d'Esceyracs liked to claim, a nonsense again unknown to Laurent, had been named for Queen Marie-Thérèse as she made her wedding journey up from the Basque country to Versailles. Laurent knew the wood was named for the Queen of Heaven, as there was a little shrine to Our Lady by the stream that circled the base of the chateau hill and formed the western boundary of Murblanc, passing the cow barn on its low mound in the winter meadow, and tipping into the Landine. Between the wood and the meadow was Bottom Field, with High Field on the ridge that ran against the house in the middle of the property, and Top Field joining the old road that linked the Castroux bridge and the plain. From the road, the Murblanc lane cut deep against the two fields to the yard, leaving a little triangle of scrub for the donkeys by the orchard wall. Behind the orchard were the small barn, the old bread oven now used for storing wood, and the vegetable plot, and at the back, before the land rose to rocks and a thin cover of ever-puny trees, Laurent's father had planted six rows of terraced vines. Though the yield was small, the concentrated sun on the bank and the moisture that filtered down from the plain produced a rich red wine that was as good as any from the big vineyards around Cahors.

Much of his time was spent within the eighty acres of the farm. Laurent's great-grandfather had come north from the Lot some time in the last century; he had been a miller, and there were still cousins at Montrattier, and two fields that Laurent's mother let to them. His great-grandfather was buried in Castroux, the headstone said 1899. His ancient grandfather still loitered about the farm, tending his beloved donkeys and even brewing in his still with his few remaining cronies when autumn came.

Laurent went up to Aucordier's on a June evening wearing a clean shirt and carrying a basket of his mother's, lined with an embroidered napkin and holding two dozen apricots. He had picked the fruit himself before supper, with the solid heat still heavy on his stripped back, and washed them carefully, one by one, at the pump. He considered wearing his leg, but it seemed better manners to walk up the hill, and the thought of the pitch of the road bearing on the stump was unpleasant. Oriane was sitting on a stool outside the front door, bent over a bucket of new broad beans. Under her arm, she saw Laurent Nadl swing and hop into her yard with his mother's best pink straw basket bobbing absurdly in the crook of his elbow, and knew he had come to marry her. She gave no sign that she was aware of him, feeling it would be rude to anticipate his tippety progress by getting up to meet him. His Sunday boot made no sound on the hardened dirt. When he was closer, he called out, and she turned, wiping her hands on her skirt, tucking a coil of hair behind her ears. When he had greeted her, he held out the basket and said, 'I brought these for you.'

Oriane thanked him and offered her stool while she fetched him a glass. She swam through the thick green air of the cool kitchen, she set the basket on the table. There was wine in the jug in the larder, protected from the flies by a white lace cloth weighed down with little glass beads, amber coloured, like the warm skin on Laurent's fruits. She stretched towards the shelf where the four thick glass tumblers stood, then paused. For a long moment she rested her forehead against the thick oak, feeling suddenly very tired, and very sad. Then, moving briskly, she went to the *buffet* in the kitchen and turned the key. Swaddled in scraps of grey blanket were her mother's wedding gifts, the pink and white china bonbonnière, the set of delicate coffee cups, and six crystal goblets, bluish tinged, contoured rough and chunky like the stonework on the church. Carefully, she extracted two, inspected them for dust, and set them on the table. One she filled, into the other she poured a few drops of treacly dark wine, then stepped out into the light.

'Well then,' said Laurent. He smoothed his trousers over his leg and the stump and raised the blue glass, took a swallow. Oriane sipped, and waited until he had drunk, standing awkwardly by the stool.

'Will you come for a walk with me?' he asked, and when she nodded, he stood up and took her hand.

At the entrance of the yard, he paused, as if uncertain of the direction, though there were only two ways to go and they had both walked them since they took their first steps. Up or down. 'Will we go there along the ridge, then?' he asked.

'That's nice. We'll look at the view,' she answered.

It pained her then that even in these first moments, she should be conscious of something unfinished, impoverished in their appearance as they moved along the hot white stones of the road. She in her dusty skirt, with her hair stranded across her forehead, and he, so much older, hurting her with his starch-collared shirt, keeping his stride effortfully ahead of her own. She wished she could see them together differently, separate from herself observing; it seemed cruel that she could not be unconscious for a little while. But they walked in silence, and that was wrong too, though she could think of nothing to say herself, she expected something from him. They went along like married people already, not jostling or whispering or pinching, and though the skin of her cheeks felt warm, she knew it was only from the sun, full on their faces now as they came up from the shade of the last poplars and emerged into the searing western light of the plain. She knew him too well for there to be anything curious or exciting in the sensation of his hard brown palm in her own, though she wished that there were not grey-green strands of bean pod squashed under her nails. They went on for ten minutes or so. A few spreads of elderflower remained in the hedge, and Oriane said, 'I should have brought my basket.'

Laurent pointed to a tumble of stones lying a little way across the sheep-cropped grass. 'Shall we sit down?' It was the remains of one of the little huts the shepherds built, there were many of them dotted over the plain. Some were neat, with stoves even, that the hunters used in winter, but most were crumbling now, one room with a roof left to slide back into the soil. They sat on a low wall with iron tethering rings let into it, spattered with lichen the colour of egg yolk. Deliberately, Laurent put his arms around Oriane's shoulders and kissed her, and just as deliberately, after a little time, pulled away. He took her hand once more. 'When shall it be, then?'

'I haven't thought. With everything as it is. And then there's William.'

'You know I'm fond of William. He's a good lad, really.'

Laurent had a plan, which he explained to her. Things would change after the war. Aucordier's was a fine big house, though it needed a lot of work. He would begin on that this winter when he had more time.

Oriane and William would move down to Murblanc in a year or so, where there was lots of room, especially as Papie couldn't last for ever. He didn't see that Cathérine would marry, but that would be a help to Oriane, having her there, when the children came. He thought Aucordier's could be let, without the land of course, but painted up, with a nice bit of garden. People were going in for what they called weekend houses now, they might get a doctor or a *notaire* from Landi, or even Cahors. The plot where the goats were kept was too steep for anything but vines, but they could have Chasselas there in a few years, and you never lost money with those, and fruit, he thought, cherries or plums, in the field above the house. He would get a workshop going in the barn, a real carpentry workshop, that was what he loved, maybe even take on a few lads, and if it was a success they could have an overseer for the farm. They began to talk about the idea, about which bedroom they would take at Murblanc, and whether the goats would get along with the cows. Oriane would plant a flower garden, a real one with a stone seat.

As they spoke, Oriane watched a carousel of kites, nine or ten of them, whirling in some complex pattern along the edge of the ridge where the rocks were turning now from white to mauve, their wings almost touching as they swooped in tight spirals. It was too simple, she thought, that must be why she did not feel happy. There was no struggle, nothing difficult. She would not have to work so hard. She would live at Murblanc with Laurent, and William would have a home, and she would no longer feel lonely and strange. At the same time, she could not really imagine anything changing, could not envisage leaving Aucordier's, so perhaps that was why she did not feel excited, because it did not as yet seem real. But it would do, she told herself, and held tight to Laurent's arm as he talked about his idea for making chairs and dressers in the small barn. She held on all the way down the road, looking up at his face and saying, 'This is my husband,' swallowing down the coil of dismay that twitched within her, a tiny serpent flexing its tail.

SUMMER HOLIDAYS

Delphine d'Esceyrac had telephoned again, to ask Aisling if the Harveys were going to the Castroux *fête* on the twenty-second of August. 'It will probably be awful,' she had said, 'but then I feel we ought to go to these things?'

'Oh yes,' answered Aisling, 'we definitely should.'

The power of that 'we' annihilated any potential dissent from Aisling's family. The Harveys would certainly attend, as in fact they had attended every year since they first moved to Murblanc, along with Alex and Claudia, the Glovers, and, Aisling thought, the Sternbachs, if they would like to come. The Sternbachs had kept quite to themselves, hardly using the pool, and driving out on excursions each day. They had eaten at all three of the restaurants in Landi, and had tried the *steak-frites* at the bar in the village. Ella said she didn't much like to cook on holiday, and besides her own efforts seemed a waste when one was in France, a remark that struck Aisling as honest and tasteful.

'I think it's quite special, really, the *fête*,' she explained to Ella when she popped down to La Maison Bleue the evening of Delphine's call. The Sternbachs changed for dinner, which Aisling also approved of; Ella was ready to go out in a black linen pinafore thing and an olive vest underneath, with another chunky ethnic necklace.

'Of course, it's nothing grand, but the dinner is jolly, and there's music and fireworks afterwards. We make a point of going along.'

Claudia had no desire to see the d'Esceyracs again, but the lake trip had been too lucky to be repeated. There would be lots of people anyway, she could always chat to Charlotte Glover, and a part of her, she admitted to herself, was curious to see Delphine play lady of the manor. She said as much to Alex as they were changing.

'Hurry up, darling, the *apéritif* kicks off at seven,' he chivvied.

'I can hardly restrain myself. Imagine if we're too late for a lukewarm kir.'

'Aisling would explode. This is the most exciting thing that's happened to her since the ducks had twins.'

'Don't be mean, Alex. I think you were a bit impressed by the chateau yourself.'

Alex didn't reply, as this was perfectly true. He liked the way Claudia saw things clearly, though she could be a bit hard on people at times. But she didn't pretend that the world permanently lived up to her expectations, which he vaguely recognized was his own strategy. He had a feeling that dissatisfaction showed up as a form of failure, an inability to impose himself sufficiently. He felt enough for Claudia to mistake contempt for honesty.

'Do me up?'

'Darling, I think you might have put on a little bit of weight.'

'Oh, fuck off, Alex, it's just your sweaty fingers.'

She had surprised herself with the vehemence of her reaction, too abrupt, too defensive. In the bathroom, Claudia squashed her breasts with one hand and yanked painfully over her head at the zip; it fastened, but the seams of her burned-orange Marni sundress were strained, and the fabric pulled over her chest in a tight, flat panel. She scooped at her flesh until the dress sat properly, extracting a vulgar amount of overspill. Still, to change it would be to concede that Alex was right, though Aisling would certainly think she was vamping, which was infuriating, as though anyone could be flattered enough by Jonathan peering at their tits to invite it.

Malcolm Glover peered at Claudia's tits, along with Jean-Marc Lesprats, the mayor, Monsieur Chauvignat, Richard Harvey, Madame Lesprats (speculatively), Robert Kendrick and his friend Dick Logan. Aisling thought that it was really too bad that the English had all been lumped together on one table, not that she had exactly expected to be seated with the d'Esceyracs, who were in the centre at what was clearly the table of honour with the mayor and his wife, but Delphine had phoned to see that they were coming, after all. And of course the Kendricks had invited the Logans, who made a great clamour of being thrilled to see Jonathan and Aisling, bustling up on the trestle bench so that there was no choice but to sit next to them. They had all had too much to drink, it was obvious, both men and women sweating pastily over their tans so their skin looked like wet chamois leather. Boozing it up in the Glovers' garden all afternoon, apparently. Dick and Mary Logan were Americans, living in a converted mill house on the other side of Landi. They were great friends with Lucy and Robert Kendrick, who belonged to what Aisling called the Landi set, the English colony living on the flat and frankly much less attractive land around the market town twelve kilometres away. They went in for quiz nights.

'Isn't this great, Aisling!' shouted Mary, waving a glass of rosé. 'Your cleaning lady said we could join them.'

The rest of the table consisted of Madame Lesprats with her son and daughter-in-law, and some ancient husk of a Lesprats relation, wrapped despite the heat in layers of pungent wool. Sabine Lesprats wore a shiny blue satin cocktail dress, which pouched over her bosom and strained over a sad little bulge of belly. Her hair was sliced aggressively short in the back, coloured a violent purplish-black, and moulded on top into a complex pompadour.

'She looks like Elvis,' Olly sniggered.

There was no room for the Sternbachs, and Aisling, wedged into the bench, was unable to do more than contort her shoulders and shrug apologetically.

'I'm sure there's seats over there,' she called, pointing to the one unoccupied table, which stood fully in the still-glaring sun. This was dreadful. Otto and Ella would think she was rude and that these loud Anglo-Saxons were the Harveys' preferred companions. Delphine would see her sitting down cheerfully with the cleaner as though they had no other French friends. And the dinner would go on for hours, there was no hope of moving until the cheese at least. The boys hovered politely enough, though Aisling saw Olly's wince when Mary Logan kissed him juicily on both cheeks. They sloped off gratefully to the group of teenagers standing around their motos, too cool to sit down.

The Lesprats family was separated from the Harveys by the Glover party, which was a blessing in the Delphine sense, but then it meant that Aisling would not be able to distance herself further from '*les Anglais*' by conversing exclusively in French. Neither the Glovers nor the Kendricks spoke any sort of French, though Charlotte at least could communicate, and Aisling could already hear Mary Logan explaining to Claudia that it was amazing how one could get by, though of course she and Dick were finally going to get around to doing lessons this winter. Aisling loathed the arrogance of the English in this respect, and winced every time they went to a restaurant with their friends and the waiter kindly brought out an English menu. How they rolled their eyes and waved their arms, as though to compensate by gestural gallicisms for their appalling grammar! And there had been a particularly excruciating incident involving Malcolm Glover's attempt to pantomime his request for a breast of chicken. In Aisling's version of France, there were no English menus, and she always had to hold back from explaining in French that they weren't tourists, actually, that they lived here. When she was alone with Jonathan it was always pleasing to think that they passed as a French couple.

Monsieur Chauvignat was standing to make the toast. Aisling translated in a loud whisper. 'Friends, it is a great pleasure to see so many of you here again on August the twenty-second. This is a day for celebration and a day for remembrance. We celebrate the great courage of those who lived through the occupation of Castroux, and we remember those who gave their lives for the freedom of France. My own father, as you know, was in Germany. Sadly he is no longer with us, but we applaud his companions. Amélie Lesprats—'The white haired bundle at their table struggled to its feet as the clapping broke out.

'See,' Aisling heard Alex say to Claudia, 'no way it was a bloke.'

'—Yves and Magalie Contier, Jean Charrot, and my own mother Cécile Chauvignat.'

'Do you see Yves?' said Charlotte Glover, pointing to the tiny, toothless old man in a wheelchair and beret. 'It's wonderful, he's a hundred and one and still bright as a button.'

'*Vieux schnoc*,' muttered Kevin to Richard. '*Il raconte les mêmes conneries chaque année.*'

Everyone sang the 'Marseillaise'. Claudia could see Aisling mouthing along, though it was evident she didn't know the words. The level of conversation rose, as with their duty done people settled to the serious business of eating. Plates of excellent foie gras were brought around, then a 'seafood surprise' whose contents, swimming in a floury *sauce Nantaise*, had obviously not seen the sea for some time. A large platter of charcuterie, with tiny *cornichons* like baby crocodiles, was served to each table, then the main course, *magret*, the thick fat rinded next to the dark red meat, and *pommes Charlotte*. Claudia was starving, she was always starving these days, it seemed, but she didn't want to gobble with Alex sitting there, after what he'd said. When the cheese and salad arrived she looked around to see how the Sternbachs were doing and noticed with relief that Ella was lighting a cigarette. 'I'll just go and see if they're OK,' she told Alex, unwedging herself from the bench, aware of the eyes on her breasts as she crossed the square.

'I hope it's not too awful for you,' she said lightly, sitting down and extracting her own cigarettes from her bag. Ella handed her a lighter.

'No, no,' said Otto seriously, 'this is just what we came for.'

'Really? I mean, this sort of thing interests you particularly?' Perhaps he was a university professor, some sort of anthropologist, not a medical doctor. She had thought that the Dutch would be too sensible to be charmed by a village *fête*.

'Yes, I'm hoping to speak to some of those older people later. You see, we didn't come here just for a holiday.'

'Don't be mysterious, Otto. And we're very pleased with La Maison Bleue, as I said to Aisling. It's lovely.'

Claudia felt she was being slow. They looked quizzical, this elegant older couple with their precise, accentless English, quizzical and conspiratorial.

'I came here to see if I could find out about my brother.'

'Your brother? You have a French brother?'

'Well, half French. My father was in the Army, yes, the German army. He was stationed here during the war and he had a child with a local girl. He was killed, but he had written a letter to my mother.'

'I'm sorry.' Claudia didn't think about whether she sounded sorry because Otto's father had been a Nazi or an adulterer, or just because he was dead. This was fascinating.

Ella looked impatient, as though her husband's deliberate speech was too slow. 'Otto's father, well, it was the war. They'd been training at Bordeaux and he met Otto's mother there, she was a nurse. Her name was Ursula. They married and when she became pregnant she returned to Germany. He was posted on, and well, this happened. So he wrote to her, to make a clean breast of things. He said there was a little boy.'

'And your mother, Otto? I thought you were Dutch, not German. Not that it matters, of course,' she said hastily.

'My mother had relatives in Antwerp and she went to them before the end of the war. She remarried and so I grew up there.'

'And so this brother, you think he lives here?'

'We don't know exactly,' Ella broke in again, excited by the story. 'We've been to the records office at Monguèriac and the *Mairie* at Landi. Otto's father didn't say exactly where he was writing from, he couldn't, but we know the name of his battalion, and we've researched their movements. It was called *Das Reich*.' Claudia thought that maybe Ella should lower her voice, considering where they were, but she was hurrying on. 'Some divisions were right here in 1943 and 1944. They had their headquarters at the chateau.'

'Really? You know, I could introduce you to the Marquis, who lives there now. I know him from Paris. I'm sure he'd know something.'

'There's no guarantee the mother stayed here. There were terrible punishments for Frenchwomen who did as she did, though it was very common. And if she did, she might be dead, or have remarried and moved away, had more children. We know so little.'

Claudia realized that this *Das Reich* business must have something to do with the deaths in the village that Aisling had told her about. She thought of mentioning Oriane

Aucordier as someone the Sternbachs might speak to, but that seemed horribly tactless.

'It's difficult to ask, too,' added Ella. 'Even though it was long ago, it doesn't seem that way to many people. They were quite rude at Monguèriac.'

Claudia wanted to ask what Otto intended to do if he found his brother, or how he would feel if this dreamed-of relative turned out to be a Le Pen voter living in a breeze-block bungalow on the *lotissement* at Landi, but she did not wish to appear prying. She reiterated her offer of an introduction to the Marquis, adding that today was not the best moment to bring the subject up, but that she could ring up later. In her interest and the satisfaction of seeming a sort of insider she had forgotten her fear of Delphine.

The tightly packed tables had now relaxed and spread and she suggested they join the Harveys. Aisling was calling across the table to Jonathan that the boys were going to miss the winner of the goat race. Claudia felt sorry for her. It was clear that Aisling had not realized that her sons were no longer of an age to be genuinely charmed by a goat race, nor yet old enough to fake it for her sake. Goat racing would be met with an embarrassment akin to physical pain. In between the clapping for the boules cup, the church decorations, and the lap of honour of the triumphant goat, the Sternbachs were introduced.

'We take guests too, you know,' announced Mary Logan to Ella, 'you must come over for dinner and test out the competition!'

'Mary's a fantastic cook,' put in her husband, when no one else appeared to get up the energy for the anticipated compliment.

'You have to taste my vichyssoise,' she crowed.

'I do like a nice leek and potato soup,' said Otto politely, 'Ella makes it very well.'

'I'm not talking leek and potato soup! I'm talking vichyssoise!' Mary glared at Otto with glazed sincerity, defying him to contradict her.

'Tell me,' said Jean-Marc Lesprats, leaning forward aggressively to Jonathan, 'what do you English want with so many toilets?'

Things got better when the band started up. As always happens at such events, sexagenarian couples waltzed with sprightly elegance around the square and everyone said how marvellous it was, to try to compensate for their own ungainliness. Claudia hated dancing with Alex, with English men in general, but she shuffled gamely through one with him and one with Jonathan. Aisling looked pleased enough with Otto and then Dick Logan, who did a sort of swing that made him the best of the expat dancers, but it was embarrassing that all the women drew the line so clearly at Malcolm Glover. It had grown dark, the air was soft and smelt of jasmine, the chestnut tree was full of brightly coloured bulbs. Aisling and Claudia exchanged a satisfactory roll of the eyes as they turned on the floor, indicating a good bitch about that appalling Mary woman later. Sitting out, smoking, Claudia thought of what Otto had told her, and of how romantic the village seemed, timeless if one ignored the Shopi frontage and the line of neon-stickered motos. Perhaps everything would be all right. In an access of goodwill she turned to Madame Lesprats' old relative, who was cheerfully sipping at a brandy. 'Are you having a nice time, Madame?' she pronounced loudly.

'Oh, it's not bad.'

It occurred to Claudia that it was odd that Oriane Aucordier and Ginette were not there. This woman must be about Oriane's age, though it was hard to tell at this juncture of decay.

'Tell me, do you know Oriane Aucordier? She told me about her brother, who was killed in the war.' Perhaps she could find out something about the scandal at the chateau? Her attempt was met with a vicious glare from the watery, almost colourless old eyes, and Amélie turned her head deliberately away. Claudia felt foolish, but decided she had been misunderstood, the old bat was probably senile anyway, and just then Charles-Louis d'Esceyrac came up and asked her to dance. She ground out her cigarette and stepped up into his arms.

He held her correctly, as she had known he would, and as they danced he made it clear, lightly and without saying anything at all, that he knew all about Sébastien and that he would be quite happy to offer himself as a replacement of sorts, in Paris, if Claudia were that way inclined one day in the future. So Delphine had sneaked. Claudia laughed softly and minded less about her dress, and surprised herself in the car on the short drive home with a vivid image of Charles-Louis fucking her. He was sexy, in an old, Merchant Ivory sort of way. The image was accompanied by a sharp snap of desire, and then the now-familiar knowledge that such things were no longer possible, and then back, bloodily, to Sébastien.

Alex wanted sex again that night. Claudia was tired, truly just tired, and she considered refusing him, but then she thought of the time that refusing would take, and the sulks and the reassurance, and then she would probably end up doing it anyway. She thought, as he shoved away, that sex was often a bit like netball at school. She had played centre for the team, or sometimes goal attack. She hadn't particularly liked netball, but she had been good at it, and it was easier to play for the team, to go along to practice and the tedious Saturday afternoon tournaments, than to contrive a way of getting out of it. They were all 'good in bed', she and her friends. They did all the things the magazines instructed them to do, oral, anal, cowgirl, spanking, blindfolds. Like a list of prostitutes' services. They sucked and they swallowed, they Kegeled and contorted. The women Claudia knew did everything, with the same diligence they applied to getting their roots done or not missing spin class. It was no big deal, just one more necessary component of being attractive. Claudia did not feel her own pleasure had been much enhanced by any of these activities. Alex tried hard to please her, succeeded at first, but the fact was that she didn't fancy him any more. That was what was extraordinary about Sébastien, that she wanted him to fuck her so badly she didn't care if they went through the checklist. It didn't even matter that he wasn't all that good at it. She saw Sébastien's face for a moment, hovering above her, and she groaned in shame and anger as Alex came, so that was just as well.

Claudia was intrigued by the Sternbachs' story. Playing detective wasn't exactly her thing, but she felt sure that if she tried to help them she would also find out more about Oriane and her son. Oriane had offered her something more than her surprising empathy, a connection that Claudia grasped at as though it might in some way help her. Or if that was being woolly, then at least it might be enough of a distraction to drown the white noise in her head. She tried to interest Olly and Richard, but their complete lack of reaction reminded her that for them the war was a sort of fiction, a maniac spitting absurd speeches, and the source of baddies in the movies. Wasn't every child supposed to be an expert on the Holocaust? Richard did say that she should probably talk to Madame Lesprats, who knew everything about everyone, and had about a million barmy old relations. She lived next door to Kevin. He offered to show her on his bike.

Madame Lesprats lived in the new *lotissement* on the other side of Castroux. *Lotissements* were one of Aisling and Jonathan's bêtes noirs. Aisling claimed that though they could not actually see the development from Murblanc, she could feel its presence. Alex had pointed out that the farm people had to live somewhere, since the English had bought all the nice old houses and priced them out of the market, but Aisling thought the government ought to have a scheme or something. And anyway it was no good the French complaining now that all the property had been bought by foreigners, when for years they had been happy to let their beautiful old houses fall to rack and ruin and live in concrete horrors in the garden. The *lotissement* was certainly hideous. Many of the small houses were still raw terracotta breeze block, standing in plots of scorched mud, made uglier by the bright plastic of discarded children's toys and several giant paddling pools, sold as '*piscines*' in Monsieur Bricolage. Each home was adorned with a satellite dish, stuck to the roof like a button on a hat.

The Lesprats' house was older, it had been there long enough for a squat bushy hedge to grow up around the plot. The French seemed to be obsessed with keeping nature out, surrounding themselves with topiary and evergreen, enclosing their homes like giftwrapped packages from the disorder beyond. Madame Lesprats had positioned several plastic swans along the crazy paving leading to the door, their backs grotesquely split and streaming with garish bougainvillea. Claudia wished for a moment that Alex was with her, it was all so Chingford.

'I was getting the lunch,' said Madame Lesprats accusingly.

'Oh, I'm so sorry. I could come back?'

'No, no, come in.' Claudia had counted on the scent of gossip overwhelming Madame Lesprats' reluctance to have her enter her home. Richard said that only family was usually allowed inside peoples' houses in Castroux. She had armed herself with a small bunch of somewhat mummified roses, tied with a broderie anglaise ribbon purloined from one of the sodding lavender bags, though she knew that the correct thing would have been a huge bunch of forced chrysanthemums from the florists in Landi, crackling in coloured cellophane.

It was stuffy indoors, the blinds drawn against the heat, and the windows tightly shut. Despite the aspirations expressed by the exterior of her house, Madame Lesprats, and, Claudia guessed, most of her neighbours, still appeared to make use of just one room. A sofa was jammed along one wall of the small kitchen, with a television muttering in front of it. The space was cramped even more by an old-fashioned free-standing stove with a huge stock pot on the ring, though there was a modern electric cooker fitted into the wall of units. The lunch table was set for three, with a tomato tart and a bowl of lettuce going brown and frilly at the edges. Claudia felt a bit sick.

'That looks lovely,' she remarked brightly. 'Is it hard to make?'

Madame Lesprats was off.

'Oh, I don't bother with that any more. I had quite enough when I was a girl. No, Jean-Marc drives me to the Carrefour at Landi once a week, it's much better. More hygienic. They've got Picard as well, and you can get everything frozen. Even artichokes. They've got Moroccan things too, though I suppose that's for the Arabs. Landi's full of them, you know, Arabs. My cousin over to Cahors is a builder and he won't have anything more to do with them, not even on the black. He says they're too much trouble.'

Claudia wanted quite badly to sit down, but she had to wait until Madame Lesprats had finished with the Arabs and the number of babies they had, how they clogged up the hospitals, her cousin's opinion on the meanness of the Dutch who bought holiday homes and expected something for nothing, the things Sabine heard in the pharmacy and a long story about another cousin of Madame Lesprats who had a Growth. In the end she sat on the sofa without being invited, and Madame Lesprats eyed her so beadily that Claudia thought Ginette must have said something.

Madame Lesprats paused to look in the stock pot, letting out a wave of thickly scented steam.

'Rabbit,' she said, prodding with a satisfied spoon, as though the animal had got what it deserved. Claudia launched in with her account of the Sternbachs' visit and her desire to help them by finding out what she could.

'No,' said Madame Lesprats firmly, 'I don't know anything about that sort of thing.'

It was obvious that she was lying. She clearly did not care that Claudia could see it.

'Perhaps I could ask your relation, the lady I saw at the *fête*? Amélie?'

'Oh no, you don't want to be bothering her. Anyway, she can't remember anything, poor old thing.'

'Do you think Mademoiselle Oriane up at Aucordier's might be able to help?'

'I think people should mind their own business,' snapped Madame Lesprats. She looked suspicious and offended and Claudia felt rude. She tried to chat for a few minutes on general topics, to make it seem as though she had really paid a social call, but it was obvious that in asking about the war she had been crass, emphasized her position as an outsider, a foreigner. She trudged back up to Murblanc feeling embarrassed and dispirited, but she did ask Aisling for the number to telephone the chateau.

1942

Cathérine received a letter from Paris. It was exciting because no one had ever written a letter to her before and she couldn't think who it might be from. She took it up to Oriane and they read it together at the kitchen table. 'Dear Cathérine,' it said, 'I am sorry to write to you now, but you were always a good hardworking girl. I am ashamed to have to write to you, but things are very bad here and my poor mother is unwell. There is nothing to be had in the shops, and we are feeling it. You wouldn't believe they are wanting eighty francs for a skinny little chicken! So if your family could spare it, I hoped you might be able to send some pâté, or some of that potted ham we used to enjoy in the good old days at Castroux, or perhaps some cheese. I will be sure to pay you back when times are better. I hope you are keeping well and working hard. Respectfully, your friend, Emilie Cleret.'

'Well,' said Cathérine, 'the cheek of her! Herself, saying she's my friend. Good old days in Castroux my arse.'

'She must mind it,' said Oriane, 'I mean, she's probably ashamed to have to ask. And her mother's sick.'

'Well, look after your own, that's what I say,' snorted Cathérine, crumpling the letter and stuffing it in the fire underneath the soup pot. 'And I was so pleased too. It might have been from my mystery man!' She laughed.

Laurent and his father had driven the Murblanc cows to Monguèriac to be sold. It had taken six days, but they had got a good price, and they had been just in time because the prices were fixed, even though things were getting more expensive, everyone said. Alice was long gone, but her daughter Albertine was still William's favourite and he had cried when he saw her plodding sadly away along the lane. Vionne's butchers had been investigated by the *Ravitaillement*, the food inspector, but they had a warning from the shop at St Urcisse. Their pork and capons were long gone when the man came to visit finding only a few veal chops and three rabbits. On Fridays a truck came from Cahors with a clerk and two *Milice* men, and the people of Castroux handed in their produce, with the sums being ticked off in a register. On Saturdays they sold everything else at the market in Landi. François Boissière asked Père Guillaume to speak about these goings on, he said it was not only dishonest but unpatriotic, it would undermine the government. Père Guillaume preached that Sunday on the merchants in the temple, which François understood as a refusal. Afterwards, when Charlotte served a crisp leg of pork with sage and garlic that she had from Cécile Chauvignat in return for some help with her certificates, he bowed to the ineveitable, took a third helping and swirled his salad in the juices.

Now she had the new goats, Oriane made up her cheeses in the dairy off the barn at Murblanc. She borrowed one of Papie's donkeys and drove it down with the churns slung across its shoulders. Papie met her every morning and always said that it was just as well the road from Aucordier's led downwards. He was as pleased with his joke after two years as the first time he made it. She wrapped the cheeses in muslin and gave them to Laurent for the market. He gave her back the money, always reminding her to put something away for the wedding. Her preserves were much better than Cathérine's, he had taken her cherries and apricots in syrup and over the winter she had made pickled walnuts and damson wine, though it was true that sugar was so dear now she wondered if it would be worth buying the extra to make something to sell next year. Laurent said there were people in Landi who came all the way from Paris to buy for the big hotels and restaurants, and if they could get the sugar they could do very well with the fruit, though it was a shame they had not got any Chasselas, they had gone for a fortune last year. Madame Nadl made her rillettes and pâtés and buttered gizzards as usual. They had heard that people from towns went bicycling about on Sundays, pretending they were out on a trip, but looking for a box of eggs or a foie gras they could hide in their saddle bags. No one had come to Castroux though, and Betty Dubois said what did you expect being stuck in the middle of nowhere, it was just their luck.

It was Betty who got the dances going, it must have been a year or so after Oriane started walking out with Laurent Nadl. She nagged and begged for weeks at her father to buy her a gramophone, even trying to persuade him that it would improve business in the café, but he said that men came to have a quiet drink and get away from a lot of women's noise, and the last thing the customers wanted was some nigger shrieking at them after a hard day's work. She consulted Andrée Charrot, who thought that maybe they could borrow the wireless from Père Guillaume, but neither of them had the nerve to ask him and they couldn't see a way to claiming that dancing was holy anyway, especially as it might encourage people to stay up late and lie in bed on Sunday morning. Magalie Contier wouldn't have Yves playing, she'd enough trouble keeping him at home as it was. So that left William Aucordier, who cost nothing and was happy to fiddle away for hours. Hilaire Charrot didn't mind letting them have the barn, and the two girls spent a whole Sunday with rags tied around their heads, sweeping and clearing, making a bonfire of crumbling discarded beams and ancient birds' nests. Betty was imagining candles with pleated paper shades, but Andrée said not to be a fool, everyone would be burned to a crisp in a minute and they weren't opening the Palais de Danse in Monguèriac. Neither of them had ever seen that when it came to it, but they had a shared idea of low lights and red velvet and tall men in impeccable evening dress. People would have to bring their own lamps and refreshments, though Monsieur Dubois grudgingly agreed to let them have a couple of the benches and trestles that were brought out for weddings and funerals for the mothers to sit on. The girls persuaded their brothers, Jean and Nic, to drag the furniture along the river bank to the barn, and Betty wanted to put up a notice in the window of the café, but Andrée scoffed at that too, on the grounds that everybody knew already and they were sure to come because what else had there ever been to do around here?

Charlotte Boissière told François that it was beneath their position as schoolteachers to go to such a thing, and didn't these giddy girls realize there was a war on? François said it would look well for them to pop in early on, for propriety's sake, since Père Guillaume could hardly be expected to attend himself. Besides, cultural activity was good for morale. This was exactly what Charlotte had expected him to say, and most satisfactory since she had already altered her violet *costume* and could now wear it whilst retaining a sense of moral superiority over the outing. The Boissières were surprised to find that they did not know everyone crowded into the barn that first Saturday night. Girls and their mothers had walked over from Auzerte and St Urcisse in their clogs, their Sunday shoes in handkerchiefs, there were boys who had come on bicycles from Landi, and three strange, silent brothers without a collar to their shirts between them who had only been seen before at the market, where they sold gnarled little cheeses rolled in ash. They came from one of the tiny forgotten hamlets in the steep cliffs above Saintonge, where there was not even a cart track through the woods, and people married their sisters. None of them danced, they just stood stiffly in a corner, smelling strongly of goat, but they stayed until the very end. William, fetched in triumph on Laurent Nadl's motorbike, took off his carefully brushed jacket and played from nine o'clock until two in the morning without once putting down his bow, sweat pooling in his ears and a huge grin on his face as he jigged his feet in time. The mothers sat along the walls, and everybody walked home in the starlight along the Landine, calling goodbye at the bridge, their voices carrying far across the hills.

With the dances, it seemed as though life began again in the valley. Soon it was nearly every week that a man would come to Aucordier's or Murblanc on a bicycle, asking if William would play on a Saturday night, and Laurent didn't seem to mind taking him on the moto. Sometimes William would get paid, twenty or thirty centimes for a night in a dirt-floored barn where the owls hooted in confusion outside, wondering where their peaceful roost had gone. Laurent put the coins in a jar for him and said that when there was enough they would go to Monguèriac in the train and buy him a new violin. Betty said it was a bit much, that other people had copied her idea like that, but she was happy to walk ten kilometres with Andrée and Amélie and Cathérine, and spend the week trimming the hem of her best dress or copying a pattern for a bolero jacket from one of the magazines, gossiping about who they had danced with and who they would see next week. After the first dance, Oriane preferred to stay at home, or sit sewing in the kitchen at Murblanc with the Nadls and Papie snoozing in the corner. She hadn't felt it was right to dance with anyone else, not that any of the boys had asked, because everyone knew she was going with Laurent. He hadn't said anything to her, but she thought it must be impossible for him, with his leg, and she hadn't wanted to hurt him by mentioning it. It wasn't the dancing though, that she was glad to avoid.

Oriane knew what went on between people. She knew it from her work in the laundry at the chateau, and if she needed reminding, from Amélie Lesprats and her dirty mouth, and from Madame Nadl's stories in the kitchen of who was expecting and who had to be married in a hurry. In Castroux, it had never even mattered much whether the baby came before the ring, so long as the wedding was managed eventually. There were some sorts of rules. At first, when Laurent called for her in the evenings, they had gone up to the hut on the plain, though they could just as well have made themselves cosy in the kitchen at Aucordier's, but that wouldn't have been right. So they sat uncomfortably on the pile of rocks, and Laurent kissed her, pushing his tongue into her mouth. She liked the taste of him, the crisp, woody smell that was always in his clothes, the muscles under his shirt and the strength of his arms. After a few times he touched her breasts under her blouse and she was surprised, ashamed, that she got wet, sopping wet so there was a patch on her skirt when she stood up to go home. Then she expected that after a while they would do everything, and though at other times she still felt a sense of lack, of dismay, when she looked at him, when they had been kissing for a while she wanted to carry on, for him to hold her and lie down on top of her. It was supposed to hurt, the first time, but she was prepared for that. So when he did not, and when later he began to stop kissing her if she unbuttoned her blouse, she was sorry for him, because she thought he was ashamed of his deformity.

The next time, Oriane thought she would help him. She put her hand in the middle of his trousers, where his thing would be, and rubbed him, whispering in his ear, 'It's all right, Laurent. I love you.' When he struck at her, missing her face and knocking himself off balance so he slipped on the stones and slumped on his knees in the grass, she felt as cold with shock as if the blow had found her. He struggled to his feet, grappling with the crutch, and pulled her shoulder, shaking her so hard she felt dizzy.

'Don't,' he shouted, 'don't ever do that again!' Then he turned away and she began to walk alone across the plain towards home, her head up and her eyes smarting. After a while, a little mean voice inside her told her she ought to laugh at him, a hard, sneering laugh, to see him scrabbling on the ground like that, poor crippled thing.

'Look at you!' she wanted to shout, 'How dare you? Look at yourself.' Then she knew it was her mother's voice she heard, and realized that there could be a terrible pleasure in cruelty, even though you knew it would hurt yourself too. When he came up behind her, the crutch tapping anxiously, she flinched when he reached out, just to hurt him because she knew he would be even more ashamed if he believed she thought he might hit her again.

'I'm not William, you know. I'm not simple,' he said softly to her back. 'Oriane, I just think that it's better we wait for that sort of thing. Until we're properly married.' His voice was tender, as though he might cry even, so she turned around and rested her face a moment against the warmth of his coat, then let him take her hand as they walked on. She was shocked at herself, to find that there could be such hate in her, where it was not deserved. So Oriane did not go to the dances, because she wanted to avoid being alone with him afterwards, coming back in the dark.

SUMMER HOLIDAYS

Otto must once have been a beautiful man, Claudia thought, though the dark, French type aged better. He looked like a Viking next to the Marquis, more so because his straight, massive shoulders were encased in a rough, dark-blue Breton shirt with a pocket in front, which would have looked ridiculous on Malcolm Glover, but seemed stylish and somehow urban on Otto. He was much heavier than Charles-Louis, but his eyes, still a sharp, sudden blue flash, and the remaining gold streaks in the grey hair on his collar, made him an attractive man. Claudia wondered if the Marquis noticed that she noticed. They had driven up to the chateau in Otto's high, smooth car early in the morning, before it grew too hot, although the windows on the lower floor were already shuttered against the banking sun.

Charles-Louis had said he would be delighted to show Otto over the house, though he doubted whether there would be anything to learn. He had fetched some books from his study, biographies of Hitler and de Gaulle, and Otto looked over them politely as he explained his story in simple but well-accented French.

'There are some rooms closed up,' Charles-Louis explained, leading them up the stairs and along a landing, 'but you can have a look if you care to.' They turned into a small, pretty room with a bow window giving on to what Claudia guessed would be the garden at the back, with a rather lovely day bed in pale green silk, figured with an old-rose pattern, and a cream tiled fireplace. A modern desk featured a wedding photograph of Delphine in a sort of Renoir confection with an outsized cartwheel hat. 'Delphine has this room,' explained Charles-Louis, though Claudia had already ascertained with relief that she and the little boys had gone to the riding stables near Landi. Charles-Louis unlocked a little door, let into the panelling next to the fireplace, which gave on to a narrow passage with bare buff-coloured walls and a tight, twisting staircase. Claudia loved the sense of secrecy of these servants' alleyways, she had seen them at Versailles and Fontainebleau. Otto hunching over, they came up into a larger space, a gallery that ran the length of the building. It was quite empty, except for an ugly green futon thing, and the air was thick and close, as though the windows had not been opened for years.

'I haven't been up here since I was a child,' remarked Charles-Louis.

The telephone rang below them, deep in the passages.

'I'll leave you,' said Charles-Louis, his feet disappearing down the stairs, 'come to find me when you're ready.'

'Shall we carry on, Otto?' asked Claudia. 'There's nothing here.'

They progressed along the gallery, leaving marks in the dust.

Now that Claudia's eyes were accustomed to the dimness, she could make out vague shapes along the walls, a palimpsest of figures beneath what looked like a hasty coat of whitewash. As Otto fiddled with the bunch of keys the Marquis had handed him, Claudia noticed a patch of wall in one of the window bays that had not been covered.

'Otto!' she called. 'Sorry, could you just give me a hand?'

The window latch had been painted into immobility, and after struggling breathily for a few minutes Otto simply struck it hard from underneath with the heel of his palm. Flakes of paint scattered on to the floor as they wrestled the window wide enough for Otto to reach through and beat open the shutters. The gallery was suddenly alive with dust motes, dancing like plankton in the dark air. Claudia squatted in the dusty corner, fumbling around in her handbag for the clear plastic wallet that held her make-up. She found her fat bronzer brush and cleaned it against her grey cotton smock before carefully dabbing at the patch. In the new light, she could see a head, a vicious, etiolated little face with curling hair and twisted horns, cocked cheekily to one side against what appeared to be a woman's flank. Claudia looked for a long time. Pretty, but probably negligible.

'Sorry, Otto. Let's go on.'

They passed through the door at the end of the space into an anteroom with a large bricked-up doorway. Claudia guessed that once this had been the formal entrance to the gallery. Another concealed passage ran for a few metres, then turned around a few steps, ran and turned again. Claudia had no sense now of where they were, and was surprised when, after more attempts with the keys, they came out into a low, wide space with cheap wooden partitions and a stack of iron bedsteads like deckchairs in a corner. Claudia peered down the boxy staircase.

'We're above the stable. Or what used to be.'

Otto was poking in a heap of odds and ends near the piled beds. He had pulled off a canvas sheet, creating more dust clouds. Effortfully, he dragged out a cumbrous wooden mangle, two large wooden tubs, bleached white on the inside, and a cardboard box. The box collapsed as he touched it, spilling a muddle of rusting iron oddments. It was chilly and Claudia was growing rather bored.

'Look here!'

'It's just blankets, Otto.' As he unwrapped the grey wool, Claudia shuddered and thought of rats.

'Look!'

Otto was turning out a drawstring bag. Three round, gold-coloured cases patted on to the blanket. Claudia picked one up, and laughed.

'What a funny thing to find. Look, Otto, make-up!'

The lid of the compact had a design of a classical nymph, holding a vase above her head, with a relief of garlands. Inside, there was a matching gold tube of lipstick, fresh and greasy, and a bed of beige powder. Claudia turned it over. There was a name she recognized, 'Bourjois', and then 'Histoire d'Amour'. It was obviously not valuable, machine-made gilt, but it was charming, vintage, the sort of thing one would find in Spitalfields market.

'What about this?' proffered Otto excitedly.

Claudia held two small rectangles of fabric, black, with white designs. One had two flashes, Deco lightning, the other a plain oblong. There were threads hanging off the back, as though they had been torn.

'This is SS,' said Otto, 'a collar badge. I can look it up when we get back. They must have been here, Claudia, this is evidence!'

Claudia failed to see why he was so excited, after all, he had known his father's battalion had been quartered at the chateau, but she was glad that he had found something to please him. There ought to have been something sinister about touching it, SS was an idea that still conjured horror, but it was so light and tiny in her hand. They shoved the things back and re-covered them, then went down into the sudden welcome heat and found the Marquis on the lawn.

'Histoire d'Amour?' he said to Claudia when she showed him the compact. 'Well, you must keep one of those.'

Delphine could feel herself growing more provincial by the second. She had never understood why the English considered it smart to be attached to the countryside. Charles-Edouard had loved that, as he loved everything English. During their courtship she had been obliged to spend many hideous weekends in freezing houses in the chillier parts of Burgundy, while he galloped about in a black coat looking for deer to kill. Occasionally the dogs chased one on to the road where it was handily run over, but Charles-Edouard would insist that it was the best meat he had ever tasted. Delphine could hardly bring herself to touch something that had been scraped off the underside of a lorry, but she told herself she put up with the weekends because they gave her fiancé so much pleasure. Naturally, she put a stop to them after they were married.

Now she had a reason to get back to Paris, she could hardly wait. The country made one brood.

This morning, she had actually found herself gossiping with Madame Lesprats about that Claudia girl. Apparently she was pregnant. She told herself she felt sorry for Claudia if she was indeed involved with Sébastien Marichalar. Was he the father? Sébastien had slept with practically every woman in Paris, though not actually with Delphine herself. She had a knack for turning pique to propriety when it suited her, and now believed she had firmly resisted his advances. The girl had a certain something, despite those dreadful droopy clothes; certainly she didn't seem to fit with the Harvey brother. Delphine wondered what Aisling thought of her, of whether she was aware of the affair with Sébastien. Not that it was anybody's business, but that was the problem with the country, everything became one's business.

Delphine was aware that Aisling had a bit of a crush and was prepared to make use of it. Her boys seemed well brought up, and in a few years they would be able to speak English with Charles-Henri and Jules. Delphine was hardly in a position to dislike her for being such an obvious climber, the other English people around here all seemed rather dreadful, drunk the whole time and terribly patronizing. Delphine wondered idly – she seemed to spend all day doing that, she really had to get back to Paris – whether Aisling's marriage was happy. It could hardly be an amusing life she led. Jonathan seemed entirely featureless to Delphine, just another overweight expat with too much time and too little to say, though there must be money. Madame Lesprats said that Monsieur Harvey had made a lot of '*grain*' in computers.

How mortified Aisling had looked, squashed in at the *fête* with the help! Though Madame Lesprats was probably better company than that pompous Chauvignat and his revolting old mother, who had dipped her bread in her wine and mumbled it in her toothless mouth. Still, she would have to get Chauvignat on her side if the hotel were to go ahead, it was amazing how much power these mayors had. How he had droned on about his father being a prisoner of war and his mother speeding heroically about on her bicycle, smuggling contraband sausages to the partisans. She had managed to keep a smile on her face by thinking of how she could work it up into an anecdote to amuse Armand. How people did seem to obsess over the war, like that Dutch chap who had come up to ask her father-in-law about it. Altogether it would be a good thing to have Aisling Harvey as a friend, she was the energetic type, and she truly had good taste. There had been some clever features in the converted barn, that cow byre, the wooden cradle used as a log basket, the lime-washed beams in the bedrooms. She would never do for Paris, naturally, but if she were to be spending time down here to get the hotel going, it would be nice to have someone to talk to. Her thoughts returned to Armand. She would mind not being Madame la Comtesse, though of course it was much better these days to pretend that one hardly noticed such things.

Alex, too, was restive. He had spent his morning wandering about on the steep road up to the plain, finding and then infuriatingly losing a signal on his mobile to call the office. He couldn't see why Claudia had made such a thing of it, they'd barely had any time alone since they had arrived. Each day was the same. He'd fancied a yacht in Croatia. It was beyond him why Jonathan had allowed Aisling to talk him into upping sticks and moving down here. He'd been into the study to catch up with the FT online and seen the 'work' Jonathan claimed to be so busy with. He'd expected lesbian schoolgirls and that sort of thing, tame enough, but he was quite shocked when he saw what his brother was involved in. It was one of those 'second life' programmes where the user takes on a character and manipulates it through a realistic alternative world. Guiltily, Alex discovered that Jonathan was Mikhail, an eastern European architect living alone in a loft space overlooking a sort of San Francisco Bay. Mikhail ran his own studio, and collected contemporary art. He went to the gym and drove a Maserati. Alex was tempted to make a joke of it to Claudia, it was the sort of thing she would say was 'delicious', but that seemed really low.

Obviously the poor chap didn't have enough to do. He thought about getting Jonathan to come in with him on something, maybe a property if he and Claudia were selling, but he had the impression that things might be a bit tight, not that Jonathan could ever bear to admit that to his little brother. He supposed he ought to start thinking about putting something aside for school fees himself once the wedding was sorted. Still, Claudia seemed happy here. She had seemed oddly nervous the last few weeks in London, but then it was a big step getting engaged. If the American markets carried on like this, he'd be looking at a fantastic bonus, maybe they could get a big place right away. Queen's Park was really coming up, you could still get whole houses there. Claudia might need a bit of persuading, it wasn't exactly the sort of place her trendy friends hung out, but in a few years, he could tell her, they'd need the room. Thinking of it, he went out to the pool to find her, and buried his face in the warm honey of her hair.

MAY 1943

Because they came over the plain, along the Cahors road, they passed by Aucordier's first. It was the day for the May flowers, there was to be a dance that night. Oriane remembered that clearly, she remembered that she had been sitting on her stool in the yard sewing a bunch of silk violets to her old dress, the dress she had worn for Mademoiselle Lafage's wedding. She listened to William playing as she unpicked the flowers from the bodice, thinking they would look better, perhaps, sprigged on to the shoulder. Laurent had brought them for her from Monguèriac, the day he took Alice to the market, and she hadn't the heart to tell him that artificial flowers made her sad since they reminded her of her mother's terrible Sunday hat. There had been a feather on that hat, too, that flapped viciously over her mother's face as she shook William by the shoulders.

'Look at you!' her mother had hissed. 'Look at you!' They had been to Mass, and William had been startled by the vehemence of the singing, he shrieked and gibbered, his ears grubby, his face shiny with spit. Oriane had dragged him kicking down the aisle and tried to calm him, but later their mother beat at him with her fists in the square, for everyone to see.

Still, Laurent had meant kindly, and when they got married she said to herself, she would have real flowers, orange blossom like Mademoiselle Lafage.

William was playing, she remembered that, he was playing as she sewed, the tune of the May-horn. She sang along to the music, 'Lou coucou! Lou coucou!' Before the dance they would go around the village with the others, singing before each home and collecting two or three eggs for the May omelette. William stopped abruptly and turned his head up towards the plain. He brought the violin over to her, carrying it preciously as he always did, then he was gone, running, out of the yard, chasing a noise. Like a hunting dog, she thought, wondering what the sound was that acted on him like scent, too distant and subtle for her to catch. But he was back in a moment, tugging at her, and she had to push him away in case he spoiled her dress with rosin. 'Lo monde,' he was crowing, 'lo monde.'

'What people, William, where?' She was half laughing, incredible that she had not known, but how could she know? She followed him with the dress in her hand to the corner of the barn, and looked where he pointed along the road.

'Come on, William, come on now.' He was too big for her to pull him, too excited by what he had seen. Her voice was wrong, she was helpless to communicate her urgency. Desperately, she cuffed him over the brow, as she had never done, and put aside the ache it gave her to see his face collapse in shock as something she would have to mind later, there was no time now. Cathérine's words were in her head, she had to hide him. Pushing him in front of her, his hands over his ears, head bowed, she forced them both into the barn and pulled the big door tight. William had begun to sob, she slapped him again and the surprise of it calmed her so her hands obeyed and fastened the twine on the inside of the door.

'Get the ladder, hurry!'

He stared at her, smeary-faced. She felt very cold, she was shaking, but she brought her fingers to her lips, 'Shhh!' Like a game, it had to be like a game. 'Get the ladder,' she whispered, pointing. When they were up, she began to drag it towards her, rung over rung, feeling the muscles in her abdomen clench with strain, until he understood and took the weight behind her as it rose. The noise was there now, vibrating in the earth beneath them. 'Lay it down, good boy, William.' He was still whimpering. '*Lou rescondat*,' she murmured, 'so we have to be quiet, see?' Hide and seek. Creeping forward to the window, lying down under the sill. She wished it was winter, so the hay would be in. Below, her dress lay where she had dropped it, a dead woman with a corsage of violets, weakly bright in the dust. William crawled up next to her, under her arm. 'Shh!' he said dramatically, sounding pleased. He would forget where she remembered, he had never needed to forgive. The noise was real now, engines and the crunch of boots, but surely her heart was louder, they would hear her heart. Her skin was drenched and clammy, she felt sick.

First there was a huge tank, like a picture in the newspapers at the café, snub and clumsy-looking as it rolled over the white road, but it moved shockingly fast, smoothly, as though it had thousands of tiny wheels. A fat little tower stuck up from the top and a man was visible to the waist, wearing a black jacket and a cap with silver braid around it. The tank was so high that Oriane could have reached down and plucked it from his head. There was silver too on his left shoulder, he looked straight ahead. On the side of the tower was the head of a black cat, snarling. Then came three cars covered close with plated metal, and another tank, then a beautiful open car, like the Marquis's, with a driver in front and two men sitting behind. They had silver braid on their shoulders, and the lapels of their jackets had pink piping, a strange, ludic note in their frightening appearance.

Oriane could hear a rat rustling in the roof above her and gripped William hard, her palm clamped around his jaw.

'Please, please be good now. We don't want them to find us, do we?' Now there were columns of men in peaked caps, four abreast, buttoned into heavy grey coats with green collars even though it was warm, with black fabric showing at the neck. Some wore high boots like heavy riding boots, others had shorter, softer-looking ones with laces. William drummed his feet in time with the boots, one two three four one two three four, they filled the road and it seemed as though the barn was vibrating with their feet. Then three lorries with green canvas sides, puffing thick fumes, then more men, a third tank. They were so close. Some of them seemed to try to look into the yard as they came by, though only their eyes were moving. Beneath their boots, her dress showed its flowers sadly, then it was pressed grey and merged with the road.

When they had passed, everything looked just the same. Two of the hens scuttled across the yard, chuckling, and began to scratch in the long grass by the barn wall. Slowly, Oriane sat up, stretching her cramped arms, and released the catch of the window, cautiously stretched her head outside to look down the road. 'Listen, William, listen. Have they gone?' He shuffled up on his knees, breathing softly, and shook his head. So they lay there in the shadow and listened to the church clock strike the quarter hours in the valley. Oriane was very thirsty, the dust was clogged in her throat and her eyes stung, but it seemed stupid to move until something happened. Her body felt heavy, she had a perverse desire to sleep. An hour passed, the bells chimed once for a quarter past nine. It seemed as though nothing was moving, even the wind in the poplars was muffled with anticipation. Craning out of the little window, Oriane could see the road until it dropped down, then the meadows of Murblanc and the *étable*, the chateau hill rising behind, the tower just visible above the trees, which were still lacy, not dense with summer leaves. William was distracted, playing a jumping game in the squares of sunlight opened by the missing tiles of the roof, hopping from one to another with his arms stretched out like a dancer. When she turned back to the valley, there was a flag flying from the chateau, a red flag with a white circle and a hooked black cross, limp but fluttering a little, determined. They had not been passing through.

As the bells chimed towards the afternoon it felt foolish, eventually, to stay in the loft. Oriane heated the soup for William and left him to drink it while she stood in the doorway with a glass of that morning's cold coffee and stared down the road. She was sure that Laurent would come and tell her what to do, but until then she was reluctant even to leave the yard. She went upstairs for a jersey of William's and fitted the wool through the darning needle, then sat back on her stool. William had retrieved his violin and was playing again, there seemed no point in stopping him, in trying to explain that they would not be going to the village tonight after all, and that there would be no dancing. It was extraordinary that just hours ago she had been here, pinning flowers on her dress, and that the music that was now so thin and sad had seemed gay. But it was cruel to prevent him after she had struck at him this morning, so he played on. Beneath the sound, the valley was still so quiet that she was sure it could be heard in Castroux. It was dreadful, surely, just to sit here?

Oriane hated the look on William's face when he saw her in the kitchen doorway. He started, his shoulders rising as he ducked his chin to his chest, ready to shield himself.

'Have you eaten your soup?' He nodded. 'Good boy. Shall you go a walk for me?' She felt shabby to make him go alone, but to leave the house empty did not feel safe. When he came back, she explained, it would be nearly time to walk to the village. He set off up to the plain with a slice of bread on which she had dolloped a big spoon of strawberry compote. It was too easy to please William, to hurt him and then take away his fear with sweets or games. He was more quickly mollified than a screaming child, but she preferred to treat him as though he were reasonable, as though he understood things. If she practised the delusion hard enough it might allow him a small and unharmed place in the world. She watched his progress up the white road, his head twisting this way and that with his comical ears sticking out like cabbage leaves, and was full of a painful love for him, for that loneliness that she thought he ought to feel and which was hers alone. When his figure was gone, she put away the dishes and wiped the crumbs from the table, then swept the floor as she had done that morning. There was the noise of an engine outside, so she crossed quickly to the yard, expecting Laurent and an explanation.

Four of them were getting down from a square, open-topped car. For a second she thought of grabbing the poker, a knife, or simply running, but her limbs had the heavy quality of a dream and she remained still, though her body was as vividly alive as a hare before the dogs. One of them came towards her. He was tall, taller than any of the men in the village, in a black tunic open at the neck to show a grey shirt and black tie. There were knots of silver in his lapels and an emblem above the bib of the black peaked cap, which he removed. His hair was the colour of new corn, short and bristling. He waited a few steps away, as though expecting her to speak. So they had come already.

'Good morning, Mademoiselle. Might I ask if your father is at home?' His voice was almost French, clear and polite. Oriane twisted her hands in her dress until the moment grew too long and she stammered out that she was alone, that she lived alone, except for her brother.

'He's at work,' she added stupidly.

The other three wore helmets, rounded with short brims. They stood by the car and watched.

'I'm sorry to intrude, Mademoiselle,' went on the man with the cap, 'but we need to look over the buildings here.'

'The buildings?'

'Yes.'

He said it with such calm and perfect authority that it did not occur to Oriane to question him, to find out why, let alone to refuse or ask for justification. Her first feeling was simple relief. The man said something to one of the others. It was the first time Oriane heard German. The rhythm of it was strange, tripled like the jigs William played. It didn't sound terrifying, it was almost funny. The helmet stepped forward with a notebook and pencil.

'Your name?

'Oriane Aucordier.'

'Your papers?'

'I have to fetch them. They're inside.' He nodded his head slowly, as though she could take her time. She brought out the identification cards and the ration books that had lain untouched in the drawer of the *buffet* for three years. The man looked at them so slowly that she felt guilty, certain there was something wrong and that they would take her away.

'How old is your brother, William Aucordier?'

'Seventeen.'

'Has he a paper of exemption?'

It would be wrong, she was certain, to tell the truth, which was that she did not understand. But was the truth about William any better? They would take him to prison.

'The paper that excuses him from serving in the Army, if he's here?' When they had gone to the *Mairie* for the cards no one had mentioned any such thing, but William was old enough now, she had to speak, to decide just this instant which was worse to admit to.

'No, sir. He's feeble minded. Simple. But he's very good, he doesn't do any harm, he's never been in trouble.'

'But you said he was at work.'

'Yes, he scares birds you know, to help. Up in the fields.' Oriane made to gesture with her arm towards the plain, but it hung like a broken wing at her side. Already she had been forced to lie, and the helmeted man was scribbling down the translation as the other spoke it. William would go to a horrible prison, he would be beaten and starved and it would be her fault for telling the truth. A hot wash of thin vomit rose in her throat, she gulped, shuddering, stretching her eyes wide to keep tears from coming.

'May we look inside?'

'Inside?' He must think she was some country throwback, not quite finished.

'Yes, Mademoiselle,' patiently, with no sign in his voice that she seemed a cretin to him, 'that's why we're here. Just to see the buildings.'

'Of course.' She held the door for him as formally as if he were the priest, and the others followed, removing their helmets as they stepped over the threshold. They walked through the rooms, the kitchen and scullery downstairs, the four bedrooms, lifting the hatch to the low, dusty attic where the rats scuttled at night. Then Oriane was to show them the barn, the ladder to the loft, the chicken house, the vegetable garden, and all the time the man asked questions in his formal, correct French. How many goats had she? What work did she do? When had her mother died? Oriane blushed as they opened the door to the privy, though it was whitewashed and the seat scrubbed smooth. One of them picked a sprig of rosemary at the door and rubbed it against his fingers until the man with the cap frowned at him and he dropped it. She still did not know the purpose of the inspection, yet her fear receded and she answered confidently, hoping that the man would see from her tone that she was respectable and had nothing to hide. Later she learned that they were doing the same all over Castroux, poking sticks up chimneys and peering into larders, rattling at windows that had been painted shut for generations.

'You two live alone, you say, Mademoiselle?'

'Yes.'

'And you are not, that is you have never?' He paused and said something in German, the helmeted men sniggered and one of them shook his head. 'Never mind. You will report to the *Mairie* tomorrow morning please, at eight o'clock? With your brother?'

'Yes.'

He saluted her and clicked his heels together smartly. 'Thank you, Mademoiselle.'

They were starting up the car when there was a raucous whooping from the road. William was hurtling into the yard, his face tight and terrified, blood streaming from his nose. Two soldiers chased him, so fast that when they saw the car and stopped short, the second of them crashed into his companion and stumbled to the ground. William threw himself at Oriane, clutching at her clothes and gasping, butting his head against her shoulder as though he was trying to hide. The hands of the men in the car reached swift and simultaneous to their hips, and Oriane realized with a sick dread that they were, truly, reaching for guns.

The man in the cap was kind, though. He bellowed at the two soldiers as they stood shiftily to attention, and apologized formally, in French, no less, to William. His attention gave her a kind of pride, as though it made her and William distinguished, that they had been singled out to be defended so. He must be an officer, she thought. The man's eyes were a sharp greenish blue, like roof slates after the rain.

SUMMER HOLIDAYS

Claudia's misery had descended to the point where she felt mechanical, divided between one self, which functioned, spoke to Aisling and Alex, swam, ate, performed efficiently, and another, which floated somewhere outside, the same questions running through its mind, wretchedly irresolute, permanently on the edge of tears. There was a sort of perverse pride in the discipline it took to keep the two selves apart, like holding a pair of magnets without permitting them to touch. What had seemed so simple and obviously apparent in London was now clouded, opaque, a treacherous quicksand that would swallow her whether she moved forward or back. The link between the d'Esceyracs and Sébastien had recalled her, horribly, to the fact that he, unlike her, was not suspended in limbo, that his life continued in the world with no sense of hesitation as to how she, Claudia, would act.

If she could not choose to love Alex, the sensible thing would be to get rid of the baby, get over Sébastien, engineer some quarrel with Alex and return to her life as though nothing had happened, but she was afraid. If she pursued that, it would be unpleasant for a time, but she knew rationally that she would recover, that no one would die of it, except the baby. There was a sort of arrogance, she thought, in people's belief in their capacity to cause others pain. Alex would not be irrevocably damaged, he would not collapse of a broken heart. He would be disappointed, angry perhaps, and uncomprehending, but not destroyed. Or she could do as she had originally intended, but then why was that now so difficult? There were worse things, surely, than to marry a man who she found embarrassing, and what did it tell her about herself that Alex's slight buffoonishness outweighed his other qualities? She could justify not marrying him on the grounds that it was insulting, such a deceit, and cruel to pretend to love him when she did not, but this argument was implausibly abstract. She did not believe it because she did not believe that Alex would ever know the difference. He would not necessarily prefer the kind of woman who would love him as he deserved.

What Alex deserved was one of the Emmas or Lucys, someone unimaginative and undemanding, who would admire him, but what he wanted, what he thought he was worth, was difficult, clever, beautiful Claudia, so was it not generous, truly, to encourage him in the delusion that she would have had him even if he weren't second prize? Maybe that was a disgusting thing to think, but it was nonetheless true. It was why she could not blame Sébastien. The only deceit had been her own towards herself, and she acknowledged that she was craven enough to have been grateful if he were to have deceived her, to have pretended to love her. Though surely in that case she would not have known and so would have been happy, as Alex was happy now. All through the settled routine of the days at Murblanc, Claudia dismantled her reasons and rebuilt them thus, and the only idea that did not occur to her was that this torturous logic grew from a need to rationalize where it had previously been valid only to feel. She had never before had to reconcile desire and possibility, to accept, simply, that she would not have what she wanted.

The peacefulness with which she was surrounded was beginning to feel oppressive. She felt banked in, as surely as the house and the village were held in their bowl of hills, moving in a slower time. Aisling seemed so contented, so preoccupied with her tiny universe, as unbearably smug and self-satisfied as Alex's London friends, and yet Claudia envied her in a way, envied her assurance of agency, however limited its scope. There was no need for gin and hot baths, Claudia had autonomy too, she could elect for that life she had before, her flat, her job, her friends, yet things were too far gone for that. She had been offered a sort of grandeur, a chance to alter herself radically, to become someone else, and mysteriously she felt superstitious about negating it. Not to move forward would be a denial she might regret. So why was she so afraid to take what a few weeks ago had seemed a simple and necessary step?

She said she felt like a walk, Alex offered dutifully to accompany her, but she could see he would be glad to continue with the phone calls that spun him across the sea to London.

Claudia climbed the hill to Aucordier's and went to find old Oriane. She had the excuse of the Sternbachs, and tried to begin by explaining their story, that she had wondered if Oriane could remember anything. Did she know another lady, Amélie Lesprats? Oriane was sitting as usual in the kitchen, the television making its perpetual murmur in the corner. Claudia brought the story around to the visit to the chateau, then petered out. Was this too indelicate, too hurtful? But the memory of the old woman's calm acceptance of her earlier outburst made her feel that she might say anything, so she simply asked.

'Was it the old Marquis, your baby's father?'

'Is that what you thought?'

'Well, I sort of guessed.'

'You were wrong.' They used the formal '*vous*' with one another. Claudia was mortified.

'I'm so sorry, I didn't mean to pry. I haven't said anything to anyone else. I just, you know, when you said about the baby—'

Oriane patted the sofa beside her. 'Come and sit here.'

Claudia got up from the hard kitchen chair where she had been sitting, fiddling uselessly with the hem of her skirt, and took the proffered place. The old lady smelt clean today, like talcum powder.

'Down the hill, behind Murblanc there, there was a good place for gathering ceps. We used to go there. We'd find them quickly, maybe half a kilo, a kilo after the rain. Cook used to put them up in butter and serve them with little potatoes and black pepper. They were delicious that way.'

Claudia tried to look interested, but her stomach was contracting like a snail pulled out of its shell and left in the sun. What was she going on about mushrooms for?

'One time, I went with my brother. He was called William, my brother. People thought he was simple, but he could be clever in his way. When they came, the Marquis asked William to move some things for him. Just boxes, but they had important papers in them, I think, and he wanted someone he could trust, someone who wouldn't talk. Poor William couldn't exactly talk. So when we'd got the ceps, we took them up the hill. I was going to share them with the girls who worked in the kitchen, although Cook had gone by then. Well, we came to the house, and William got excited, he was pulling at me, wanting to show me something, so I followed him into the stables. I wasn't supposed to go in there, it was where they slept, see?'

Claudia nodded, although she didn't see.

'And he showed me a little cupboard, and in the cupboard was a key.'

'A key. Good.'

'I couldn't see why he wanted to show me that. But then he took me down into the woods and he showed me the place the key fitted, a sort of cellar, where the Marquis had put his boxes.'

'Did you look inside?'

'There were just papers, like I say. Some of them in English, I think. I think he thought they would be important if he got killed. But I kept the key. And that was where I met him. Jacky's father, he was one of them, see?'

Claudia took a moment to concentrate, still confused by the mushrooms. She had not expected this sort of chattiness, really. She began to babble about her visit to the chateau, describing what she and Otto had found. 'Look,' she said brightly, trying to distract Oriane, 'there were three of these.' She tumbled the compacts on to the dingy cushion between them.

Oriane picked one up, opened it, examined the design, turned it over and read out the name on the underside. She surveyed her face in the mirror.

'*Regarde toi*,' she said softly.

Claudia was chattering, 'I wonder where they came from? How they got there? It's a funny thing to find, no?'

'I know how they got there,' answered Oriane, and her voice was curt again.

She reached for her stick and pulled herself up, slowly, manoeuvring with her unbandaged arm. For a while Claudia was left alone with the half-light from the shutters and Gérard Depardieu. There seemed to be only about eight actors in France, she thought. She could hear Oriane moving about upstairs, and then the shuffle and tap as she returned.

'Are you all right? Should I fetch you some water?' Oriane's face was flushed, bruised-looking.

'Do you love the other one then?'

'Yes.'

'Does he love you?'

'No.'

'Then have a look at this.'

Claudia held the compact, identical to the others. Inside it, scratched in amateurish gothic letters, was 'Oriane'. Fuck.

'He didn't love me either, not enough anyway. But I didn't care.'

Claudia on her feet, backing away, murmuring I'm sorry, I'm so sorry. Oriane said nothing to help her until she was almost at the door. She could not believe she had been so crass, so selfish, so involved with her own wretched, meagre story that she had failed to see that time was something more than a story of people's activities that had been scrapped, that the world was not the sole property of the living. Ghosts had shares in the present. She was stupid and wicked and cruel and blind. How could she have exposed Oriane like that, how could she not have picked it up?

'It's all right,' said Oriane, her voice so warm and gentle that it sounded young. 'I'm not sorry. I'm not sorry for any of it, now.'

PART TWO

JUNE–JULY 1943

'Try it, then.'

'I can't see. Bring the candle.'

It was night here. Karl held up the candle to the side of the little mirror and Oriane saw her mouth inside the gold rim. He rubbed a finger across her lips. Close up, the powder sat chalkily on her skin, pinker-toned, but if she held the mirror away, her face looked soft, warmer. The lipstick matched the compact, a twisting design around the tube, and when she rubbed it carefully across her lower lip it smelt of greasy flowers.

'Don't look yet. Close your eyes.' She felt bold with her painted face. His boots were lying next to his folded clothes, they felt huge as she dragged them up her bare legs, over her knees where the leather chafed against her skin. Her dress and bodice and drawers were dropped untidily, her hair covered her breasts and she spread it out, imagining her white skin in the candlelight.

'Not yet. Wait.' He grabbed at her as she moved past him,

she swung her hips neatly out of the way and lay down on the blanket, leaning back on bent arms, her throat exposed.

'Now look.'

Karl saw Oriane naked except for his jackboots, her eyes on his face, her red mouth a little open. The skin of her thighs looked luminous, catching the polish of the black leather, she parted her knees, lolled them open, then stretched her legs wide, her eyes following his own, showing him everything. Down there her hair was black and thick, he could make out the gleam of the opening.

'Huur,' he whispered, and she smiled stupidly. He knelt between her legs and she reached forward to unfasten his trousers, pulling open the white drawers until his cock was released, holding his belt on one side.

'Watch.' Her hand was dipping between her legs, when she brought it up the fingers were shining. She reached to his mouth and smeared her wetness across his lips, beneath his nose. Taking more, she traced a finger across his straining cock. 'See? See what you do?' He rubbed the backs of his knuckles against her, held them above her face so she stretched her tongue to lick her own juice off the curved heel of his palm.

'Well, I don't care,' Andrée had said defiantly, 'it's true.'

'You shouldn't say things like that, though. It's wrong.'

'Why? I think they're the handsomest men I've ever seen. There.'

By June, there was a photograph in the window of the café, next to the picture of Maréchal Pétain. It showed Herr Hitler in a uniform, his arm raised straight out in the German salute. Underneath, Monsieur Dubois had written on a piece of cardboard: 'We welcome our friends the Germans'. In the evenings, Betty served wine and cognac to the officers, she said they couldn't get enough of her omelettes and duck rillettes. She recited the strange names to her friends, '*Haupsturmführer*', '*Standartenführer*', which Monsieur Dubois had asked them to write on a piece of paper. Only the officers were permitted to drink in the village, Betty said, and they put white cloths on the tables for them. The bench outside the door was usually empty now. Bernard and Yves no longer wheeled poor Jean-Marc there of an evening, though Betty said her father said that the others drank more and left quicker, so that was better. Camille Lesprats still sat in his corner every night, his nose splayed and bulbous, like a potato forgotten in the cellar for a whole winter. At first he had been alone, but as the weeks passed the men resumed their accustomed places and played *pétanque* outside in the dust.

'They were quite polite, you know,' ventured Oriane, 'when they came up to me.'

Betty and Andrée had heard before how Oriane had sent William to see if they were camped on the plain, and William had blundered right through the lorries and tent poles. Oriane guessed they had tried to question him and then become mocking, pushing and taunting him, making a sport of his bewilderment. Cathérine Nadl had been wrong though, William had not been taken away. The interest in the Aucordiers having been the first to see them had been swallowed by everything else that had happened in Castroux in the weeks since they had arrived. Since the night in the square when everyone had said that France was lost, little had changed as

Oriane thought it might. It seemed so long since she had come down the avenue from the chateau that next day, expecting to find a different world, dangerous and terrible, and finding nothing altered, or at least it seemed so then.

There was a game they had played in the spring, *l'esterbel*. You took the stone of an apricot or a plum and rubbed at it with a pebble to make two holes in the husk, exposing the creamy almond at the centre, which could be sucked or teased out until the core was hollow. Then you passed a thread through each hole and wound it around the first finger of each hand, and then, if you pulled the strings tight in a certain way, the stone would spin, revolving so quickly that its motion blurred to the eye, and letting off a reedy, high-pitched hum. William had loved *esterbels*, she would bring hers home from the schoolhouse and make it turn for him, kneeling on the kitchen floor. Time had done that, Oriane thought, hollowed and chiselled slowly through the years so that only now, when the strings pulled taut and the spinning began, you could see that this was not sudden or surprising, but had been gathering there all along.

Oriane did not tell her friends how she had quarrelled with Laurent about going back to work up at the chateau. He had said she ought not, that it was wrong and besides there was no need. What would people think knowing that she was engaged to him? Oriane had been unable to explain, completely, how confined she felt by the farmhouse. The endless list of tasks woke her before dawn. She counted them in her head, but they never seemed finished, no matter how early she got up. Some days it seemed indulgent even to take the time to wash, and she trudged about the yard with a grubby face, conscious of the smell of her own body. Some days she did not even go beyond the perimeter of the yard. William continued to go down to Murblanc, but the burden of his presence, his messes, his clothes to be picked up and washed, his food to be prepared and cooked and the dishes to be rinsed, his bed to be aired and changed, made her angry with him, her poor overgrown child. The effort of concealing her anger exhausted her until there had come to be afternoons when she sat helplessly by the cold fireplace, watching flies hum over the squalor of crumbs on the table. She sensed a recalcitrance in the house, as though it resisted becoming bright and orderly like Madame Nadl's kitchen, but slumped always towards despair and disarray, like her father sneaking endlessly back towards his bottle. She felt exhausted all day, dragging about the place, but when she fell gratefully into bed at last, sleep would not come.

Laurent had seemed to think that her wish to leave it just for a while, just for the morning, was a reproach to him, a protest against the postponement of their marriage. He had tried, in the end, to be kind to her, to permit her to go. Oriane took this as easier, accepted his explanation of her feelings and even added to them, saying that the money she could save would be useful when he started the workshop. She could not attempt to explain how much she wanted to recover the feeling of being between places, of walking alone through the woods in the early morning with the sense that for this time at least, she belonged to nobody.

Betty and Andrée were much more interested in the intimacy that her work gave her with the officers. Andrée was right, they were handsome, though when she had seen them that first day on the plain she had been too afraid to notice. Castroux men, by and large, were dark and squat, their broad shoulders matching the wide hips of their women. They had big hands and feet with thick, splayed fingers. Short-legged, powerful men with a certain brief freshness in their outdoor skins their only claim to looks. The officers were more like Monsieur d'Esceyrac, or like beautiful horses, long and fine limbed, their hair all the colours of wheat. Oriane touched their things, knew the shape of their shoulders and the line of their waists through the tunics with the plaited silver cord on the seam that she brushed, the grey shirts marked inside with what at first seemed indecipherable combinations of initials. They wore a heavy, dull silver badge on both lapels of their jacket, an ugly thing; though this was removed before cleaning, Oriane would have to unpin one occasionally before she rubbed in the alum.

Magalie Contier was working, along with Cécile Chauvignat from the pig farm, whose husband Emile had volunteered for the work service in Germany. Shirts and underclothes were boiled together in the copper, though the women turned away their eyes when they sorted the underpants. Oriane was glad of Magalie, though she missed Cathérine, and it was strange after a while how little the chateau seemed to have changed, the noise of their work and the scent of the steam from the irons remained the same, the pine smell of oil soap mingling with the potato hiss of starch on a collar.

Betty fancied Officer Hummel, she thought he looked sad with his high cheekbones and pale moustache. Oriane knew all their names from the hieroglyphs of their laundry marks. The piano had been moved from the salon to the Marquise's sitting room to make way for desks, and Oriane could tell Betty that she had heard Officer Hummel playing it sometimes, not really a whole tune because that probably wasn't allowed in the daytime, but you could definitely tell he knew how to do it. They liked to sing, the officers, Betty said. Oriane was glad in the end that she hadn't said anything about Karl Sternbach, though Andrée had picked him out as the best-looking of the lot, like a picture of a film star in a magazine, she said.

Betty was mad for those magazines, though Oriane couldn't see the point, if films were like the one Père Guillaume had got up in the schoolhouse the winter before they came. It was about the work of the Poor Clares, the convent in Landi for which they collected every year. Everyone in Castroux had gone, squashed together on the benches, with the men and the big boys at the back, pretending not to be interested. Looking rather dusty, the Sisters held up a selection of little black babies to the camera, smiling encouragingly. A voice told of how many new Catholics were being born every year on the Ivory Coast. 'Look at the state of them,' Andrée whispered, 'no wonder they got sent to Africa. Too ugly even for the convent!' Père Guillaume said loudly in the smelly dimness that he would cancel the projection if certain people didn't stop their ignorant comments. It was true, Oriane remembered, that several of the nuns had particularly bad teeth, but compared to the officers, most of the people in Castroux looked like gargoyles when they opened their mouths. Karl Sternbach's teeth were white and straight, and his lips were full, often slightly parted so that you could see the gleam of them. At the back of his neck his cropped hair was as tender as the new feathers of a duckling.

Betty said it was a shame they couldn't ask the officers to the dances, it was rotten having to have girls for partners. Andrée said was she stupid, that even if they knew about the dances, which they didn't, and even if they were allowed to come, which they weren't, what made Betty think that officers would want to be dancing with the likes of them? Officers would be used to dancing with ladies, not hobbledehoys like Betty. Betty said if that was what Andrée thought then she could hobble back to her flour bin and not hear what she had heard her father telling her mother about a woman in Landi who was doing business above her café, and with officers too, so there. Oriane was happy the conversation could continue without her, she could allow herself to think about the hollow place at the back of Karl's neck, and how it felt when she put her mouth there.

She had known as soon as she went back to work at the chateau that he liked her, the beautiful soldier in the cap who had protected William. The long dormitory above the stables was in use again, and she saw him watching her as she crossed the yard to the wash house. The women were not allowed in to collect the wash, but she knew he slept there. One morning she was struggling with a big basket of kindling for the copper and he came forward and took it from her hands, swinging it up so easily. He called her Mademoiselle.

'Let me help you with that, Mademoiselle Aucordier.' He had remembered her name. She was terribly conscious of the damp rag barely covering her escaped hair and the freckles on her arms where she had pushed up the sleeves of her overall to try to keep a little cool. When she looked up into his face her heart stopped beating, truly skipped and churned in her chest. She wished she could tell Betty about it, who would know what she meant. The next day he was waiting for her at the top of the track with a little fistful of marguerites. Apart from Monsieur Boissière, Oriane didn't know anybody who picked flowers, just like that, for no reason. She thought of Laurent and his apricots. You could eat apricots. She kept the posy in the pocket of her skirt until it shrivelled and dried, and when she went home that day she saw as if for the first time that the meadow at Murblanc was filled with marguerites, as though someone had thrown a huge lace tablecloth across the grass.

Cécile Chauvignat had sharp eyes and a nasty way with her. Oriane knew that Magalie didn't like her either. She was worried that Cécile would notice how often *Unterscharführer* Sternbach seemed to have a few moments to help with a bulging sack of bedding, or soothe the valve on the copper when it started to blow out menacing clouds of steam. Then he kissed her in the woods, and it was nothing like kissing Laurent, she dropped her basket and didn't even pretend to push him away. She imagined Cécile staring horrified from behind a tree, and the words were out of her mouth before she thought what she was saying.

'I know somewhere we could go. To be private.'

He stepped back from her as though he could feel the heat of the blood in her face.

'Do you, then?' he asked, as if something was funny.

Since her mother's death, Oriane had taken what she saw as a practical view of sin. Sin seemed to be connected to shame, which was usually something people couldn't help and yet which made others think badly of them. People couldn't help being what they were, look at William. It was wrong to hurt others, but she did not see anything shameful or wicked in going to have a look in the little hidden room under the bridge. Her mother had been eaten up by the idea of sin, until the shame of it had gobbled her insides and she died of it. If Oriane had told Père Guillaume about her visits to the chateau wood he would have said she was a natural Jesuit. She knew she should feel shame for what they had done. Shame for Laurent and for something even worse than that. All she felt was Karl's eyes and hands and mouth on her, the taste of his skin and his voice telling her she was beautiful. This was what she was then. She was flesh under his body and the sound that caught in the back of his throat when he stopped moving inside her, she was his spit and his sweat and the blood between her legs. You couldn't blame anyone for being what they were.

'I'll go first.'

'Yes, it's better.'

'I'd better hide these.'

'You could leave them here.'

'No, if someone did find them?'

'Shall you come tomorrow?'

'Wait on the bridge if you can. I'll come back this way after work.'

When the candles were out Oriane opened the door, closing her eyes first so as not to be blinded by the light. The lipstick and compact were in her basket, beneath the same torn pillowcase she had been carrying up and down the hill for a week now. There was no reason she should not be in the grounds at this time, she worked here after all, but it seemed more plausible to her if she had something to show if she were stopped, a prop of some kind. It was important not to hurry, nor to look up towards the house. There was a faint footpath through the woods to the Murblanc track, but now, in July, it was almost overgrown and the thorns were vicious. Before she joined the track, she pulled her hat further over her brow and rubbed her mouth with the back of her hand. Karl's handkerchief had got most of the make-up off, but she had to fetch William. With the remains of the water in her bottle she rinsed her mouth and spat. The compact was in the pocket of her apron, she rubbed it, a talisman, over and over.

SEPTEMBER–OCTOBER 1943

Karl dressed himself with professional swiftness, slipping the key into the pocket of his tunic. He looked about quickly before locking the little door and moved out from beneath the bridge, the heat already gathering around him as he came into the thinning shade. Soldiering, it seemed to him, was mostly a matter of being too bloody hot or too bloody cold. He had time to get to his billet in the long room above the stables before he had to report. He was lucky to be here, as one of the division translators, most of the lads were sweating their arses off in the tents on the plain. He replaced the key in his tin box under the cot. There were three of the gold compacts left. They had been a good buy, those, quality stuff, though best not to ask where they came from. Lifted from one of the big department stores in Lyons, no doubt. Fashionable. The lipstick had its name written on a label at the base, which made him smile, 'Histoire d'Amour'. And that had been a nice touch of Willi's, scratching the names with a pin on the inside, making it more personal. He smiled as he said them to himself – Heike, Elodie, Marie-Cathérine, Ursula, Aurélie, Jeanne. Poor old Ursula. Then Oriane. She'd got to him for sure, this one. Dirtiest of the lot with those big eyes and all that black hair. Wearing his boots like that. At least he had boots still.

One time she licked him all over, her tongue rasping on him like a mother cat cleaning a kitten, all the way from his toes, which had white hair at their joints, up to the hollow of his collarbone. Her tongue lapped at the blue numbers inked in his armpit, just next to the soft gold hair that sprouted there. He explained that it was a tattoo, that all the men who had volunteered had them. He and Willi had been tattooed at the same time when they joined the division. She asked him how he spoke such good French, and he explained that he had taken lessons for six months in Bordeaux, and that was how he was promoted. The piping on his short, double-buttoned jacket was pink, but that wasn't because he was a translator, it showed that he was part of the Panzer section. He had been in Russia with his tank. Oriane asked him about Russia, she had some idea of snow and people in big furry hats, but Karl liked better to tell her about his tank.

The tanks were the most important section of the whole army, he said. He told her how fast the tank could go, how tall it was, and how much petrol it needed, more than four litres to drive one kilometre, which sounded impossible. He had a badge, a black tank in a silver wreath with an eagle and the same sign as on the chateau flag, with the number fifty. That showed how many battles he had been in on the Eastern Front. She laughed and said maybe it was dangerous to tell her things, she might be a spy.

'You?' he said. 'You're not a spy. You're a slut.' He laughed.
'Yes,' she said happily, 'yes, I am.'

Willi was unimpressed that he was carrying on with a girl
from the village. He said he knew how it would end.

'And what about Ursula?' he asked. 'It's not like you can go
getting married again.'

Willi and Karl were friends, but since Russia that friendship
seemed to Karl to have been based on a mutual will to silence.
There were too many things it seemed impossible to say. They
could talk a bit about girls, or the officers, but now, after the
taut, baking summer, there seemed to be a great wave of silence
between them, waiting and roiling, ready to engulf them. Karl
found that he couldn't say to Willi that it wasn't just a bit of
fun, that there was something – he looked for the thought
– there was something *clean* about Oriane. Not innocent, but
pure somehow, the way she wasn't ashamed of it, her greed
for him. She didn't seem to need him, there was none of the
bother with love talk that girls usually required. He had been
touched by her, the first time he saw her in the yard, she was
so obviously afraid and so defiantly trying to hide it. And then
her mouth, that hair. He got hard just thinking about her.

Until the first frost coated the leaves in the rose garden at the
chateau with white, Oriane could still not fully believe in the
meaning of the black fear she had pushed down inside herself
since the summer turned. Each day on her way home from
work she sat beside the little Madonna watching over her pool
and prayed for a miracle. She hauled the heaviest loads into
the copper and her heart leaped whenever she felt an answering

stab of pain in her back or the muscles of her abdomen, every morning she snatched up her nightdress in the hope of a spot of blood, but there was nothing. When Karl hung about in the stable yard, she avoided his eyes and shook her head swiftly to show that it wasn't safe, and after a week or so she saw him less and less often.

She brewed *verjus* with Cathérine, they gathered the tiny golden mirabelles and made syrup, and stewed jam from the huge overblown marrows that squatted late in the vegetable garden, but it was impossible to speak to her. Amélie might have been understanding, but she was a gossip and too stupid to help. A girl at Ligeac, over to Auzerte, had hanged herself in the cherry orchard, her feet dangling under the turning leaves. Andrée said gleefully that the crows had pecked her eyes out by the time they cut her down.

Oriane had no wish to do away with herself, and even if she had there was William. It did not occur to her to try to leave Castroux. She found herself thinking that if only Laurent would crash into a tree on his motorbike and die, then everyone would feel sorry for her and she wouldn't have to marry him either. It didn't even feel wicked to think it. But Laurent wouldn't marry her now, and then people would talk and ask questions. There had been so few of those between moments in her life, the times when no one knew where she was or what she was doing. That had been part of Karl. She doubted her power to create more of them. Maybe she could walk to Landi and make up a story about a strange man who had given her too much wine and taken advantage? That sounded like something in one of Papie's songs. Laurent had done nothing to deserve such shame, which would come to him anyway if there was a baby at Aucordier's and no more talk of a wedding. The fear hummed in her head until she was numb and dizzy, but she had to do something, before it showed.

After so long avoiding him, Karl seemed hard to find. At first he had been everywhere, now he seemed to have vanished back into the anonymous grey and black mass of his companions. Uselessly, she waited about the doorway of the laundry until Cécile Chauvignat gave her a sharp look and asked if there was someone she hoped to see? Oriane felt truly frightened then. If Cécile guessed, would she go to prison? Her secret was making her stupid, as once, ensorcelled, it had made her reckless. She had feared shame in Castroux, but now, looking at Cécile's calculating eyes, she understood that she had committed a crime. She hurried off through the woods, not even glancing up at the bridge, and it was five more hideous days before she heard footsteps behind her as she hung out a wash and knew that it was him.

'*Ça va*, Oriane?' he asked gently.

'No.' She put her hand on her stomach and looked into his face. He understood immediately.

'Meet me later, when you finish. I'll wait for you.'

Karl tried to give her money. He explained, though she knew it already, that there was nothing he could do. They would be leaving any day now, he said, any day. She crumpled the notes and threw them on the floor, despising him when he scrabbled in the mouldy ground to retrieve them. Then she caught his face turned up in the candlelight and saw that it was wet, so she knelt down and took him in her arms, to have him inside her just one last time. When they were lying together, her head in the crook of his arm, he pulled up to look at her and she knew what he wanted to say.

'Please don't,' she said, 'don't say it. There's no point, see.'

He held her tighter, but didn't speak, and for a little while he slept, as she rested her lips against his skin of his skull under the delicate newborn hair. When he was still, she moved gently from under him, pulled down her skirt, pushed back her hair. The key was still in the pocket of his tunic, but that didn't seem to matter any more.

HARVEST 1943

The grapes were in, but there would be no celebration of the *vendange* this year. Still, Madame Nadl said, there could be no objections to a few friends having a quiet supper in their own kitchen. If people wanted to call in for a drink on their way home from the vines, that wasn't her fault. So Laurent and his father set up the long trestle in the passage that ran through the house from the Murblanc kitchen, and Cathérine and Oriane stewed six rabbits in *verjus* and garlic as they did every year. There was duck neck stuffed with pâté and Madame Nadl made her fruit cake, heavy with brandy and dried figs. Jean Charrot had worked on the Murblanc vines, so he was there with Andrée, and Camille Lesprats turned up as usual whenever there was a chance of a free drink, but they tolerated him for Papie's sake. Murblanc was a big farm and usually they would have asked the mayor, but Madame Nadl thought best not. Monsieur Larivière appeared anyway and said he was come to supervise the vintage, which made everyone laugh. The men sat at the table and the women took their food in the kitchen. When they had eaten, they carried the jugs through and Monsieur Larivière thanked Madame Nadl politely, and made the toast, 'To a long drought and a lake of wine'. Then the women returned to the kitchen and each of them took up their sewing, their fingers moving as swiftly as their tongues, pausing now and then to nibble a chunk of cake.

'It's quite like old times,' said Madame Nadl, and Oriane knew she was talking about the old custom on winter evenings where people would crowd together in one house or another, often with the animals beneath them for warmth, the men drinking and playing cards, the women sewing and talking in low voices of their men. No one had ever come up to Aucordier's though, and her mother had been too shy and afraid to take her children for a bit of warmth and company.

William was playing and the men began to sing. Oriane waited on them, taking away the jugs to refill them. Camille's face was purple and the others were flushed too, they had opened the front door to let in a breath of air, and Papie was maudlin.

'The next time you open that door,' he sighed, 'it will be for me. I won't last another winter.' They all laughed because Papie said this every year too.

'To the good old days, eh, Papie?' called Jean, but Papie did not raise his glass.

'The old times won't come again, that's for sure,' put in Camille. For a moment the men were silent, nodding slowly, the room full of the presence on the hill.

They perked up as Papie began to tell his stories of the old days, how the men of Castroux would travel for a whole day in wagons to the big estates around Cahors and sleep every night amongst the vines with their heads on their boots. 'And we knew how to celebrate, too,' he admonished, wagging a finger. 'Oh yes, when we were finished I remember I lay dead drunk under a hedge for three days.'

'And the girls,' cackled Camille, 'do you remember them, Nadl?' Monsieur Larivière cast him a warning look, pointing to Oriane framed in the candlelight from the kitchen.

Laurent was smoking, sitting a little apart and letting the scent of the tobacco drift out into the night. He looked much more sober than the others.

'Tell you what, Nadl,' old Camille was saying, 'how about we try some of your good stuff? Keep the chill off your old bones.'

'I'll fetch it,' said Oriane quickly.

She skirted the few trees that divided the house from the bottom field and began to cross the empty meadow, unbuttoning her jersey gratefully as soon as she was out of sight of the house. The warm air was still cooling to the sweat that seemed to fizz on her skin. Her breasts felt much heavier, prickling and rubbing against her bodice, her hair felt heavy too, and she wished she could unfasten it and let the breeze unravel it down her back. The barn was still so thick with the soft grassy breath of the cows, it was hard to believe the stalls were empty. Papie kept his store in an old wardrobe with fruits and flowers carved into the rim, so old even he could not remember where it had come from. There were strange little creatures peeping among the garlands of apples, with pointy, deer like faces. Oriane's fingers traced them a moment in the dark, she thought them pretty, though Laurent said the thing was so rickety it would fall down one day and kill someone, that it was only good for the fire. The stoneware flagon was heavy and she carried it back up to the house cradled into the hollow of her hip. The trees were too thick to see if there was any light from the chateau.

'They're well away,' said Andrée later, as the singing grew louder. 'How will I get him home?'

'You can come in with me,' said Cathérine, 'Jean can go in the little barn. He won't mind, the state he's in.'

'I'd best go,' said Oriane. 'Once William's gone, they won't stop.'

'Make Laurent take you up,' said Madame Nadl. 'He could do with the fresh air. Mind he doesn't fall over himself.'

Oriane waited until All Saints' Day to tell him. She would have to leave it long enough to seem to be sure. It was a bleak day, the brown fields sodden. A hard little wind tweaked at the women's hats and handkerchieves and beat the chrysanthemum petals in the flowerpots they carried until the poor little blooms were ragged scarecrows of themselves, their bronze and yellow dulled to the tone of tobacco smoke. Père Guillaume led the procession from the church once around the square and then stood at the gate of the cemetery as the congregation filed past, the women with their flowers, the men carrying the candles. Outside the café, Betty's father served wine to a bored huddle of heavy grey overcoats. Oriane bent to kiss the earth of her mother's grave, followed by William. They had no proper flowers, so she had done up a bunch of rosemary in a ribbon, for remembrance. She wondered if William understood that his mother was here, and if he was sorry. None of the candles stayed lit, some of the men swore as they scrabbled in the gravel covering the graves, trying to make a hollow to protect the flame. Next year, thought Oriane, I will come with my baby in my arms, and the next year I will hold his little sticky hand as he walks next to me, with his scarf tied tight. I will love you, she said to herself, oh I will love you love you love you.

Everyone slipped away in small groups, not talking much, glancing at the group inside the café. Oriane, William and the Nadls set off for the bridge, walking slowly to pretend they were allowing Papie to keep up, Madame Nadl clutching at her best hat. As they came in sight of the wash house, Oriane tugged gently at Laurent's sleeve, guiding him into the nuns' garden. 'Laurent, I need to tell you something. Let the others go on a bit.'

It was warmer here, the air sheltered between the stone walls was softer with the clean earthy scent of wet herbs. For a moment, when she said the words she had prepared, carefully, as though she were concealing happiness with embarrassment, his face was bright with such joy that she could believe herself. Safe, she thought, safe, safe. But then his face twisted into a bitter, suspicious grimace, and, though he continued holding her arm, his own was as lifeless as his wooden leg.

'You'll be wanting to have the wedding, then?' he said coldly.

He couldn't know, that was the thing. He had been dead drunk, had fallen asleep snoring as he was kissing her on the bed. She had tugged off his trousers and drawers, trying not to look at the thick purpled sole of the stump, and had arranged the covers over him. The sheet was prepared with a dab of rabbit's blood she had poured into a medicine bottle when she and Cathérine had prepared the stew. When he awoke she was downstairs with her hair tidy under a handkerchief, and she blushed at him as she served his coffee.

'There's no need for that. With things the way they are, everyone will understand if we wait, like we planned.'

'I'll tell my mother. She'll be pleased, I daresay.'

'Are you pleased, Laurent?'

'What do you think?'

She didn't dare to answer, just followed him meekly out of the garden.

There was a massive oak beam out in the barn, the strut of a mill-wheel. It had been lying there for years but the wood was supple and dry. Flexing the powerful muscles of his abdomen until they held him firm, Laurent swung the axe. It was too bad. Everyone in Castroux would be having a joke at his expense, saying he went rutting like a swine after one too many with old Lesprats. Disgusting. He was terribly disappointed that Oriane had allowed this to happen, men could not help themselves after all, it was up to the women to see that they behaved. Laurent had been shocked on his recent trips to the market at Landi, to see how some of them carried on. There were girls in Landi, bold girls from big cities who had come back to their country relations in 1940. They swaggered about arm in arm, with powdered faces and cigarettes stuck in greasy red mouths. He had even seen Cécile Chauvignat furtively smoking as she unpacked her sausages. Laurent might trade with them in Landi, but he still saw himself as set apart from those sluts, who seemed to represent everything that was wrong with things lately.

Worse than the women were the men, who sat back and watched French women demean themselves, conniving at the disgusting behaviour. As usual, Laurent felt cheated. As he saw it, the high-ups had talked plenty about the noble sweat of the French farmer when they wanted to line them all up and cart them off to Alsace to be shot to bits. Now the very same men said they had to submit to price fixing, practically giving that famous old sweat away while people went hungry. Laurent's argument did not admit the fact that no one in Castroux was any hungrier than they had ever been. So it was one thing to get yourself a fair price and not be cheated by those liars in Vichy, but it was quite another to lie down and let them fuck you. There was a part of Laurent that believed they had got what they deserved, really. When you looked at how weak and sloppy and stupid people were, they weren't fit to be in charge themselves. It was confusing, but more than ever, you had to keep your self-respect. He would make it up, though. Once he had the centre out he could hollow it out with the lathe, to make a real little cradle.

JANUARY 1944

William was confused. There was a man asleep in the goat house. Usually, he rattled his stick gleefully in the scrap bucket as he made his way down the path and the goats bounded up to meet him, nosing for crusts. Today all he had was a bundle of hay, because Oriane said there were no scraps for the goats any more. William hoped they would not be hungry. The man was not dead, like the black goat that William had found in the straw, he was snoring. William heard the snores all the way up in the yard, a rich stew of a sound, so he set the hay down silently and opened the door just a crack to see. The goats were snickering, butting their heads towards the light.

'Shh!' William whispered to them, and pulled the door just wide enough for them to slip out. The man was wrapped in a blanket with his boots sticking out at the bottom, and a cap over his face, but William could see that he had a beard. He didn't know what to do. Oriane was away to work and he was all alone, so he was not supposed to leave the yard, but there shouldn't be a man in the goat house. He might be a bad man.

Was it a secret? He shut the door slowly, slowly so it didn't creak, and walked away with his feet splayed and soft in his boots, pressing the earth so he would not make a noise, though the snoring continued regular. The mist was so thick down here that the goats had disappeared, but William could hear their jaws working as they chewed sadly at the bare twigs poking out of the hedge. Poor goats.

It was very cold, William was grateful to get back to the kitchen fire. He wanted to play the violin, but his head was too full of the snoring man. He opened his mouth halfway and made an experimental snorting sound, rattling the air at the top of his nose. Perhaps he should hide in the barn, but it was so icy outside, he couldn't bear to leave the room again. He sat on the edge of the fireplace and snored to himself, making a little grunting tune, up and down, until he heard the noise of a boot on the frozen ground. He knew the sound of Laurent's walk, the heavy sole and the lighter tap of the crutch, so he wasn't afraid when the door was pushed open. Laurent was carrying an armful of logs.

'Come on, William, give me a hand. What are you doing sitting around like a granny?'

William considered. He snored again, loud enough to make Laurent start, but Laurent didn't seem to understand. 'Shh!' he added, triumphantly.

'That's right, William, but not now. Now I need you to help me with the wood, see?'

'Man,' said William, 'do-do man.' He sang a little bit of the song to help Laurent see, 'Do-do, nenet do.'

'William, so help me I'll come over there and clout you if you don't get off your lazy backside right now. Stop it!'

Now Laurent had an angry voice and William felt tears in his eyes, he was trying so hard. He took the logs from Laurent, put one on the fire and stacked the others neatly to the side.

'That's better, now,' Laurent's voice was soft again.

Why didn't he see? He tried a bleating sound, like a goat.

'The goats, William? Is there something?' William nodded so hard his head rattled inside, and they went out together.

The snoring man was still there. Laurent looked about for a stick, but the clear patch in front of the shed was bare. 'Stay here, William,' he whispered, then threw the door wide, shouting, 'Hey, you! What do you think you're doing?'

The man woke as swift and silent as a cat, coming upright and snatching the cap from his face in one move, rising to a stooped stand under the low ceiling. He held both hands wide away from his body. Laurent could see the whites of his eyes in the dimness, their brightness shocking him just for a second so that he stepped back. He recovered and kept his voice loud, 'Get out here then, where we can see you.'

The man moved towards him, leaving the blanket coiled in the shape of his body like a discarded shell. As he stepped into the light he laughed.

'You can stop that then,' he said in Occitan. '*Bonjorn*, Laurent.'

All the explanation Laurent needed was in the cock of Jean-Claude's head towards William, the speculative widening of the eyes. Whilst he understood, he was uncertain how to act. It was cold, JC was probably hungry, but immediately the simple solution to this became tangled with difficulty. At least it was William who had found him, not Oriane. He put an arm around JC, clapping him on the shoulder, trying to seem hearty.

'It's fine, William. This is my friend. He came to look for me, see?' Oriane would not return for several hours, they had a little time.

William banged the logs down as loudly as he dared. The snoring man was not a bad man because he was eating terrine by the fire with Laurent, with lumps of rabbit in it, but William had found him and he was piling the logs while they sat there. He had tried to show the man his violin, but Laurent told him to unload the wood from the wagon and stack it in the barn. Snoring man's voice was higher and lighter than Laurent's. He was talking and talking while Laurent said yes yes, he didn't stop even when his mouth was full of bread and something else that William suspected might be walnuts from the jar in the *buffet* in brown wine, just talked with gummy teeth and crumbs in his beard. William could hear every word of the conversation perfectly, and would have perhaps understood a great deal more than Laurent suspected, but words were the least interesting of noises, even when they were addressed directly to him. Still, sometimes he had to speak. His fingers were crabbed and purple from the icy air, stiffening so they hardly bent around the wood. He opened the door. 'Lazy backside!' he crowed loudly, knowing quite well that this was rude.

The snoring man laughed, 'He's right, Laurent. I should be off.'

'Where will you go?'

'Best not to say. But you'll do as I told you?'

'I'll try. Here, take some bread. And my coat, take my coat.'

The snoring man stuffed the bread into his pocket. Laurent was pitched awkwardly on his crutch, trying to wriggle out of his jacket.

'No, better not. I'll do fine. *Adieu*, Laurent.'

'*Adieu.*'

They shook hands. The snoring man waved to William as he passed him in the yard, but he did not go out to the road, he turned back to the path and disappeared down the hill past the goat house.

'Come on, William. Do you want to go for a ride?'

William took his violin as usual, and Laurent did not prevent him. They set off towards Murblanc to fetch the motorbike.

The Larivière house was on the edge of the village, above the church on the Landi road, a fine building with a row of tall, green-shuttered windows on the first floor. By the time they arrived, their ears were skinned from the frost. William stretched his legs to the ground as Laurent had shown him, steadying the bike so that he could dismount more easily. When Madame Larivière opened the door, a rich mist of stew steamed around their noses. 'We were about to have lunch,' she said wearily.

'I'm sorry,' Laurent began, 'but I need to speak to the mayor. Could you take William into the kitchen, please, Madame?'

'Well, no, I don't think so. This isn't a soup kitchen, you know, Laurent Nadl. You can both come back later.'

Laurent didn't have the words for this, didn't know how to make her understand. He leaned forward, 'I've seen Jean-Claude.'

He shouldn't have come out with it like that, she called out and began to cry, and it was some while before Monsieur Larivière persuaded her to sit quiet in the kitchen while Laurent explained. The two men went into the parlour, which was as cold as the tomb, despite the thick crocheted curtains at the window. Laurent thought longingly of the kitchen fire and chicken in thick gravy with shallots.

'Well, Laurent?' Larivière was upright in an armchair, his fingers digging in to the worn red upholstery. Laurent handed over the letter Jean-Claude had given him, and stood politely by the window. The valley looked different from here, raw and flat where the land ran to the Landine, the fields scoured with cold. The chateau hill seemed steep and aggressive, though perhaps that was because from the mayor's window the flag was squarely in view, its red more vivid than ever in the thick white winter light. Laurent stared out, feeling the silence thicken behind him, hoping that the other man would not weep. He did not turn back until Larivière spoke.

'So he was in Spain?'

'He said so, yes. In Paris before that.' Jean-Claude had told him very little. All Laurent's memories were contained by the moment in which he saw Jean-Claude's face. Already he mourned his unappeased longing to speak, to know that Jean-Claude remembered. He sensed that JC's past was occupied, pressured down by what had happened since, so that what was huge in Laurent took up only a small space, now, in him. He had said nothing about the leg, though perhaps that too was because a time when Laurent was whole was no longer present or interesting to him. Laurent had listened, and agreed without thinking, and now he had begun it.

'He said that what he wanted to tell you was in the letter. He was very sorry that he could not pass by to see his mother.' JC had said nothing of the kind. 'But he had come to tell you something else, that is, I'm supposed to tell you, so you know what to do. He said he was lucky to find me up at Aucordier's, he was planning to come down to Murblanc tonight.'

'Go on.'

JC had asked Laurent to repeat what he told him, slow and clear, with the names. Since the recruiters had come for the *Relève*, when Emile Chauvignat had left alone, it seemed as though Castroux had been forgotten. But with the failure of the new law, the government was finding even conscription for the STO inadequate. More workers were necessary for Germany to win the war.

'They're desperate, do you see?' JC had asked excitedly, spitting crumbs. 'Sauckel can't meet the quotas, the Reich is demanding more and more labour. It's the beginning of the end.'

There was a list of names of *réfractaires*, and the *Milice* had resorted to *shanghaillage*. Laurent pronounced it carefully. It meant raids on whole quarters in the towns. A cinema audience had been impounded in Toulouse and the men marched away to the train there and then.

'And how does Jean-Claude know all this, about the *Service du Travail*?'

'He's been in Cahors. He said he'd come from there. He told me a list.'

'Of Castroux men?'

Laurent felt as though he was repeating a lesson. 'Not you

or me. No one over sixty. François Boissière, Nic Dubois, Jean Charrot, Yves Contier, Bernard and Marcel Vionne—'

'Hilaire?'

'Charrot? Yes, but he might be able to get exemption if he proves he mills as well as bakes. Otherwise yes. Not William Aucordier, obviously, and the other lads are seventeen.'

'So seven, if we count Charrot.'

Laurent felt out of breath, but not relieved. He had done what JC had asked, but in doing it he saw now, he had begun something that would not stop, and that made him want to draw the bobbled wool curtains closed.

'And this, this "*shanghaillage*"?'

'He doesn't know exactly. He said soon.'

'And did my son give you any more instructions?'

'No. He had to go, he said you would know what to do.' Larivière was turning JC's letter in his hand, there was no gladness in his face, and Laurent pitied him his wife waiting eagerly in the kitchen, pitied the single scrawled sheet.

'You see what he's done, don't you, Nadl?' Larivière spat out angrily. 'He's left us no choice. Do you see that?'

Laurent did see, and yet did not feel tricked, or trapped, though he had begun to be afraid. Oddly, he felt happy. He realized that he had been waiting for something without knowing really that he was waiting. JC had known that he, Laurent would understand, that he could look with clear eyes, easy even, and imperative because of what they both knew. So he had not forgotten.

JANUARY 1944

Georges Tinville debated between the two sheets of *La Dépêche* his wife had retrieved from the coal scuttle. He had reprimanded her that morning for lining the cat's box from the pile of newspapers. Minette had given birth to two tabby kittens on the portrait of Monsieur Henriot, the new Minister of Information. Georges suspected that grey tom he had seen hanging around on the quay. It was going to be a bright day, the sun was already striking off the Lot through the bedroom window, causing the looking glass to glare as he strapped on his leather belt. Georges enjoyed wearing his uniform. He fastened his black tie carefully over the khaki shirt and smoothed down his trousers under his stomach. His dark blue jacket was neatly pressed on the bed, next to the holster. That was a shame now, but one couldn't expect everything with times as they were, and appearances were what mattered. He considered November 1940,'*Toulouse a fait au Maréchal Pétain l'Accueil le Plus Enthousiaste*' and June 1942, '*Le Maréchal est Acclamé avec un Ferveur et un Enthousiasme Indescriptibles*'. He settled on the later piece, as being less significant a date and rolled it tightly, working the paper into the holster until it was satisfyingly full. With the belt in place it didn't look too bad, nothing like what he'd handled in 1916, but still.

They would be two hours or more in the truck from Cahors to the village, and Georges opened his lunch packet before they had passed under the viaduct. Sausage, wonderful really, but the smell alerted the others and Georges had reluctantly to offer his greased paper until there was hardly a decent bite left. Selfishness, that was the problem. It was just a matter of making them see that, these *réfractaires*, that with a bit of cooperation things would be better for everyone. It came down to patriotism in the end. Georges saw himself putting a firm hand on one of these young men's shoulders, explaining that he understood his reluctance to leave, but that it would work out better if they all did their bit. There would be no need for strong arming. They were peasants, after all, probably had barely left their little village, it was natural they should be apprehensive, but duty was duty. The sausage was a bit oily, and as the truck began to climb along the twining roads above the town Georges felt queer. He stared hard at the white stones beside the wheels as they bumped along, shoulders rod-straight, setting an example.

It was after eleven when they reached the division camp on the plain. Georges gulped gratefully at the cold air, saluted the sentry smartly and asked for *Obersturmführer* Hummel, who was waiting as arranged with the map and the list. The first checkpoint was a big farmhouse on a rise above the Landine river. It looked a prosperous sort of place, Georges wouldn't have minded betting there was a cow or two with no certificate, but he had his orders. They were not to raise an alarm. Two women came out at the sound of the truck, mother and daughter, they looked like, plain as brass nails both.

'*Milice*,' said Georges, and saw that their papers were in order. 'Does Laurent Nadl live here?'

The older of the two women answered,'Yes, with his father and grandfather. They're both over sixty. Then there's me and Cathérine.'

'I need to see him.'

'Well, you'd best come in then, Monsieur. He's having a bad day with his leg.'

Georges could see that they lived in the one room, like all country people, though the house was a good size. Nadl was lying on a truckle bed in the corner of the kitchen, his good leg stretched out and the stump discreetly covered with a blanket. He wore a muffler and a thick jersey despite the heat from the range. A crutch was propped against the table.

'Your exemption paper?'

'I'm sorry, you'll have to ask my mother to fetch it. I'm bad today.'

'Where?' asked Georges, when he had seen the second category classification.

'Verdun.'

Georges leaned forward and shook his hand.

'Vive Pétain.' They looked into one another's eyes for a moment.

'Vive Pétain.'

As they drove away, Georges explained to the others, 'Verdun, that means something, that does. He's a hero, that man.' He ran his finger ponderously over the map, to where the bakery was marked in the village square.

In the kitchen at Murblanc, Yves Contier whipped off the blanket and fumbled frantically at his left leg, strapped tight beneath him and tucked into a pillowcase.

'Christ, I've had my big toe in my bollocks for hours.'

'Shh,' hissed Cathérine, though she was laughing, 'you'll have to stick it back in a minute. They might come back this way.'

The village wasn't much to speak of. A scrappy square with a few chestnut trees, Vionne's *boucherie* with a home-made sign in the window reminding the housewives to bring their coupons, the café with the usual row of old has-beens on the bench outside. The *boulangerie*, Georges noted with approval, had a large photograph of the Maréchal above the counter.

'*Milice*,' he said importantly to the skinny girl who watched over three *flûtes* and a quartet of deflated-looking brioche. 'We need to see Hilaire Charrot and Jean Charrot.'

'My father's at the mill,' she replied. 'He's there every day now, since Jean left.'

'Jean is your brother? Jean Charrot?'

She rubbed a dusty hand over her face. 'Yes. It's been hard without him.'

'I'm sorry, Mademoiselle, but we have our duty to do.' He flicked his head authoritatively towards the raffia curtain that separated the shop from the family kitchen.

'Search it.'

While the other three went through, he stared at the girl, who returned his gaze incuriously with bright, curranty eyes.

Georges had recovered from the effects of the sausage and the sharp air had made him feel peckish. He eyed the brioche.

'Would you care to try one, sir? Of course, they're not what they were, since we can't get the butter, but you're very welcome.'

'Don't mind if I do.'

When his colleagues returned, rather floury about the jackets, Georges saw that Thierry was looking disapprovingly at a few crumbs, which had somehow become lodged in the shirt crease above his belly. He straightened his shoulders and looked stern. 'Well?'

'Nothing.'

'Where's this mill then?'

The girl came out from behind the counter, popping up a wooden hatch, and pointed through the doorway. 'Down to the river and then right back on yourself along the bank, past the old barn. You can't miss it, though it's a bit of a walk.'

'There's no road?'

'No sir. Father uses the wagon to get along, but you'll have a hard time of it with your lorry. The ruts are something terrible with the rain we've had, and now all frozen up. It's best to walk.'

Georges thought he might send the others and wait behind, but the matter of the crumb had already undermined him. Several miles on rough, icy ground was more than he could bear to think of.

'Come on then, where's your brother? We're serious, you know. The *Milice* doesn't have time to play games.'

'I told you sir, he's not here. He went off with his friends Marcel Vionne, and Nic Dubois oh, months ago now. To

Toulouse they said. They were going together to look for work in the factories, but we've not heard a thing. Nor Betty next door at the café neither.'

'You can tell your father we'll be back, and he'd better be here with his papers. If he's a miller it should be in order. Good day.'

Georges marched out, letting the door slam. The bell tinkled shrilly, and the girl kept her face towards the ground. Georges struck his pencil through three of the names on his list and made a question mark against the miller. Thierry rolled his eyes.

Madame Teulière had wheeled Bernard Vionne outside, despite the cold. They'd had a time of it lifting poor Jean-Marc into the attic. Madame Teuliere had said why couldn't Bernard hide in the attic for that matter, but Laurent's plan was that some of the *refractaires* had to be recognized as other people, if they all just vanished it would be too suspicious. They had to make a distraction. Bernard sat upright in the chair, his ears stretched in opposite directions like a snail's eyes, one for the sound of a truck and one up the stairs, anticipating the first of his old friend's cries that would have him on the train to Germany. His fingers were wound tightly together beneath the rug that covered his knees. There were four of them climbing down, three younger and the one in charge, a great wineskin of a fellow with a huge swag of belly juddering above his belt. Reluctantly, Bernard closed his eyes and let his head loll down to his shoulder. He could hear Madame Teulière speaking to them, smell a cigarette. He pushed his breath deliberately through his nostrils, feeling it warm in the three day's growth on his upper lip. A hand touched his shoulder.

'Jean-Marc,' Madame Teulière said softly.

He opened his eyes, taking care not to focus on her face, but keeping them fixed in the middle distance.

'Can he understand me then?' asked the fat one.

'He seems to, sometimes. We hope so.'

'Jean-Marc Teulière!' bellowed in his ear so that involuntarily, Bernard jumped. 'He heard that all right.'

'Oh, you shouldn't frighten him. You'll set him off!'

The cold was digging at Bernard's neck like a knuckle grinding into his sinew. How was it possible they could not hear his heart? He gripped the handles of the chair, forcing his weight into his stomach, controlling the desire to jump and run. He tried to keep his eyes soft and wandering vaguely over the faces of the waiting men. Madame Teulière was whispering Jean-Marc's story, the nightmares, the useless flailing limbs. As she spoke, Bernard caught the sound of a wail beginning from the house, hatefully familiar, the snuffling gulps of a grown man preparing to scream like a child. He sensed that Jean-Marc's mother heard it too, for she raised her voice determinedly and stroked the blanket, patting, soothing. The fat man's blunder was his salvation then. As the first cry swelled from the house, he opened his mouth and roared, adding an upward kick of his leg for good measure. The men jumped back, shocked, and Bernard screamed with all his strength, drowning the sound of Jean-Marc's echoing sob, joining swiftly with his mother's shrill complaints.

'You see, you see what you've done. I said he'd go off! Shame on you!'

As he screamed, it seemed to go dark before his eyes. A scent came to him, a scent he thought he had forgotten, but which now swelled to a vile stench in his nostrils. That smell of livid, peeling flesh, the smell of Laurent's leg, skewed across Bernard's body in the trench, Laurent's face in still, astonished agony somehow too far away from the limb that weighed on Bernard like a live thing, creeping over him. He rolled in the stifling mud, trying to breathe, and sucked in a gobbet of warm flesh. He screamed and screamed, until he felt Madame Teulière's hands on his shoulders, shaking at him.

'You can stop now. Stop! They're gone. Stop it.'

Bernard could not breathe, could not pant out the smell from his lungs. He floundered and gasped until he subsided, sobbing, into Madame Teulière's surprised arms.

'It's funny,' said Thierry as they bumped down the track, 'I could have sworn there were two of them, just then.'

Eric laughed, 'Watch it, you're going gaga too! Aaagh,' he cried, waving his arms, 'the gas, the gas! It's coming for me!'

Georges thought he ought to reprimand them, but he was beginning to feel slightly defeated. The next hour was spent searching fruitlessly and infuriatingly for Contier and Vionne. It was as much as they could do to get any of the Castroux people to admit to knowing them, most of their questions were met with a shrug and a muttered '*sais pas*' which was as near as most of them seemed to get to speaking French at all.

The bell was ringing as they arrived at the schoolhouse. A dozen or so children were filing out, stooping to step into their clogs at the door, the bigger girls helping the little ones with jackets and mufflers tied across the breast like miniature bandoliers. Georges guessed that several of them would have a bitter walk home, long kilometres across the fields. Odd that he felt a stab of fear as they stepped down into the schoolroom, a forgotten anxiety returning to him even before his body gratefully registered the warmth of the fat iron stove. Behind his back, his hands washed themselves, the pressure reconjuring the burning tenderness of palms red-stripped from the cane. The feeling heightened when the figure bending to rearrange some books in a cupboard resolved itself as a priest, a tall narrow man with greying hair brushed aristocratically back from his temples. Georges saluted and the priest came forward, smiling pleasantly.

'Good morning. Or is it just afternoon? What can I do for you, gentlemen?'

Georges felt Thierry and Eric behind him, and the consciousness of their morning's failure fought with his natural respect for the collar and the cassock. 'We're very busy, Father,' he began gravely, 'so we won't take up your time. I'll come straight to the point.'

'Please do.'

Georges felt his throat contracting dustily as it always had when it was his turn to recite the catechism. Thierry interrupted, 'We need Boissière. François Boissière, the schoolteacher. And don't mess us about, with respect, padre.'

If the priest was affronted, he didn't show it. 'Monsieur Boissière? I see. I had better fetch his wife, if you can wait a few moments.' He passed down the room to a yellow painted door at the right of the stove that presumably connected the schoolroom with the teachers' living quarters. Georges cleared his throat and strolled over to the bookcase to look over a copy of Molière, turning the pages with slow attention and not glancing at the others, nor did he stir at the sound of the door.

'Dear old Harpagon?' asked the priest. 'One of his finest comedies, I think.'

'I prefer the tragedies, myself,' said Georges.

'Of course, of course. You are the er, the superior officer, sir?'

'Indeed.'

'Well perhaps you would like to come and sit down in private. This is rather a delicate matter, you understand.'

Boissière's wife was in the small sitting room of the schoolhouse, like a man in the armchair, with her big feet planted flat on the floor and her hands clasped beneath her knees. Later, to make a joke, Georges said he could see why Boissière would have preferred to get into bed with Uncle Joe. Now, he removed his cap and gratefully took the weight off his feet at her invitation. There was an arrangement of dried twigs in the empty grate. Artistic, he supposed, though the room was freezing.

'You are looking for my husband, I imagine?' Her educated voice showed that she was not local.

'Yes, Madame. He is in our files, you see.' Georges liked the sound of that.

The woman attempted to speak and then began to weep, scrambling a grubby handkerchief from the nubbly brown sleeve of her buttoned sweater and pressing it to her eyes. The priest took over.

'I'm sorry, Monsieur, but we have all had a terrible shock. We learned recently that Madame Boissière's husband was, is,' he lowered his voice and cast a pained glance at the snuffling woman.

'Yes?' said Georges.

'Not to put too fine a point on it, you understand—'

'Yes?'

'—a Communist.'

Père Guillaume had said it was impossible for them to light a brazier in the crypt. François Boissière had felt awkward at first to be confined so closely with his three former pupils, but the cold and the injunction against speech and cigarettes united them swiftly. Marcel had thoughtfully brought a pack of cards, and they played hand after hand of *vingt-et-un*, laying the cards down separately so they would not slap even slightly on the floor. None of them concentrated on the game, but it gave their eyes something to focus on besides one another's faces, and the movement of their hands marked the time. François wanted to talk to the lads, to ask them how they thought it was that they found themselves here, but he knew better than to expect an explanation, even if they were not hiding underneath Castroux church whilst they were variously denounced and impersonated to the *Milice*.

He could not ascertain satisfactorily even to himself why his convictions had failed to make even a token show of themselves when René Larivière called on him to explain the warning. Nor did he understand why, when they had all met in the presbytery, Bibles clutched absurdly in their hands, he had taken a certain pleasure in selecting the Communist cover story for himself. He, who had tried to explain to the Castroux farmers that the world had changed definitively, for better or worse, that France was beaten and this must be accepted, that at least they were on the winning side in the coming battle against Communism, had suddenly found himself amused by the idea that he had run off to join the Party. He was rationalizing his own cowardice, he knew that. What he thought he believed to be correct was a puff of air, and François Boissière was revealed to himself as a man of no principle who was terrified of what he had taken pride in ignoring until it came too close.

If he could have asked the others why exactly they were here now, he knew they could not answer him. He remembered too clearly their blushes when he asked them to respond to a question, the way they had sprawled their already-powerful bodies over the forms, shoulders and biceps arguing more impressively against their imprisonment in this little room than their tongues could ever have done. At fourteen, Jean Charrot had had an almost full moustache. None of them had taken their Certificate, and in the case of Nic Dubois, François had felt guilty when he filled in the customary 'knows how to read and write' on the leaving paper, though the lad did have a good head for figures, which would be useful to him in the café. None of them was lazy or would ever consider himself a coward, that much François thought. If they refused their obligations now, he doubted whether they did so after any considered analysis of what was their duty. Partly it was the mulishness with which their type, the peasant type, greeted an injunction of authority, and partly the foxy delight that class took in getting the better of the same.

It was all very well for the likes of de Chazoumes to sentimentalize the rural poor, but there was no denying that they were often a bad lot. François had re-read *La Terre* before coming to Castroux, and had often discussed with Charlotte his surprise at the continuing accuracy of Zola's depiction. They liked to get one over whenever they could, these people, and they didn't consider it dishonest, just looking out for their own. That was their only principle, though it seemed that in the end he himself was no better. François did not consider then or afterwards for how many it had begun like that, doing what you could to get by until you found yourself suddenly on the wrong side of the law, with the game changed beyond recognition.

Georges was at a loss. The chair into which he had squeezed himself was very low, and the narrow wings confined him so that he was unsure that he would be able to get up with any dignity. Moreover, his paper-stuffed holster had been pushed up by the flesh of his thigh and had risen obscenely against his belly, right in the schoolmistress's line of vision. The poor woman was obviously desperately ashamed, she repeated again and again that she was trying to compensate now by being ever stricter with the pupils, for who knew how he might have indoctrinated the big boys whilst she took the little ones for their nature walks? She had jumped up and pulled papers from her desk; extracts from the Maréchal's speeches made by the children, her own notes on the education laws of 1940. The priest had taken over some of her husband's lessons, and with God's grace they were getting by, but it was a struggle to recover from such a terrible betrayal. There was more of this, a good deal more. Georges attempted to look knowledgeably at the extracts whilst thinking of a way to tell the woman that if her husband were to return it would be her duty to report him, and that he would surely go to prison.

He had impressed that on the mayor, he thought later, made that fact thoroughly clear. This observation was repeated in various formulations throughout the drive home in the humiliatingly empty truck. If any of them, Dubois, Charrot, the Vionnes, Contier, Boissière, so much as showed their faces there or anywhere else then they were under arrest. The mayor would be under arrest if he failed to report any information pertaining to their capture.

'Is it clear, Monsieur,' Georges had asked grandly, 'that these men of the Saintonge commune are considered outside the law by the state. Outside the law!' Thierry and Eric had thankfully not witnessed the priest's effort to extract him from the armchair. Georges was unaware that they were presently puffing out their cheeks in the doorway and muttering 'Outside the law!'

Eric was a serious young man, Georges thought, but he had his doubts about Thierry. Too keen, yet in the wrong way.

JANUARY 1944

Dispatches came by motorbicycle and sidecar twice a day, from Cahors and Monguèriac. In theory, they were to arrive by eight o'clock in the morning and three in the afternoon in winter, but the weather and the condition of the roads had made this improbable since December. Had *Obersturmbannführer* von Scheurenberg not been waiting irritably in his first-floor office at Esceyrac for the post to appear, smoking his fifth cigarette of the morning and watching a dimly visible work party ploddingly clear leaves from the avenue, he would have thrown the letter away after a first reading. Von Scheurenberg liked his room, with its long windows and thick pale walls and the two elongated Mannerist nymphs, delicate of wrist and ankle and robust about the hips, let into the relief around the fireplace. He guessed, from their appearance and counting the distance from Esceyrac to Fontainebleau, that they were likely late-sixteenth century. It was the sort of thing he would have liked to look up, if he had the time. But the room was overheated and stuffy, and when he opened the casement in the broader panel of glass to get some air, the January mist snaked in from the dark, straight behind his eyes so that his incipient headache became urgent. He felt dehydrated, as though his breath was foul, and pressed the bell for his orderly to fetch a carafe of water.

When it came, he asked the man if the post had arrived, although he knew that it hadn't. There had been a letter, addressed to him personally, found in the hallway that morning. Von Scheurenberg felt able to work up quite a good rage about that, shouting that he didn't expect to find correspondence dropped off at random like invitations to a birthday party, and where had the watch been so as not to notice people sneaking around in the grounds delivering letters in the middle of the night, and what did the man think they were here for, a rest cure? He took some time over the explosion, then sent for Wurster to have him look into it, lit another cigarette when he was alone again and thought he might as well open the white envelope, though he knew what he would find.

Monsieur Obersturmbannführer Führer,
I have the honour to draw to your attention the activities of some people who are encouraging drunkenness and idleness in this village. If you look in the barn at Nadl's farm you will see for yourself. There are certainly some lazy people who try to escape the law.
Respectfully,
An Honest Frenchwoman

Von Scheurenberg had seen hundreds of these things, in Paris and then at Bordeaux, but this was the first he had received here and his disgust was freshened. Who were these mealy-mouthed types who had no loyalty to their own? The Nadl property was the big farm visible in the valley to the left of the chateau, he thought. Hummel had reported that some *Milice* men from Cahors had been there yesterday, checking up on the STO. There were two pointless organizations, both of them a wearisome waste of energy and resources. There was still no sign of the blasted post. He left the office and crossed the stone-flagged passage to the staircase, admiring as always the smoothness of the bevelled poplar wood under his hand as he descended. Hummel was at his desk in what had been the *salon*, and as he scraped his chair back to come to attention, von Scheurenberg was glad once more that he had decided not to replace the valuable old carpets on the parquet.

'Is that Nadl's farm, down there?'

'Yes, sir.'

'You'd better take a couple of men and go along to see what's going on. Contraband alcohol.'

'That will be the old man's still, sir.'

'What?'

'If you look through the window, sir, you can see the smoke. Look. He makes schnapps, sir.'

The lower reaches of the valley were still stuffed with mist, but it was lighter now, with no wind, and sure enough there were two plumes of smoke rising from the farm, one from the main building and the other, finer, from a distance away. Von Scheurenberg recalled the melon drink he had tasted in the summer, sweetish and rather charming, and the stiffer plum brandy, like a slivovitz, of which he had drunk several glasses whenever he went to the café this winter. He considered surprise followed by a lenient warning. Still, it wouldn't do to seem sloppy.

'Well if he hasn't got a permit, you'd better arrest him. You can use the cellar room. Then ring up Cahors and have the *Milice* deal with him. And ask them what the hell is going on with their dispatches.'

'Yes sir.'

There was refuge in irritation, von Scheurenberg was aware of that. He feared the contents of the post, feared his own truly righteous anger, because they revealed to him that hope had abruptly departed. He could muster no sincerity for the bumblings of the *Milice* or anonymous letters, felt himself lean and urgent with the tension of what was to come sprung constantly inside him. The men, he thought, were beginning to be afraid, and he wanted that fear from them, though he had to control it, to direct it through discipline so that it would never be dissipated by despair. Von Scheurenberg had been in Russia, but he thought that this would be worse in the end, though he could not admit of the conclusion of such thinking, as he lit his seventh cigarette and sat in his chair to wait for news.

Most of Papie's still was older than he was, and there were parts of it, he said, which were made before the Revolution, though it had been patched and cobbled so many times that it was impossible to discern what its original form may have been. In summer, for the melons, he brewed outside because of the heat and the terrible flies. Papie preferred the winter brewing, when the still was wheeled on the huge solid rubber tyres, which had carried Papie's son's perambulator in the last century into the big barn and a fire was lit in the blackened grate. There were two roof tiles kept loose so the tin beak of the still could poke out to the sky, though it had been twenty years since Papie had climbed up himself to remove them. It was cosy then, waiting through the short day in the warm, the metallic pungency of the alcohol filling the air, so that when he stepped outside to empty the pulp bucket the cold would strike him with the same surprising, invigorating force as if he had drunk his potion, not merely breathed it. Not that Papie was stingy in giving away a nip or two. There were usually three or four old-timers sitting around the fire in the afternoons, though nowadays it seemed to be mostly just Camille Lesprats. Lately there had been William too, and the music, which was a compensation for Camille. There was a blackened copper ladle, dipped straight into the bucket, and a collection of filthy little glasses that no one had ever thought to wash. Outside, the juicy skins mounted into a pile, amber or purple, depending on whether he was brewing from the prunes or the Chasselas, though his visitors would know from the scent long before they even crossed the Landine. As it grew dark Papie shovelled the skins into a barrow and wheeled it around to the compost heap by the orchard wall. He had tried the skins on the cows one year, but they got the squits something terrible and fell down drunk in their own liquid dirt. A good story to tell, but not to repeat.

Papie told himself that he was not troubled when four soldiers arrived to take him away. He could remember 1870 perfectly well, and considered himself to be too old to be afraid of anyone much, even of them. Besides, he had been arrested for distilling before the first war, and the customs men had started coming back every season a couple of seasons after it ended. They had fallen into a pleasant relationship over the years, the same twosome setting up their hide on the high bank below Aucordier's, so on sunny days Papie could see the wink of their field glasses and wave. They didn't bother him, and in turn he made sure that any more irregular customers, who came with big flagons rather than stone bottles, appeared only during their dinner break, from noon until two, or after they had left their post with the light, around four. On several particularly cold days Cathérine had struggled up the bank with a flask of hot coffee, which had been most politely and thankfully received. After the last day's brewing he would leave a full litre pot on the fence post, and its punctual empty arrival on the barn lintel the following January would have acted as a reminder, had he needed one, that it was time to bank the charcoal in the belly of the still.

It was not yet ten o'clock when they arrived, and though Papie had been about since seven, he had only just finished wheeling the last barrowload of Chasselas down from the orchard store. He had to go slowly these days and his hands no longer moved so deftly amongst the fruit, he warmed them over the fire to get them supple. When he heard a movement behind him, he did not turn, assuming it was William as usual, but no hand plucked caressingly at the sleeve of his jacket, William's silent greeting since he had been a little boy, and when he looked around there they were in the doorway in their black caps and long grey coats. The lieutenant or whatever he was had silver piping around his cap, you could see he was in charge although he was so young, but it was another of them who stepped forward and spoke to Papie in surprisingly clear French. For a moment it seemed an idea to pretend not to understand, to hump into himself and refuse to look at them, but pride got the better of that and Papie walked as smartly as he could outside to the truck. He had never ridden in a truck, but he grasped the sides at the open back to show them he knew just what to do, and pulled hinself up in one movement, though the effort of it made his eyes bulge nearly out of his head, and he had to suck as much air as possible through his nose so that they should not hear him panting. He said not one word to them, but sat up straight with his cap on his head and his hands folded between his legs.

Cathérine came hurtling down the field, her skirt flapping and a rag in her hand, crying out. Laurent was doing his best to keep up with her. The soldiers strode up to meet them, so that Papie was unable to catch their words, although the day was so still. He waved to his grandchildren and shouted in patois, 'Don't worry about me. Tell your mother I'll be back for supper!' Then they came back and got into the truck, the silver braid cap next to the driver in front and the other two on either side of him. They held on to the rail with a hand each, so he felt he could do the same without appearing nervous. The boards vibrated beneath their feet as the engine started and they moved forward slowly enough over the track, but when they came to the road they ran with such smoothness and speed, streaming along so the wind made him breathless and icicles formed and melted in his eyelashes as quick as the silvered earth flew by. It was beautiful. Papie turned his head about, astonished at how things rushed up then flew behind, at the ease, when they had slowed and turned into the gates, with which they picked up speed again and whirred up the avenue of the chateau. He opened his mouth wide to the wind.

Karl had felt horribly uncomfortable when *Obersturmführer* Hummel had fetched him to translate at the Nadl farm. He knew that Oriane's brother, the simpleton, used to go down there when she worked, but he had no news of her. There was no excuse he could contrive to give him a reason to ask, and though he hoped every day to be ordered up to the camp, there was more work than there had ever been at the chateau, something big was up. It surprised him how much he ached to see her, but he was also ashamed at his own proxy closeness to these people. Arriving at the farm he saw that he was associated in some way now with this smelly old man and his disreputable activities, that there was a connection between them that differed from that of ruler and ruled, which was how it was when one came down to think of it. Like those men on the plantations who slept with the black slaves. Castroux seemed different in the winter, not old-fashioned and charming, but mean and dirty, the people grubbing squatly over the land like so many bundled trolls. He took less trouble than usual to be polite to the old man, and when they got him back he let the two privates take him away immediately Hummel ordered it, knowing that they would be able to offer him no words of explanation or encouragement.

Having never been inside the chateau, Papie was disappointed when he was led under the archway to the stable yard and directly through a door and down a flight of steps. A second door was unlocked and they went along a damp passage with the aid of an oil lamp, passing vaulted, musty spaces until a third door was opened and he was pushed through it. From the smell, Papie knew it was the wine cellar, and that made him smile, though when one of the soldiers handed him a lighted candle he saw that the ranks of bins were empty, though their rich scent lingered. The room was swept clean, flagged in thick cool limestone, though, since it was not oozing damp, Papie reckoned it had been dug in properly, raised on a bed of sand and gravel. There was a stove, but it was cold. The d'Esceyracs had done themselves right, no doubt of that, lighting a fire just to keep their precious bottles warm. There was a wooden stool, and, Papie saw when he set the candle holder on the floor, a white chamber pot at the edge of where the shadow fell. As he looked around, the soldier said something in his own language and the door was shut. Papie heard a key turn and two bolts being shot. Instinctively, he moved to the door and pushed stupidly against it, noticing in the next moment that there was a bottle of water and a cup on the protruding stone where in old times there would have been a statue of the Virgin. Every room in Castroux had one of those. For a few moments Papie prowled about with the candle, imagining a forgotten bottle of champagne or burgundy, but the room, though high for a cellar, was not large, and he swiftly saw that it was bare. That had been a fine bottle, that one young William had brought down from the chateau. They might be cowards, these aristos, but at least the Marquis hadn't left the bastards anything decent to drink. He poured a little of the water and sat down on the stool. There was no sound except the slight wheeze of his own breath, and after some time he began to wonder what would happen when the candle burned out.

★

Obersturmführer Hummel gave himself permission to use the telephone. It was a waste in some ways, but he had to concede that he was not blocking any more vital information from the exchange and moreover, the sooner the *Milice* took away the poor old man in the cellar the better. He shared *Obersturmbannführer* von Scheurenberg's unspoken yet palpable conviction that such matters were beneath their dignity, insulting even. Minor insurrection was not SS business. These people had no reason to be especially afraid since Hummel and his men had simply not attempted to make them feel afraid. To suggest that silly breaches of discipline were a shortcoming on their own part was demeaning. It was quite clear to Hummel. If they had been made to feel afraid you could bet there would be no more of this sort of business, it was nonsense to mess around with half measures. Hummel did not despise the old chap any more than he despised the rest of the people in Castroux, he reserved what contemptuous attention he had for the *Milice* men. He looked about for the day's orders to check the telephone password, anticipating the smugness in the voice that would use the code on the other end of the line. They took such pathetic pleasure in it, playing at soldiers, as if it wasn't obvious who was telephoning, as the line was only connected three ways. Hummel peered at the smudgy sheet, which was clearly marked with an inky fingerprint in the top left-hand corner. Wurster was a dreadful typist.

Laurent thought that if he considered the possible consequences, the problem would not be solved. The translator fellow had said that Papie's transgression would be a *Milice* matter, which meant, immediately, that they would be back.

Yves would have to take Laurent's place again, in case they came to Murblanc, but Bernard had put on a good show yesterday, they were unlikely to return to the Teulière house, so that could be risked if both Bernard and Jean-Marc were kept out of sight. Hilaire the baker could make a show of goodwill by presenting his papers, though Laurent himself had no idea whether he had a document to prove he was milling, but Hilaire would have to deal with that himself, there was no time for anything elaborate. That left the other four, Boissière, Nic, Marcel and Jean. They would have to move quickly, hide. Did Larivière know where his son was? Laurent wished he could speak to JC, perhaps a telephone call could be made from the *Mairie*, but even as he pictured himself talking urgently into the instrument he knew it was impossible, JC would not have been so careless. So that left him responsible, as the mayor had said. His mother was bewildered, she had been all for marching up to the chateau and demanding Papie's release, but they couldn't see the connection, that this was about life and death. Laurent smiled a little. Old Papie would be giving them hell, anyway, those buggers.

'What about Georges? We should get permission.'

'Christ, Eric, you're as much of an old pussy as he is. We don't need that fat gut-sack.'

'I don't know.'

'But I told you what he said on the phone. Just as well I took the call. I went upstairs to ask, but there was no one there. We'll explain when we get back. What, do you think we should leave a note? Have you never heard of security? Come on. You can drive.'

'I don't know. Maybe you should count me out.'

'Eric. This is a serious matter, very serious. Do you want people to, you know, start casting doubts?'

'If you're sure.'

'Course I'm sure.'

Thierry had taken the phone call from *Obersturmfuuhrer* Hummel, and it was true that he had gone next door ('upstairs' was a satisfactory metaphor, British-style, Thierry did not consider whether his pleasure in it was appropriate) to ask permission, though he had taken the precaution of waiting until the two senior duty officers had left for their lunch at noon. They would not return before three. He had been furious all the way back to Cahors, wedged into the truck next to that disgusting Georges Tinville. It was obvious that there had been funny business going on, that those wily country bastards had pulled a fast one. Tinville had been too busy stuffing himself as usual to notice. Now a man had been denounced for illegal alcohol production in the same village, right under the noses of the battalion. It was too much. Thierry felt keenly that the *Milice* were considered a bit of a laughing stock, and he believed that it was the lack of discipline and strict example amongst what he had learned to call the populace that were driving things to the bad. It was no surprise that schoolteacher had turned out to be a Communist, and Thierry wouldn't mind betting there were a few more of them in that village. It was time to teach someone a lesson, and Thierry knew that he was the right man to do it. It was tempting to tell Eric about the pistol, though maybe that was better revealed when they were on the way.

★

Papie could not say he had been treated badly. They had brought him soup and bread at what he guessed was midday, and a slice of omelette later. He had been given a blanket to sleep on, and when they had opened the door after the hours until morning had dozed past, there was a bowl of water to wash in, cold but with a clean towel, and more bread, even warm coffee. Still, he was cold and hungry. It was hard to keep track of the time going by, in the darkness, and the stool was so uncomfortable he had propped himself on the stone flags with the blanket rolled into a bolster. He had relieved himself several times into the pot, and though he had tried to carry it to the furthest corner of the cellar, some of it had slopped and spilled, and he was disgusted by the smell, ashamed that they would see he had soiled the floor. His legs hurt, deep in the marrow, though he tried to walk up and down every now and then to stay warm. He slipped in and out of sleep, though never so thoroughly that when he opened his eyes to find merely a different quality of darkness he did not know immediately where he was. The last few times he had felt tears in his eyes and made a groaning sort of sound that surprised him in the silence and the black. He was still not exactly afraid, though he could not understand why nothing had happened, why no one had come for him. He grew wearier and wearier and the time spent staring dully at the sinking candle shrank to shorter intervals.

When the door opened again, he had no idea of how much time had passed, though his bladder was aching and he felt dizzy as he pushed himself effortfully from the floor. The candle was gone, and he blinked into the dull yellow light from the passage. One of them was speaking in thickly accented French. 'In here.'

Two figures moved towards him, darkly dressed, one of them holding up an oil lamp.

'Hercule Nadl?' They were French, thank God. Papie peered up at them eagerly, stretched his hands towards the first man as though the other might help him to stand. In the lamp light he could see their uniforms. *Milice*.

'Have you come to get me out?'

'Not likely. Contraband brewing is a serious offence.' It was the young one who spoke. Deliberately, Papie let his eyes travel to the holster at the boy's waist.

'Given you a real gun, have they? Call yourselves Frenchmen?' Papie sucked his cheeks for a good gob and spat accurately on the polished boots.

'Watch it, you old bastard.'

Papie stood as straight as he could manage. 'How old are you? 'Bout twenty-five? Where was your mother in 1918? Spreading her legs for the Boche, was she?'

There was no time for his satisfaction in the remark to be replaced by surprise as the butt of the pistol cracked up against his jaw.

JANUARY 1944

The goats were eating hay now, it was so bleak there was nothing else left for them. Oriane thought it would be as well to get the last of it down to the floor of the barn before she got too big to be climbing ladders. There was no one about to help, but she could roll the bales over the edge, and if they split so much the better. It was hard to force herself out into the yard again. When she had let the chickens out earlier the wind had been so bitter her face felt scalded with it. She was so tired, all she wanted to do was sit quiet, as close to the fire as she could. She told herself not to be lazy, and took one of William's grubby jerseys from the hook behind the door, pulling it down over her wrists and bunching the wool around her fingers. She climbed the ladder more carefully than usual, conscious of every step, so when she saw Monsieur Boissière sitting in the straw at the top her first sensation was anger, that the shock could have made her slip.

The schoolteacher looked extremely cold and miserable, as did Jean Charrot, Nic Dubois, and Marcel Vionne, who were hunched up with their arms around their knees and their caps pulled down over their faces, staring at the plank floor of the loft.

'Oh, it's you, Oriane,' said Monsieur Boissière, sounding relieved.

'Well, I do live here. What's all this, Monsieur Boissière?'

'Shh, you can't call me that!'

'Why ever not? What am I supposed to call you? Does Madame Boissière know you're here, sir? And what about you lot?' she finished in Occitan.

Oriane thought that they must have got drunk together, somehow, and rolled home along the Cahors road, stopping to sleep it off. But what would the schoolteacher be doing, boozing with lads from the village?

'Laurent said—'

Marcel interrupted with obvious relish, 'Remember, Prof.'

'Ah, yes, La Moto said, we had to stay here until further instructions.'

'La Moto? Monsieur Boissière, I'm sorry to ask, but have you had a few glasses?'

'Certainly not.'

'Or anything to eat, come to that,' put in Nic.

'Shut up, Ceba.'

'Ceba? Onion?' Oriane put her hands on her hips. 'Get out, the lot of you. You should be ashamed, Monsieur Boissière, showing yourself up. Just you go home to your wife now. And as for you three, your mothers will be hearing about this. Go on, out!'

'Oriane, we really can't. Up there, the tents. We can't be seen on the road.'

'Is this business to do with Papie Nadl, then?'

'You could say that.'

'And you want to stay here? You could come into the kitchen you know. There's no sense freezing out here.'

'We can't.'

'Well, make yourselves useful then. You three, get that lot of hay down for me. It'll warm you up. I suppose I'll go and see if there's some soup in the house, will I?'

They nodded sheepishly, tired little boys, but later, when she returned for the empty soup pot, the hay was on the floor of the barn, and the four men were gone.

'He's pissed himself.'

'Never mind that. Is he breathing?'

'I don't know. I think he hit his head. Look. We shouldn't of did it, Thierry, we shouldn't of come.'

Eric felt his arms wet with moisture, though his skin felt strangely hot in the freezing air of the cellar. He started to cry. 'I think we've killed him, Thierry. You killed him, you did.'

The bones of Thierry's face stood out sharp in the lamp light, his eyes were bright pinpricks and his breath came rapidly, as though he had been running. Eric sat on the floor next to the old man's body and hid his face in his arms, gasping. Thierry kicked at him savagely. 'Get up, get up, you stupid cunt. We have to get him out, put him in the truck. Move!'

The sour smelling form huddled in the damp blanket was pathetically light. Eric supported it under one shoulder, cooperating at least, though his face was dazed and smeared with tears. Thierry's thoughts were already moving ahead, probing the walk across the yard. They would have to get rid of it. There were plenty of places they could hide it, up on the plain, one of the shepherds' huts, maybe, where no one would come until the spring. Eric wouldn't talk, he was sure of that, though he needed a story he could understand, something he could go along with.

'We could say he was a Communist,' said Eric doubtfully, 'like that schoolteacher.'

Thierry considered. There was no way they could get the body out of the chateau unnoticed, no possibility of merely hiding it and expecting it to vanish. He spoke gently to Eric, his own fear passed.

'There's no need. We didn't kill him. He's old, he was probably a bit frightened. His heart gave out when he, when he fell. That's all.'

'Is it?'

'Yes. It's a shame. We'll make a report, then we'll get on home.'

Von Scheurenberg was able to notice, from the part of himself that somehow stood back from all that was happening, the significance of his own lack of dismay. He would have bawled them out once, these two snivelling incompetents in their pathetic uniforms, but as it was he simply needed them to be gone. It wasn't important any more, one old man.

'Tell them to see the mayor, then,' he told Hummel swiftly. 'Then get him home. They'd better take Sternbach to translate. Just get the lot of them out of my sight.'

Hummel clicked his heels and the door closed. Von Scheurenberg looked at his watch and saw that it was several hours before he could decently have a drink.

★

When Laurent arrived back at Murblanc that night, pleased with what he had accomplished, it was to find his mother and Cathérine sitting shocked in the kitchen. They had not even lit a lamp. Papie lay stretched out on the table. There was no need for an explanation.

'William was here,' said Cathérine. 'He kept trying to wake Papie up.'

Laurent looked at his grandfather, shrivelled and broken. As far as he knew, the old man had never done harm to anyone. His mother was weeping behind her hands.

'Go for the priest,' he told his mother. 'Cathérine, put me a clean shirt and something to eat in a bag. I have to go out, but I'll be back as soon as I can.'

He approached his mother, trying to think of some words of comfort, but he settled for touching her gently on the shoulder. She did not look up.

Outside, as he kicked the bike into life, he could feel the sweat on his skin turning to ice. He knew he wouldn't find JC in Cahors, but if he waited a while, he would find someone who could. Papie's donkeys raised their heads at him as he rode up the lane, and he looked for their sad patient eyes in the dark.

January 1944

François twisted in his blanket and looked around the low room. The moon was so bright through the one tiny window that he could clearly see the smoke-stained beams standing out on the whitewashed ceiling. The other three appeared to be sleeping. At least it was finally warm. They had come to Aucordier's, two of the strange brothers he had noticed so long ago at the dance in the barn. He didn't know their real names. The older called himself Pastre, the younger, whose eyes were peculiar, one brown and one blue, huge and startled in his wan face, said he was Lebre. 'Hare,' Marcel had told him. They had filed in silence down the rise where Oriane Aucordier kept her goats and then tracked along the hedgerows to the river. The two brothers had hardly broken their stride, just waded in, though the stream was running strong and the painful water was waist deep. François's trousers were stiff as they began to climb towards Saintonge, emerging from the fields to cross the road at a run below the Chauvignat place, then along a cart track for a while until Pastre pointed to a tiny path that wandered off through the chalk. They took it as the night fell around them, panting and stumbling with only the steady sound of the brothers' boots ahead to keep them in line. After what seemed like an hour or so, François felt the trees recede and the moonlight came clear.

They were in a hollow, with two ivy-covered ghosts of houses, a suggestion of walls and a doorway, and beside them a tiny hump of a building with a cross standing out clear from the roof against the sky. The doorway was a round, elfin-sized arch with an empty niche beside it. François guessed this must be one of the ancient chapels on the pilgrim route, forgotten for a thousand years. The brothers passed on, disappearing into the thick wood. When François and the others came up, stumbling, they saw a low house, the ground floor banked so deep into the earth that only half its wooden door was visible, with a flight of stone steps in the old manner leading to the second floor. There was one room, not even a fireplace, just a hole in the ceiling. Beneath them, unseen animals stirred, the grassy mildewed breath of cows and the sharp stink of goat.

Pastre and Lebre lit a candle stuck into a saucer, took some ancient bread from a wooden press and warmed a thin, greasy soup in an iron cauldron over a trivet set on the heap of smouldering charcoal, which filled the room with a thick woody stench. The bread was edible soaked in the sour liquid, and they passed around a jug of wine, drinking straight from the lip. The brothers solemnly handed each of them a blanket, then took themselves to sleep at one end of the room. Beyond their names, they had not spoken a word. François thought of Charlotte, of when he might see her again. Though he tried, he was unable to believe that this was anything more than an adventure, a sort of camping trip that he might have undertaken with his pupils, Baden-Powell style. Perhaps because if he believed it, he would have to begin to be afraid.

They stayed a week at the hamlet before Laurent and the other one came. François wound his watch carefully every evening, since they were buried so deep here they could hear no church bells and it was his only way of counting the days. With nothing to read, he was wretchedly bored. The lads, Nic, Marcel and Jean, or Ceba, Nenet and Pan as he tried to call them, seemed unconcerned by the total lack of distraction. They helped Pastre and Lebre with the two cows and four goats, mucking out the filthy byre, collecting firewood from the perimeter of the clearing, then sitting silent for hours, dozing and staring at the coals, or playing hand after hand of cards. The living space reeked with tobacco and the salty, cheesy fug of six men. François insisted they boil water in the cauldron each day to wash at least their hands and faces, which seemed a novelty to Pastre and Lebre, but there was no means of shaving and the prospect of a strip wash in the slashing, icy wind was unbearable. He grew used to the stench, and it was preferable to shivering outside and looking at the mud.

Each day two loaves and a pot of wine were left in the doorway of the little chapel. François guessed they were delivered by the third brother, who was perhaps young enough to have remained legitimately in the world. Sometimes there were a few greyish carrots or a bag of squelching, half-rotten potatoes. They ate one loaf in the morning, soaked in coffee with fresh milk, and in the evening there was the inevitable vile soup, and scrapes of curdy, ammoniac cheese. At first

François was irritable from the combination of permanent hunger and lack of a book. After a few days he was grateful for the meagre food, it made him duller and more anxious to sleep. One night he thought he heard Marcel crying, and another he heard little mews and gasps, rustling fumbles from the brothers' corner. Beastly, but then what did one expect, if this existence had been their whole life?

François was overjoyed when he went down to the chapel one morning to collect the supplies and saw Laurent Nadl and another man sitting on the lintel above the miniature door. They were breakfasting on one of the loaves. Laurent's companion was about the same age, neatly dressed in a jacket over a thick sweater, though when he sprang down François could see the weariness around his eyes and the greyness of his skin.

'Morning, Prof!' he called cheerfully.

'This is Jean-Claude, sorry, Mula,' said Laurent, scrabbling down less gracefully.

'Laurent. Is it over? Can we go home? Charlotte…'

'Call him Moto,' said the other man curtly. Laurent smiled as though he had said something funny.

'Look, Laurent, can't we just stop all this business with the names? We all know each other anyway, so what's the point? Are we leaving now?'

'The point,' said Mula slowly, 'is that you forget everything. You're Prof, see? So when they capture you, and you get tortured, you can't tell them anything. Get it?'

François was appalled. He looked to Laurent for help, but Mula started laughing and Laurent joined in.

'We had you there, eh, Prof? You should see your face.'

So François began to laugh too and for the first time, in that cold morning, nowhere, it began to feel all right.

They moved that night. Mula remained with them, but Moto had stumped off down the path, back to the real world. Once again, the two brothers led the way and they followed in a line, heads down, shoving their frozen hands into their pockets whenever the track was clear enough to avoid the risk of falling. Mula walked in front of François, who was shocked to see he carried a long hunting knife, the blade winking horribly whenever it caught the light of the now-thin moon. 'Boar,' Mula hissed at him, but François sensed he had the knife out more for pleasure than protection. They walked for hours, and though François had no sense any more of their direction, it seemed they were going in a sort of circle, bearing left above where he thought Saintonge had been and dropping down once more into the valley. He looked at his watch when Mula stopped to light a cigarette. Four in the morning. 'Nearly there, Prof.'

'There' was one of the shepherds' hovels, hidden beneath an overhang of rock. François guessed they were now below the plain. There was no door, but the roof was sound. Mula said they couldn't light a fire, but Pastre produced a little brass pot of coals from the blanket tied around his back, like the ones François had seen in the orchards, warming the pale petals of the plum trees. They slumped around it, pulling their blankets tight.

'Right then,' said Mula. He was the leader, had been the leader from the moment he arrived. François felt curiously light, obeying him. He realized it had weighed on him, that sense of always having to maintain a position of authority, before.

'I'll be back here at midnight. There's some grub in a basket there. Get some rest and don't leave the hut.'

In a few seconds, the night had swallowed even the sound of his boots. For the first time since he had left the schoolhouse, François slept well.

Hummel didn't think he should say so, but in his view it was a poor show. This was serious enough for von Scheurenberg to be taking an interest, surely? He should be with them. His presence would be a reassurance to the men at the camp, who were apparently vengeful and restive. As it was, von Scheurenberg had merely told him to make a full report. The boss was behaving strangely, that was for sure, and it would have been good to discuss it with a superior officer. Grenadier Koller was waiting for him at attention in the mess tent, looking stiff and guilty. Hummel took out his notebook.

'At ease, Grenadier. Now, tell me exactly what happened. Take your time.'

The private cleared his throat, still rod-straight despite the order, obviously scared.

'It was o-four-hundred hours, sir and I was patrolling the perimeter with Grenadier Bloch.' He paused, as if uncertain how to go on.

'Forget the official speak, Koller. Just say what happened.'

'We had the third patrol, sir. We'd just made a round and I was standing outside the cabin. I was having a smoke.'

'What was Grenadier Bloch doing?'

'He was taking a piss, sir.'

'So he was a way off?'

'Yes, sir, by the fence.'

'Go on.'

'I heard something and I turned around. I couldn't see Rudi – Grenadier Bloch – so I shone my torch, but then something hit me on the head and I fell down. I don't know what happened for a bit, I felt myself being dragged across the ground. They stuffed something in my mouth, it might've been a scarf, and there was something tied around my eyes. I struggled to reach my gun, but it was hard to breathe, it happened so quick. Then I heard them moving about in the cabin. I don't know how they broke the lock. We don't have the keys, the *Oberscharführer* keeps them. There were a few of them, I think, because I could hear different footsteps moving about. Then they hit me again, see?'

He bent his head and Hummel saw a huge greenish bruise at the base of the harshly shaved skull.

'They'd taken off the blindfold, but I still couldn't see, it was pitch dark. They'd tied my arms and legs. I tried to stand up, then I rolled to the wall and started kicking as hard as I could. After a bit, the others came and we found Grenadier Bloch, sir.'

Hummel knew already what they had found. Bloch had been garrotted with a thin wire and there was a single deep wound beneath his left ear. Someone had known what he was doing. The man was propped up inside the cabin under a V-sign, daubed on the wood in his own blood. He dismissed Koller under guard. He would be disciplined, Hummel thought, though he didn't think the man could be blamed for having a cigarette.

They had not taken much, just what could be carried. Six rifles, four service pistols, and the mortars. They must have had a vehicle, or they couldn't have got away quickly enough. No one had heard anything, the men maintained. There was something else that Hummel found no one to tell, which was that he was impressed.

When Oriane awakened to the sound of the latch downstairs, she hoped for a few short, stupid seconds, that it would be Karl. She did not call out his name. Rubbing her hands across her face dispelled any guilty signal of disappointment. When Laurent told her that he needed her to take her big laundry basket down to Murblanc that day she was grateful that he seemed to need her help. He said she was to put a few things in the basket, sheets or something, and he made her wait outside the humped shape of the old bread oven and took the basket inside. When he emerged he was listing, struggling to maintain his balance against his crutch. She could see the tendons standing out in his wrists.

'I'll help you carry it up the hill, it's heavy. Put it in the kitchen and don't look inside. Do you understand, Oriane? Don't look inside. I'll be back for it sometime.' They said nothing as they walked up the hill, and Oriane tried not to show her fatigue, holding her arm stiffly away from her body, as though her belly wasn't there.

'Do you want to eat?' she asked when they reached the thin warmth of the fire.

'I could do with something.'

She heated up the soup, the cabbage leaves roiling under the spoon, broke the bread into it so it would soften. He was sitting at the table, she was conscious of his silence at her back, and that the last time they had been alone together like this she had made him coffee and he believed himself her lover. There had been nothing since but silence between them, never anything but silence. As she set the dish on the table the baby kicked under her ribs and she giggled without meaning to.

'What's up?'

'Here.' Slow, she drew his hand towards her belly, somehow feeling he would pull back angrily, but he allowed his big warm palm to come to rest on her blouse and the baby spun and tumbled beneath their skins.

'He's playing! I can feel it.'

The baby somersaulted, as though he was rolling down a bank, a meadow in summer full of flowers. They would watch that together, one day. Laurent removed his hand softly and took her own, and they looked at one another for the first time in months, too full of words to speak.

'You're a good girl, Oriane. You'll see, it'll all be different soon.' He watched her shyly. 'I've been making him a cradle, well, a little basket, in good oak. He won't be able to fall out if he tries.'

'We can put him outside, under the trees. He'll like that.'

She watched him eat his soup. After he had gone she waited ten minutes or so until she looked beneath the soiled clothes where the snout of the gun peering out at her was no surprise. So now she knew something about Laurent, something she was sure was connected with Papie's death and the disappearance of the lads from the village, and Monsieur Boissière's confused face in the hay. She pushed the basket into the corner under the stairs and laid a brush across it, to

look as if she had been interrupted at her work. Of course
they would not think to look here, she imagined Laurent was
counting on that, that it would be too obvious. He had told
her not to look because he wanted to protect her, because he
was afraid.

MARCH 1944

Jacky came at the beginning of spring, a few months after Papie Nadl's death. Oriane was surprised at how kind everyone was. Betty and Andrée and Amélie came up nearly every day, one of them, and sat with her by the fire in the last weeks, knitting little things and telling her the latest gossip from the village. Amélie even kept her dirty remarks to herself, because the war was on and everyone understood that she and Laurent would have to wait to be married. Betty and Andrée were more sober now, with their brothers gone, though it didn't stop them chattering about the dances. Madame Boissière was very busy with the school, but she came up with a bag of soap and rubbing alcohol from the chemists in Landi, and told Betty and Andrée to scrub Oriane's bedroom within an inch of their lives.

When the pains began, Laurent went to fetch Magalie Contier on the motorbike, then sat in the kitchen at Aucordier's with William. They drank red wine because that was the thing to do. Cathérine and his mother went up and down the stairs with horrible red bundles of rags. Oriane screamed above them and Cathérine said, 'I bet you're sorry now, aren't you, you dirty bugger?' William was so upset by the noise that in the end Madame Nadl fetched him back to Murblanc. Oriane squatted, clutching the bedpost, with the knotted bolster cover between her teeth. Magalie told her about her own first time, there had been a doctor in the village then, and Yves had insisted on having him out, he was so proud to be getting a baby. Yves and the doctor sat drinking in the kitchen while Magalie howled on the bedroom floor, and when she asked if she could have a bit of something for the pain the doctor said it wasn't suitable for women, so when the child came they were both dead drunk, he and Yves, rolling under the *buffet*. Magalie had to pull her son out herself. Oriane tried to smile.

Afterwards, Laurent was allowed to see Oriane for a few minutes. The tiny baby snuffled at her breast, but her face was old and far away, bruised as though she had been beaten. Laurent reached out to touch his son, but Magalie swiped his hand away and said to get downstairs and make himself useful, the poor girl had had a shocking time. Jacky was no more than a bag of skin in her deft hands, his dark hair plastered over his scrunched up face. Laurent took the soup pot from Cathérine's hands and, for the first time in his life, stirred food at the fire. There were potatoes in goose fat. He squashed them into lumps. He managed to get upstairs with a steaming plate and sat as gently as he could on the edge of the clean sheet holding out the dripping spoon.

14 JUNE 1944

The war had been good news for the pigeons, Père Guillaume thought as he struggled up to the belltower. The *Milice* had impounded every hunting rifle in the south, or so they claimed. René Larivière had been obliged to announce the abandonment of the annual Castroux Pigeon Feast last August. This was usually a delirious occasion, when the *chasseurs* warmed up their trigger fingers by blasting every bird in sight, and on more than one occasion in Père Guillaume's memory, one another. The women spent a frenzied day of plucking and roasting and there was a five franc prize for the biggest bag. Unculled, the pigeons were fatter and saucier than ever, as witness the pulpy-bodied yellow chick squatting contentedly in the nest its parents had seen fit to build on top of the wireless set. Other than squirming its greasy stumps of feather, it seemed undisturbed when the priest tuned in. Père Guillaume was panting as he arrived in the loft space beneath the bell. He had hoped to hide the set in the crypt, but there was no reception, so it was as well he had slimmed down a little in the past few years. The chick squeaked and opened its beak expectantly. Père Guillaume considered pigeons to be a disreputable sort of bird, and he enjoyed the Feast as much as anyone, but he took a heel of bread from his cassock and crumbled it in the smelly nest, glad that no one could see his foolishness.

Even with the volume turned as low as possible, it was terrifying to imagine how sound carried across the valley. As ever, he refused to let himself think of it, though if he were to crawl to the porthole that was the pigeons' doorway he would have a clear view of the flag on the tower and its twin high up on the plain. He tried to keep his mind only on the facts, on the connected logic of what he knew, but he wished he could speak English. He listened often to London, hoping that one day the clipped sounds would suddenly resolve, Pentecostally, into sense. He had even tried writing down words phonetically, then trying hopelessly to find them in the dictionary. Madame Boissière could speak a little English, he believed, and it had been very tempting to invite her to listen in, especially these last few wondrous, agonizing days, but Larivière persuaded him that they would be unfair in exposing her to the risk, particularly with François gone. But now they were there, the Allies were really in Normandy, and it had to be only a matter of time. This was confirmed by the fact that they had blocked the road to Landi a week ago, the day after the landings, though Père Guillaume was uncertain if the people understood the reason for the two heavy armoured trucks stationed above the village. He had resolved with René that they wouldn't spread the news for the moment. It was hateful to think, but since Papie Nadl's death in the chateau,

René said it was obvious that there was an informer in Castroux, maybe more than one. So the wireless was their secret, their only link now with the world beyond the valley.

Today he was hoping to hear Père François-Xavier. Although it must be a code name, Père Guillaume felt he knew the exiled priest as a friend. He imagined him sitting in a tall house with London damp and misty outside, drinking a cup of tea. It had been so long since he had heard Mass from anyone other than himself, it was a great comfort to pray with that confident, educated voice so far away. Last week he and René had knelt down weeping in the pigeon droppings and thanked God together. The announcer's voice came over in French, and Père Guillaume hunched over the set, steering his mind from the vehicles that squatted like hellish toads just a few hundred metres away. Père François-Xavier began to speak.

'Today we have received a report from the Bishopric of Limoges. On the tenth of June, at Oradour-sur-Glane...'

The broadcast ended, but Père Guillaume was unable for some time to switch off the set. He slumped on the floor as the alien English voices continued. He could make out the words 'Normandy', 'Americans', 'Allies'. When he eventually stood he felt faint and had to grasp at the low roof beam to stop himself from falling. Tentatively, he reached out and touched the chick's head with his finger. It regarded him placidly. Pere Guillaume told himself that he must not give way to despair. As he prayed to Sainte Claude de la Colombière, he found a smile for the tiny pigeon. 'Your mercy is boundless, no sinner no matter how great his offences should have reason to despair of pardon—' He broke off and his palms came away wet where they had covered his eyes. What pardon could he find, what redemption?

The square looked just as usual, except that there were no uniformed men drinking in the shade outside the café. No soldiers had stopped in the village for a week now, just driven back and forth to change the watch on the road. He found René a few paces away at the *Mairie*, fiddling aimlessly at some papers. It had been impossible for either of them to work these last days.

'Come in a few minutes,' he said.

To be sure though, he let himself into the presbytery and followed the passage through to the garden, where there was a door let in to the vestry. No one would see them entering the church together. For a while they had used the confessional, but that had felt absurdly conspiratorial, and the few old biddies who came to pass the time confessing to uncharitable thoughts had remarked on the mayor's sudden piety. Now they sat in the vestry, where Père Guillaume had tacked a thick piece of baize, which had once served as an undercloth on the altar, to the inside of the door. With the garden door locked and the hinges of the heavy church door left deliberately unoiled, it would be difficult for anyone to creep in and eavesdrop.

When René came, his face eager for good news, Père Guillaume set himself to recite the facts of what he had heard. They had come to a place called Oradour. The houses were searched for arms, although none were found. The people were taken to a field and divided into groups. The men were taken to six different buildings and shot. The buildings were fired. Several hundred women and children were crowded into the church. Then the church was burned. Anyone trying to escape was shot. They shot them against the altar of the church. Six people had escaped, five men and one woman. The woman had lain hidden in a garden with bullet wounds until the following evening. The woman's husband was dead, her son and two daughters were dead, her grandson aged seven months was dead. The number of the dead was more than six hundred. Many of the corpses could not be identified. They were being buried by volunteers from the seminary at Limoges. The village had been burned to the ground.

15 JUNE 1944

The orders had finally arrived. They were to move up to the front in Normandy in two days. From where he stood on the terrace of the chateau, von Scheurenberg could see the men breaking camp on the plain, beginning the preparations to entrain at Monguèriac. He wondered how long the journey would take. He knew that he was going to die in Normandy. When that came, his fear would return, but for now it waited somewhere beyond him, strangely comforting in its certainty, like the promise of love. It was only the journey that frightened him just now. How many hours in the stinking, stifling train with nothing to do but smoke and wonder how it would come to him? Shockingly, it had crossed his mind to see to it with his own pistol, but he knew even as he luxuriated in the fantasy that he would be too afraid. He had not been afraid in Russia; it was reflection that bred cowardice. He would have liked to have spoken about that to someone, how strange it was, except there was no one to tell. So, there were still things to do. He would address the men before they left. The

Wehrmacht soldiers had been taught to say 'I surrender' in English, but von Scheurenberg knew there was not even that possibility for SS troops. Stand or die, *Führerbefahl*. They knew as well as he that they were marked men, literally, he would not have to exhort them to fight to the bitter end, to make themselves inhuman again after this soft time.

He had sensed the bewilderment from the ranks of those who had been with the division in the East, the sense of confusion when you have been in heavy fighting so long that it becomes all you know, all you understand, and after living breathless for so long in the fighting, the time to breathe lies heavy, and the sound of the wind in the trees is more terrifying than the mortars that pull your heart up into your skull and drive out fear. There were things to do. He was wearing his walking out cap, more in deference to the chateau than his visitors, and as he went in he wondered if Wurster had managed to scare the kitchen into producing something decent for lunch.

'Excellent duck,' observed *Standartenführer* Bernd, 'it was one of the pities at Cahors that the wine was so excellent, but there was so little to drink it with.'

'It was very thoughtful of you to bring the wine, sir,' answered von Scheurenberg, thinking how ill-bred the man was. The duck had been good, with fresh peas and a rich gravy. Bernd looked more like a butcher than a high-rank Gestapo officer. He had somehow managed to grow even fatter in the time he had spent in Cahors. Von Scheurenberg didn't believe in fat officers, it looked bad to the men, suggesting both weakness and the wrong kind of power. Bernd poured himself another glass of wine and began to smear a whole fresh goat's cheese on a sliver of bread. It oozed out of the sides of his wet mouth as he munched, and von Scheurenberg shuddered in disgust. He considered lighting a cigarette to disguise the odour of sour sweat that always seemed to hang around fat people, but other people's bad manners were no excuse for one's own.

'Before you leave, then?' There was garlic in the cheese, it poured across the table in the question.

'Everything is in order.'

'I understand you've had very little trouble here.'

'As you saw in my reports, sir.'

'I came with twenty men.'

'Yes, sir?'

'They want examples made. What do you have?'

Von Scheurenberg managed a dry smile. 'There are no Jews left in the Midi. We've a village idiot, but he's harmless.'

'What about the Maquis activity?'

'Sir, as you know, very little. Except for poor old Bloch.'

'What do you know?'

'Again, very little, sir. I judged the moment was too sensitive to stir things up in the village. There was no suggestion of any activity here, never has been. Only that unfortunate nonsense with the Cahors *Milice*. I imagine it was one of the groups over in the Lot. Misguided reprisal. They'll be long gone now. It was in the report.'

Bernd had clearly not studied the report thoroughly because von Scheurenberg had to explain about the death of the old man. He didn't add that whatever happened in Normandy, it was his own belief that the French would destroy the country before long with this habit of fighting amongst themselves.

'Do the men know it was *Milice*?' Bernd's vile fat-cushioned eyes were cunning.

'No.'

'They know Bloch was killed by Maquis?'

'Yes.'

'Interesting. You know they put a sign up in Cahors? On some statue?'

'Léon Gambetta, sir, I believe.'

'Yes, well, the sign said "*Nach* Berlin".'

'Quite funny, really, for peasants.'

Von Scheurenberg thought he had misspoken, until Bernd smiled, wanting to be sophisticated.

'I'll have my men search the village anyway. If nothing comes up, we'll have to make do with the idiot, eh, von Scheurenberg?' He laughed loudly to show he, too, was joking, spraying the tablecloth with crumbs.

Laurent had heard about the dance from Betty. He made a point of popping into the café regularly now, neatly dressed and clean-shaven. JC said it was essential to look as though you belonged to normal society on the outside. Betty was wiping down the tables, her fat backside straining under her apron.

'It's dangerous, you know, Betty,' he said in a low voice, tapping a coin on the counter to make it obvious he was ordering a drink.

She blew her hair out of her eyes.

'Pouf, don't be such an old bore. Nothing ever happens.' It

was hard to remember that the people in Castroux knew nothing at all, he couldn't warn Betty any further without giving something away.

'Will you fetch William down, then?'

'I could do.'

'Oh, go on. Oriane won't let him otherwise, in the dark.'

Laurent drank a glass of *eau de noix* as he tried to calculate the risk. Above all, he had to behave normally. Apart from Larivière and the priest, no one knew about the truth of Normandy, the few newspapers that made their way into the village recently were all Pétainiste propaganda. The dances had been going on in secret for over a year. Laurent assumed that they knew all about it and sensibly turned a blind eye, and Betty was crazy for dancing, for all she was so plump. If he tried to talk her out of it she would ask questions, he couldn't afford that, he had to keep his eyes on the priority. He could coast down the hill with the engine off as he'd planned anyway, then push the bike along the track and cut around Saintonge. It would be more effort, with his leg, but it would be even safer.

'Go on, then,' he said to Betty, so she gave him the drink on the house.

Laurent reached Monguèriac about eleven, slowing down carefully as soon as he came in sight of the roadblock. They had cut off the bridge over the Tarn beneath the first of its high fancy towers. The clock ticked loudly in his head as he handed over the papers JC had provided. They were authorized by a *Milice* man and a doctor in Landi. 'One of ours,' JC said. He was going to the hospital to see about an infection in his stump. The French speaker asked why he was so late. That was easy, the bike had broken down and he had to fix it. He would go to the hospital now and wait until morning. Don't be too eager, JC had warned, they'll suspect if you seem too honest, try to seem a bit rude.

'Search the bike.'

Laurent thanked God he had remembered to get rid of the gun. The gun Lebre had taken before he slid his neat little gutting knife into the hollow below the soldier's ear. How could he almost have been so stupid? JC had said he should have it as his own, for Papie. But it was all right, he'd slipped it into William's violin case as they reached the barn. The boy held his instrument like a baby all the time, it would be easy to take it back when things were over. He was safe, there was nothing in his pannier but some bread and butter and a clean shirt.

'Show us the leg.' It took a few minutes to dismount and take off his trousers, though Laurent did so as swiftly as he could, in case they suspected he was a diversion. He was proud of the leg, though it itched something terrible. For a week he had kept the stump bound in damp rags until it began to stink, and when he had unwrapped it this evening there was the expected cheesy fungus coating the spongy flesh. He had ripped at it with his nails until the white rind was tattered and oozing bright blood, then bound it back up with a morsel of greening bacon hidden in the bandage. In the torchlight it had the desired effect.

'For fuck's sake put that away!'

As they waved him on he looked at Papie's watch and could hardly believe that just five minutes had passed. The hospital was on the other side of the cathedral square, towards the railway. He was on time and, incredibly, it looked as though it was going to happen.

JUNE 1944

Cécile Chauvignat killed the last of her secret pigs. She'd had a good price for them, over to Landi, but now the road was blocked the meat could be put to better use. She planned to give a good bit to Madame Larivière as an insurance policy. Cécile had devised a wire noose that slipped over the pig's snout, pulled tight, and silenced the screams.

'Die, pig,' she muttered urgently.

She felt regretful as she straddled the animal and worked the knife through the throat, the eyes bulging out of its head. It was a shame to kill it so early. Cécile was very frightened. She was sure that no one connected her with Papie Nadl's death, which was not what she had intended at all by her letter, but no one would believe her if it came out. And now they were leaving it was bound to come out. She had no idea what had happened to Papie, but she knew his arrest must be because of her letter. That was why the Germans had killed him. You had to look out for yourself, Emile had said, that was why he had accepted the STO call up.

That was all the letter had been, Cécile told herself, looking out. She had no understanding that her pigs, if they came to light, would be a *Milice* matter, not for the soldiers. She had thought that if she were caught, they would have her letter and that would prove that she was an honest citizen, keeping her eye on others' misdoings, so she would not be punished. Besides, Laurent Nadl was walking out with that Aucordier girl, who'd proved she was no better than she should be, just like her mother, who hadn't been too proud to accept work from her and Emile, for all her daughter marched about the place as though she and that brother of hers made their own laws. That was what you got for charity.

So it was as well to kill the pig in case anyone came snooping around, and she thought Madame Larivière would speak up for her if there was any trouble. She collected the blood in its basin and regretfully poured it down the privy; there was no time for making up puddings. As it was, the meat would be too bloody, there was no time to hang it right, but she set swiftly to work hacking at the carcass, wrapping a whole leg in a sack and adding a big slice of oozing loin. She would go over to the Larivière house on her bicycle after dark.

She set off after a late supper, about ten o'clock. The pork was well-covered, but it would be impossible to disguise it if anyone looked. As she cycled down the lane from Saintonge, she saw the dim lights of two vehicles crossing the bridge over the Landine. Cécile panicked. She skewed the bicycle around and bumped along the verge, nearly falling into the ditch, which was alive with frogs at this time of year. One of the parcels fell into the water, but there was no time to retrieve it, she dragged the bike up the bank and plunged into the Teulière poplar plantation. Weaving through the trees, she thought she would stop at the old barn. She could hide the meat there, or, if it seemed safe, continue along the river bank until she was below the mayor's home. Mosquitoes dived at her face, the frogs gurgled loud and happy. The barn came into view below her and she hurried, desperate to be safe inside its walls, but she saw that the walls were already illuminated with a soft glow from the open door, and there was the unmistakeable sound of William Aucordier's violin.

Cécile sat on the ground at the edge of the trees. There were cigarettes in her apron and she lit one. It was a habit she had picked up from Emile, and she needed her little cigarette now, it was one of the good things about her trips to Landi with the meat. They must be dancing again in the barn. She sucked at the smoke. Why? Everyone knew it was forbidden, she was taking a big risk herself being out at this time. Laurent Nadl must be behind it somehow. She had her suspicions about him, she had seen him coming out of the woods at Saintonge early in the morning a few months ago. He had raised a hand to her and driven off on that motorbike of his, looking quite normal, but now she began to wonder. Everyone in Castroux knew how he and Larivière had tricked the *Milice*, but they had vanished for good afterwards, the schoolteacher, Marcel Vionne, Nic Dubois, Jean Charrot. They were up to something, all of them. She had thought of writing another letter, but after what happened to Papie she had been afraid, and besides, they wouldn't be able to prove anything. It was very warm, she smelt the tinny scent of the fresh pork through the sacking and began cautiously to push the bicycle towards the river. Either way then, she had a secret.

Cécile was safely back in her kitchen by midnight. She changed into her nightgown, put her dirty clothes to soak, and washed her face and hands. As she splashed at the basin she thought she heard a noise, but it was not until she was reaching for the towel that it resolved itself into the sound of an engine. She blew out the lamp and leaped under the bedclothes, sure that the sound of her heart could be heard above the counterpane. There was a banging at the door. 'Open up, open up!' She mussed her hair to make it look more that she had been sleeping and took the bedside candle. As soon as she opened the door, three men in black clothes swept into the room like a gale. In a few seconds, it seemed, everything in her kitchen was overturned, plates smashed, the log basket and the chairs kicked over, pots spinning and ringing across the floor.

'Sorry, Madame,' one of them sneered, 'we just need to check you've nothing to hide. Your papers?'

As Cécile went to the *buffet*, she saw through to the scullery. A black tunic was bent over the bucket under the sink.

'What's this?'

'Clothes, my work clothes.'

'There's blood here. Why?'

'Pigs. We've a pig farm.'

'Fucking too right.' The tunic laughed, sniffing the air ostentatiously. It struck Cécile that he knew French very well, to swear like that.

'I was killing a pig. I could show you the certificate. It's all in order.' Praying, praying that they wouldn't ask to count the animals.

'Let's have them then.' The one who had spoken first held out his hand.

'I'll just get a lamp. I need my shoes. Everything's in the barn.' The barn. Cécile turned around, squaring up to them. 'Anyway, I don't know what you're bothering me for. My husband's in Germany you know, a volunteer. Emile Chauvignat, you can check that too. Bothering people in their beds when there's all sorts going on down there.' She stopped as though she had made a mistake.

'What do you mean?'

'Nothing. I'll get those certificates.'

A black arm shot out and shoved at her, backing her against the edge of the fireplace. The cornerstone was warm behind her head.

'What did you mean?'

After that it was easy. Cécile took them up to the *grenier* from where, if they screwed up their big bodies to peer through the half-moon let in the stone, they could clearly see beyond the steep fall of poplars to the lights in the barn. After that, the pigs were forgotten.

Karl was with Willi. They decided to drive back to the square and report to *Haupsturmführer* Hummel. Then, Willi said, they would surely go straight to the barn. Willi was excited, his eyes swift and gleaming. In the darkness of the truck Karl suddenly remembered him roaring from the trammel of the tank, firing blind, his sweater slick with blood like a seal. 'Here we go again, boys,' Willi muttered as the car swung down the lane. 'Here we go.'

JUNE 1944

Prof felt sick as he inched his way along the parapet of the viaduct. The gun was strapped across his chest. He must not look down. He couldn't understand why Moto had selected this task for him. Even after the months of target practice he could barely hit a rabbit for the pot. At least a man was bigger. Moto had tried to explain, 'You're too slow, Prof. All those books.' He patted the remains of Prof's belly. 'It'll take you with it.'

'I don't care,' said Prof stoutly, 'if that's what's necessary.'

'No good playing the hero. We need your brains.'

It was true. Prof was proud of how he had worked out the plan for Moto. When they had the news that the Allies had truly landed in Normandy, Mula said that all units were concentrating on stopping reinforcements from reaching the coast. This would be the last big push. The idea was easy, but it was Prof who worked out the details against the timetable, which they had obtained from the coded telegram from Mula's contact at the station in Toulouse. He had thought of how to time it, everything. But now it all depended on him getting it right, and he only had one chance.

It was now ten minutes to midnight. Prof's feet moved with heavenly relief into the wider space of the central alcove. He unstrapped the gun, knelt down in position, set the torch at his left. Lucky it was a clear night, he could easily make out the figure, dark silhouette against dark, as it moved along the bridge to the signal box. It was time. He depressed the button on the powerful torch, wiping his trembling hand swiftly on his trousers before bringing it up to the shaft. The figure turned immediately, one arm up over the eyes, the other going for his pistol.

'Who's there?' it called as Prof fired, aiming just below the pale blur of a face. He closed his eyes as he squeezed the trigger. When he opened them, the figure was no longer visible. Almost immediately he heard the first of the explosions behind him. He was shaking. 'Don't hurry, don't look,' he repeated aloud, 'don't hurry, don't look.' The chant became the rhythm of the approaching train as the rails began to hum, fields of space below him. He gained the bank and scrambled up, rolling down and sideways into the scrub, covering his ears as it blew. The noise took every part of his body and hammered it into the ground. His face was in the earth, he tried to breathe, but his heart was banging in his head with the vibration, he couldn't force it back into his chest. Gasping, he spread his arms and clawed at the earth, trying to pitch his weight against the booming echo that threatened to pull him up with the tornado of sound. Then he was gone from himself, gone beyond thought until he arrived, sprinting beneath the sky alive with fireworks of bullets, at the track above the viaduct where Moto was waiting. 'Good work, Prof.' He heard only his own blood in his ears, louder by far than the screams of the dying.

For the present, Hummel was reporting to Bernd. He knew the orders. He had thirty men, ten of his own division as well as Bernd's Gestapo. He had strolled along the river bank many times, enjoying the picture of the tall poplars along the stream turning through the seasons. He moved the boys at a jog, weapons down. They fanned out silently around the building and Hummel was proud to see how swift and supple they were, moving softly through the dark. They were not to shoot, though they all knew well how to make it look as though they were going to. When he saw that the doors were open he had a better idea than storming in. He beckoned the men back.

Watching for a moment, Hummel thought that the scene inside the barn looked like a painting, a Brueghel illuminated by La Tour. The few oil lamps set on the bosses of the uneven pale stone walls blended the end of the space into deep gentle shadow from which the faces of the dancers emerged briefly, a kaleidoscope of feature and expressions. A row of wooden clogs stood along a wall, a table was covered in jugs and cheap thick water glasses, stained with wine that changed from ruby to plum as the dancers wove in and out of the light, moonbeams through stained glass. To Hummel's surprise, the music was supplied by the idiot lad he had seen around the village, one huge ear cocked towards a violin that he handled in an odd, undisciplined manner. For a long while, as the dancers gradually stopped and fell silent, the boy played on, oblivious, played all the while the black ghosts ranked still in the doorway, and when he stopped, his sleeve plucked gently by one of the young women, he looked astonished, it seemed to Hummel, not by the presence of the soldiers or the sour fear that came off his companions, but by the quality of the silence.

Hummel looked to Sternbach. 'Tell them to separate, women on the left, men on the right.' Sternbach repeated the order in French and the people obeyed like chastened children. Separated, there were far fewer men than women, none of them young. The idiot held his violin to his chest like a baby. First, Hummel's men worked along the two lines, examining papers. Many were unable to produce anything. They emptied out the bags and bundles heaped by the clogs, shone their torches along the point where the walls met the beaten earth floor. One of the women called out something, Hummel inferred that she was explaining she was not from Castroux, that she had come from one of the other villages. The violin case was found and the boy made a high chirruping noise, craning his head forward anxiously as the men on either side of him patted at his shoulders as though soothing a horse. When Hummel saw what the case contained he was relieved. This was what Bernd had wanted, and he had found it.

As always when she woke in the night, Madame Larivière thought that Jean-Claude must have come home. René had taken to locking the door of an evening, so he must have used his key. She looked around the bedroom for René, bewildered, before she realized that the shouting she heard below must be connected with the banging she had heard faintly through her dream. Still there was time to feel the quick clenching ache of loss. She pulled her shawl over her nightgown and went down to the kitchen. The air was cool, a soft breeze from where the door had been. René was bent over the table in his pyjamas, his arm twisted up behind his back, held there by a blond man in a black tunic. Madame Larivière screamed. There were more of them crowding through the doorway, pushing into the house, surging over it like huge beetles. 'It's all right,' René called, 'just get me my clothes.' Madame Larivière was unable to move or to understand what was happening.

'Go on.'

She moved back to the staircase, but one of them blocked her way. He followed her into the bedroom and stood behind her as she fumbled for the trousers and shirt René had draped over the chair. She caught a glimpse of him in the glass and saw he had his gun out. It was pointing at her.

One of them spoke French. He asked her for her husband's papers.

'He's the mayor,' she said stupidly.

'Tell the priest,' said René in Occitan.

'What was that?'

'Nothing.'

The man struck René across his face with the end of his pistol. Madame Larivière watched as her husband's mouth bloomed red. Then they said something in their own language and she felt herself being pushed outside, a hand on either arm. René was climbing into a car, trying to keep one hand to his bleeding jaw. Behind her she could smell burning, she was too frightened to look back. 'It has begun,' she thought. As she was marched along the road in her nightgown she said the Hail Mary to herself, and though the stones hurt her bare feet she was determined not to stumble, in case it looked as though she was afraid. It was only when she saw where they were taking her, saw the faces gathered inside, that she tried to struggle. But the faces were watching her, then she tried to make it look as though she was shaking off those black arms so as to make her way into the church alone.

JUNE 1944

Normandy. Everyone knew they were going to Normandy. The Americans would be there. Karl thought he would write to his parents in the train if he made it, but now he sat on his cot and awkwardly scribbled a letter to Ursula, clutching a candle in his left hand. His wife. Willi had been right of course, but he couldn't really say he had any feelings for her, or the child, beyond a sense of duty that seemed increasingly abstract in all respects. The thing he would do now was for Oriane.

Willi collapsed on his cot without even bothering to undress, and in a few minutes he was snoring. Karl waited a little while more, then moved out into the darkness without bothering to try to be quiet. It would look better if it seemed as though he was going for a piss or a last cigarette. It took him fifteen minutes on foot to reach the *Mairie*. He wondered if the women were watching him from where they had been rounded up in the church. The lads outside were smoking in a huddle, giving a desultory glance now and then to both the locked doors. He caught a little of their conversation. Normandy, Normandy.

Karl explained that William Aucordier, the idiot, was wanted at the chateau. They didn't question him, just went inside and in a few minutes the boy was marched out between them, still clutching his violin. Karl spoke in French, 'Hello, William. Don't worry. Oriane is waiting for you.'

When he heard his sister's name, the boy's grey, tear-stained face became radiant with a smile and he took Karl's proffered hand trustingly, though Karl tried to twist his own features into an expression of disgust for the benefit of the watch.

At the bridge they took the track that led around the hill, making their way slowly past the shrine to where the path led up into the chateau wood. The frogs splashed and sang around them in the brook and Karl shone his torch cautiously from time to time, anxious not to slip into the teeming slimed water. He had the key in his pocket. As they moved into the thicker cover of the trees, Karl heard the sound of a motorbike somewhere on the other side of the hill. He pulled William down next to him in the prickling scrub, close enough to smell the sweat in his jacket, praying the boy would not make any of his stupid noises. But William seemed to think they were playing a game, he lay silent with his ear cocked to the ground and it occurred to Karl that this peculiar musician could hear things that other people could not. They breathed for ten minutes or so in the leaf mould.

Just as Karl was about to move on, there was an explosion of life from the direction of the house. He heard cars starting up, whistles blowing the reveille, though it was still the middle of the night. There must have been a message then, on the bike. New orders? Karl thought of Bloch, of the gun they had found in William's case. If something had happened, he could shoot William now, make something up, get away with it. Then, distinctly, the sound of boots marching towards them. He scrabbled desperately further into the undergrowth, thorns tearing at his face and hair, and clapped a hand over William's mouth as a dull moon of torchlight appeared beside them. He held his breath as the party came past, six of them.

'This Nadl's got something to do with it, for sure.'

'We'll have him.'

'They've gone for the other one too. Larivière.'

'Bastards.'

So they were heading for Murblanc, the farm where the old man had lived.

Whatever was happening, Karl saw that it was imperative he get back to be seen and counted. He hardly waited for the sound of the men to die away before dragging William up and almost sprinting the last steep stretch to the abandoned bridge. His hand was so wet he dropped the key twice before he got the door open. At the last minute he grabbed the violin from his arms, trust him to start plucking it or some idiocy. He wanted to throw it in the bushes, but if it was found nearby it would be too risky. He would hide it, then break it into pieces when he had time. Now he had to get back to the house.

He scrambled out of the woods at the back of the stables and bent over with his head between his knees to catch his breath. There was a mirror in the stall the division had converted into a shower-room, he should try to tidy himself up before anyone saw him, he was all over scratches, and his hair was full of moss and leaves.

Karl was splashing water on his face when he saw Willi in the mirror behind him, spooky in the lamp light.

'Christ, you made me jump, mate.'

There was something strange about Willi's eyes.

'What you got there? Mate.'

Karl knew it was all done with before he began to turn around, so when he did he was not surprised to see the end of Willi's pistol, hovering a hair's breadth from the fabric of his tunic. The violin lay on the slippery flagged floor between them.

'It's that girl, isn't it? The one with the kid? Her brother?'

Karl nodded slowly. Perhaps there was a chance of sympathy.

'You don't know what's happened, do you?'

'There was a message?' Karl replied.

Willi lowered the snout of the gun. His face was twisted with contempt. 'Your barmy pal has just got the fucking Toulouse train blown up at Monguèriac, see? There was a group of them in it. It was full of our lads.'

He raised the gun. 'I should shoot you, you cunt.'

Karl thought of protesting, that he didn't know, how could he have known, but he knew Willi. Their friendship was dead, and the only reason Willi refused to let his own anger get the better of him and blow Karl's head off right here was because he believed in honour. Karl had never gone in for all that, had even teased Willi about his old-fashioned code, but it occurred to him now that he would be allowed to die like a gentleman. There was nothing to be afraid of.

'Put it down then. You know you don't need it.'

Willi put his hand to Karl's face. Karl flinched, expecting a blow or even a caress.

Almost tenderly, Willi hooked his hand into the pips on his collar and pulled. 'And you won't be needing these.'

'There's a letter, on my bed. Could you see to that? Please, Willi?'

Willi smiled, a gentle, faraway, cruel smile. Then he saluted, banging his heels together.

'Come.'

So they walked together side by side across the dark patch on the cobblestones where William had helped the Marquis to pour away his wine.

JUNE 1944

The sound of the bells of Castroux church counted von Scheurenberg through the night. The quarter hour struck with an extra ring for each fifteen-minute section of what was left of his life, the hour sounded deeper. It had seemed pointless to undress and lie on the bed, but if he did not he knew he would sit out the night with his cigarettes and the brandy bottle. Bernd was bad enough without a hangover. So it was precisely half past two when Hummel came in with the news of the explosion on the Monguèriac line. It had happened at midnight, a motorcyclist had just arrived. Suddenly, he felt truly sleepy on top of his exhaustion. The cruel bed now looked the gentlest, most inviting place in the world. If he could just close his eyes. Instead he rubbed at them roughly, splashed water on his face and lit a cigarette, opened the window. The air was cool now and he had seen enough night skies here to know where the constellations hovered above the landmarks in the valley, circling slowly, raptorlike, as the year moved around. There was Orion right above him.

'Sir, excuse me, sir?' Hummel was hovering in the doorway, undismissed. Von Scheurenberg pulled himself together, like an actor about to step out into the lights. He cleared his throat and began the barking of orders.

René had been left alone for some time, he heard the church bell strike two, then three. He wished he had a cigarette. There had been commotion, engines and running and whistles and it occurred to him that he might escape in the confusion, but he had refused to try the door and, as the time wore on, it became a strange point of honour, that he would remain here of his own free will. It was locked anyway, because he heard the key turn before a hugely obese man lumbered in, bulging out of his uniform. His fat fingers fluttered delicately on the gilt doorhandle.

'Tell me about Monguèriac.'

'Monguèriac?'

'Please, Monsieur *le Maire*, you know what I am talking about.'

The fat man spoke French well, though his accent should have been comic. René had been surprised to find himself in this warm, pleasant room, he had imagined some medieval dungeon concealed in the cellars, dripping with slime and rats, but they were on the first floor of the chateau, in what he thought might once have been Madame La Marquise's sitting room. The room had a deep bow window and retained an air of femininity, with its pale green walls and cream tiled fireplace. The grate was filled with a dusty oriental fan that must have been left over when the family scarpered. René had had ample time to study the little Chinese figures on the silk, busy in their pleated world. The fat man was crammed into a delicate white love seat upholstered in an apricot-coloured fabric. He looked ridiculous in this place, with the dawn just beginning to show through the long window behind him, but the quietness of his voice and the faint scent of lavender made him even more menacing.

'Then tell me about the gun we found in the barn.'

'Please believe me, sir. I really don't know what you are talking about.'

'Do you know William Aucordier?'

'Yes.'

'Where is he?'

'At home, I should think.'

'No.'

'Then I have no idea.'

'Very well.'

The fat man heaved himself unselfconsciously to his feet. René heard the painted wood crack, released from the strain. The fat man waddled towards the door and held it open. René was incredulous. They couldn't be allowing him to go. Up a little twisting flight of stairs the space opened up into a long hall, dim in a single oil lamp. Réne could see paintings on the walls, Greek-looking people twined with hints of flowers. The fat man indicated another door at the end and René walked into a smaller room that had been made into an office.

'Open the shutters, please. You see the village?'

'Yes.'

'All the women and the children are in the church. The men are in your little *Mairie*, with a few exceptions.' He pulled a list from his pocket and read slowly. 'William Aucordier,

Laurent Nadl, François Boissière, Marcel Vionne, Jean Charrot, Nicolas Dubois. Where are they?'

'I don't know. I was asleep. I don't know.'

The fat man made a show of looking disappointed. He looked back into the passage and beckoned to the two men who had pushed René up the staircase. He spoke to them and turned to René. 'I have told them that Monsieur *le Maire* needs a little help refreshing his memory. When you remember, just say yes. They'll stop helping you then.'

Von Scheurenberg was furious. Bernd's zeal was turning the whole situation into a farce. There was the mayor in the drawing room, the women in the church, shenanigans in some disused barn, and now *Unterscharführer* Sternbach was holed up in the cellar, confessing to a dreary little love affair. Like some absurd boulevard comedy. He vaguely remembered the pregnant girl going quietly up and down the stairs with her laundry basket. She had pretty hair.

'I don't have time for this,' he snapped at Hummel, welcoming the fury into him. 'Get the girl, see if she'll talk. Leave it to Bernd, shoot the pair of them if you have to. Just get rid of it.' It was odd, Sternbach's behaviour, he had been a fine translator and a good Panzer man. But he had Cahors on the line, it seemed they would have to swing around and use the roads as far as Limoges. How long? He stared irritably at the map in front of him, trying to calculate extra time the lost days would add to his life.

Oriane thought that things might have been different if she hadn't had to take Jacky. His little body was warm against her, tied in her shawl, one little soft arm escaped and his fingers played curiously with the fringe. She cupped her hand around his head as she stood in the cold stone room, looking at Karl. Karl's face was scratched and his hands were cuffed behind his back. He stood still with his head bent, his eyes on the ground. She had known something was wrong when William hadn't come home, but she had believed that Laurent was with him. Then William had been found at the dance with a gun and Karl had tried to save him. It was perfectly clear and made no sense.

Karl had tried to save him. She didn't dare speak to him, and he kept his face down. His thick hair looked wet, at the parting she could see the reddish tinge where his scalp had burned in the hot sun. Later and later and later, when she remembered that, it was all there was. He would not look at her. She felt no wish to reach out to him, to touch that hair, which she had filled her mouth with, to hold up his child to his eyes that were already gone. Before everything else began, she needed to see his blue eyes. She stared at him pointlessly for a while, then one of them touched her arm and led her back to the passage, past a wooden door. She thought she could hear someone moaning. Was this where they had taken Papie?

The fat man seemed quite kind, he spoke French. He said he understood Karl was the baby's father? She nodded. He reached out and stroked Jacky's cheek with his fat paw, it was all Oriane could do not to jerk the child away. He could see she was a good girl, the fat man was saying, that she wouldn't be the sort to want trouble. Did she know that her brother was a *maquisard*, one of Nadl's men?

This man was a liar, Oriane thought. He was trying to trick her, but he was clever. She shouldn't pretend not to know what he meant, he might get angry.

'I'm sorry, sir, but I don't see how that's possible. William is, well, he's a bit backward. He wouldn't understand.'

'Nevertheless, we have evidence.'

Did that mean he knew about the other guns, the stolen guns Oriane had kept for Laurent? Jacky had fallen asleep, his breath quick and soft against her breast, she had to be careful, so careful.

'Sternbach was trying to help you. You know that's a crime?' She nodded again. 'Now you can help him. Where is your brother?'

'I don't know, sir. Truly I don't.'

The fat man poked his head into the passage and another man came in. Oriane recognized Karl's friend Willi. Willi grabbed her suddenly and held her arms behind her back, she couldn't struggle in case Jacky tipped out. The fat man reached into her shawl, his hand suddenly deft and quick as a heron's beak stabbing at a pond, and pulled Jacky free. The baby began to cry, squirming and struggling, Oriane was terrified he would fall on to the stone floor. The fat man swung him back and forth like a pendulum, his legs in their tiny red woollen trousers pumping frantically at the air. Jacky was screaming, and the fat man handed him to Willi, who carried him away, closing the door. His wails grew fainter.

'Where is your brother?'

When she couldn't hear him crying she would have no more time left to decide. There was no great moment of choice. William died as she opened her mouth. What woke her screaming for the rest of her life was not what happened later, as Ginette came to believe, but her uncertainty afterwards that as she looked into the fat man's expectant face it was not Karl she meant to save, that she wanted to see his eyes on her one last time, with hunger in them.

JUNE 1944

René had read very few books in his life, but when they went
on their yearly holiday to his wife's family at Narbonne he
enjoyed reading the detective magazines. Whenever the villains
temporarily got the better of the detective, they would knock
him unconscious with an ornate lamp or a sudden blow to
the head. Unconsciousness did not seem to be so easily
obtained in real life. He waited for it between the blows, for
the black mist that would surely descend on him, but it didn't
come. Instead he felt himself shrinking, shrivelling up into a
concentrated ball of pain. His wife was in the church with
the children. The men were in the *Mairie*. Only he and Père
Guillaume knew what had happened at Oradour. Something
had happened at Monguèriac. He tried to guess what it might
be, the detective would know, he would produce a train
timetable from his well-cut suit and prove that the villain
could not have been on the 6.45 to Paris. His wife was in the
church. They would be going in trains to Normandy where
the fighting was, Laurent Nadl had hidden a gun in the barn.

'Yes,' he shouted, though it seemed to make no noise. 'Please, yes. I've remembered.' They were laughing and they gave him a glass of water. That was how it was, they would be kind now, they were allowing him to lie on the ground, so cool under his face.

The rat wandered about sniffing at the boxes, twitching its whiskers. 'Shhh,' whispered William. The rat's feet were loud. It turned and squeaked so he could see its long yellow rat teeth. 'Shh!' he said more strongly, kicking at it with his boot. The rat ran away. William was pleased. The black man had said to be very very quiet. He stroked about the damp ground on either side of him until his fingers remembered that the violin was gone. Papie might be looking after it. He was a bit hungry but it wasn't time to eat so he lay on the ground and slept, playing a little tune on the fret with his fingers until they twitched into stillness. After a while he was even more hungry and he wished the rat would come back to keep him company, so he sang a little rat song, chirruping and slurping his lips like the skin of a boiled potato. Then cold grey light came through the open door. Oriane was there with the little baby and some more black men. William crowed with joy and ran towards her. Finally she had come to fetch him home.

By ten o'clock in the morning there was a terrible stench in the church. Nearly all the children had soiled themselves and the women had resorted to using the flower vases. They put them in the confessional for privacy and removed them when they were full. Madame Larivière had broken down and was sobbing intermittently, recounting the story of the mayor's arrest over and over. Those who had been at the dance joined in, saying the same things again and again as they tried to hush the hungry children, trying to find a connection, an explanation. Charlotte Boissière had done her best. She had sent Betty Dubois to the vestry for the communion wine and the wafers, which they shared out amongst the little ones. There was holy water in the stoups. Some of the older women protested, but Charlotte said firmly that God would want them to keep their strength up and anyway it wasn't Mass so it wasn't as though they were eating Him personally. She was uncertain about the theology of that, but it was better they have something to squabble about amongst themselves. She and Magalie Contier had made a precarious ziggurat of pews from which they took turns to look out of the window into the square, though the hours dragged on and nothing happened except the bored sentries changed places with their doubles. There were two windows on either side of the door of the *Mairie*, and Charlotte could discern the bodies of the men inside, changing places every few minutes to allow others to look out.

Several cars drew up in the square. The driver of the first climbed down and held the door open for an immensely fat man, who went straight to the café bench in the shade of the chestnut tree. Charlotte could see the sweat oozing from his forehead, which he dabbed with a white handkerchief. Two more soldiers descended and spoke to the sentries outside the *Mairie*.

'What's happening?'

'What can you see?'

'They're bringing the men out,' answered Charlotte,

clutching the window ledge for support as her knees began to jerk like a marionette's.

'Can you see Yves?'

'Can you see Bernard?'

Charlotte flapped her hand behind her for quiet. The men were prodded into rows in the middle of the square, a gun trained at each corner of their ranks. From the second car the men helped what was obviously a prisoner, the white blindfold of his face vanishing into the silver-gold of his hair. 'Please,' Charlotte whispered to herself, 'please, please,' though she could not have said what it was she was pleading for.

The prisoner was positioned with his face to the wall of the *Mairie*. Charlotte turned her head to the fat man's face and closed her eyes as she saw him nod, heard the instruction and then staggered and almost fell at the sound of the gunfire. Behind her the church was silent except for the panting of the women's breath. Charlotte allowed herself to look at the black heap against the dripping red wall.

'It was one of them,' she managed to say, she felt faint and wanted to step down, but her fingers seemed frozen to the window ledge, the whole weight of her body supported by the contact.

William Aucordier was brought from the third car. Charlotte thought how the noise must have hurt his poor sensitive ears. He was supported on either side by soldiers, and one of them reached on to the seat of the car and brought out William's violin. The fat man was smiling, and Charlotte understood what evil he was about to do. They turned him towards the church so that Charlotte could see his puzzled face just a few metres away. Reckless, she rapped on the window, and William smiled uncertainly as he recognized her, holding up his violin. 'Good boy,' she mouthed.

'Give us a tune then, William!' It was one of the Castroux men. William had no bow, but he plucked a little, pizzicato, searching for a tune. The men took up the note and began to sing, not in Occitan but in French, William's long fingers moving faster, his eyes closed. They were taking it away from the fat man, transforming his torturing joke for William's sake. Charlotte knew the song, she had heard it many times in her years in Castroux, the story of a soldier who comes home from the wars to find his bride at her wedding feast with another. 'Go on, William!' cried Charlotte, though she could hardly force her lips to make the words and her eyes were swamped with tears of love for William and for all the men of the village. For a few seconds it was beautiful. Then they shot William in the head from close behind so that Charlotte recoiled from the flesh that spattered the window, but she could not stop watching as the front of his face flew off intact, the surprised eyes left behind in the sockets, coming to rest in the dust and lying there white like a carnival mask.

JUNE 1944

Laurent struggled on through the dawn. His leg itched frantically, it was surely infected, though it had been worth it. His bewilderment was deepened by the exhilaration of their success, and now he was soaked too, having forded the river below Saintonge. He tried to think it through clearly. He and Prof had arrived back at 'base camp', as they called Pastre's farm, without a hitch, and the others, who had ridden in the truck, scrambled into the clearing an hour later. The truck had been fired down a bank on the old Monguèriac road and, as they had expected, Pastre, Lebre, Nenet, Pan and Ceba had been able to watch the dispatch rider pass on his way to the chateau from their hiding place in the woods. It had been about four o'clock, Laurent reckoned, when he set off on foot back to the village. Physically he was exhausted, but he felt wide awake, fearless. The plan was for him to return to Murblanc and wait until the village was clear. JC said the Americans were only days away. But as he came to Chauvignat's, he saw that there were lights in the village. He scrambled back into the tree cover and worked his way slowly along, hampered by his crutch in the summer growth, until he was above Teulière, from where he could make out that there were lights in the *Mairie*. It would be too risky to go through the village, so he doubled back and now, after an agonized hour of pushing along the hedgerows, he was at Aucordier's. Oriane might know something.

The kitchen door stood open and Laurent knew before he entered that there was no one inside, but he still went through the big rooms, calling softly, hoping that William would hear his footsteps and jump out to surprise him. The cradle he had made for Jacky was empty except for a little grey flannel rabbit with two mismatched buttons for eyes. Oriane must have stitched it. The breakfast coffee was waiting in the pot by the fire, and Laurent was poking up the wood to heat it when he heard activity on the road.

It came to him in the same few seconds it took to haul himself back up the stairs, when he realized the car was not stopping in the yard. They knew no one was here, they hadn't come looking. They had found the gun. They had searched the dance and found the gun, they would know where it came from. Then they would have had the news from the railway. They would know immediately that there was a connection because of the dead one. That would lead them to Papie. They would see that the dead soldier was revenge because they had killed Papie. Then they would just have to look at the *Milice* list of the STO evaders for the names and if they were quick they would guess, and now, with the railway, they would know who to look for. It must be because of him they had taken Oriane, they would be questioning her, assuming she knew.

Thank God he had never told her everything, but it was possible she might tell about the guns. They had Jacky too, she would surely tell about the guns, and he couldn't blame her.

They had his son, his baby boy. He thought of trying to get into the barn, from where he would be able to see any movement on the road, but it was a risk that would tell him nothing. Laurent was not afraid for himself, though his body told him otherwise. He could go to the chateau and give himself up, but that could betray the others. He groaned drily, wished that JC was there. The only thing he could do was wait out the hours in the knowledge that whatever was happening in Castroux, to William and Oriane and their child, it was all his fault.

René knew Officer Hummel well. They had spoken in the *Mairie* many times about regulations, the permission for the procession at *Toussaint*. Hummel had expressed his personal condolences about the terrible business of Papie Nadl and the *Milice*. He seemed a correct young man. René imagined he was well-educated, a gentleman in his own country, and apparently he played the piano. Riding next to him in the truck, Hummel stared frigidly ahead like a passenger in a crowded train whose neighbour has committed the indecency of falling asleep and slobbering on his shoulder.

'I think this is the place.'

The other trucks pulled in behind. As they began the climb through the woods, René concentrated on placing his feet carefully, scanning the undergrowth for the right opening of the steep path. He knew all the hunting tracks around the village, but there was a part of him that wanted his eyes to miss the place, so they could just shoot him here in the woods. Perhaps they would find it and he would have been wrong, his guess misplaced, and then they would shoot him too. Or even if he was right they might still kill him. If he lived, he would have to explain. Père Guillaume would support him. No one else in Castroux knew about Oradour. If this was the only way to save them, then surely it had to be the right, the only, the impossible choice?

JUNE 1944

Thanks to the deep shade, the chestnuts in the avenue were still magnificent, their parchment-coloured candles preserved intact. Von Scheurenberg had liked to walk here in the twilight with a cigarette, watching the smoke curl into the canopy, the throb of the bees calming as the sun went down. He was revolted by what Bernd had done. The man was always a barbarian, but this had a histrionic pettiness to it that von Scheurenberg found mortifying. He no longer cared to disguise his contempt, though he doubted this would penetrate through Bernd's lappings of flesh. How fond he had been of those chestnut trees. It irked him that not only had Bernd made them appear weak, but had spoiled the last beautiful thing he could reasonably expect to see. Von Scheurenberg kept his eyes front, but when the driver stalled as he turned on to the bridge something knocked against the window and it took all von Scheurenberg's self-control not to recoil as the crimson face of the village drunk bobbed at the pane, purpled orbs of eye-flesh oozing inches from his own.

'Was it necessary,' he asked when they were finally on the road to Landi, 'to hang them upside down?'

Bernd's jowls undulated in a placid chuckle.

'Well, we shot them first.'

For hours after the men had been marched out of the square, Charlotte and Magalie kept watch at the window. A few bold pigeons hopped around the two bodies, and the Charrots' skinny tabby, bulging like a sack of apples with another load of doomed kittens, came out to sun herself against the pot of pink geraniums outside the café. When the convoy began to roll past, heading for Landi, Charlotte saw the eyes of the men slide to the corpse tumbled against the wall of the *Mairie*. None of them looked towards William. Charlotte was surprised that she no longer recognized any of the faces, apart from the head officer and the fat man who had ridden in the first car. They had melded back together, these men she had seen on the roads and about the village, of whom she had forgotten to be afraid. One of them had helped Magalie's youngest boy pick up his books when he dropped his satchel, Charlotte had seen him from the schoolhouse window. The smart officers had played cards in the lamp light of the café, a younger one had carried an armful of baguettes on Christmas Eve. She and Magalie changed places every ten minutes, though there was nothing new to see, even the tanks had become familiar to them. Finally, Charlotte watched the last of the cars go by, craning her neck as it turned the corner to the road. The sound of the engine died like a dream, with only the two heaps in the square as proof that any of it had ever happened.

★

René was huddled on the stone parapet outside the tiny chapel in the woods. As the hours passed he told himself that he would get up in a moment and begin to drag the bodies together, do what he could to make them decent, as soon as he stopped shaking, but the shaking continued and occasionally he burst into dry, choked sobs. The gunfire had begun as soon as they reached the clearing. They had no chance. He saw Boissière fall, and a fist-sized hole open in Nic Dubois's chest. Then René had fallen to the ground, where he lay for what seemed only a few astonishing seconds until the pounding stopped and he knew dismally that he was still alive. They left him there, that seemed right to René, because this Hell was of his own making. Several times he attempted to rise, but his head swam and he clutched the parapet for support. His left eye was swollen shut and he was very thirsty, there might be water in the house but that would mean dragging himself between the six bodies. The air lilted with the hum of insects, he watched the sun twist the shadows of the trees across the ground. One of the Luthier brothers had a knife, he could see the sheath twisted half under his hip. His legs had scrabbled a while in the dust before he was still. He could cheat them, he could escape from Hell, if he could get to the knife. Slowly he pushed his hands along the stone, so warm under his bloodless fingers, until he managed to stand. Not to look. That was the thing, then only a few more steps. That was how the priest found him, kneeling beside a headless corpse with a hunting knife in his hand, praying for the strength to drive it home.

It was the shots that had woken Laurent. He was starving hungry, and the breeze that stirred over the Landine as he limped across the bridge added to the odd feeling of cleanness inside him. He had seen dead men before. Somehow he felt distanced from everything, his senses blurred so that he could concentrate easily on the next thing, his crutch on the pale road, Oriane and the little baby hunched on the ground outside the church. Relief came then, but her swollen eyes as she turned to him were red coals of hate, she pushed him away, so hard that he sprawled at her feet, scrabbling in circles to right himself like a maimed rabbit. She bent forward over him so her hair fell around his face.

'You did this. You killed William. Just you keep away from me and Jacky now.'

She bent closer so he could feel the vicious lap of her tongue in his ear. 'He's no son of yours, see? You're a joke of a man. He's one of theirs, understand? But you killed my William, not them. I hate you, Laurent Nadl.'

There were hands pulling him up, trying to lift him, and he heard the baby screeching, far away. René's voice came, babbling 'I did right, Laurent. You see? I had to. I did right.' The square was full of the women, René's face was joyful. 'You see, Laurent, you see! I did right. I can see them, I can see my wife!' Laurent saw the women, their heads bare, pulling silently at a horseless wagon. When one of them, the schoolteacher it was, stooped from beneath the shaft, he saw what they were pulling, and knew.

They had lined the men up in the avenue and asked who amongst them had fought in the first war. Yves Contier stood forward at once, so did Bernard and so did Camille Lesprats. No one contradicted him. Nine others did not choose. They were all shot where they stood, with the remaining Castroux men looking on. When the last car had driven away, the women had streamed from the church to find their men, except for Oriane Aucordier, who knelt over her brother's body in the dust. They went to the chateau and found them there, hanging, bobbing among the chestnut flowers in the sound of the bees.

AUGUST 1944

The village of Castroux was liberated by American troops on the twenty-second of August 1944. *Das Reich* had been gone since the seventeenth of June. Jean-Claude Larivière, former hero of Verdun, rode triumphantly into the square in an open topped American jeep, a *tricolore* wrapped around his shoulders. He no longer used the code name 'Mula'; he preferred to be addressed as 'Capitaine'. Beside him sat Laurent Nadl, the only other living member of Maquis group 'Le Moto'. As they approached the village, Laurent watched the unharvested sunflowers in Teulière's field, their swollen blackened heads bowed in the painful heat. They shuffled in the dull breeze, a desert army of corpses. Castroux seemed drab after the colour and busyness of his weeks in Cahors, bleached out beneath the thickened August sky. A few women emerged from the houses and watched the Americans as they jumped energetically from their vehicles, but they were silent, their eyes as colourless as their dreary bundled clothes. The presbytery door opened and Père Guillaume came out in his black cassock, supporting

Madame Larivière by the arm. Laurent watched bleakly as she threw herself against Jean-Claude's chest.

The Americans were surprised and somewhat offended by the lack of interest or gratitude shown by the people of the village, until Jean-Claude explained to them in English, another startling acquisition of his transformation, that Castroux was still recovering from the shock of the departing troops' revenge. In addition to the slaughter of six Le Moto members, they had shot a seventh comrade – Jean-Claude adjusted his vocabulary here in response to a surprised look from the American sergeant, a seventh brother – right here in the square. They had done it in front of the eyes of all the women and children who had been imprisoned for days in the church without food or water, and who included the man's own sister and her tiny baby. But still this was not the worst, Jean-Claude went on. All the remaining men of the village had been forced to watch as twelve of their number had been shot and then hanged by the feet in the avenue of the chateau, which was that castle up on the hill, yes. It belonged to Monsieur d'Esceyrac (even now Jean-Claude could not bring himself to use the title), who had fought with the Division Blindée in Normandy under Leclerc.

The Americans took photographs of everything. They puffed up to the bell tower to see where the courageous priest, Père Guillaume, had hidden his radio set, and Jean-Claude explained how it was he who had provided the supplies for Le Moto's camp, collected from the presbytery each evening by the third surviving Luthier brother. Jean-Claude hoped he would not have to introduce Luthier, since no one, it seemed, distinguished the brothers by Christian names. Père Guillaume said he would be surprised if they had any, and later, when it came time to put up the memorial, this proved to be true. He asked the remaining brother if he thought Pierre and Léon were nice names, but Luthier expressed the opinion in his few words of French that it didn't matter much, 'being as they's deaded'. He continued to live on his own up at the hamlet for many years, appearing at the market with his cheeses, and people took to leaving little offerings at the bottom of the track for 'Luthier le Vivant'.

Jean-Claude no longer spoke in Occitan with Laurent, he said it was an outdated patois and that people should show their patriotism by speaking French. He explained this as they lined up outside the church for the photograph of 'Le Maquis', holding their borrowed American rifles. There were men from Cahors with them, men from the brotherhood with whom Jean-Claude had been working for four years, and they stood in for François, for Nic and Marcel and Jean, the Luthiers and William. Laurent thought of saying that William had not really been a member of the gang, but it didn't seem to matter. He posed at the end of the group beside the R44C, the bike pulled up in front of him to hide his bad leg. Children pattered about in the white midday heat, encouraged by Jean-Claude and a liberal sprinkling of 'candeez' to raise a cheer as the flag was hoisted over the *Mairie*. Two days later, the Americans left and General de Gaulle entered Paris. The Marquis d'Esceyrac marched with him along the Champs Elysées.

Jean-Claude and his men waited until their liberators had departed before turning to the unpleasant side of the business. There was no need to let them see the depths to which some

French people had sunk. He could not listen either to his mother or Père Guillaume, who pleaded that René had acted as he thought best, in an attempt to save the people of Castroux from the fate of those in Oradour. It was not his fault he had been tricked into giving away the others.

Although no blame could conceivably attach to himself, Jean-Claude was aware that any mercy would involve him with suspicion that would be the ruin of his ambitions. He had been unconcerned with Laurent's trembling admission of how the gun came to be in William's violin case, and insisted that what happened at the chateau was a response to the railway explosion and therefore nothing to do with Laurent personally. William had been granted a hero's death, defending France in his own poor way, elevated to the rank of a partisan brother. And besides, he said, Laurent shouldn't trouble about it, these idiot types usually died young.

In the case of his own father, he could afford no leniency. René had been locked up in the *Mairie*, and was referred to as 'the prisoner'. Cécile Chauvignat gave evidence that René was involved in the black market, that he had claimed to have powerful connections in Germany. Cécile had been forced to hide pigs for him, fearing René's threats against her husband, conscripted to the STO against his will. The very night of the raid on the dance she had been forced to make a delivery of meat to the mayor's own house. Jean-Claude's men spoke to several people in Castroux who remembered the mayor's furtive appearance on the night war broke out. They had looked to him for guidance, and instead he had looked as if he had something to hide. They had had their suspicions even then. He had certainly spent time closeted in the *Mairie* with one of the officers. Betty Dubois testified that when she had fetched a glass of water for the Marquis d'Esceyrac, that night, the mayor was trying to ask him questions, surely spying on what was going on in Paris. The Marquis was a hero now, so maybe he knew some secrets.

Magalie Contier and Charlotte Boissière quarrelled in the square when the schoolmistress said that witch-hunting wasn't going to bring Yves back and if anyone was to blame it was the *maquisards* of whom her own husband was one. Père Guillaume insisted it was all nonsense, that he and René had worked together to hide the radio, which was their only connection with the truth, and one of the Cahors brothers looked at him pityingly and said that charity was all very well, but there was no reason for even a priest to be naïve. Larivière was clearly a double agent, he had even tricked his own son, and any help he had given to Laurent and his band was part of a double bluff. It was just as well they had not told him of the planned attack on Monguèriac, which had been instrumental in the defeat in Normandy.

Hitler had been replaced with De Gaulle in Dubois's café. Jean-Claude had made his feelings clear, and so, though nothing was said, a few of the Cahors men slipped away from the cluster of drinkers under the chestnut tree, and after an hour or so, they slipped back. Laurent wondered if the body would ever be found. He was drinking hard, trying to avoid Jean-Claude's eye. Jean-Claude had hinted at an alternative, but Laurent could not bring himself to accept it, and unlike Jean-Claude, he would have to join in. He was beginning to feel nauseated, it was an effort to swallow the thick wine that

Betty could not pour enough of, but he held his breath when it threatened to rise up in his throat. Jean-Claude made it seem so clever, all those long evenings in Cahors.

Since the morning in the freezing goat house, Laurent had been for Jean-Claude because that was what made sense. JC refused to talk about the past, he said it was only the future that mattered now, but Laurent knew he had not forgotten, and that was the thing. He had insisted Laurent accompany him back to Cahors, where they shared a room in the old customs house on the river behind the cathedral. Laurent was left alone in the days as Jean-Claude bustled about with the comrades, but in the evenings they drank and drank, and Jean-Claude talked about how there would be big changes in the Midi now, that the worker would finally have his day. He talked of his days organizing in Paris, and described his months in Spain. Laurent swallowed and listened, and one night told JC the truth. 'Well, we'll fix her, mate,' JC said, 'we'll fix that bitch for you.'

Laurent had wept then, saying not to call her that, but JC had an answer. 'It's simple,' he always said, 'what you do is what you are. If what you do is right, you win. Action is morality.'

And Jean-Claude had been proved right. Laurent concentrated on what Oriane had done, on what she was, drinking his wine, conjuring hate. Hate was his pal, it had kept him strong in the weeks he had been away from the village, hate persuaded him he was alive and explained it wasn't his fault, so he sought it and drank it and listened. When he could bear no more, he gave the signal without waiting for Jean-Claude.

'Attaboy, Laurent. Sit tight and I'll fetch out the girls.'

AUGUST 1944

Waiting, Oriane tried to find herself, walking along the road to meet her mother in the twilight, and recalled nothing but the sometime scent of cherry blossom, and the blood that came in her cheeks in winter as she looked down through the mist for the figure moving slowly up the hill. William had been with her, eagerly clutching her hand. William would have heard them, above the wind in the poplars. And what if the moon shone, so they saw her, or if they came without light so that she would not see them? It was futile, was it not, this game of hide and seek? They would have Jacky for William and the others. She should go, go now, take the child and start walking. But Oriane stayed there, looking down over the valley, staring dully at the flat grey sky. In a while, she carried Jacky upstairs and fed him. His hand patted at her breast as he sucked, contented as William beating with his spoon. Oriane's throat contracted, she gulped for air, breathing raggedly and trying to hold his body steady against her own until the heaving calmed. She lay down with him in the circle of her arms, watching the pallid light grow blue.

The church bell chimed a quarter. Oriane knew when she awoke that the last she had heard was half past eleven. She did not know if she had slept an hour, or if it was nearly morning. Magalie Contier stood in the doorway holding a candle. She had last come up to Aucordier's when Jacky was born. Magalie moved towards the bed. Oriane said 'Here?', but Magalie set her candle down, keeping her eyes to the side, and held out her arms. Gently, so as not to wake him, Oriane sat up, lifted Jacky from the bed clothes and passed him to Magalie. He snuffled and beat the air with his fists. 'Wait please,' she said, her voice low, and went to the chest. The drawer stuck, her hands sliding on the cold china knob. She turned back to the bed and shook the bolster from its case, collapsing it on the sheet. She passed the tube of fabric to Magalie, who gathered it efficiently around Jacky's back, then stepped back to allow Oriane to pass first down the stairs. Six women stood just inside the door, they shuffled a little to let Magalie pass out with the child. The air stirred the smell of ashes from the fireplace.

Amélie was there, and Betty, and Andrée, and Cathérine Nadl. Oriane knew them in one sweep of her eyes. They had men's greatcoats over their skirts, but their shapes were as familiar as the hills around the valley. Two more shapes had their faces bundled in shawls. Oriane felt her fear contract slightly, since they needed this ritual of disguise. Amélie was holding her scissors, solemnly as though she were to lay them on a grave like flowers at *Toussaint*. Oriane sought for something to say, something dignified that they could repeat to one another afterwards, but she knew they would never speak of the still moments here, so she sat in silence on the wooden chair they had placed in the middle of the room. She closed her eyes, felt them gather. The warmth retained by the half-charred firewood relaxed the fibres in their coats and Oriane smelt acrid male sweat, grass, autumn dampness. She felt a hand on her head, a plume of hair lifted from her neck. She screwed up her eyes, knowing she must not see, must not let them know that she distinguished them, the order of it coming to her easily, as though she had learned it alongside them around the stove in the schoolhouse. The oldest game of all, if I close my eyes you cannot see me, and they all needed the sense of it. As the hand tightened, Oriane's head jerked at the wrench and she pressed her tongue against the roof of her mouth, lips tight, seeking her courage in her mother's face when her arm reached out irresistibly, irremediably, for her William's body. She made no sound, contracting her breath inside her abdomen, forcing it slow through her nose. Her head lolled doll-like, pulled back and forth as the hand worked quickly, joined by another hand and then another, though they did not strike her. Quickly, her head felt light and cool.

Two fingers on either side of her jaw, firmly pressing on the skin against her back teeth. The heel of a hand under her chin, pushing her head back, unresisting. Her throat felt long. When she heard the snap of the razor opening, Oriane started, tried to struggle, but her shoulders were gripped from behind, the wrists squeezed together, her legs forced apart and held around the knees so that her wrestling was reduced to a helpless, obscene bucking of her pelvis. 'We won't,' one of them gasped, Oriane too confused now to recognize the voice. She collapsed back against the seat and felt the sweat that had started out all over her skin run cool down her ribs. They would not cut her throat, and so great was her relief that she barely felt the scratch of the blade on her scalp, or the cut that must have released the blood she could feel running hot and thin down her forehead. When they moved away from her, Oriane did not look up. She heard their feet pat to the door. It was done.

Then the door opened once more, so Oriane knew it was not finished. She opened her eyes. Four of them. She watched them stupidly, her hand passing over the bristle on her head, finding the raw welt that bled there. Blood gathered like ink in the runnel of her palm. Their faces were covered, bound about anyhow with scarves wrapped and tied behind so that only their eyes showed, scarecrow men. Nearest the door, pathetically concealing himself, was Laurent. She knew him from the uneven line of his shoulders, the give that he made in his weight for his lost leg. Oriane understood. She rose from the chair, holding the hem of her nightdress and stepped towards him. His quick lurching flinch and the smell of his breath, ripe with drink, confirmed it. Her arms felt compact now, strong as she reached for the knot of cloth strained tight against his hair. It was a moment, a flirtation of a movement, to unravel it and hold it up in her hand, swiftly stepping back like a matador with the dull blue wool dangling before her.

'I know him,' Oriane said in French, 'but I won't know you.'

She knelt on the hearthrug, arranged Jacky's cushion as a pillow, closed her eyes, and tied the scarf around them, then lay back. It was not a shock when the first blow came, but the pain of the cuff was surprising. Laurent had struck her that once, for shame, but in the hot burst of this was the knowledge that she had invited it, had shamed them. They were weak because they needed her pain. A boot found the softness above her hip bone, probed the flesh, then kicked, knocking a sound from her, but she closed her mouth, folding her lips inside against her teeth to keep silence. Her breast took the next, a leaden pain dropping over her heart, then another strike across her face. This time she screamed.

A hand fumbled at her collar then, her nightdress was torn, order restored. Their relief was in the changed quality of their silence, a gathering, a thickening of their focus and she cried out, struggled to cover her breasts, feigning fear to overlay what terror was left. This she could endure.

One. Her thighs pushed apart. She heard him spit on his hand, and swallowed hard as he rubbed the mucus against her. He pushed it in, and she barely felt the chafing. He bucked a little, gasped and was gone. She did not move, lay there, gaping.

Two. Much bigger, he passed an arm beneath her waist and tilted her backwards, ramming hard until he really did hurt her, this one, and she cried out again, 'Stop, please stop,' knowing as the tears came that this was her punishment and she could not trick them from it. Her body must accept, that was all, and then it would be over. He pulled back, she breathed, he shoved with all his weight, all the way up inside her and she howled, trying to get away but he struck her so hard across the face that she was dizzy, her cry abbreviated into a gulp, and then she was sobbing, as he went on and on, grinding into her, pulling at her shoulders to drive her weight down on to him, and the pain came and went, came and went, twisting like scorching wire through her womb to a rhythm that stung in her ears, and there still even she was safe until stupid, stupid, she remembered Jacky, and that Magalie had taken him away, and she let her head fall back to the stone floor.

Roused with a crack against her cheekbone. There was milk trickling from her breasts, cooling on her skin and soaking the rug beneath her. This was shame. She felt stubble on her tender skin as one of them bent to feed on her, his teeth tugging at her nipple as her flesh softened, as she retched at the comfort of the release and struggled to breathe through her sobs. Behind the scarf, her eyelids struggled to open, to show that she was willing to remain conscious, craven now.

Three. She was a raw hole. Three was Laurent, she smelt him under the high reek of their sweat. His skin always smelt of new wood. He lay down on top of her, his chin pressing on her collarbone, the folds of his coat falling around them. It was a moment before she knew there was nothing inside her, that the movement of his hips against hers was a feint. She cried out again, 'No, please, please, no.' It was all she could do for him, now, there was even a conceit in it, at her own nobility. Yet when he lay still against her, she felt his mouth against her skin, and his lips felt as disgusting as a slug, and she hated him. She brought her shoulder up hard, knocking his head back, and spat at him, a dry hiss of contempt.

Four. The bone at the base of her spine burned as it grated against the sodden rug. She felt dizzy again, almost sleepy. It stopped, and she thought it was over, then fingers closed over her nose, he shuffled forward, she stretched and gagged for air and then her mouth was full of it, hitting the back of her throat and running down her chin, then she screamed, screamed, for her mouth was full of burning ash, live and searing, choking her and scorching down her blocked throat, snorting up her nose full of the slime of him, she retched and vomited, spitting and sucking at the same time, her tongue a white coal, her chest stabbed with tiny filaments of white hot agony, writhing and swallowing the vomit over and over until she turned, released, and with her head dropping between her arms began to heave acid, iron blood over her hands.

The men passed quickly from the house and set off down the hill. They did not look at the women, or speak to them. Magalie waited until their shapes became one hump against the moonlight. Jacky was screaming. She laid him on the bed, wedging the bolster against him so that he should not fall. The thing on the floor raised an arm, pointing upwards. Magalie nodded, 'He's all right, you know,' stern, as one who had washed and fed and cradled many children to a fussy first-timer who ought to know better than to take fright at a cry. Magalie pulled Oriane on to her knees. The head looked horribly large, hideously tufted like a nestling pigeon. One eye was closed, the other peered through a crust of blood. A foul pool of blood and vomit, stinking of ash, had collected on the dripping breasts, and it began to slide down the naked belly, still soft and puffy from the baby, so white. Oriane's nightgown was gathered about her waist, there was a long smear of blood inside her thigh, and trails of something else too. Oriane made a little gasping sound, and the rug darkened between her spread legs. 'That's disgusting,' said Magalie, 'making it worse, aren't you?'

She pumped water and carried it back in the bucket. Oriane had passed her hands across her face. Her lip was cut, but the mouth was invisible beneath a swift foam of blisters. Magalie scooped water into a bowl, held it to the burned hole. Oriane sucked, inhaled a shrill cry, spat, swallowed. The water was leaden, but Magalie could not make a fire to heat it. She reached down a cloth and rubbed Oriane all over, even between her legs. No one was there to watch, so she did not purse her mouth in disgust, just washed firmly, as women do the stinking old, the dead. The drawer in the bedroom did not stick under her cool hands. She grabbed Oriane's blue print dress and dragged it over the head, then stooped her own head under the armpit and strained, pulling Oriane to her feet. She wavered, turned, and dumped her back on the chair. When the rug was folded over the mess and carried outside, she went behind for a broom and swept the floor. Now the room looked just the same.

'Come on, then,' said Magalie. She pulled Oriane to her feet and got her to the bed, whimpering and reaching for Jacky.

'It's more than you deserved, you know.' Magalie spoke loudly, hopefully even, but there was no response.

On the way home, Magalie stopped on the bridge. She hitched up her skirt awkwardly, twisting against the little parapet, and turned out her pocket. Oriane Aucordier's beautiful dark hair mingled noiselessly with the moon-blue water.

When it was done, Laurent walked down the hill with the others in the darkness. Jean-Claude tried to speak to him, put an arm on his shoulder, but he shrugged it off in disgust and turned into the Murblanc lane without speaking. He did not go along to the house, just waited until they were gone, then began to drag himself along the road, moving like the cripple he was, bent and painful, a mauled creature whose only will for life is concentrated in the need to die. Oriane had forgiven him, he had understood that. She had pretended that he was capable of hurting her like the others. It was too late to stop then.

He wished that he had done this when he came home, all that time ago, but he knew that it had been his punishment to live, and he had served it out. They would understand, Jean-Marc and Bernard and Yves, it had been wrong to push them away for so long. He wanted to whistle to them, one of the old songs to let them know he was coming, but he found it made him cry, and that would never do.

The barn smelt like cows and like Papie. Laurent worked so swiftly, so purposefully that he did not even register surprise when he felt his leg return to him, steady, where he had always known it would come. The byre was low, but if he knelt he could manage it.

He closed his eyes and saw himself walking the road up to the plain with a basket of apricots, her sitting there on a stool in the yard with her hands all over bean skins and her black hair blowing in the ever present wind.

PART THREE

SUMMER HOLIDAYS

Aisling had cooked little escalopes of veal in a sauce of cream, sage and white wine, with some wilted lemony sorrel. Alex rubbed his hands as she set the platter on the table.

'Luvverly jubberly,' he said in what he obviously thought was a Cockney accent. 'Nice bit o' grub.'

Aisling looked at him in irritation. Why was he talking in that stupid voice?

'Jamie Oliver,' he said, 'you know, bit o' this, bit o' that.'

'No,' said Aisling, 'I don't know.'

'He's all the rage in England,' said Claudia, cringing for Alex, 'he's a sort of wide-boy chef. It's the latest thing in gastroporn.'

'Gastroporn?' asked Jonathan hopefully. 'We must keep up more, darling.'

Now that his joke had fallen flat, Alex didn't bother to disguise his boredom at dinner.

Aisling served cheeses and salad, then a peach *semifreddo*

with tiny almond meringues. She thought Alex very pompous. He knew nothing about food really, for all his talk of the grand restaurants he went to with City clients. They probably went to strip clubs too, thought Aisling, though you didn't catch him showing off about that. His air of patronage towards Jonathan was becoming irritating, and he had made several remarks questioning the financial viability of the PGs. Aisling liked to think that her business was profitable, though Alex had pointed out that she didn't include many of the extras in the books, and did she price the food she served them? If she was honest with herself, the profit from the PGs wasn't that big, but it was something, and though the Harveys were by no means badly off, certainly compared to people like the Glovers, the boys' school fees were a bit of a struggle. Jonathan was fond of telling her that he had sold his computer business at just the right time, though it was hard not to be wistful when all that dot com stuff really exploded a few years later.

Jonathan seemed reluctant to talk business with his brother, at least in front of her, as though he had not once been possessed of a similar brashness. Perhaps that was her fault, a bit. She had been so passionate about Murblanc, so keen for him to retire, that maybe she had forced this role on him, of not appearing to care any more about making money. His fiddling in the study certainly didn't amount to much, but they had enough. It seemed small of Alex, in Aisling's opinion, not to help Jonathan improve their investments, though it did not occur to her that if she wanted his help she would be better off humouring his conceit.

Everyone was rather silent over coffee. The Sternbachs' car was gone, they were obviously dining out. Claudia yawned ostentatiously, she and Aisling began to gather the plates and glasses.

'Oh Christ!' said Jonathan. 'Not again. She's hovering around this place like a bloody banshee. Can't you do something, darling?'

Ginette and her bicycle were once again in evidence. She plodded dolefully right up to the table.

'Excuse me, Madame Harvey, but may I speak to Mademoiselle Claudia for a moment?'

'Is everything all right, Ginette? No trouble with Mademoiselle Oriane?'

'Yes, I'm sorry. Everything's fine. I just need a word.'

'I'll finish this then, Claudia.'

'Do give her a hand, Alex.'

They were left alone on the terrace. Ginette looked a little too wide-eyed, Claudia hoped she wasn't going to have another one of her turns. 'Are those people here?' she asked, looking about as though there might be spies concealed in the ivy.

'What people? Ginette, what is the matter, please?'

'Those Dutch people?

'No, they're out. Why?'

'I need to speak to you.'

'Yes, Ginette. Would you like to sit down, at least?' This was all very tiresome.

'I saw Madame Lesprats in the village.'

Claudia felt cold. Had Ginette come to make some sort of announcement for Alex's benefit? She had to get her away from the house. She wanted a cigarette.

'Come on then. We can go to that bar in Castroux. I'll just

get my bag and the bike.' She tried to smile encouragingly, 'I'll buy you a drink.'

Ginette ordered a small coffee.

'I've never been in here,' she said conspiratorially, as though Claudia had dragged her to a den of vice. They sat outside on the little terrace, away from the group of men clustered around the television inside. Claudia was surprised when she asked for a cigarette from the packet of Marlboro Lights open on the table. She sipped her red wine while Ginette got it lit.

'Well?'

'Look, I need to explain something. Those people, the visitors of Madame Harvey?'

'Yes, yes. Go on.'

'Well, Madame Lesprats told me they're asking questions, that you were asking questions for them.'

'Have I upset you in some way?'

'No, please listen.' Claudia despaired of her ever getting to the point, it seemed better to sit in silence and let her talk.

'Well, I know who they're looking for. It's Mademoiselle Oriane. If I tell you this, you have to keep it secret.' Ginette looked suddenly, unpleasantly sly. 'I think you can keep secrets?'

'OK.'

'Mademoiselle Oriane had a son. Jacky. My Jacky. He didn't know for years and years, but his father was a German soldier. Mademoiselle Oriane told him at first just that he was killed in the war, but Jacky found out the truth. This man, he was a good man, although he was a German. He was killed, but they did it, the Germans, I mean. He was killed because he was trying to help Mademoiselle Oriane's brother to escape. It was the end of the war, there were terrible things happening everywhere around here. Mademoiselle Oriane loved him so much, it was true love, and he had promised that after the war they would go away together, but then he was killed. Mademoiselle Oriane was very brave in the war, she did things to help the Maquis, that's the men who fought against the Germans in the Resistance.'

'I know. I know that's what they were called, I mean. Did she really?'

'But it didn't matter. They punished her, punished her dreadfully.'

'I've read about that sort of thing.'

'And then my parents found out about me and Jacky. They used to live at Saintonge, at the farm. There's English people there now. They took me to the priest and made me say I'd been going with Jacky. Then Jacky went away.'

Ginette was struggling to control herself. Claudia gently removed the burned out cigarette from her shaking fingers and stubbed it in the ashtray. She held Ginette's hand.

'I was, well, you know that sometimes I'm not very well? It was bad. Mademoiselle Oriane took me in, she said I could live up there with her. And we stayed there, the two of us. And now these people say that this man was a liar, that he already had a family, that he didn't really mean to go away with her. It's cruel, that's what it is, coming here with their questions, poking their noses after all this time.'

'But I can't stop them. I mean if everyone in the village knows. Madame Lesprats knows.'

'People won't say, not to strangers. You went to the *fête*, didn't you? Well, the mayor, the one who gave the speech,

Monsieur Chauvignat? That's my brother. I haven't spoken to him for thirty years. People mind their business around here.'

'What do you want me to do, Ginette?'

'Tell them they've made a mistake. They can't come around, it's all she's got, now my Jacky's gone.'

'Do you know what happened to Jacky?'

'We were going to be married. He went to Marseille, we know that, but then – we didn't hear any more.'

'So he just never came home?'

'Yes. He never came home.'

Claudia thought of the compact, and the scratched-in name. She tried to make her voice as gentle as possible. 'Ginette, thank you for telling me. I respect your confidence. But I've already talked about this with Mademoiselle Oriane. She knows, Ginette, doesn't she? She knows all about it.'

Ginette's jaw began to shake. Claudia felt so cruel, but she had to go on.

'So it wouldn't be so bad, would it? The Sternbachs – that's the Dutch people, could probably find Jacky. They can do all sorts of things, with the internet, if they know he's in Marseille. And Mademoiselle Oriane would even have a chance to see her son? That's not what you're afraid of, is it, Ginette?'

Ginette bit down on her lower lip.

'No,' she answered, in a little bitter voice. 'That's not what I'm afraid of. Look at me. Just look at me.'

It was almost dark when they left the bar. Ginette mounted her bicycle and freewheeled down the hill. Claudia watched her as she crossed the bridge, then pushed her own bike up towards the village. She had seen the war memorial next to the church, a squat obelisk surrounded by a little chain fence. Squinting a little in the dusk, she began to count the names. 'Aucordier, William' was the first, but as she read down the list, Claudia was appalled by how many there were, so many for such a tiny place. She felt as though the air around her had become heavy, it was pressing down on her, and she bit her lip and tensed the muscles in her shoulders to stop herself crying. The image of that terrible barren room up on the hill, of those two ruined bodies sitting patiently in the strip light waiting for nothing, was unbearable. That pathetic, treasured little gift, that she had thrown in Oriane's face like a silly child. She felt contemptible, inhuman. They would have shaved her head, that's what was done to those women, they shaved her head, and her little baby grew up to hate her, and Ginette's life was spoiled. Each of these names was a spoiled life.

That was trite, she thought, and then hated the goblin that sat on her shoulder, the pretty, well-dressed sneering goblin that allowed nothing to touch her, nothing ever to be quite real. It was wicked, what she had been planning to do to Alex, wicked. Crazily, she tried to push open the door of the church, but of course it was locked for the night. Then the tears that had been hovering inside her eyelids began to roll down her face and she remembered how she had cried for Sébastien, who had never loved her, and that she would have to go on and on because there was no pity. The goblin chattered like a monkey and pushed long bony fingers into her hair. She was incapable of love, and she would have to go on and on. Oriane had loved her German boy, and Claudia was too cold even to imagine what she must have suffered. She pulled the bike around and pushed off hard so that she felt the breeze dry her tears into track marks on her face as she pedalled down the slope. Her hair was in her eyes and she had a fistful of it, pulling it back as the bike sped over the crossroads, when she turned her head just in time to see the lights of a car coming at her in the blue night.

She had no impression of the impact, she was on the ground before she understood what had happened. It felt obvious that she wasn't dead. Though she was breathless, and there was a dull pain at the bottom of her back, her head felt quite clear. The car had stopped because she had heard the brakes and now there were people running towards her along the road. 'I'm fine,' she called in French, 'I'm fine.' Her back hurt a lot, and the pain seemed to spread around to her waist and tighten like a metal belt, then she gasped and vomited as the goblin's hand reached inside her. The twig-like fingers twined through the membranes, writhing and searching, then abruptly squeezed a clenched fist at the base of her belly and pulled. She could smell the lemon from Aisling's veal. Claudia didn't need to wait for the first rush of liquid to know what was happening.

Malcolm Glover repeated many times afterwards that she must have been in terrible shock, because even though she had blood all over her and sick on her face, when he reached her she was sitting up and laughing.

Claudia stayed in bed at Murblanc for a few days, bleeding. Aisling felt truly sorry for her, though perhaps it was better that the poor girl hadn't even suspected she was pregnant. She wouldn't feel the loss so much. It was brave of her to insist on not telling Alex too, denying herself the comfort he could offer for his own sake.

Malcolm and Charlotte had been in a terrible state. When the doctor had left and Claudia was resting with a sleeping pill, they had to hear over and over again how she had just shot out into the road without looking, there was no time to stop, thank God Malcolm had his wits about him or it could have been unthinkable. Aisling suspected the sharpness of Malcolm's wits, since the Glovers had been at the pizzeria in Landi with those Logans, not that it stopped him swigging half a bottle of cognac for the shock. What exactly Claudia had been doing whizzing about the village in the dark was a mystery, though Richard told her that Kevin had seen her crying in front of the war memorial. Richard and Olly said that Claudia was always crying, and she was probably a bit mental. Aisling thought Claudia resolutely self-possessed, but perhaps she was on Prozac.

The Glovers came back the next day (at lunchtime, Aisling observed), to relive the accident over a glass or three of PG white. The Marquis and Delphine turned up just as they were polishing off a warm salad with walnuts and smoked *magret*. Just as well, because Aisling wouldn't have liked to have had to ask them to sit down with Malcolm and Charlotte, who was wearing ceramic earrings she had made herself in the shape of little pumpkins. Delphine had heard about the crash that morning from Madame Lesprats, who had heard about it on her mobile from Sabine at the pharmacy in Landi.

'She should be a spy, that cleaning lady!' laughed Malcolm, as though he were the first person ever to realize that Madame Lesprats was nosy. Delphine wanted to go up, but Alex, who had been sitting with Claudia, said that he didn't think she was up to it, though it was very kind. That looked rude, Aisling thought, since she had bothered to come, so she took advantage of Malcolm showing the Marquis exactly which bit of car had struck the bicycle to whisper the words '*fausse-couche*' in Delphine's ear. She had looked up 'miscarriage' specially in the Larousse that morning. Delphine understood then, naturally. She suggested Aisling call around soon, if she wasn't too busy, as there was something she would like to discuss with her. Everyone stood around on the drive for a while, until Malcolm rubbed his hands briskly and announced that they had to be getting on, which meant Delphine had to move her car.

As the d'Esceyracs were leaving, Delphine had called out in English that Aisling shouldn't worry about the dogs when she came up to the chateau, as they only barked at strangers. Charlotte Glover had definitely heard.

SUMMER HOLIDAYS

As soon as Claudia felt recovered, she popped down to La Maison Bleue and told the Sternbachs everything. They drove to the village, and as soon as Madame Lesprats answered the door she knew the game was up. Madame Lesprats had heard everything, long ago, from her great-aunt Amélie, even the parts that she felt sure Oriane had concealed all that time from Ginette. Madame Lesprats had never been able to like Oriane, but she was a great believer in romance. Free to talk, she confirmed everything that Claudia had heard from Oriane, including a great deal of detail about the mayor, who'd turned out to be a *collabo,* and the terrible things that had gone on at the chateau.

When they eventually escaped, they had a drink in the bar. Ella and Otto were planning to leave. They decided that the best thing was to continue their research when they returned home, now they had the details there was no need to disturb the old lady, though Ella thought it would be nice to send a letter introducing themselves. If they discovered anything tangible, they would try to visit Jacky themselves, and then think how to go on.

They told Aisling they were cutting their visit short to spend a few days with some friends who had a house over in the Lot. Aisling said they had paid up to the end of the week anyway, but she was obviously needled that La Maison Bleue had been in some way insufficient for them.

'The Lot's more fashionable of course,' she said peevishly to Claudia, 'but I thought they were the sort of people who wanted something a bit more authentic. I shan't bother to do them a barbecue.'

Claudia felt it was unlikely that Otto and Ella would be devastated by this.

It was a bit mean, Aisling would feel less slighted if she knew the truth, but since the wondrous release of the accident, Claudia had a feeling she wouldn't have to be bothering with Aisling much longer.

Alex and Claudia went to Cahors for the day. As they wandered rather boredly around the medieval centre of the little city, she remembered the passionate grief that had possessed her as she stood before the war memorial in the village.

'Why don't we see if the museum's open?' she suggested.

The museum had more earnestness than exhibits, most of which were painstakingly handwritten accounts by local amateur historians suspended as leaflets from chains set in the wall. Many were bad photocopies, their pages frayed and greasy from indifferent tourist fingers. One wall had a home-made sign in felt tip reading 'Le Maquis', with a collection of photos pinned beneath.

'Look,' called Claudia, 'here's Castroux.' She translated the description into English for Alex's benefit.

'Maquis le Moto, 1944. The group "Le Moto" was responsible for one of the crucial acts of sabotage following the Normandy landings in 1944. Panzer Division "Das Reich" was due to travel north by train, but was delayed by six days due to the destruction of a train and lines at Monguèriac, coordinated and carried out by "Le Moto". Seven members of "Le Moto" were shot as part of the infamous "Das Reich" reprisals before the division left the region.'

'That was Larivière,' Claudia explained. 'The mayor told us that he was the one who betrayed the local partisans.'

Alex wandered away, but Claudia studied the picture. It was strange how small men looked, even such a short time ago. Their heads looked normal, but their bodies were shrunken, child-sized, smothered in their ill-fitting jackets. The group was posed before the church in Castroux. Eight men knelt in a row holding rifles, a ninth stood at one end, propped on a crutch, his body half hidden behind what was presumably the famous Moto. They smiled crumbling Orwellian smiles at the camera, several clutched cigarettes cocked over the barrels of their guns. Claudia recognized the names from the memorial: Aucordier, Boissière, Charrot, Dubois, Nadl, Vionne. The photo must have been taken before the attack on the railway, before the German reprisals. She wondered which one was Oriane's brother. That part was true then, but it all seemed so impossibly far away that it was hard to believe there were still living people who mourned these men. Claudia reached out to trace the lines of the photo, but a warning of 'Don't touch' immediately rattled out from the attendant in the corner.

Claudia and Alex mooched dutifully around the cathedral until she thought they had better get on with it and suggested they stop for a coffee. Naturally, the charming café with a wisteria-draped terrace overlooking the river was closed, and they sat too near the traffic outside a horrible little pizzeria. Arabic music played loudly and the coffee came in plastic cups. She plunged in. What was it about leaving people that meant they always showed themselves at their best just when you needed to believe the worst of them? Alex asked if she was sure she meant what she said, that it wasn't just the shock of the accident, would she prefer to discuss this in London? Then he said that he understood, and Claudia watched him try not to burst into tears. He didn't bluster or say anything spiteful, just held her hand and told her that he loved her, that he was unspeakably sorry. Claudia began to cry and tugged off her ring.

'Don't be theatrical, darling.'

'What do you want me to do with it? Throw it in the river?' Her nose was running.

'Do what you like with it. It's yours. You might wear it sometimes, to think of me.'

Claudia sobbed harder and said she was sorry, sorry, sorry, though she wasn't tempted to tell him everything, even now when he seemed noble and she was full of her own awfulness. He fetched some paper napkins from the pizza maker and held them out to her.

'I can't keep it anyway. I'll have to get another for the next one.' He was trying to smile.

'You could ask Sarah Ashworth.'

'Too late, darling. I am irremediably corrupted, thanks to you. She's just too Clapham.'

Claudia felt a little prod of regret, after all he had been to Oxford.

'Not Chiswick?' she said.

They both laughed, at first forced and then really, and held hands as they went to find the car. Claudia felt huge affection for him, stroking the sleeve of his shirt, feeling his palm warm and firm against her own smaller one. Having told him she would never marry him, she suddenly liked him enough to wish she could. They were silent on the drive home though, along the tiny green roads in their hired car.

'I'm going to sell my flat,' said Claudia. 'I think I'm going to find somewhere in Paris.' As she spoke she realized she meant it.

'I thought you might,' answered Alex, and Claudia realized she was a very great fool. But all he said then was that he would give her a number of someone who would be able to get her a good deal.

At Murblanc, Aisling was having a crisis on the terrace. She was clutching what was obviously not her first glass of wine, and as they helped themselves from the jug of rosé, to Claudia's astonishment, Aisling took one of her cigarettes. She smoked it like the men in the photo, held between thumb and finger, her hand curled over the smouldering end. Jonathan was clearly at a loss. Aisling explained she had been to see Delphine, for a coffee. Delphine had shown her over the house, she had opened up a wonderful long gallery in the old part of the chateau. Even though Aisling was furious, she wasn't totally able to curb the admiration in her voice. The gallery was full of frescoes, painted over, but you could see through in the light, it looked almost like Fontainebleau.

'Never mind, Aisling, darling,' said Alex, 'what happened? Did Delphine leave you off the WI cake list?'

Aisling glared at him. 'Delphine wants to make the chateau into a hotel. She asked if we might think of selling one of our fields. They want to make a golf course and a gym and a new driveway.'

'How awful,' Claudia murmured.

'She's going to Paris tomorrow. There are some Americans interested in investing, she said.'

'Americans!' said Alex, and Claudia gave him a look before she remembered they were now split up.

'She thought I'd be pleased. She even asked if I wanted to help as a sort of consultant. She offered me a job, to work for her! As if she thinks I'm Madame Lesprats!'

'Steady on.'

'Oh, shut up, Jonathan. As if you care how hard I've worked to make this place what it is! You'd probably be happy to spend the rest of your life playing Scrabble with the likes of Malcolm Glover.'

'You know, it mightn't be a bad idea, darling. The golf course. This place could do with a bit of investment. Everything's dying around here. '

Aisling stood up and threw her rosé in Jonathan's hapless face. 'You're disgusting!' she screamed, and ran into the house. They heard her feet on the stairs and the slam of her sitting room door.

★

Claudia assembled some bread and ham and tomatoes and set it out on trays by the pool, then took a cup of tea up to Aisling. 'How are you feeling?' she asked softly.

'I'm sorry. So embarrassing, in front of you two. And after what you've been through. It's just, he doesn't see it, any of it, how hard I work, how hard I try. It might not be much, it's not everyone's idea of a good life, but it's mine and I try so hard.'

Claudia winced a bit at that.

'I hate him sometimes,' Aisling went on, ' I really do. Sometimes I catch myself wishing he would just drop dead, it would be so much easier than having to leave him. He has no idea how much work he makes for me, pretending to think he's doing anything in that study all day but look at pornography, that's work! And the fact that he can't amuse himself, I'm always having to get things up for him, he's worse than the boys.'

Claudia was embarrassed for her now, she wanted these surprising confidences to stop before Aisling said something she would mind later. 'But you and Jonathan seem happy, on the whole,' she managed, trying to keep the phrase 'rub along' out of the conversation.

'Oh, we rub along. Maybe he doesn't really look at porn sites all day. It's just, when he said that, I realized I've lived with him all this time and he has no idea of who I am. And then you realize that's marriage. You give your life to a stranger,' she added dramatically, swigging the tea, 'and now that hateful woman wants to spoil it all.'

Claudia hugged her, and Aisling wept loud and snottily in her arms. After a while she fished about for a hanky, producing a scrap of embroidered pansies Claudia recognized from Cahors market. She thought that if Aisling had been born in a different age, she would have made a good colonial wife, keeping up standards to the bitter end until she was hacked to bits by rebel swords.

'Well,' Aisling said, wiping her face, 'it'll be over my dead body, that's all, no matter what that bastard thinks about bloody investments.'

'Aisling, I know it might sound funny, but tell me again about those frescoes.'

'Peaceful,' said Alex by the pool as the distant howls subsided.

'As far as I can see,' said Jonathan, 'the problem with this place is there's always some bloody woman crying.'

'Maybe it's cursed, Dad,' offered Richard, spearing a salty tomato. 'Maybe there's ghosts here.'

'Does that mean we're moving back to London?' asked Olly.

'I doubt it. Imagine how potty your mother would go there.'

SUMMER HOLIDAYS

That night, Aisling sat alone in the kitchen when the others had gone to bed. She had made a pot of coffee and filched another cigarette from Claudia's handbag. Everyone seemed to be doing that, she thought ruefully. Spread open before her were the blue and orange notebooks. She had Alex to thank, really, with his stupid impersonations. She began to circle recipes with her pencil. *Tagliata* of Charolais beef with morel sauce, salad of pigeon breast with pear and hazelnut, mint sorbet with iced cherry compote. She could do this, she realized. Bugger Comtesse fucking Delphine and bugger Jonathan too. Though he was right in a way, it was about time she pulled her weight. Her book would be called *La Maison Bleue: Recipes from a French Kitchen*. The cover would be a photograph, one of the ones she had taken for Mrs Highland that first season, the shutters the exact colour of a summer sky. With a delicious sense of wickedness, she allowed the fag end to buzz out in her coffee cup. It was handy, in the end, that she wasn't pretty, the way Claudia was. The viewers would feel reassured by that, like Delia.

Alex left the next morning. He felt there was no point sitting out the last few days for the sake of it, and it was easy to say he had been called back to the office. Claudia was still wearing her ring, Alex said he preferred not to make any awkwardness and that he could phone up Jonathan after she had caught her train. She was submissive, solicitous in her comfort of his bereavement.

'It's just as well we didn't tell too many people,' he said.

'Alex, I can't just keep telling you how sorry I am. It won't make it any less awful, I know that. But I do believe you deserve better.'

He looked at her in disappointment for the first time, and she told herself she had no right to mind it.

'Claudia, do you think I'm blind? Of course I deserve better. I always knew that you didn't love me as much, as much as someone else. You spend all your time making people think you're perfect, and so long as they do you're satisfied, and you don't care how unreal you make yourself. I felt sorry for you, I thought that if you knew you could rely on me loving you that you might just relax a bit. I didn't want better, Claudia, I wanted you.'

'Shall we meet in London?' Craven. Alex was right.

'I don't think there's much point, do you? But you can always call me if you need anything.'

They made a decent job of concealing from the Harveys their relief to be away from each other. After he had driven away, Claudia took the bicycle to the chateau. The leaves in the avenue were tea coloured, beginning to drift down and coat the grass. It seemed for ever away, Giles Froggett and his ankle. It was a beautiful place, Claudia could see how the avenue would look in a brochure, shot at dusk with the shadows thick and the house opening up at the top like a lost castle. Claudia wondered if Delphine was planning to put the SS slaughter in her brochure. She was still amazed by how relieved she felt, by how lightly she had got off. Everything was suddenly, wonderfully simple, she could even feel sorry for herself if she wanted to − Aisling certainly did.

The Marquis came out to meet her, holding a dog by its collar in each hand. He was very pleased to see her, though, correctly, he said nothing about what he had intimated at the *fête*. They sat on the lawn with glasses of stickily un-iced lemonade, and he asked politely about the Sternbachs.

'I wonder if they'll be glad in the end?' he said, when she explained. 'It's terrible, the things that were done here. Not so well known as Oradour, of course, but dreadful, dreadful.' There was a sort of pride in his voice. Claudia didn't want to get started on the war, so she asked him quite directly about the hotel, what he thought?

'Delphine seems very confident. There are the boys to think of, naturally. In a way it's no longer my business.'

She asked if he would take her inside. She had brought her camera and a notebook, a torch from the Harveys' barn, and the puffy bronzer brush she had washed carefully in shampoo and dried with her hairdryer. They were indoors for nearly an hour, and, when they came out squinting on to the steps, the Marquis shook her hand and said that in any case, they would have to meet now, in Paris. He mentioned La Perouse, which was as good a hint as any. Claudia pretended she didn't know the anecdote about '*Bel Ami*', and the courtesans scratching their diamonds on the mirrors to see if they were real. Rather obvious, but the old chap had style. Claudia grinned all the way down the hill, thinking perhaps I will and perhaps I won't.

The Sternbachs were gone too, with a basket of biscuits and preserves that suggested Aisling felt guilty about her neglect of the barbecue. Aisling was down at La Maison Bleue supervizing Madame Lesprats and no doubt getting every last bit of information about the plans at the chateau. Claudia did a bit of peering from the balcony and ascertained that Ginette's bicycle was also there. She used the house phone to call Sébastien and thought while she was waiting for the connection that he would surely answer, as surely as he would not have done before Malcolm Glover, unlikely messenger of the gods, knocked her down. He picked up on the third ring.

'Claudia! You're in France.'

'Bravo, Sherlock.' It seemed strange after all she had felt and struggled with that her voice sounded just as usual.

'Are you being bucolic?'

'Dangerously. Listen, I have to ask you something. You know someone at the *Patrimoine*, right?'

She told him about the frescoes. 'Obviously not Primatice, but definitely school of. Real Mannerist. The Marquis was pretty certain they were originals. The dates are all right.'

'He's such an old fraud with his Bonnards. Had it never occurred to him before?'

'He says not. That part of the house is usually shut up,

anyway, it hadn't been used since before the war. Apparently Delphine went rooting about because she thought it would be marvellous for the spa.'

'I'll give Jean-Jacques a ring and call you back.'

'Perfect.'

When they hung up, Claudia said out loud to Delphine, 'That's the end of you, then.' She couldn't tell anyone about her idea just yet, in case she was wrong, but after seeing the paintings twice she knew she wasn't. These things did happen, Rembrandts turning up under coffee tables. The d'Esceyracs had had the house since the early seventeenth century, but the gallery and the tower were at least fifty years earlier, the Marquis said, built by the Vicomtes who had held the land since early mediaeval times. It was amazing how little he seemed to know about it. In England, it would all be written up in a guidebook and you would be able to pay to go around and buy fudge. Aisling would mind much less about a museum, she was tremendously fond of frescoes after all. Claudia looked out again for the bicycle, then set off up the road to find Oriane.

She knocked cautiously at the door of the farmhouse, then pushed it open when there was no response. The kitchen room was dim and stuffy, shutters closed against the sun. She found Oriane on a whitish plastic chair around the side of the house, positioned in the shade of a dilapidated tenement of dirty old rabbit hutches.

'Hello,' she called cheerfully as she approached, not wanting to startle the old lady.

'Claudia. How are you? Ginette told me all about the accident.'

Claudia looked for somewhere to sit and perched on the concrete base of the hutches, holding her knees under her chin.

'I lost the baby.'

'Are you sorry?'

'No. I mean, I probably should be, but I'm glad. I'm glad it wasn't my fault though, if you understand what I mean.'

'Yes.'

'It hurt more than I expected. It hurt a lot.'

'Not as much as it would have done, all the same.'

'I wanted to ask before, how did you know, that I was pregnant, I mean?'

'Did you think I was a witch?'

Claudia smiled, 'Maybe.'

'It was your face, that was all. I had the same thing. The skin goes darker, around the cheeks and the forehead, they call it the mask of pregnancy. English people normally have such pale skin.'

Claudia realized she was right. So simple. She had noticed a crop of freckles on her cheekbones, but thought it was just a tan and had been irritated because she had spent forty pounds on a La Prairie sunblock.

'So you had it too?'

'My baby was conceived in the summer.'

'Yes, in the war.'

'Are you still going to marry him then, Monsieur Harvey's brother?'

'No. No I'm not going to marry him. I suppose it isn't necessary now, to be honest. That sounds awful, doesn't it?'

'I didn't think you young people bothered about all that any more.'

Claudia had hunched herself down on the packed dirt, she looked between her knees and said nothing. 'All that' she had to admit in the end, was minding that she wouldn't have had enough money.

'What about the other one?' Oriane asked.

'I don't know. He's not in love with me.'

'So what will you do, then?'

Claudia thought. The right thing, the empowered emancipated independent adult thing, would be to tell Sébastien, fondly, to get stuffed. She knew that would not happen. For so long it seemed, she had been lost to herself, casting herself as a tormented heroine, unable to see her own smallness. She needed Sébastien, and she thought there was little use in feeling ashamed of that, of pretending she was otherwise. But there was something else, something that had been growing in her since the night of the accident. After what had happened with Alex, she knew that even marriage with Sébastien was not actually what she wanted. What she wanted was to make her own thing of that need, to choose other lovers, be hurt, but bearably, at least as long as she was pretty enough for it not to matter. And she would have a child, but she would choose when and with whom. Sébastien would suit this new self very well, for a time, and then, and she was excited at the knowledge as it came to her, he would not. She thought of Aisling. It wasn't much, but she could try, she thought, to be a little less parochial in her feelings, to live up to the person she had tried to pretend for so long that she really was. Alex was wrong. She did not dislike herself so much that she wanted to convince the world she was perfect, quite the contrary. She had merely been afraid of not conforming to his vision of what she needed, because at heart she had been too much of a coward to believe she could be happy any other way.

'I'll be fine.'

They sat in silence, looking down the valley. There had been no wind at Murblanc, but up here it puffed around the house, blowing withered straw from the rabbit hovels.

'Jacky's father, he tried to make it up to me, in a strange way, but my boy said he hated me, when he went. That I had spoiled his life and Ginette's. He spat at me, my Jacky.'

Claudia thought she would sit here a while longer and then ride her bicycle along the lanes and take the train to Paris. It was a kind of selfishness, trying to manufacture a happy ending because she herself could not stand the pity and the waste, the sad boys in the photographs and the loneliness of this place.

'I wanted to say thank you,' she said awkwardly.

'Why?'

'I had a very difficult time here, I was really unhappy. I know I don't know you, but being able to speak to you so honestly has been a help, the things you've told me, I don't really understand why, but I'm glad. So thank you.'

This was the moment for Oriane to say something wise, then Claudia would be released, absolved.

'*Uat aihvair*,' said Oriane.

'I'm sorry, what was that? Is it Occitan?'

The old woman was chuckling. 'No, it's English. From that programme, the American one where all the friends live in the same apartment. Ginette loves it. Uat aihvair!'

'Right,' said Claudia, 'yes, right. Whatever.'

AUGUST 1947 /AUGUST 2000

Behind the church at Castroux, as in most country churchyards, was the plot reserved for suicides. Mostly, the names on the plain stones were men's. Girls got themselves into trouble, but on the whole, Oriane thought, men gave up more easily than women, and then they were found hanging in the barns, or with their heads blown off with a hunting rifle. Laurent had been buried in the Nadl family plot though, next to Papie. Jean-Claude Larivière had seen to that, because he was a hero of the Resistance. Jean-Claude was an important man now, in Cahors, for all that his own poor father had killed himself for shame. Jacky was playing on the steps of the witch's house, jumping down with his fat little legs together so his head wobbled at every bounce. That's what the children called it, they frightened themselves, daring one another to go in there, though it was really nothing more than a tiny old cottage used as a toolshed. There had been a sorcerer in Castroux once, Charlotte said, but he had lived out in the woods and people

413

went to him so he could read the cards. He had cursed the bellringer for not bringing him a gift of meat, and the next Sunday when he went to ring the bells one of them fell on his head and killed him stone dead. Charlotte was writing a book on the old customs of the village, she said they would all die out now the war was over. It kept her busy in the evenings after school. Oriane found she had lots of stories to tell her when she went down to the schoolhouse sometimes, of men who changed into wolves at night, and how she always tied Jacky's hat with a green ribbon, because that was what you did to ward off the grass snakes who slithered into babies' cribs as their mothers worked in the vines, to suck the milk from their throats.

Cook said they had an electrical washing machine now, up at the chateau. Oriane's hair reached the tips of her ears and curled out under her handkerchief. The scars around her mouth were fading, tight, pink and smooth. She didn't miss the weight of her hair, in the heat. Cook had asked if she would like to go to the chateau again, now the family was back, but she couldn't leave Jacky. Clara had not returned, and she had never written either, but Cook said that was because she was Jewish, though you never would have guessed.

At first Cathérine had turned her head away ostentatiously when they met in the village, but now she looked through her, as though she wasn't there. Oriane missed her, and Amélie, and Andrée. Amélie was married now, to one of her innumerable Lesprats cousins, she was already expecting. Oriane hoped she didn't get another poor William. Betty was gone, up to Paris with her parents to find a bar to run. For sure she would see plenty of dancing there. The bakery was empty, waiting for someone to buy it, so a van came around the village twice a week with bread that was already old and stale. Andrée's father had gone to work in a factory in Toulouse. Cécile Chauvignat had one baby now, a girl, and another on the way, she wore her medal all the time, pinned to the front of her bulging jumper. She was the one who had distracted the soldiers long enough to allow Laurent to get away to Monguèriac, at least everyone believed that, but they said William was a hero too, when all he had done was play his violin.

There was to be a monument, with William's name on it too. Oriane had asked that William not be put with their parents, there was no sense in Sophie Aucordier frightening him for all eternity, so William and his shattered violin lay over by the wall of the witch's house, in the highest part of the churchyard, where Oriane hoped the wind would reach him in the night and remind him of home. She put lavender on William's grave and a bunch of rosemary from the nuns' garden for Laurent. Jacky tugged at her skirt. It was so hot, she had him just in his little smock with his tanned legs sticking out in their sturdy wood and leather *galoches*. His hair was dark, but he had his father's pale northern eyes.

They went to Karl's grave last. Oriane suspected Père Guillaume knew that Karl was Jacky's father, though she had never said a word to anyone. Père Guillaume had buried the body himself, there was a bare wooden cross because no one had known the soldier's name, or why they had shot him. Oriane could not think badly of Karl. He had made her no promises, told her no lies. In her anger she had forgotten to ask him for the key, simply forgotten, and that was what he had used to try to save William's life. She had thought the Marquis might come to ask her about it, but since the door was broken in she assumed he had collected his box of old papers and been too relieved to think about what had happened.

Oriane had to believe that he must have loved her then, in a way, because of what he had done, but she couldn't feel glad about that. When she tried to unravel things, she saw that they would have killed William anyway if Karl had not acted, and that the person who had chosen his death was herself. Time twisted up and things got remembered wrongly, because what happened was always more simple than the reasons why. If the Marquis had not wanted to hide his stupid box, if she had gone to live at Murblanc when Jacky was born. Even a place as small as Castroux was impossibly dense with connections and chances, of tiny plenteous moments that became lives or deaths.

There was no one in the square as they walked down through the village, everyone was eating their lunch or sleeping. Jacky held her hand on the scorched white road as they walked up home. You couldn't try to be happy, you couldn't make yourself believe it. Sometimes, the between times, you were, and that had to be enough.

Years later, seated with a rug across his knees in the garden of the convent in Rome where he had come to die, Père Guillaume remembered a woman weeping. On his lap was a picture postcard, sent by a Jesuit friend from Venice, showing a painting of a woman, a woman with lustrously waving gold hair and a wonderful luminosity in her skin, the Magdalene, his friend wrote, and Père Guillaume held it a long time between hands now delicately blush-veined, and sought in himself to recognize the origin of the sensation the painting made in him, a sensation he was sure he had felt once before, quite differently, long ago.

Père Guillaume had never once, from the time he declared his vocation, been troubled by the flesh. He was happily able to admire a pretty girl in the safe knowledge that her hair or mouth would not return to pester his dreams. He had easily resisted a streetwalker who had once flicked up her skirt over her boots, calling to him softly in the cathedral walk in Toulouse. He was inured to the whispered obscenity of the propositions that came to him occasionally through the grille of the confessional. If he had sinned at all, it was in pride at his own inviolability. Yet the picture stirred something in him, too soft, he thought slowly, to be wicked now, a desire to smooth that glowing face with his hand, to know just a little, through his own skin and nerves, what was meant by beauty. He sat on there in the garden with the yellow-white jasmine on the walls until a thousand church bells sang the angelus and he remembered that he had felt this before, for a woman whose hair was straight and wet-black, who was nothing at all like the holy image before him, whose flesh shone over hard cheekbones with the mercury of tears in a room that smelt of ashes. Her eyes were wet flowers. He was too tired to trouble himself for her name.

Claudia's mobile began to chirrup as soon as the train drew in range of a signal. She began to check her messages as it rang.

'Claudia, I'm very impressed. Jean-Jacques was so excited he's cut short his holiday. He had some idea about Fiorentino. The man himself – not that he could have done the work, but there's some cartoons in the Louvre that he thinks look like the photos you mailed me. Will you still know me when you're famous?'

'Are they sending someone then?'

'I gave Jean-Jacques all the details. No hotel for Madame la Comtesse.'

'What if I told you I was motivated entirely by spite?'

'She deserves it. Apparently she gave old Charles-Edouard such a time I think he dropped dead just to be rid of her.'

'Do tell.'

'Come to Paris then.'

'I'm in the train.'

'Where shall we have dinner?'

'Sébastien, I don't know.'

'Old Faithful?'

'Actually, I'm not getting married to Alex.'

'Oh dear. Or are you pleased?'

'I just couldn't. I didn't love him.'

'I thought that was rather the point.'

'It was, but then it wasn't. Well, I just didn't like it, or myself, much.'

'Claudia, darling girl, don't tell me. You're still persisting with true love?'

Claudia took the phone away from her ear and looked at it. The train was running parallel with a motorway, clogged on one side with returning holiday-makers. Beyond the road were the huge hangar sheds of a commercial centre, Leclerc,

Décathlon, Buffalo Grill, Ikea. The air looked sluggish and dirty.

'Of course not. What about L'Ami Louis? You owe me.'

'Ten o'clock?'

'Perfect. I'll have time to change.'

Acknowledgements

Many thanks to Erica Lewis, Linda Hilton, Patrizia Moro, Michael Alcock, Anna Power, Georgina Capel, Laura Palmer. In the Tarn-et-Garonne, my thanks especially to Mme Andree Pouchet, M. Claude Desprats, the staffs of the Public Records office at Montauban and the Museum of the Resistance in Cahors, and to all my neighbours in Trejouls and Cazes Mondenard who contributed their memories to this story. Thanks most of all to Andrew Roberts, who made me take it out of the drawer.